RED DEMON

Sill Bihagia

OriaPress.com

Cover design by Maria Spada, with illustrative elements by Kateryna Vitkovskaya (silhouette) and Sill Bihagia (mycelium maze motif, mycelium vectors, final tweaks).
Map art by Adriano Bezerra.
Interior illustrations by Sill Bihagia.
Proofreading by Danai Christopoulou.

Published by Oria Press
oriapress.com | info@oriapress.com
7310 Ritchie Hwy Ste 200
PMB 1019
Glen Burnie, MD 21061

ISBN: 978-1-968468-00-2 (paperback) | 978-1-968468-01-9 (hardcover) | 978-1-968468-03-3 (ebook)]

Library of Congress Control Number: 2025918879

First edition, September 2025.

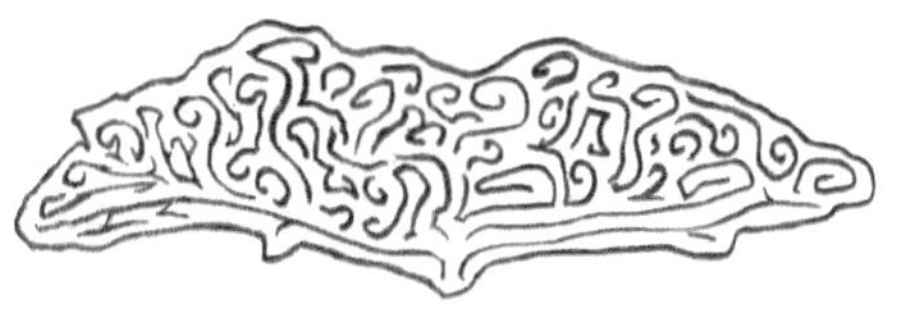

Dedication

*To everyone who must choose
between white lies and uncomfortable truths
in response to casual questions.*

Content Warnings: Depictions of death (including children), graphic violence, one chapter of graphic gore, bioengineered animal death (they aren't cute), profanity, graphic sexual content (M/F), off-page rape references, threats of sexual violence, and inappropriate physical contact.

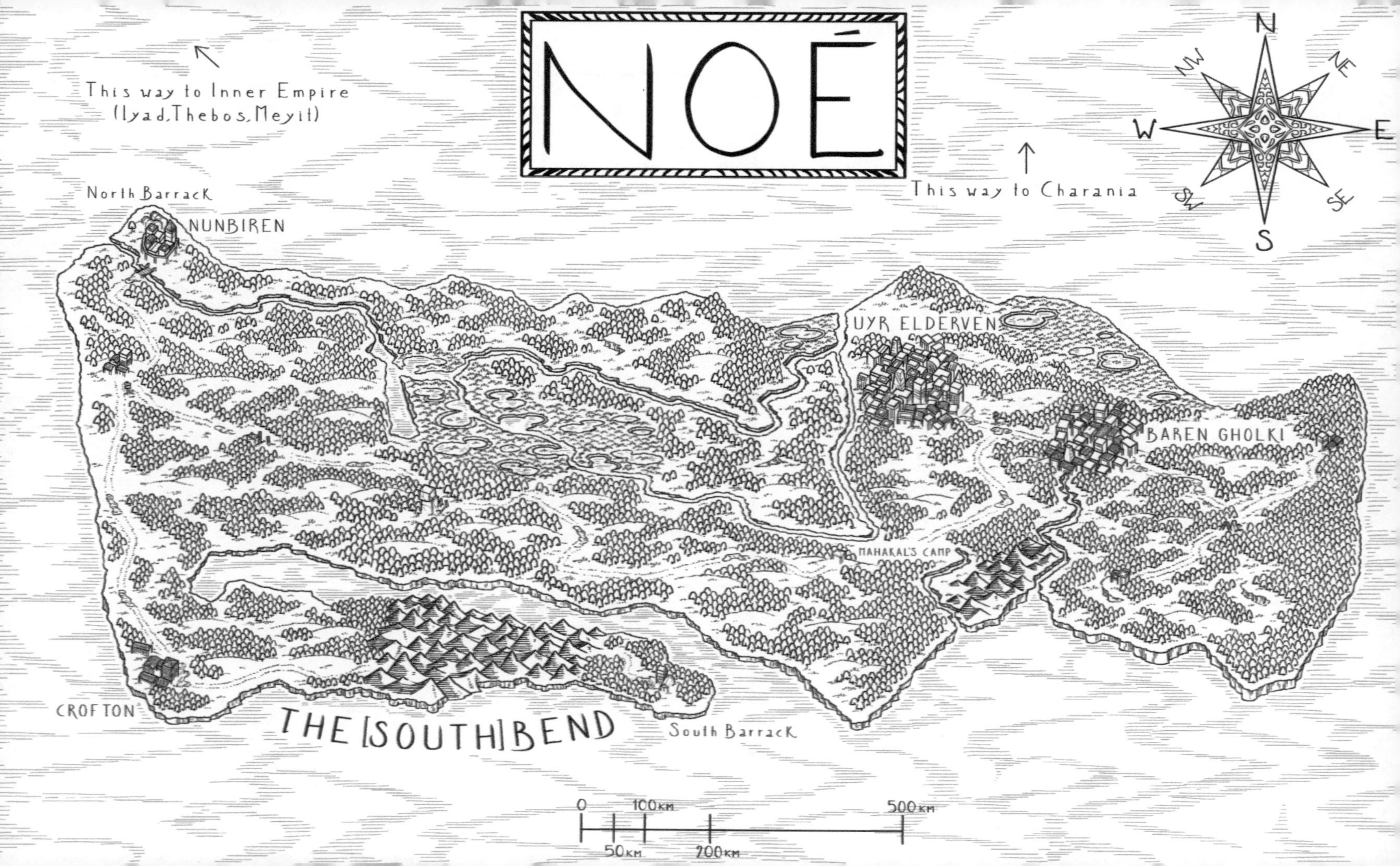

NOÉ
This way to Inner Empire
(Iyad, Thebos, Meyit)
This way to Charania
N NE E SE S SW W NW
North Barrack
NUNBIREN
UYR ELDERVEN
BAREN GHOLKI
MAHAKAL'S CAMP
CROFTON
THE [SOUTH] BEND
South Barrack
0 100 km 500 km
50 km 200 km

Contents

Glossary

Spoiler Free

Pronunciation Notes

Long vowels are marked with macrons: **ā** as in say, **ē** as in see, **ī** as in eye, **ō** as in go, **ū** as in blue. Short vowels are unmarked: **a** as in cat, **e** as in bed, **i** as in sit, **o** as in hot, **u** as in cup.

Ä - "Ah" sound as in father.

ə - short, neutral vowel like the beginning and ending sound in "arena."

KH - a throaty K common in many non-English languages. Found in the Scottish "loch," the Vietnamese KH, or the German CH in "Bach," for example. Voiceless velar fricative.

þ - soft th, as in "thin."

Ç - This Asri consonant falls somewhere between the English *"Ch"* and *"Sh,"* and I'll write it either way—whatever looks better. Most will pronounce it wrong, but look at you—my fellow nerd—reading this glossary. You know the truth, that the canonical pronunciation for both **Charania** and Ea **Sh**adohe is technically "voiceless post-alveolar fricative."

Academy - Boarding schools and career guilds that originated within the Chaeten culture. Academies raise and train children year-round in the same facility, allowing the most prestigious in that discipline to practice their work on site. Academies are often associated with a specific military, academic, or religious order, and details vary widely between these orders.

Academy Mother (or Father) – An advisor assigned to oversee the progress of a student in an Academy.

A's'aan Khel (*Ä-s-ÄN KHEL*) – A perception filter works both at the level of neurological systems and photoreceptors to expand the human blind spot. Anyone staring an an A's'aan khel will not see the hidden area, and not be aware that something is missing in their field of view.

Attiq-ka (*ä-tē-KÄ*) – Reincarnated immortals whose memories/souls were preserved in Oria. Since the Ghost War and the destruction of specific Asri tech, there has been no record of an Attiq-ka reincarnation. Physiologically, Attiq-ka were indistinguishable from the humans they coexisted with on Nara Mnaet at the time of birth and were born into Asri families. Culturally, the Attiq-ka preferred to choose names from among the oldest of Earth's heroes and gods. The vast majority of surviving Attiq-ka did not support Azara and Jeron Alexander in their rise to power, and remain hunted outlaws.

Asri-ka (*ÄS-rē-KÄ*) – The original inhabitants of Nara Mnaet before the Chaeten arrived. This term covers both immortal humans (Attiq-ka) and mortals (Sedo-ka). Asri maintained much of the core genetics of their home planet and focused any genetic engineering on preventing disease rather than further experimentation and refinement. They would appear similar to the people of Earth in terms of range of skin tones and hair, although far more diverse in terms of ethnic heritage. Their eyes have darker limbal rings and layered irises in otherwise natural colors.

Azara (*ä-ZÄ-rä*) – The only known Chaeten to survive to adulthood and merge with the reincarnated soul of an Attiq-ka. Her unique lineage was originally a symbol of peace that helped her garner support among both Chaeten and humans in the years following the Ghost War.

(Magic) Blocker - A Chaeten machine that emits a frequency that mimics and disrupts the delta rhythm specific to Chout Attiq-ka. Enhancement/use of magic employs this rhythm, and anyone using magic within the radius of the frequency would experience an intense, focal seizure. Even with short exposure and immediate treatment, the magic user would experience neuronal death and possible bleeding within the brain. Anyone incapable of—or untrained in—using magic would not be affected, and trained wielders not currently using magic would be less affected than those actively using their skills.

Chaeten *(CHĀ-ten)* - A species of humans that came to Nara Mnaet as refugees two hundred years prior to the Ghost War, following the destruction of their home planet. They quickly adapted their genetics to survive on the planet, introgressing their genes to the Asri. Chaeten were allowed to settle in Thebos, but wide scale peaceful, mutual cohabitation was never achieved before the reign of Azara.

Chaeten-Sa *(CHĀ-ten-SÄ)* - A deliberately ambiguous term! This originally referred to any Chaeten deemed inhuman (and to the most radical Asri at the time of the Ghost War, this meant all Chaeten). Since the Ghost War, it refers to a specifically genetically enhanced line of immortals created by the Chaeten to mimic Attiq-ka longevity and abilities. Jeron Alexander chose the term to refer to his spec line as a way of taking back power from those who intended it as a slur. Although the Chaeten-sa spec line was designed to limit their skin tones to those among the Asri, the eyes for that spec line were always bright yellow-green and their hair always red.

Charania *(Çä-RÄ-ē-ə)* - A large island in the northern hemisphere with the oldest temples and the least Chaeten influence.

Chout *(CHOWT)* - Discipline. See "magic."

[The Attiq-ka] Council - The government prior to Azara's reign, comprising a group of reincarnated elders who voted on major judicial and executive decisions in partnership with local governments. Local government generally (and often intentionally) comprised mortal elders.

Dahn *(DÄN)* – A magical power that is innate and does not require meditation or training to use at its most basic level. (See also: magic.)

Earth – Although the reader can be safely told both the Chaeten and Asri ancestors originated from the third planet orbiting Sol, the general population on Nara Mnaet does not generally think this far back. It has been hundreds of thousands of years since humans first ventured into the stars. The Asri/Attiq-ka are aware that they originated from the "Planet of a Thousand Names" and have some highly overtranslated accounts of what the planet was like.

Ea Shadohe *(Ē-ə-shä-DŌ-hā)* – Capital of the Nine Islands, and of Nara Mnaet, located on the island of Iyad.

Ghosts – Spirits/souls that are either not welcomed into Oria, incompatible, or whose minds are too damaged to rejoin it. Composed of subatomic energy signatures, ghosts can interact with minds and brains attuned to them and have minimal to no impact on anything else in the natural world. They also have little protection from both Asri magic and Chaeten tech outside of a mind or brain, so further degradation of memories or functions is inevitable unless the ghost finds a host. (In Asri – *Ruren.*)

Ghost War – A brutal war between the Chaeten and Attiq-ka prior to Azara's rise to power that wiped out 90 percent of the world population over the course of several years. There were many factors that contributed to the start of the war, but all agree the creation of the Chaeten-sa immortal line was one of the final fractures, causing the majority of Attiq-ka to call for their extinction. It's the reason most of the immortals on the planet (particularly Chaeten-sa) are now dead.

Inner Empire – The equatorial islands of Iyad, Meyit, and Thebos. Chaeten cities and culture are more concentrated in these regions.

Iyad *(Ī-ad)* – Largest of the Nine Islands, located on the equator. Contains the world capital Ea Shadohe.

Jeron Alexander *(JĀR-on)* – General of Azara's armies and royal consort, and the second most powerful immortal on the planet.

Ka *(KÄ)* – This term is most commonly translated as "human." Layered with both the ethical and philosophical connotations in "mind" or "soul," but not encompassing intangibility or immutability. The most literal translation would be "the sum of the connections between synapses in a human mind," and the programs and systems that could be translated to Oria. A *ka* can briefly live on beyond the scope of the human brain as a ghost. Although the term can be used on an individual level, the most common usage is to assign humanity to a group. Example: *Noé-ka* would be understood to mean humans who live on the island of Noé, and *Chaeten-ka* would be one or more humans from the Chaeten culture.

Khel *(KHEL)* – A wall or a barrier. The broad term is usually used in the context of Asri magic (chout). Depending on the type of energy employed, it might harm minds that pass through it, interact with certain technologies, or alter perception.

Long Hour – The hour in the daily cycle with nineteen extra minutes, so that the day has twenty-four hours; the third hour after midnight. The original inhabitants of Nara Mnaet tried to incorporate a time system similar to the planet they came from (Earth) where seconds and minutes were identical to their original system.

Magic – Any technology whose mechanics are generally not fully understood by the user from a technical standpoint but are integrated within the mind. Asri purists will prefer the term "Chout," meaning "discipline." Although the Chaeten are aware that magic runs in Asri families, they have never isolated a gene or marker associated with its use. The Attiq-ka retained skills gained during prior lives and generally had higher discipline/a broader array of magical skills. Magic use is restricted within the empire, with more powerful skills only allowed to be performed by elite Z'har priests or Azara herself.

(The) Nara *(NÄ-rə)* – Short form of Nara Mnaet, and the more commonly used term to refer to the planet.

Nara Mnaet *(NÄ-rə m-NĀ-et)* – The original name of the planet, translating to "New Beginning." Nara Mnaet is roughly Mars-sized with similar concentrations of iron oxide dust, but it has a thicker atmosphere than the original planet Earth. The vast majority of Nara Mnaet is covered with misty, shallow seas.

Niire Mai *(NĒ-rā MĪ)* – The mandate for Asri to do no [intentional] harm. Although the principles that comprise this are complex, the main ones that factor in this book are to never kill and never eat anything with a brain, with guidelines to limit intentional harm to brains. There's some other exceptions to the rules beyond "Sa" being excluded from this prohibition, but for the purpose of *Red Demon*, don't worry about it.

Nine Islands – Although other islands in the Nara were occupied prior to the war, the Nine Islands in Azara's empire remain the only human-occupied land in the Nara.

Oria *(ō-RĪ-ə)* – The underground mycelial bionetwork array that contains the memories of ancestors whose souls were welcomed back. A living, sentient database composed of the sum of the knowledge of the dead. Oria is a symbiotic life form developed by the ancient Asri, consisting of a native life form fused with a fungal strain originating from the "Planet of a Thousand Names." Oria derives energy both from the heat of the planet's core and chemical decomposition at the surface.

Pathfinder – One of the positions on the Attiq-ka Council, which must be held by someone with a magical ability to model and/or make credible predictions about the future.

Red Demon – A figure in an increasing number of bedtime or campfire stories, with a long trail of blood behind her. A lone Chaeten-sa who wanders the wilds and kills indiscriminately and quietly, often without saying a word.

Reic *(RĀ-ik)* – Attiq-ka founder of one of the Underground networks.

Ruren-sa *(RŪ-ren-SÄ)* – Although any dead spirit might choose to be malicious, the majority of those that wander the wild in Jesse's world are left behind from the Ghost War. 90 percent of the population was destroyed at that time, and some souls that were once in Oria were damaged. Many Ruren-sa want revenge but have a blind, driving desire to preserve themselves by joining a human mind—or failing that—a brain. They cannot join a mind without causing harm, inflicting rage and hatred without much context.

Sa *(SÄ)* – A derogatory Asri word translated in Chaeten to "demon." The Attiq-ka originally used it to describe humans who committed crimes/sins that stripped them of their humanity, precluding them from access to Oria. The term *Sa* was later expanded to refer to any humans genetically modified to a point where it was impossible for them to live according to the principles of Niire Mai.

Sedo-ka *(SĀ-dō-KÄ)* – The Asri word for non-immortal humans, which were the majority of humans at any given time. It literally means "Dead (past tense) soul," with the connotation of a pre-life death. Any Sedo-ka whose soul is accepted into Oria has the potential to reincarnate as an Attiq-ka.

Shortgrain – Originally derived from wheat, it has been heavily genetically modified to maximize both shelf-life and nutrition. The crop reaches maturity in about two months.

Ruren *(RŪ-ren)* – See "ghost."

Ruren-sa *(RŪ-ren-SÄ)* – Ghosts that are corrupted in such a way that they cannot enter a host without killing the mind they inhabit—and prove willing to do it anyway. Demon ghosts.

Thebos *(þĀ-bōs)* – A densely populated urban island with Chaeten tech on full display and many Z'har academies.

Year – Because the author allowed themself to be lazy somewhere, the time it takes Nara Mnaet to fully orbit its star is only negligibly different from an Earth year in terms of minutes. The day is nineteen minutes longer, but the Nara Mnaet year is 360.243 days shorter to make up for that—so, 360 days with a leap year about every four years. Twenty-eight-day months, seven days in each week, with twenty-four days left over for festivals not formally incorporated into those months or weeks. This author does not plan to name the days of the week if they can avoid it.

Z'har *(z'-HÄR)* – One who is formally pledged to the service of the empire through one of several religious, academic, or military fraternal orders. Z'har, while not expected to be celibate, are not allowed to marry or raise their own children.

CHAPTER 1

Everyone Died

When everyone in town died, we heard no scream. We should have, every sound carried up that forest gorge. Winters in the south bend of Noé carry no birdsong, no rustle of leaves, just the crinkle of my feet rolling over the snow as softly as possible so as not to spook the deer. My brother Iden tipped his bow in the quiet, as still as the trees staring down. The deer died in the silence of that winter morning. A village of three thousand did too.

At fourteen, I stood almost to my full height, my lanky frame already capable of lugging back game, wood, or baskets of whatever herbs, berries or mushrooms we could gather from the forest. Iden, a year older, stood just as tall and strong—though the scrubby blond stubble he called a goatee still eluded me. Each day, we tested our muscles to hunt or gather what we could until we were old enough to do our part in the mineral mines. I gutted the doe that morning amid trees as wide as I stood tall. Iden prepped the pole to carry it between our shoulders.

I inhaled earthy blood as we trudged back to the cobble road, eager to get that deer butchered in our shed. We made it down the road a ways, talking about the venison stew Mom would soon bubble over the fire, adding chives, potatoes, and wild root vegetables to make it perfect. I dreamed about a good shortgrain bread to go with it, but

Iden reminded me we'd have to wait until spring to save up. Imports were expensive, and money was tight since Dad died last year.

Death wouldn't be new to me that day, just the scale of it. We'd all banded together after Dad's death because we knew all Chaeten had to. Our ancestors already survived the death of a planet, coming to a new one as refugees, and a war when the native humans on Nara Mnaet couldn't agree if we were coded human enough to say so. Through these last few generations, we'd changed everything about our genetic code to live here, to make ourselves belong. Dad always said Chaeten don't break, we mod ourselves stronger and move on. We'd stood tall in that town for three generations, stubborn enough to flourish in a place where our Asri neighbors once slaughtered as many of us as they could.

"It shouldn't be this quiet," Iden said as we reached the maple grove.

I shifted the deer on my shoulders. "I'm fine with quiet. The twins just learned to whistle."

He groaned. "Yeah, they woke me up this morning with a new whistle-song."

"Yep. Told them you'd love that." I'd relished my little sisters' smiles just as much as Iden's annoyance.

"You shit." He laughed, but he'd been right about the quiet. There were no work trucks on the road, or rumbles under our feet from the mine. A breeze chimed through the icy trees, then running footsteps. The moment I first saw the Red Demon will be etched in my mind forever—every slow second of it.

I didn't know what she was then, or what to call her, but I recognized she was something special, powerful, beyond the human I was. My eyes were sharp enough to see her on the far edge of the field, to make out the maze of scars down her golden arms and the long, wine-red hair streaming behind her. I hadn't seen hair that shade before, glowing a little more than it should, hovering with something brilliant on the edge of perception. Her hair bloomed as all colors do when we're children, warm and shining bright. She moved fluid, precise, flawlessly fast. I couldn't pinpoint the otherness of it, but I couldn't look away, even when she swerved to charge us.

She came from the village, all lean muscle and grace across the field of white powdered snow. She crossed twin swords in front of her, their blades glinting with blood. I'd dropped the pole from my shoulder, but I still stood there like an idiot, too transfixed to be afraid. Iden drew his bow.

Mid-stride, she wiped one blade in the snow with a flash of sunlight. Another step, she flipped it and cleaned the blood off the other side. Lunge, wipe; lunge, wipe, all without changing pace.

"Get your knife out, Jesse," Iden said. His voice sounded calm, too calm. All the same, his green eyes flitted with panic when I didn't jump immediately.

I unsheathed my knife, my heart pounding when only a few paces remained between her and my neck.

She stopped, letting out one slow, frosty breath. Her blades shone clean as she stared at us with vacant yellow-green eyes, meeting our wide-eyes for a moment before her gaze flitted down the road beyond us.

Iden breathed in deep beside me, his bowstring taut, every muscle prepared as we waited for her to speak or take one step forward to meet his arrow.

That armor of hers, once well-crafted, hung tattered and torn: a studded leather bodice and bracers over a ragged shirt. Iden could still target a mortal wound to her neck or her eye, but she'd left little else exposed. She wore black Chaeten leather pants: a thin, alloyed fabric, patched with dyed deer hide. I could also aim for that patch on the inner thigh if the bow missed. But by then, I was shaking. I'd seen how fast she could move.

"Who are you?" I smiled, hoping for the best. "I'm Jesse. That's Iden."

Iden's eyes flitted to me in warning, then back to the Red Demon, his bow still trained on her.

I nodded at my brother. "He's friendlier than he looks." I hoped I looked calm even as my heart galloped in my chest.

The Red Demon glanced my way, then beyond, emotionless. She sheathed both blades at once with a thud, so fast I could barely track it. Then she veered off with long strides toward the trees, hair flaming behind. We watched every step.

Iden kept his bow trained on her. "Wait until we know the Chaeten-sa isn't circling back."

Chaeten-sa. I suppose I should have put it together the instant I saw that hair, but the portraits in my history books of the warriors that won our right to live on this planet painted a different picture. General Alexander, second in command to our queen, has similar hair and features. However, our Chaeten-sa general stands immaculate and grinning in his portraits— nonchalant in front of the white stone palace, a bustling capital in the background. Although "sa" meant "demon" to his Asri enemies, General Alexander co-opted that slur with pride, formally adopting the name for everyone in his genetic spec line.

She shouldn't be here. Chaeten-sa veterans should be in places of power, not roaming the frontier in ragged armor.

I could no longer hear her footsteps among the trees. "Whose blood do you suppose that was?"

He twitched a frown, lowering the bow half-way. "Let's find out." He nodded toward the town, and we crept down the road, leaving our deer behind.

On the first street, a young girl lay face down in the snow, long brown hair under her cap. Iden and I ran, then flipped over her frigid body, not yet stiff. It took us a moment to accept what should have been clear from her pallid skin, but no blood stained her clothes, no wounds. We could see nothing to explain how she died. I didn't remember the girl's name, but knew her parents ran the corner store.

"Help!" I yelled.

"Someone, please help!" Iden called out.

Our voices echoed between the frosted gorges. A dog barked, but no one called back. We started running. By the time we reached the market, the dead lay everywhere.

Do you know what most people do in a crisis, when the right thing to do is act fast? They fucking stand there. They freeze, until someone tells them what to do or shows them by doing it first. There must be some primitive part of our brains our engineers have yet to mod away, though I've since tried to train it out of me.

We stood there, mouths agape, at the dozens of friends and neighbors leaning on the market booths, apples toppled into the street where my old tutor lay slumped by a cart. Then there was Marc, that little girl's dad, lying in the street in a puddle of blood, fresh and freezing on his coat. He lay next to a bright display of flowers, the sign for his corner store streaked with the last of his life. The two women beside him were unmarked: no blood or wounds, neither bruises nor signs of broken bones. They just stared up at the sky with frost-glazed eyes.

I made myself forget much of what I saw in that square, but Marc was important: that blood. He lay stabbed while most others were not, and I knew who stabbed him.

"Keep your knife up, little brother," Iden said, his voice as icy as the wind in his hair.

"What good is that? A knife didn't do that," I whispered, gesturing to the woman crumbled by the apple cart without a mark on her. Ms. Carter had lived three houses down. I was breathing hard, struggling to stay calm. "What happened to her?"

Iden opened his mouth and closed it again, his eyes darting as fast as mine. "Home," he said, his jaw set. "Let's go home."

Iden turned into an alley, his bow up in front of him. I followed, my mind racing, thinking about Mom and my sisters. I didn't see a point in his ducking down under windows, or choosing the alley over the street. The enemy would find us if they wanted. They'd gotten everyone else. When the alley ended, we jogged in the open, down the road home.

I tried to make sense of the threat. It would have taken some heavy tech to kill our town. But what, and who had it? Queen Azara had outlawed anything she thought the Asri could abuse to hurt us, and she'd outlawed anything she thought we Chaeten could use to hurt them. The priests said Asri magic can corrupt even little things, like electricity, without the right protections. On the fringe of an empire surrounded by Asri towns, we did without a lot of tech our ancestors found essential, to prevent tragedies like this.

"Asri tech—magic, whatever." I couldn't get that thought out of my head. "It has to be." They didn't teach us at school how that magic worked. They didn't want to give anyone the key to abusing it. But it had wiped out communities before.

At first, I thought Iden would keep his mouth clamped shut as we rushed on. "Maybe," he said. "Let's go home. Hurry."

We ran.

We crossed the alley between the school and the temple. Ice clinked in the branches of the bushes along the street. A cat mewed from a porch with a door wide open to the winter cold, the body of Dr. Garla lying in the doorway. I recognized the purple in her hair and blue tint to her skin—a more traditional Chaeten, wearing bold, unrepentant colors when the rest of us were coded to blend in.

A pram drifted slowly across the road toward us, blood smearing the outside. We slowed our pace, but I avoided stepping closer to that carriage, too fearful to look and confirm if it was a baby's blood that stained those blankets. A woman lay cloaked in indigo down the road, blood on her arms and chest—the mom, perhaps.

On every street we jogged down, only the dead greeted us. Then we were home.

Our gate creaked on its hinges. My pulse pounded in my ears. And then I saw my sisters.

The twins, Cara and Samantha, lay sprawled in the front yard, a dusting of snow on their winter clothes. At five, the twins doted on the youngest, Sora. She lay dead beside the twins on the icy ground, her thin blonde hair rustling in the wind. Brushing the snow off did nothing to warm their little bodies.

I wanted to lose it, to scream, but I didn't. Iden's chest heaved, and I gripped a hand on his shoulder. Mom taught me there will always be someone else to cling to when a pillar of our life falls down, and she taught me to be that pillar in turn. We kept it together, holding each other up.

Mom lay dead in the kitchen, near the fire... very near the fire. I've never had a nightmare that hollowed me out as much as pulling her red, blistered body away from the embers, seeing the mutilated face of someone I loved so much.

I can tell you what it felt like when I realized she wouldn't be there to turn to. My hope died. It didn't feel possible that I was here, and she was gone. I don't think I'll ever stop missing her, or stop feeling as if she is missing, even if I know she'd hate that. The Chaeten way would be to let her go and never look back. She left me too young to see that lesson home, to teach me how that's possible.

Resilience is often mistaken for coldheartedness, especially so for us Chaeten. We coded ourselves to survive our near-extinction, never surrendering to fear or heartbreak. When they cut us down and we'd hold our heads high at the end, the Asri saw it as inhumanity, not bravery. But heartbreak sums the same for all of us. I didn't break that day, but the cost would come later, in my dreams, and in so many quiet moments where I could never fully surrender to joy.

"I'll check the basement," Iden said.

"I'll check the other rooms."

The bedroom door just off the kitchen creaked as I opened it to see what, at this point, I was expecting. My sister Bella died at twelve, tucking in the young neighbor kids for their nap. There were always extra kids around the house, whose parents were on shift in the mines.

That's how Mom earned coin. Bella's long blonde hair spilled across the multicolored blanket, her head down as if resting her eyes. I checked her cold body for blood, then lifted a bright-squared quilt to look for clues on the children's faces and little bodies. Nothing; I'd hoped it felt like sleeping for all of them when they died.

It started snowing out the window. I stayed until I heard Iden's footsteps behind me.

"Downstairs is clear." Iden sheathed his knife and stood for a moment, eyes fixed and overcome. He gripped the doorframe, painted over in bold green and blue geometric designs.

"Should we burn them?" I asked, trying to be practical, to not fall apart.

"The mines." It looked like he considered his own words as if they hadn't just come from his mouth. "Mal and Oren won't be back for hours. They might be—Jesse, they might be okay."

I bit my lip. All seven of my siblings lived at home with me, odd for Chaeten standards, I know, but the frontier was different.

Iden paced the room. "The Asri don't use our tech. They wouldn't want our mine. They'd just want to kill us."

"The Chaeten-sa had blood on her sword. That's no accident, and she's no Asri rebel."

Iden massaged his forehead. "She didn't attack us, though. Maybe she killed off the people who did it."

"Then where are their bodies?"

Iden turned to the bodies of the children in bed, his eyes unfocused. "So, the kids, that bloody baby—" He shuddered. "You're right. It has to be her." It still didn't explain the ones with no wounds. Squatting beside the bed, I held Bella's cold hand, too exhausted to speculate further. I pushed blond, curly hair from both our faces.

"Mr. Gell was lying by the temple. I saw him." Iden gripped the door frame so tight I wondered if it would splinter.

"I liked him," I said. Mr. Gell was the only Asri in town, a bearded man with a bright smile and hazel-ringed eyes that came alive when he taught his classes on history or the Asri language. He left out the parts my mother taught me—things Asri called us in the war—things that rebels still called us in secret, but he meant well. If the killers didn't check Mr. Gell's irises for those two shades of color, I suppose they wouldn't have noticed which kind of human he was.

The embers in the kitchen provided little warmth through the open doorway. I'd have to see my mother's body again to stoke the fire. I wanted to sink into the chilled wood floor, numb and cold as the dead. Iden had the same glazed-over look as I must have. Seeing him snapped me out of it.

"Iden, we should go."

Iden nodded, pursing his lips. "Go-bags. Mines."

Dad had made sure we were prepared for emergencies. I was grateful for a routine that took little thought. I packed food and water, wrapped in the best blankets. Iden took our best hunting gear, our warmest clothes. I picked up a bracelet from Mom's jewelry box, the only memento I allowed myself that didn't serve a practical purpose. Not everything in our house would fit in our packs. I took the rest in my memory, vowing to never forget the walls painted in a rainbow of little hand prints, the smell of spices in the pantry, the feeling of being in a room worn down with love and laughter.

Because I knew this house would never be home again.

Chapter 2

The Mine

As a young kid, the colossal mining trucks fascinated me. I'd stop whatever I was doing to watch them lumber past, kicking up dust on the road as the ground vibrated under me. That day, twin headlights stared at me across the falling snow in the dying light, chilling in a way the wind could never be. Behind the truck, the mine lay dark and quiet, with metal doors stretched open like a wild dog's yawn.

Inside, our steps echoed between stone walls. Slanting beams from ventilation shafts speared the gloom, painting vague figures on the walls. I took the lack of bodies as a good sign, but Iden frowned, his eyes fixed forward, adjusting to the dark. Both of us had inherited the vision our parents and grandparents had modded for their work. We waited a moment until we could see the fuzzy shapes of a world in black and white.

The drill rigs should have been running. I should have felt that vibration to my bones, a low roar audible from a kilometer away. Those rigs self-piloted most of their work, sensing seams of the right densities to explore, knowing the path of stone and earth to tunnel to avoid other machines or structural failures. They'd return to the maintenance level only when they were full, low on fuel, or when a human told them to stop.

"Someone stopped the rigs," I said.

Iden looked through me, his gaze falling hard down the entrance hall toward the office wing.

"Did you hear me? Mal said it takes hours for a rig to get back."

"So?" Iden kept walking.

"So, if they died like the others, the machines would still be going. They had the time to stop them. Our people must be hiding, planning something."

Iden flicked his gaze to me, then away. Silence never bothered me when the two of us were hunting, but it felt as heavy as my pack just then.

"You're too optimistic. Asri magic could kill them and stop the machines too, as far as we know." Iden twitched his fingers across the hilt of the knife at his hip.

We opened the door to the admin suite; the shadows held tight to corners, but the shafts' faint glow traced edges of desks and chairs. I tried the light panel, heard the click, and still saw darkness. I went for my pack to dig out a lantern.

"Not yet," Iden whispered, gesturing to sunroofs at the far end of the office. "If anyone is here, we need to see them first."

We reached the door of the main office without seeing a soul. Dust danced in the thin light, motes swirling like tiny stars in a galaxy between desks and strewn chairs. Coffee mugs sat full and abandoned on desks—each a disquieting testament. Iden trembled, staring into nowhere. I poured a mug from the sideboard that he refused to take.

"It's just going to waste." I took a swig of the cold brew.

His fingers drummed the surface of a dead monitor. He didn't look up at my forced smile.

"Iden. Take a moment, think. No one's here. Let's work through what's next." I drained the mug to make my point when he kept staring out into the dark. Despite my cool bravado, I was just as freaked out as he was, with my heart thumping to keep time with the tremor in Iden's hand. I knew if I surrendered to that feeling, it would pull me under. I needed to keep his head above water too.

Iden let out a breath, finally looking at me. He picked up an empty mug and poured from a pot on the side table. Mug in hand, he sank into a creaking office chair. "If I were here, and we lost power, I'd have gone to the surface. I'd have gone to town—and I'd have died with everyone else."

"There are no tracks in the snow."

"Maybe they all left this morning, before the snow."

"I don't remember seeing any mining uniforms among all those dead. Besides, they have all this tech here we don't, right?" I waved around to the office, full of tablets and screens that no longer worked. "Maybe they saw what was coming, and knew it wasn't safe to come home. Maybe they are waiting this all out in one of the lower levels."

Iden set his jaw, lost in thought. But as he opened his mouth to reply, we heard the shriek of metal tearing against metal.

We knew the sounds of a happy drill rig, and that wasn't it.

The sound rumbled deep below our feet and through the stone walls, shaking straight through my chest. Adrenaline flowed bitter in my veins. I ducked down, not sure what else to do as the floor shook under me. Papers fluttered, a few chairs rolled, but no walls tumbled down onto me like in my nightmares about Dad's last day on the job. Then it was silent again.

"We should go." Iden rose from the ground beside me, gripping the desk. He picked up his bag, jogging toward the glass office doors.

I rushed after him. Grabbing his arm, I dug in, stance wide. "Iden! Mal and Oren might be stuck down there in the dark, terrified."

Iden hesitated, then muttered a curse. "Fine."

He paced for a moment. When hunting, he'd come up with excellent strategies if I allowed time for his thoughts to brew. But that tic in his face, clear enough to see even in this light, told me he was as lost as I was.

"Alright, we stay dark—silent as possible," Iden said. "No flashlight in case Asri magic can disrupt that too. We use the lantern when we must. If Mal and Oren aren't at their station on level three, or if we see anyone at all we don't know, we head for the woods. Good?"

"Yeah, good." I let out a breath.

We crept deeper into the office to reach the emergency stairs, and I wondered if we were walking toward the explosion or further away. The vibration had seemed to come from everywhere, but I thought I could at least pinpoint the sound to not-that-stairwell. There was dwindling light as we crossed the office, and all I could make out were hazy flickers as Iden crept beside me. My heart skipped with each creak of the office floorboards—wood and scaffolding under our feet, not earth or stone.

We opened the steel door to the stairwell. Too dark.

"Lantern time," I whispered to the open door. The sound echoed down the cement walls as Iden glared.

And then I could just make out some movement, a muffled breath a level below. A dark figure hurled up the stairs toward me, long steps pounding fast.

"Jesse!" Iden hissed. I tried to close the door, but there was no lock, not even a latch. Taking a step back, I fumbled out my knife as the door flung open. The lantern fell, stuttering out.

The dark figure rushed me, hitting me hard in the chest. They threw me to the floor, and I heard my hunting knife spin across the floor and clank into a cabinet. We fell in a tangle of limbs and grunts. He was well-muscled, and I glanced one blow off his arm before he twisted away. I got up, lunging at him, a roar escaping my throat. My fist caught the man's torso as I sidestepped. He stumbled back, grunting. I caught a flash of terrified eyes through the hazy silver light. But no, it couldn't—

"Mal!" Iden roared.

"Mal?" I said, just before his fist pummeled my jaw. I tasted my blood, metallic and sour. By instinct, I curled my body to protect my vital organs, not yet sure if I should aim at his. It couldn't be Mal, just someone Mal-sized and just as—*Fuck, ouch.* I grimaced at my throbbing stomach, but escaped the next blow, forcing a desk between us.

The shadowed man pulled something from his belt, a glinting—a knife. *Voids, a fucking knife.* I wasn't sure why he didn't lead with that. He charged, clearing the desk in a bound.

I grappled for the blade as he hesitated, feeling the sharp metal slide beneath my fingers while I used all my power to keep it away. The blade flashed silver in the darkness, but I rotated away from his swipe. The man kicked. I stumbled back, and he lunged forward, toppling over me. I pried the knife free from him as he flailed, kicking him away. He fell hard onto the floor.

A burst of light. I turned to Iden, lantern in hand, shadows flickering around the office. The attacker shrank away.

Mal, definitely Mal scuttling back behind a desk, but this was not the brother I knew. His eyes, once sparkling with a mischief I appreciated, glazed over with fear as he rose. Dust, grime, and blood matted his beard and sandy hair, usually so neat and trim that it deserved frequent teasing. My oldest brother, my friend, was a stranger in this skin of fear.

He froze, eyes wide. Recognition. The knife trembled in my hand, but I didn't let go just yet. Time slowed. My world shrank to just the three of us within the boundaries of the flickering lantern.

"You look like shit, Mal," I said, breath rasping.

Mal slumped back to sit on a desk, eyes only on the knife, terrified.

"Okay." I let the blade clatter to the floor, its metallic echo jarring. I put my empty hands up when he startled at the noise, drawing a fist. "It's okay, Mal, It's just me. Just Jesse, and Iden—"

Iden took a wary step forward, eyes darting between us.

Mal looked beyond us to the stairwell. His fist clenched.

"What ... what happened to you?" I said.

Mal shrank back, the fight shattering from him like one of those dropped coffee mugs. "You aren't here to kill me?"

Iden and I shared a look, then looked back to Mal. "Why would we do that?" I said.

Mal rubbed his shoulder, shuddering.

"Mal, who else is down there?" Iden said. "Oren?"

Mal stopped breathing, his entire body frozen at that name. My mind raced as Mal sat there, staring at us with frantic eyes, offering neither answers nor questions of his own.

Only when Iden started moving toward the stairwell did he speak. "Don't. Oren's dead."

I saw more than just grief on his face, but I wasn't sure what. He rubbed his beard, dried blood on his hands.

"How'd he die?" I asked. My voice, quiet, echoed in my chest.

Mal stared at the ground as if his eyes could bore through the levels beneath. "I think that's the Red Demon down there, killing people." He looked at Iden.

"The Chaeten-sa? We saw her," Iden said. "Did she kill Oren?"

Mal stared off into the dark.

"Mal?" I tried again.

I'd never seen Mal wear that look before. Distant, broken. "Most of them just died—dropped like hail. Not us. Oren was shaken up, but the Chaeten-sa didn't get him."

"So how'd he die?" Iden growled.

Mal shifted back on the desk, his eyes latched on Iden. "I killed him." His whisper cut the air between us.

"No." I refused to understand. I could see the guilt in Mal. Maybe he watched Oren die. Maybe Mal just felt guilty that he couldn't save him. "No," I repeated, uncertain, when nothing in Mal's expression so much as flickered.

Iden shook his head, kept shaking it. "Keep it together, Mal." He reached a hand to Mal, who just stared at it. "If he's dead, we'll get out of here, and we'll figure the rest out."

Mal hoisted himself to a stand. "I killed Oren with my knife." He motioned to a stain on his thigh, a slash through the clothing. "He tried to kill me first. That's all he got in on me." He shuddered, collapsing back down into a chair.

"Why?" I whispered. All my memories of Oren had smile lines: the only dark-haired one among us. He'd be sitting across the table at dinner laughing, or letting me ride on his shoulders through the forest.

The metallic screech rent the air again, closer this time, shuddering through the floorboards and shaking the stone walls.

My heart beat wild as shelves clattered to the ground, mugs shattered and tables toppled. Raw panic spurred us into a run.

Iden's lantern wove swaying shadows in the dust-thickened air. We reached the office door then scanned the hallway: clear. The glass in the front windows shattered on the floor.

"What is happening?" I yelled at Mal, but I'm not sure he heard. That rasp in my throat was nothing compared to the rhythmic clang that pained my ears, or the groan of twisted metal as it shredded the structural beams, collapsing the office floor behind us.

"The rigs!" Iden yelled over the noise.

We ran past the truck bay. The floor beneath us shuddered, but we kept our feet, dust raining down from the ceiling. It made little sense. The machines wouldn't do this unless—*unless someone programmed them to.*

Fuck.

Fear pulled air from my lungs. Our drill rigs were tearing this place down beam by beam. The ceiling at the other end of the hall caved in, and the ground beneath me shuddered. I coughed through a cloud of dust.

The sounds of grinding metal echoed louder through the stone floor, but stone wouldn't stop machines that could carve a meter a minute through solid granite and crack through imperfections much faster. We sprinted toward the fading light of the mine entrance. Iden stooped to grab my bag from the front; his was long gone in the collapsed office.

We burst into waning twilight. Mal, a few long strides ahead of us, stumbled on the bone-shaking ground.

"Mal, get up!" I knelt down, lifting him to his feet before chasing after Iden.

I slowed my steps on the quaking, icy road. Whirling around, I expected to find Mal there. He was at least twenty paces behind now, limping. My gaze shifted to the broad mine entrance, billowing dust.

A figure leaped out into the twilight, her bright red hair streaming behind her. The Red Demon charged in her begrimed leather armor, hands on the hilts of both her swords.

"Jesse! Mal!"

I faltered.

"Run!" Iden yelled.

My feet planted to a stop, my instincts warring between escape and going back for Mal. The Red Demon had swords, prime engineering in her code, and I had nothing to defend my brother. My hunting knife lay buried in mine rubble. I moved my traitorous feet like Iden told me to: ten more paces, twenty. When I turned again, trees leaned uprooted on the dented hills above the mine entrance, their angry branches clawing the red winter sky. My heart stuttered when I found Mal—standing, knife out, too far away.

A flash of silver, a burst of crimson. My blood turned as cold as the void, an icy vacuum stealing my breath. I was close enough to see the Red Demon's impassive face when she killed my brother. I was close enough to see the maze of little scars, like old Asri art, on her muscled arms. And I was close enough to see the spray of blood as she cut Mal down like a sapling on her path. It replays in my nightmares to this day: one swipe across his chest, one thrust between his ribs. A kick to his chest to remove her blades. His knees buckled as he fell with a hollow gasp, the light in his eyes fading. He reached for me. His eyes found mine.

My mind stilled, hollow. I stared at the Red Demon glittering with my brother's blood, trying to understand. For a moment, I got the sense that I did; that nothing was real but her and me. Maybe that's the same thing that smaller animals feel when they face down a predator and stop running. They make it all make sense; get high on their own hormones before they die.

The Red Demon didn't charge. She didn't look like she wanted to, standing tall and cocking her head at me. She was terrifying, enchanting, and other words that sprang to mind that shame me even now. My brother was dead at her feet, his blood still coming in gushes, and my traitorous brain chose that moment to find her beautiful.

Time slowed, the clang of the rising rigs scarcely registered. One long exhale escaped me, then my breaths came fast and shallow. Iden screamed beside me, a hoarse roar that overcame the sheer impossibility of it all. The snow drifted down around us. Iden pulled my arm, his face desperate and pleading.

When we ran, the Red Demon followed, but she didn't outpace us. She could have.

We kept catching glimpses of movement behind us, so we kept on running. When Iden lagged behind, he let me shoulder the pack instead. We walked a few paces for the exchange, and ran again along the rocks and deer path, sliding down hills and angling up them to avoid slipping on the ice. About an hour later, Iden was wheezing and slouched, and I coughed with my sides throbbing. Below the mist of our breath arced a rippling stream. We stopped there, standing alone under the stars.

I put my arms around Iden as the flurries of snow stilled. He leaned in, his head on my shoulder. When he shuddered against me, I gripped tighter, pulling the cold sweat of his forehead to mine. We stayed like that for a moment, keeping ourselves warm through shared breaths, holding each other up.

I looked back at our footprints in the snow, to the trail that would tell the Red Demon exactly where to find us.

CHAPTER 3

Deer Stand

Iden washed the mine dust from his face in the icy river, leaving only his exhaustion behind.

Looking around at the snow-blanketed hills, I felt grateful that Iden paid attention to where we were going. The tall cedars that creaked far up into the night sky were outlines I recognized, the smaller pines underneath familiar friends.

"Dad's deer stand isn't too far from here." I was ready to collapse.

"Yeah," Iden said.

We walked along the rocks of the river to hide the last part of our journey, hoping that was enough.

The deer stand along that glittering stream wasn't what it once was; it had been about five years since we built it with Dad. And by we, I mean Dad, Oren, and Mal—all using their powerful muscles to saw and plane logs. I'd watched them anchor the boards into the wide trunk, hammering with a crack that echoed through the forest. Meanwhile, Iden and I played at fetching things, but spent most of our time pretending sticks were swords. Maybe if Iden and I were more helpful that day, Dad would have found time for a second layer of sealant so that the caulk didn't peel off, and there wouldn't be cracks in the tarpaper roof. But mossy boards were better than the snowy ground, and there were walls. Walls with holes to shoot deer from, but walls.

We settled in with the single blanket we had in the one pack, huddling together as best we could. Mushroom flour flatbread and jerky satisfied what little appetite we had, followed by metallic-tasting water from the canteen. The structure swayed with the branches in the wind, with each gust seeping through the weathered bones of the frame.

We lay back to back rather than risk a fire the Red Demon could see. The silence felt hollow as our shivering kept us awake, but any words I tried tasted like ash on my tongue. I had no words for Iden that were both hopeful and true. My thoughts drifted to the cold beds in my childhood home, the silence of all those dark rooms in all those dark houses, and my sisters' bodies lying underneath the fresh snow. We'd need to get back to burn them before the wild dogs and crows found them.

"You think—" I said, my voice cracking in the dry air. "How much longer do you think it will be until the empire sends help?"

A ragged sigh escaped Iden and dissolved into the night. "They'd be here already if half of what the priests said was true. Exaggerating fucks."

I'd come to the same conclusion myself, but I needed to hear that anyway. General Alexander had a satellite system monitoring for any major attack, ensuring he didn't lose the peace that he and the queen had fought so hard for. History at school or news at the temple were full of stories of Jeron Alexander's armies coming to destroy clusters of rebels, or our queen defending Chaeten from century-old bigotry. Even if civilians lived with minimal tech to not give magic a foothold, the empire should have trucks, drones, at least horses to mobilize fast from the nearest Z'har barrack.

By now, we should have heard army trucks rumbling along the road between the gorges or seen airships lighting the milky, star-flecked sky.

"Did you hear that?" Iden said.

I focused, unsure if I was imagining the flicker of fear in his voice. I heard nothing but the sigh of the wind through the branches. "Hear what?"

Iden sat up, startled. "Thought I heard a kid's voice," he muttered, shaking his head.

The treehouse creaked. Rising, I shivered as a breeze tickled my neck.

"Just the wind, I think." My laugh sounded brittle.

Iden shivered. "There's a man whispering now. From there..." He pointed wide-eyed through the gap in the boards, toward the dense shadows at the edge of the clearing.

Only gnarled shapes of trees reached out from the darkness; the dancing shadows cast by the moon. I looked back, bewildered.

"M–Maybe I just need sleep." His voice lacked conviction. But his eyes, even in the faint moonlight, held a ghost of something I couldn't name, something that reminded me of Mal. I rubbed the bruised abdomen where Mal had punched me, the last touch from my brother.

Sleep felt like a betrayal. Dreams waved in and out of waking thoughts, fitful cycles of Mal's final, choked gasp before I'd raise my head to scan the woods once more. I'd see Mal's wild eyes flickering in the dark, pulling that knife on me. Then he'd be standing sentinel in our tree stand, staring into the darkness where Iden heard the voices. In that place between waking and dream, I felt a presence haunting the forest. When the first rays of dawn bruised the sky, Iden was gone.

"Iden?" I hissed. I didn't dare yell, but his tracks were clear in the drifting snow.

I shoved the blanket back into our bag, then shimmied down the bark where the steps had fallen off, landing with a crunch of ice. Iden's tracks led me upstream where he sat by the bank, an empty canteen beside him.

"What's wrong?" I asked. A stupid question if there ever was one.

Iden didn't respond, his eyes fixed on the trickle of water between planes of fresh ice.

"They've been waiting for me all night," he said, voice raw in the cold.

"Who?"

He pointed to something in the snow, footsteps, not ours, circling back through the wood near our tree. "They're afraid of the Red Demon too." Iden turned his haunted eyes to me. "She's watching us now, somewhere near that ridge."

"Is that who you heard last night? Her?" It clicked into place, the prickling of unease beyond the cold; the feeling of being watched.

"A whole crowd of them are watching me, but it only takes one," Iden whispered. He scratched his hair, pulled it. "And there's only my set of tracks, so..." A bitter laugh escaped him.

"What the fuck, Iden?" He winced. I took a deep breath. "I don't understand what you're talking about."

He opened his mouth, stopped himself, tried again. "I've been trying to remember everything we learned about Chaeten-sa, to make sense of this. Not the General, the rest of them. I wished I'd paid more attention."

My mouth opened. "Why?"

"Most of those others went crazy, or died too young to see battle," he said. "They'd break in different ways, even after the war, right? Did Ms. Orozca ever tell us why?"

I remembered the lesson from school. Suicide rates among Chaeten-sa were very high after the war. Some would see things that weren't there. Some seemed healthy, then killed friends—unprovoked.

"Dad said we're unbreakable. They got stronger mods than any of us. They still broke." Iden's head jerked up, looking around.

I saw nothing. My breath hitched, lost. "So? They're not you."

Iden held my stare. "I'm breaking, Jesse."

"You're fine," I said, too quickly. I followed his gaze to the sky, the clouds tinged with red. "I won't let you break."

He didn't look at me. "She's close."

I scanned the woods for the Red Demon—the one who must have done this to him. The trees watched in silence on the ridge where Iden focused his attention.

"So why won't she come out?" I asked, loud enough to echo.

Iden rocked his knees against his body. "One of the louder ones says that when you look into her eyes, you know when it's your time."

"Who?"

He gestured to the surrounding air, his jaw clenching. A crow cawed and flew off before he turned back, staring past me over my shoulder.

"Iden..." My voice trembled in the cold.

Iden stood up, his face resolute. "Get out of here. Take the bag and go."

His words were like a punch to the gut. I couldn't speak.

"Keep going north. Stick to the woods," he said in a rush, watching the trees behind me. "Stay away from the Asri towns. Get help from a Chaeten colony with lots of Z'har, or a military barrack. You got that?"

The Z'har were those who pledged their lives to keep the empire safe, serving Queen Azara and General Alexander as priests, soldiers, or scholars. They hadn't kept us safe.

"You could book passage to the Inner Empire after. There's more of us there." A flicker of warmth. Iden had dreamed of seeing the shining city lights in Thebos or the palace in Ea Shadohe, but I watched those dreams die behind his eyes.

"C'mon, Iden," I said, shaking. I couldn't make myself understand.

"Jesse." He turned, his voice so fucking calm. "Don't—" his voice choked off, he put his fist in his hand.

The wind tinkled in the frozen branches. I didn't move. Iden stepped closer.

His hand on my cheek stopped my head from shaking. His gloved palm felt warm against the biting wind. "Jesse," he whispered, the grit in his voice chafing my hope. "Don't watch me die."

Wet eyes blurring the image of a resolve I didn't have the strength to crack.

"Come with me, Iden." My voice felt strangled. "Keep it together. Just get through today."

Iden shook his head. "Don't watch me die," he pleaded, his gaze flicking to the dark line of trees behind me.

A rustle, soft as a sigh in the wind, a last breath of fear. I spun, my heart pounding on the doors of my chest, and there she was, looking straight at Iden.

She stalked from the trees, one slow step, then another. Her long scarlet hair cascaded down her back, with dawn glowing on her face. I analyzed every ragged scrap of that antique, studded armor. I memorized every scar I could see on her lean muscled frame, her golden skin stretched over high cheekbones. Her piercing yellow-green eyes met mine.

I stood taller, too angry to be afraid. "What do you want?"

The slow, deliberate way she unsheathed her twin swords, the glint of cold steel catching the sunlight, was her only reply. I didn't bother to go for my pocket knife, not after how I saw her move against Mal. I had neither the skills nor the weapons to make a difference.

"What do you want with us?!" I repeated, putting my body in front of Iden. She cocked her head at me, curious.

"Go, Jesse," Iden said, resolute, past all fear.

The Red Demon took another measured step forward, her boots crunching on the frozen ground. Her gaze brushed past me, fixed on Iden. At that moment, I believed my brother was right. I could see my fate in her eyes: she'd marked him; I was inconsequential.

"Pick up the bag, Jesse. Go!" Iden drew his hunting knife from his belt with a shaking hand.

He didn't draw on her. He drew on me.

I watched him, stunned, as he took a second hand to pry the knife from his own grip, flipping the hilt toward me instead of the blade.

I clasped the handle, which he struggled to let go of. Confusion disrupted any lingering excuses. The Red Demon waited in silence as I picked up that bag with shaking hands. I clasped Iden's shoulder one last time, thinking about pulling him with me, but his muscles tensed under my hand.

"Go!" he roared at me.

With a choked sob, I forced my legs to move ahead of my mind, carrying me away from the stream, away from the last person alive who knew my name. I crashed through undergrowth, pushing icy air through my lungs, the forest a blur of ice and pine.

Iden got his last wish. I didn't see him die. But his scream rumbled through the trees and echoed off the gorges. That sound has yet to stop haunting my dreams.

Chapter 4

Another Dream

Faruhar

I don't ask her name. I imagine she doesn't even have one.

"May I tell you everything?" The words catch in my throat—I haven't used my voice in a while, I guess.

"Why, Chaeten-sa?" she asks, her gaze a soft blur above a red dress. Every detail shifts like smoke. Her eyes, the color of moss after rain, might have been brown a heartbeat ago. I watch as they drift to blue ringing a sandy gold in the next moment: Asri eyes instead of the Chaeten green they started. The surrounding tavern lights breathe with me, shadows flickering and details of the room shifting with an impatience I can't control. Today is a bad day, one where it's difficult to focus on what's real. I try to hold her details steady: the black hair, the blue dress.

I give up.

There is a woman with warm brown skin I want to see most of all, one whose smile glowed, a woman who held me when I was small. I can't make the woman in front of me be the one I trust. I've never had that much control. But the shifting figure in front of me is not trying to kill me yet. Good enough.

"I want to tell you everything because you aren't real," I say. "It still helps, sometimes."

She's laughing—a breathy, amused sound that does little to chase away the unease clawing at my insides. "You were always such a strange girl," she says, her words tinged with … something. A threat, I guess. When in doubt, it's that.

"Always? Do you know me?" She wouldn't be the first person I forgot.

If she answers, I lose the words in the wind's rush, a phantom gust that chills me. Then the lights in the room dim, flicker like dying stars. I lose focus on her brown eyes, her green dress.

"I told you not to come back," a different woman says. She kneels down to me on the floor, although I was sitting in a chair a moment ago. I've become small, and I hate that. It's easier for people to hurt me when I'm young. They attack more often. So I, in turn, attack more often too.

At some level, I know this means this must be a memory or a dream, nothing real and happening now. It all feels the same, though.

"They know what you are," the woman says.

"So tell them to stay away," I hear myself say in a child's voice.

"You should go before they try to kill you." Her image shifts too fast to know if that's concern in her face, or if I need to kill her too.

"Again? I just got here." The word tastes sour on my tongue.

I can see her face now. Hard, resigned. But a soft face that looks similar to the one I trust. I study it, hoping to recognize her. No, this other woman simmers anger in a way the one I trust never could, even when I deserved it. The one I trust was crying when I saw her last, and that was my fault. The woman I trust had a name, even if I lost it.

"Who did you kill this time?" The woman wears a cloak now, a scarlet shadow obscuring her form. Someone else, and I'm overwhelmed by it all.

It's easier to look away, to let none of them be real. I can react to threats as they come and allow myself to feel nothing. But for my sister's sake—for Bria—I pay attention, just in case I see someone real, not another shadow that deserves death. For her sake, I do everything. There's no blood around me yet, and no bodies. So far, so good.

It's a man's face I see now, Chaeten with dark skin and short black hair, his arms crossed. There's no hate in him, just confusion. So I talk.

"Here's everything I know. I can focus better if I stay near the same people every day. When things stay the same between days, a place or a person, I remember more. My sister said I should make myself useful." When I turn, the man is gone. No one stays long.

I wish I could control what I feel on bad days. There should be a way to create something other than the feeling of running alone in frozen woods. I can only keep the feeling of what happened, the rooms and scars those memories leave behind, the starving cold sky.

The woman I trusted as a child would know what to say. She never killed anyone, even the people that needed killing. Is she dead now? Did I kill her too? I know what I'm good at.

I'm back indoors at a table. Warm. A man, bronze skinned now, passes me a bag of coin and a portrait. "Can you kill him?"

"Yes," I say. "Why?"

He just nods at the envelope, and I open it, the words blurring like wet ink after I read them. "Okay," I say. I accept it. He must have given me a good reason. At least I can do half of what Bria wants by helping this man. I'm around people, and it's useful: the best I can do. It's too difficult to follow all the rules at once.

I'm in a little cabin now, at night. I hear footsteps in the darkness. Someone watches from the other side of the room.

I get up, the slick metallic scent unmistakable. My eyes adjust to the darkness to see the slumped form of a man, my blade in his chest. I clean it on the rug by the fire. Sheathing it, I wonder who he was.

I force my eyes closed until I'm somewhere else.

"Okay then. Tell me everything." A man's voice, but not unkind. When I open my eyes, the blood is gone. It's a little outdoor gazebo, tea on the table before me. My skin feels clean and clothes fresh, a cushion under my legs.

With a sigh, I plod on.

"I know what I'm good at, but I don't want to hurt anyone," I say with a shudder. The images in my head are not ones I like, the last blink of so many eyes, the crack of so many bones in my hands. That's all I have to share with him. The man looks back at me with kind Chaeten eyes—someone good. I want to help him any way I can.

He flicks his shining black hair away and smiles like someone I'm sure I once knew. I decide to trust him when he reaches for my hand. "You can stay, but we'll need to keep this secret. There are true dangers here, and I'm not talking about the wild dogs." He chuckles, although I don't understand the joke. His hand feels warm in mine, his grip strong and protective.

"Do you mean Mahakal?" I say. There are a few names I remember, but I fear that name. I don't think the man in front of me fears much of anything.

We leave the gazebo and walk on through the woods on a summer afternoon. I listen to him and answer his questions, retaining only the feel of the words as they leave me. My name, why I'm there: I lose it all downstream. Perhaps this is a memory, and I remembered back then—perhaps it's all lies. I watch his face when he accepts it—accepts who he thinks I am.

When he smiles, it's dazzling.

The images rush, but I sift out what I can. I can see the silver trunk of the trees, the rippling of the water. Memories of good days with him. An open door to a stone cottage, painted over in green and yellow, bright colors he thought I liked, and I suppose I do. They remind me of him. I know the feel of every room in that house, the taste of the water, the softness of a bed that's all my own. I remember a workshop, the smell of steel and leather, not blood.

My friend turns to me, with a few more lines on his face than I expect. I know what his smiles feel like. He's never looked at me like this before.

"I'm sorry." I mean that more than anything else I must have said before.

He doesn't look at me as he pushes his hair out of his face in the way he always does, a few streaks of white speckled in with the dark. "I don't think you are." His voice falters. "You should have warned me."

I can't make out my next words, or his accusation. I struggle to hold on to the details, to reach out to him as he walks away, disgusted.

The cottage falls dark. I get up, knowing I've been here before, with the slick metallic scent between my fingers. I let my eyes adjust to the darkness and see the slumped form of a man against the wall. That man—the friend who I couldn't name—a blade glittering in his chest. I clean it on the rug by the fire, then sheath it like before.

Like so many times before. I decide that next time I will write their names down before I forget. Keep a record of my wrongs.

I close my eyes, focusing on the sound of laughter in a tavern. There are happy people here. People I shouldn't kill. I focus on that, knowing that if I wish for silence, I might create it—I open my eyes to find them dead, too.

"Bria, I need you," I whisper her name, my throat dry.

The darkness thickens, pressing in on me, candles gutter in protest. I let it all go, turn to the icy air where there is no one to harm; no one to harm me. It's winter now, cold snow under my running feet. There's evergreen and cedar and blood in the snow where I clean my blades next to dead strangers.

"Bria, can you help me?" I plead, my voice a tremor in the stillness.

When I break her rules too much, she hides from me. I must have failed her again.

"Bria. Sister, I need your help," I whisper, the words rasping like sandpaper against my throat. "It's cold. I can't focus. Tell me what's real."

Snowflakes sting my bare arms. The ground rumbles under me in the darkness where I've left the machinery of the mine behind.

From the top of a mossy deer stand, I glance down to see a pale-skinned man with blond curls lying dead by the stream, and there's my little sister Bria beside him, her crescent eyes filled with tears as she looks over the boy's body. I climb down and run to her.

My sister is a frail child, her copper skin muted with cold, her lips blue. She says nothing, just shivers with me in the expanse of white, her thin rags with swirling designs doing nothing to protect her from the wind.

I smile at her. "Bria."

She steps away from the man and walks over.

"It will be over soon," Bria says, offering her hand. "Let's go."

And we step into another dream. And another.

CHAPTER 5

A Dirt Path Between Worlds

Jesse

Heartache is not a metaphor. I've since learned not everyone knows sadness can manifest as actual pain. Although I tried to keep my head clear, I wore my despair with every breath, and that sadness tried to pound its way out of my chest when I'd lie under the stars.

I knew I'd live to see better days, that I had the power to make that true—or die before I caught the lie in it. That belief kept me going every lonely morning and every frigid night. Grief wouldn't fill the hollowness that echoed between every beat of my heart, a good hunt would. Despair wouldn't return feeling to my hands or stinging face when I couldn't stay dry and warm, a better shelter would. Tears wouldn't bring back my mom or siblings because nothing would, ever.

Iden hurt most of all, the last pillar of my life, fallen.

To get through it, I'd go to bed thinking about what I needed to do next to stay alive. And by bed, I mean a pile of leaves under an arrangement of branches that I'd crawl into the middle of for insulation. On a clear night in deep forest, I'd build that shelter by a campfire, bulking the blanket and tarp with whatever I could find. The wet days were the hardest, when I couldn't get a fire started, when my fingers and toes would start to freeze. The numbness would last for days, but I always managed to heal back to normal—for a time.

Those stars were beautiful, though. I could see deep into the void on those nights: the milky trails of gas between solar systems, people like me deep in the black spaces in between. Other people overcame that hollowness, the nothing in between the pinpricks. I'd do the same. Step one: survive the night. Step one thousand: kill the Red Demon. Somewhere in between, I'd do what Iden suggested: find other Chaeten, avoid Asri, get help from the empire.

I knew if I stayed on the road where any empire vehicles could see me, anyone else might see me too. Yet I saw only hoof prints in mud beside those roads rather than imprints of truck wheels, and those horses were most likely owned by Asri. So I traveled near enough to the road to hear a passing vehicle driven by other Chaeten, but not near enough to be seen, sticking to deer paths and streams. Days bled into weeks as I avoided the patchwork of settlements along the roads. Thus far, they were all Asri, and I'd yet to hear the rumble of a single engine by road or sky.

I assumed Asri enemies were always near, creeping with the same quiet steps I used while hunting game. Hiding my bag outside of camp while foraging proved insightful, after I found my shelter destroyed and ransacked one day. I kept moving, which meant I could not process big game and struggled to hunt enough to keep my muscles full and strong. Fish, snared rabbits, snow-buried greens, and winter berries kept me alive.

Chaeten settlements like mine were few and far between on Noé. Most of us lived in the inner empire: in Thebos, our first foothold as refugees, or the cities on the islands of Iyad or Meyit. But we'd won our right to breathe the Nara's air long ago, and I knew I'd find a sign of my people soon. Maybe over that next ridge, I'd see a wall painted in ochre red for the empire's Z'har, and beyond it wooden houses in a rainbow of colors. I'd smell cooked meat over a fire and hear words I recognized. Day after day I'd try to wish that into being, finding only ruins from the decades-old war, or Asri towns with millennia-old stone cottages. Between lines of snow lay brown harvested rows of lentils and vegetables, or hills piled with compost and straw for their mushrooms.

I lasted about a month before I developed a cough that racked me throughout the icy night. The next morning I felt weaker, and the morning after that, I barely found strength to rise. That afternoon, I found myself too close to town to light a fire without giving myself away, and I was afraid I'd die in that snow unless I risked it.

So I risked it.

The woods thinned as I walked the main road, revealing a sprawl of smoke-stained rooftops within the Asri town. I thought back to all of Mr. Gell's lessons I could remember, all the foreign phrases I pushed rather than rolled off my tongue. He wasn't the only Asri who didn't want to kill me, I hoped more than believed. At that point, I figured I wasn't long for the void either way. I wondered if we were at war, if my queen was dead.

A coughing fit overtook me as I approached the town gate, fear sour in my throat. A guard manned the perch above the gate, wearing a thick swirling robe of glittering black. I dared not meet his ringed Asri eyes for more than a moment.

He scowled, but didn't stop me. The snow crunched as I stepped under the arch. Worn cobbled streets edged in moss snaked between weathered stone houses, their windows glowing with a warmth that my rasping lungs dearly missed. I walked past a cluster of people loading up a horse cart. No drones or machines anywhere that I could see, just animals and people wearing folded robes in muted colors. Heads of braided hair swiveled under cloaks that looked nothing like my once bright blue coat. Whispers pricked my skin like dry leaves skittering down the cobblestone.

On the next street, a long-haired boy no older than five pointed a stubby finger, his eyes wide. I walked with a slight limp—bedraggled, colorful, and Chaeten. A smile from me was enough to make the poor kid scream and run off. I wondered if that was my grime, or something I'd never be able to wash off.

I kept my chin held high as I studied the swirling scrawl of Asri script on the signs above the building, hoping to find the word for healer. My smile felt brittle, but I plastered it on my frost-cracked lips when anyone walked close. Mr. Gell always told me if you can't remember how to say something, a smile is universal. I hid my shaking cracked hands in the pockets of my cloak, borrowing Mr. Gell's optimism, because I only made out bits and pieces of the rapid murmurs around me.

The smell of spices and baked bread assaulted my senses as I found an open air market. Crossing under carved stone awnings, I looked around booths and shops selling clothes, housewares, and warm drinks. I only had a little coin, but now seemed like the time to spend it.

"Do you have coffee?" I asked a man at the drink stand. The word for coffee was the same in each language: they stole ours.

"No," he said.

How the Asri live without coffee after rediscovering it remains one of the things I will never understand about them. I made out the word for tea among a string of other script I didn't recognize, but I tried to hide my unease. He was barely a man, a little older than me, with bright blue in the center of his ringed amber eyes.

"How much for tea?" I asked in Asri.

He frowned, replying with a slow cadence. Nodding, I handed over a couple coins. I didn't remember how to ask for honey, but he pointed at things for me to nod to. He gestured down the road and said something I could only smile at, catching the words for "temple" and "walk". I brushed off some snow on a nearby bench, the stone cold under me as I sat. The tea tasted milky, sweet with ginger and turmeric. I savored it as long as I could.

A wizened, white-haired woman, hair spun up in braids, caught my gaze from where she arranged clay pots and kitchen supplies a few booths down. Her gaze pierced the street between us, questioning. When I was done, I walked her way.

"Good afternoon," I said, my voice raspy from disuse and the cold. "I, uh, I need a…" I couldn't remember the word for a pot. "I need to cook."

The woman's expression flickered, surprised but not unkind. "You need this?" she said in Asri. I recognized the word when she used it. "*Komaldi, na.* Pot," she repeated in Chaeten.

"Thank you." A nervous laugh escaped my lips after I stifled my cough. "I need a small one."

A hint of a frown graced the woman's lips as she pulled one down from the wall across from her booth, folding the handle down. "Why small? A boy cooking alone in winter, why?" She chose small Asri words, her voice rough and warm. Still, I wasn't an idiot. I couldn't admit I was vulnerable, that I had no one to avenge me if they killed me outright in that market.

"How much?" I asked, smiling.

She told me, then asked her question again with a few other words I didn't understand, her brow furrowed. "You here alone? Why this?" she asked again in Chaeten.

I stammered out a thank you as I fished the coins from my pocket and hustled away.

There were curious glances as I wandered the streets, and one woman who reared her horse away from me on the road with a curse. Someone followed me down the road a few blocks, but no one threatened me.

I finally found a pharmacy, grateful I had enough coin to buy some herbs for my cough. As I walked out of the Asri town—close to sunset, with the folding pan under my arm and the bag of herbs in my pocket, a flicker of hope warmed my aching ribs. I felt brave enough to light a fire that night outside of town. I brewed some tea in my pot and cobbled together some scallions, mushroom and animal fat to make something of a soup.

The next morning, my cough was less racking. By the following day, it was gone.

When the Asri ancestors terraformed Nara Mnaet, they built forests full of useful things that would yield food in any season. After I'd recovered from my cough, I gathered what I could find in the woods outside the town: cranberries, chives, and a patch of wintergreen. I walked back into the same Asri town where I bought my medicine, found the market, and laid the bundles on my blanket in an empty spot on the ground. I sat by my wares, waiting.

Although I'd yet to risk hypothermia from bathing in an icy river, I'd made sure I was presentable. I'd heated water in my new pot and cobbled soap from wood ash and animal fat. While the traces of charcoal left their mark on my clothes, I trusted they'd smell my berries and mint before me.

To my delight, it worked. I sold some of those chives and berries. Around noon, I broke down and ate a basket myself before selling a few more. In the early afternoon, an old woman in an elaborately swirled cloak approached: a town elder, I think.

She smiled; I smiled back. I didn't understand all her questions, but I understood when she asked me to leave.

After I found my way through the woods and back to camp, I refused to risk staying another night. Maybe some Asri here wanted to do more than ask me to leave; maybe they'd hunt me. Packing up, I kept walking toward the coast, hearing birdsong the following morning for the first time in months.

In the next town, they too asked me to leave after three days of sales. I kept that going, continuing north. I learned to fold wax leaves into baskets for a cleaner presentation and learned which nuts would still look edible if I could rescue them from under the snow. Hot meals in taverns got me through the coldest days, especially when the snow fell wet and heavy. Even when I had enough coin for a few night's stay at an inn, I saved that in case I needed passage on a ship to the inner empire. I'd survived this long outdoors.

Animal pelts and game: those I'd learned not to bother with; not to wear, and certainly not to sell. The Asri did not believe in harming any creature with a brain. *"Niire Mai"* is how they say that; "Never harm," more or less. My leather bag alone was enough for me to be turned away at a town gate once. Lesson learned.

My worst encounter, in a grove-shadowed town built around a whispering river, left me feeling like a kicked dog. The market smelled of spice and horse waste, with stalls overflowing with goods. I approached a century fabric booth. I'd read about it in school, but never saw it up close until that day. It appeared delicate and thin like silk, most woven in a maze-like design of animals and plants. Yet it was durable enough to outlive the owner, hence the name. Before the Asri lost their tower in the war, they used to wear the same robe from life to life, reincarnating, growing up and claiming it back from their family homes. Their immortals weren't reincarnating anymore, but they still made the robes.

Manipulating the fabric between my fingers, I asked the shopkeeper if they ever thought to thicken it up and make armor with it like Chaeten leather. It seemed to me their fabric would work just as well for armor. His bearded, sun-weathered face contorted in distaste. So did the braided woman in the booth next to him, selling pottery. They lashed their words at me, sharp and too fast for me to make out beyond the curses or *"Niire Mai"*. The fingers pointing out of the shop made the message clear enough. They followed me, yelling, until I was outside of the gates. Shame lit my cheeks as I'd retreated to the cold.

The Asri make swords for battle—they have exceptions to their rules against killing, as any Chaeten knows. So there should be nothing wrong with my question if I had the vocabulary to best frame it. Beyond "how much is this?" and the phrases I used to sell my forest goods, any attempt at conversation would resort to pantomime at some point—false starts that left me feeling like a babbling idiot.

So I needed to keep whittling down the language barrier, and to do that, I'd need to keep talking to people—Asri people.

Each quiet night, the forest became my classroom. I mimicked the rhythms of Asri speech, the lilt and dip of their voices, the way their hands danced in the air to paint spaces between certain phrases. I found comfort in the patterns, in repetition, in practicing something new. And at some point, that goal of bridging that understanding became just as important as what Iden suggested I do: find Z'har and tell them everything. I'd yet to stumble on a Chaeten soldier or police in their red uniforms, and I didn't trust the Asri enough to tell them where I'd come from even if I could get the words out. The North Barrack—the largest in Noé—must have known about the attack on my town by now, with as long as I'd been on the run. Besides that, I was in no rush to hop on a ship to a Chaeten city when all I knew was Noé. These tall trees smelled like home, the icy streams murmured words I knew, even when the Asri didn't.

I hadn't given up on finding my own people. I couldn't afford the license for a good tracking device, but I finally found a fabric printed map in my next Asri town that marked out a Chaeten settlement nearby.

Near the end of the three-day walk, I clutched the strap of my bag between gloved, numb fingers. I pushed through the brush onto the frozen road, reminding myself it should be safe to be out in the open now. The sun dipped lower, casting long shadows beside me as the cold scratched my throat. I quickened my pace, hoping to arrive at the town before nightfall.

Then, I smelled it. Thick, greasy smoke, not the comforting burn of a fireplace. My heart raced away, trying to escape my panic. Fire meant people, but smoke like that...

Curiosity, tainted by fear, propelled me forward. The road twisted, the air heavy with the acrid odor, threatening to resurrect my cough. The trees thinned, and the settlement lay broken before me.

Desolation everywhere: skeletons of Chaeten houses, once painted in cheerful hues, stood charred, their roofs collapsed inward. My stomach lurched. I knew the scent of rancid blood, what was left of a deer weeks later if scavengers didn't find it first. Spoiled meat and burnt garbage filled my nostrils as I walked closer.

Voids, I should not be on this road, but there was only open land between me and the debris-littered wreckage. I walked closer in the gray light, past the blackened and rusted carcass of a truck and some other machine too broken to identify.

In the center of the town was the pyre, a macabre monument of bones. The edges of the pyre never fully burned, the bodies contorted and blackened where the snow had quenched the fire. Acid rose in my throat.

I ran for the woods. This wasn't war. This was a massacre, a calculated act of cruelty that spared the Asri towns around me, who were carrying on their lives and buying my fucking berries. How many killers had smiled at me, thinking of this?

I jogged north, planning in the dark, trying to put as much distance between myself and that town until my body gave out. Iden was right. I needed to go to the North Barrack, to take that ship to the central empire, to Thebos or Ea Shadohe. I waited for the courage to accompany that decision, to give me the strength to tear out the last bit of my life that felt familiar. Noé was not safe; home was a place I'd never been.

CHAPTER 6

Raven

Many weeks into my ritual of survival, a brush of morning sun-light seeped through my closed eyes. The sky above me rolled clear: violet splashed with streaks of rose and gold clouds. With a sigh, I crawled out of my piles of leaves to my feet, the damp chill of earth seeping through my worn cloak as I brushed off the debris. I'd traded for an Asri style cloak a few days before, wearing it over my Chaeten coat. I found it put strangers at ease if I looked like everyone else from a distance. It put me at ease too.

The death scream of a rabbit found its way through my dreams last night, and I found it caught in my snare. I untangled it, field dressed it, and cooked it for breakfast.

I was two days from the North Barrack, and only a little light on cash. By a fallen oak, I hid my meager belongings under a pile of leaves. Then, I took my emptied backpack and walked into the woods to forage. As usual, I took that time to stoke my hope to a healthy fire, reminding myself that better days were coming.

The stream I followed wound through the forest, sunlight dappling on the water and sprinkling shadows through the leaves overhead. I thinned a patch of early morels that was too bountiful to harvest all at once. For variety, I selected some pale gooseberries and juicy strawberries, and I washed and packed them in my homemade boxes of woven wax leaves.

I could taste the promise of spring as I walked, serenaded by an orchestra of chirps and whistles and rustling leaves far above me. Then, the trees fell away, and the town bloomed before me.

The sun glinted off pale stone walls built to endure against time. Carvings ran the length of the marble walls on the first buildings, intricate swirls and spirals dating back thousands of years before a Chaeten ever dreamed of the Nara.

I offered a brief nod to the guard as I strolled past the stone gate, moss growing in every groove, the elaborate faded carvings telling stories of people I've never heard of and strange beasts I'd never seen. Few places in the Nara had recovered the population it held before the war a century ago, and this town was no exception. A couple of old cottages stood with boarded windows for every one with smoke coming out of the chimney.

I walked toward the open-air market that I'd learned would always be in the center of an Asri town. The scent of spices mingled with the earthy aroma of freshly baked mushroom and shortgrain bread as I passed the first booths, a smell that made my stomach rumble with hunger. Iden used to hate mushroom flour, even though the Asri staple was too affordable to ignore. I'd since learned to love it. The Asri cooked it much better. Children with sun-kissed skin chased each other through the square as I laid out my blanket and wares on a clear patch of grass, their laughter oblivious to the death of my Chaeten kin in villages to the south. Their parents mingled between the stalls.

I sat down next to my little baskets of mushrooms and berries. A middle-aged woman with dark hair caught my eye, approaching until her ringed eyes noted the pale green of mine. I kept my head high as she took a moment to look me over, frowning in suspicion. I just smiled as she kept walking.

A shadow blocked the sun. Black wings stretched before me, suspended in the sky. The huge raven descended in front of me with unsettling silence, resting at my feet. The beast that hopped onto the edge of my blanket was as large as a house cat, and it cocked intense black eyes at me, sizing me up as if I were prey. It let out a dry, guttural caw, loud enough to echo through the market. Its feathers gleamed green and blue and violet as it turned to fixate on a plump strawberry. With a snatch of its sharp beak, it unfurled massive wings, and I felt the beat of the air against my skin as it launched.

I swore under my breath when the raven arced around the market rather than fly away. It dipped again to fall onto a shoulder I recognized as Chaeten-sa.

For a moment, I couldn't breathe.

It wasn't her. I had to repeat that to myself. The Chaeten-sa man had the same yellow-green eyes etched with the strength of the cold void—the same grace as the woman who had killed my brothers. He stroked a gentle hand over his bird. Spiky red hair, bronze skin, and clean full armor, colored black and shimmering like the feathers of his pet. The queen's sigil on his armor wasn't enough to keep my blood from churning thick in my veins.

He wasn't alone: a ripple of silence spread through the sparse crowd as the unit of Z'har soldiers strode through the market in the traditional red, the Chaeten-sa at their center, black insignia of Azara's Introgression Tree on each soldier's shoulder. These were people I could trust, those who gave their lives in service of the empire. And one—no, two Asri soldiers strode among them with the same confidence, a testament to how much Queen Azara had done to bridge the divide between our cultures.

I reminded myself to stop staring like an idiot. This was what I was waiting for. Steeling myself as I jogged toward them, my voice cracked with an "Excuse me!"

A few heads turned, but not the Chaeten-sa's. I focused on a soldier with the most detailed uniform, a captain probably. A gruff man with tawny skin, and a jagged scar across his lips.

"Excuse me, sir," I said, after clearing my throat, "Do you have any news about the attack down south? Because—"

The Chaeten-sa's eyes whipped to me, the same inhuman motion as the woman who killed my brothers. I felt burned under his gaze and stopped talking. Beside him, the scar-faced captain moved his hand ever so slightly to the shining blade strapped across his thigh. He brought his hand back, forced a smile. I felt wary eyes on me as the surrounding crowd stopped to listen in.

"Which attack do you mean, friend?" the captain asked, voice rough as gravel. "Which village?"

My heart pounded at the gruff response. Their eyes were all narrow with suspicion, or darting onward, perhaps annoyed. I was someone whom it was their job to protect; someone they failed to protect.

"I have some friends in the Bend, spread about," I said, deciding not to risk the full truth out in the open air. Most of the Z'har soldiers appeared to relax, but not the Chaeten-sa. I felt the eyes I refused to meet burning into my face.

"Do you know who killed them? Are the attacks still happening?" I swallowed the lump of fear in my throat.

A grim silence descended. The captain's curt nod, sharp as a knife, confirmed my worst fears.

"How do you know so little?" The Chaeten-sa's voice was deep, piercing.

"I don't venture into town much," I said, still unable to meet his eyes for more than a moment.

The captain clamped his lips shut, and looked to the Chaeten-sa. "Shall I handle this for you, Major Mahakal?"

The Chaeten-sa, Mahakal I guess, took a moment before he tore his eyes away from me. "Yes please, Captain Havoc." He started walking away. "Meet us in the temple. Ren: stay with your captain."

"Yes sir, Major Mahakal," the captain said, in unison with the Asri Lieutenant Ren, a woman with straw-colored braids.

"Thank you for staying to talk, Captain Havoc," I said, heart pounding. "I'm worried my friends might be dead."

Captain Havoc furrowed his eyebrows. "It's possible. The rebels have hijacked quite a bit of tech in Chaeten settlements. Communication is limited, but the temples are tracking the casualty list."

I tried to hide my frustration at how incomplete that explanation was. "What can you tell me?"

"Only what any temple bulletin could. Every Chaeten town south of the Noé Bend was hit by rebels now in some capacity. Same bioweapon as the first attack on Crofton."

Crofton. My town. "What bioweapon? Why?"

The captain considered, looking as if I asked him to choose what to have for lunch.

"Where did you say you were from, friend?" Ren adjusted the pin in her hair that held her braid tight to her head.

I gulped, knowing the townspeople were listening too. "Can we talk in private somewhere? I live in the forest. Just out of the loop."

"I've never seen you before," Ren said.

The crowd whispered, but I didn't dare look up.

Captain Havoc frowned at his colleague before looking back at me. "All you need to know now is the rebels are spreading a disease. In most cases, the virus kills in seconds or minutes, but some infected can take up to a couple weeks, spreading disease all the while. The Bend is now in full quarantine, and we're about to start evacuation of the Asri towns too, one by one. Keep yourself above the Bend, make sure the temples inspect and license any tech you own, and tell anyone else *out-of-the-loop* the same." He put a suspicious stress on the "out-of-the-loop" part.

I made every effort to clear my thoughts from my face. *Could there really be a disease that kills people in minutes ... or seconds?* I thought of the bodies in the market, still holding their coins in their hands. And what of the Red Demon? I'd seen her kill my brothers, but they never mentioned her. Did they really know what was happening?

Fuck. My thoughts raced in circles. Maybe the truth was so much worse, and they just weren't going to tell me.

"You should check bulletins at the temple to stay informed, and you can inquire about your friends there for the usual search fee." The captain shifted on his feet, looking toward the direction the Chaeten-sa Major had gone.

"Will the temple tell me what happened to them? Or just whether they are alive?" I'd let too much anger into my voice. As the silence drew on, I did my best to hide my panic.

"They'll tell you anything safe to share," the captain said, saluting. "I'm sorry for your loss."

I didn't push further to ask about the Red Demon. They were already walking away.

But as I moved to head back to my blanket of wares, the Asri soldier called back. "Don't worry, friend," she said in fluent Chaeten, her voice softer than before. "The queen will ensure justice, as will Major Mahakal." She emphasized the titles with a reverence that seemed to warm her, make her stand taller. "Just get your information from the right place. The less gossip going around, the better."

Ren gave me an Asri salute, touching above her mind and heart before extending her hand out to me. I saluted back, and she turned to follow her captain. I studied the other soldiers' backs as they walked away.

The ground beneath my feet seemed to crack and shift as I retreated to the meager wares on my spread blanket. Whispers clung to the air of the market like the tail end of a storm. A few in the crowd stared at me, their eyes darting away when I looked up.

I was still mulling over what I'd learned when a shadow fell across my little bundles. I looked up to find an Asri boy about my age, tall, with the quiet intensity of a watchful cat. Something about his demeanor held a depth that reminded me, with a pang, of Iden, even if he looked nothing like him apart from some curls in his dark brown and sun-kissed hair. His skin was a shade darker than mine, and his amber eyes twinkled at me with gold-flecked centers.

He shifted nervously, fingers plucking at the hem of his cloak. "Those look good," he mumbled in Chaeten, his voice soft, hesitant.

"They're sweet," I replied in Asri, yanking a smile to my lips. "Just picked this morning."

He picked out a small basket of the plumpest strawberries and handed me a few coins. The juice stained his fingers as he picked the ripest one and tasted it. He offered me a shy nod.

I smiled.

"I heard what you said to the soldiers," he said, just above a whisper.

My smile faltered. I glanced around, masking my apprehension. "Heard what?"

"About the attacks," he said, his gaze unwavering as it met mine. "It was your family, wasn't it? Siblings or parents, not just friends?" He spoke that last part in Chaeten, making sure I understood. Chaeten has a word for kin, but not "family."

A lump formed in my throat. I nodded, unable to find my voice.

He took a step closer. "I'm sorry," he said, the words imbued with a sincerity that resonated deep within me. "For everything that's happening."

I swallowed, the ache in my chest a dull throb. "It's not like it's your fault," I said, surprised by the tremor in my voice. I pinched my eyes tight, trying to get a hold of myself. This boy was a stranger, not a friend. I missed friends.

He waited until I met his gaze again, his amber eyes holding me steady. "No. But I still... I want to end it rather than sit by and wait. The soldiers don't tell us much. But they're right about it all being contained to the Bend. You'll be safe if you stay here, near the coast."

A moment of silent communion passed between us. I didn't need to stay safe. I wanted to end this too.

He leaned in. "I think the rumors are right. It's ghosts in the Bend."

"Ghosts?"

He said it again, in Chaeten this time. "Just like in the Ghost War."

"I see," I said, my heart pounding. That's what the Asri called the war between the Chaeten and the Asri a century ago. I'd heard plenty of things about ghosts, all exaggerated and glorified and not something I could act on—things that belonged either in the past or in stories for children. But I knew the Chaeten destroyed an Asri tower early in the war, something that harnessed reincarnation, allowing Asri to be reborn as immortal Attiq-ka. A horde of Asri ghosts, their minds crazed and shattered, killed swathes of people the world over—mostly Asri, since there were more of them to begin with.

"I'm Asher. What's your name?" A smile played on his lips.

"Jesse." The name tasted foreign on my tongue after weeks of disuse. He'd been the first to ask.

Asher nodded, tucking the berries inside his cloak. "Your Asri is pretty good, you know."

"Don't you Asri believe it's wrong to lie?" I asked with a wry smile. I found it impossible not to warm up to him.

He gave a noncommittal gesture, borrowing Iden's smile again.

"The only Asri in my old town was my school teacher. I honestly never thought I'd use it with anyone else."

Asher huffed, a bright sound that warmed the air between us. "I enjoyed learning Chaeten," he admitted, using my language. "True, there are no words for so many things I want to say, but sometimes they have words in Chaeten for things we don't have. Both our worlds get bigger, you know?"

I raised an eyebrow. "Yeah?"

Asher shrugged, his grin turning mischievous. "Yeah. We're stronger now, right?" His eyes widened before he looked away. "Until the recent violence, anyway."

I smiled at his blush. Before I could reply, a booming voice interrupted our conversation. "Ash! Let's go!"

A burly Asri man stood at the edge of the market, black-bearded, with flecks of white in his tied-back hair. He looked at me and crossed muscular arms over his maze-designed robe, frowning.

"That's my dad. I have to go," Asher mumbled. "But don't tell anyone you came from the Bend. The soldiers will quarantine you to a refugee camp if they find out."

I frowned, trying to understand. Asher's father called his name again. "How did you know I came from the Bend?"

"It's my *dahn*," he said, but I didn't know that word. "Maybe we can talk again sometime? If you come back?"

"Maybe." A flicker of hope sparked in my chest. But that hope faltered when I glanced at Asher's father, and his deepening scowl.

Asher scampered off toward his father, then turned and saluted, as if he knew I watched him the whole way. I needed the curious warmth he left me with, the feeling that I wasn't entirely alone.

CHAPTER 7

The Forge

Rain slapped my face, rousing me from a restless sleep. My shelter of layered wax leaves had sprung leaks, and my new socks—ones I'd spent my foraging money on yesterday—were already damp and soggy. I groaned, cursing the fickle sky and my lack of engineering skills. Only the parts of my body beneath my cloak were still dry.

The embers of last night's fire still smoldered under the wax-leaf overhang, their faint glow swallowed by the morning mist and rain. I could coax the trickling smoke back to life with some wood under my tarp. I'd start there, wash and dry my clothes, have some breakfast, and patch the shelter before beginning foraging. No one had kicked me out of the market yet, so I planned to stay a day or two to build up my savings.

I stumbled out into the rain, now pelting down. The forest floor sloshed under my feet, damp leaves squelching in complaint.

That's when I heard it: the clang of steel striking steel, carried on the wind through dripping leaves—distant, but unmistakable. A shout. My pulse quickened, curiosity overcoming my sense of self-preservation. Grabbing my rope and knife, I crept closer to the sounds of the fray.

I needed to get a good look at what was happening without being seen. Using my rope, I draped it loosely around a cedar wider than both my arms. There was no knot or branch until further up, so I swung the rope around the other side, muscles straining as I shimmied up the rough bark. I'd climbed trees this size back when the worst I worried about was a wayward garter snake or a startled raccoon, but I didn't dare look down as I climbed higher and higher, stabbing into the bark with my knife when my grip slipped on mossy wood. I paused to relax my muscles, then kept going until I had a perch with a good view of the forest.

The rain thinned as I climbed, the sun filtering pink through dense clouds. Wind chilled through my damp clothes as the forest spread beneath me. Beyond it, I could spy the slate roofs atop their engraved white walls, the town washed clean by the rain. And in between, in a little clearing at the edge of the forest, I saw the source of the clangs and shouts.

I counted eight, no, nine figures moving around that clearing. The rain blurred their movements, but my Chaeten eyes, modded for the mines, could make out the swords in their hands. My heart skipped a beat when I saw the boy from yesterday: Asher, his wavy hair plastered to his forehead, his wooden sword spinning in his hands. And beside him, taller and broader, stood Asher's father, black and pepper hair and arms folded across his thick chest.

Asher's dad barked commands to three pairs of sparring partners, moving between the groups, his own sword a blur of silver as he demonstrated a swift attack and parry. Everyone wore armor. Asher and his sparring partner used wooden blades while the others used steel. I watched, mesmerized, as Asher stumbled back from a devastating blow, then rallied, launching himself forward with a yell. Asher held himself well, light on his feet between strikes. I couldn't help but smile, rooting for him.

They all fought as if their lives depended on it. I watched transfixed as a woman rolled from a brutal attack, getting back up and swinging at record speed.

But then, another thought struck me. Why were they training at all? There was a unit of soldiers just down the road, and none of them were present. *Oh fuck, were these guys the rebels those soldiers talked about? Is that why they were training at dawn?* That would mean Asher was involved in this too.

Asher radiated so much kindness. That couldn't be right.

I stayed perched in my leafy aerie a few minutes more, the lingering rain beading on my face. Then I scuttled down to get my camp in order, vowing to get back into town as fast as I could.

Mist dampened my cloak when I reached the gate. Chestnuts made up the bulk of my offerings for the day, supplemented by a few morels and strawberries. The gooseberries hadn't garnered any sales yesterday, so I hadn't bothered to harvest them again.

I took a turn down another muddy street, dodging out of the way of a loaded horse cart. Then I smelled something I recognized—fire and steel, like the buildings around the mine. I kept walking, passing a woman hunched over a food stall, the scent of roasted flatbread and spicy lentil curry battling the damp air. I approached, drawn by the flickering warmth and the covered pagoda where others sat to eat out of the rain.

"Looks like the weather got the best of you, boy," she said.

"*Ae*," I agreed in Asri. "Not snow, at least." I fished out some coin for lunch. I wasn't planning on buying anything, but that curry smelled so much better than the thought of more berries or chestnuts—which I'd burned more than roasted for my breakfast that morning.

She chuckled, a friendly sound that stopped as she took in the state of my clothes when I swept my cloak back to stash my wallet. I'd been wearing the same coat underneath since the day I left Iden, and there was some grime and dirt that I'd never managed to scrub out. I didn't meet her eyes as she passed the ceramic bowl over her stall.

"Are you looking for work, friend?" Her eyes flickered down the street. Smoke billowed from a chimney at the end of the street, a gray plume against the storm-wracked sky. "That forge is looking for a hand, I know. And there are a few farms on the edge of Nunbiren that might take you."

Nunbiren: the town name. The ceramic bowl of curry warmed my fingers.

"Thank you," I mumbled. I hadn't considered that any Asri town would allow a Chaeten stray to stick around. But I thought of Asher, and let myself feel the warmth of that woman's smile as she formed more flat loaves to cook over her fire.

When I finished my meal, I turned toward the blacksmith's shop. It was worth a shot. I needed to move beyond surviving, find some stability to have any hope of facing the Red Demon someday.

The forge door opened with a ring of a bell, blasting me with a wave of warm, dry air. *When was the last time I was this warm?* I already didn't want to leave.

Pushing past the threshold, I saw two rooms. To the right: a clean storefront with simple tools and weapons hanging in bins and baskets along the walls. To the left was the workshop, a huge glimmering machine at the center. I'd never seen tech quite like it, but the Chaeten workmanship was unmistakable. *Wait, was that Asher?* Serendipity had the audacity to creep in.

Asher didn't look up. He hunched beside the Chaeten machine, near pipes that fed up to a vent along the ceiling, a display with lights pulsing on a dashboard. Molten metal glowed red between thick, tempered glass panels as Asher pushed a button to open the machine's doors. He removed metal rods with tongs, taking them out to vise and twist them on a table with a simple crank.

He measured the hilt and set it beside a grip he looked ready to affix by hand. That seemed inefficient to me if they had electricity. I supposed even with Chaeten tech, the Asri were going to find ways to be Asri.

Asher's father emerged from the back storeroom with a Z'har soldier flanking him. I recognized the Asri Lieutenant I met yesterday, Ren, clad in a red Chaeten leather uniform. She examined a gleaming blade on the far side of the shop, her brows furrowed as Asher's dad explained something to do with density and well, numbers. There were numbers involved, but some of the Asri speech was too fast for me to follow.

"The Major is very pleased with the last shipment, Galen," Ren said. "He wanted me to ensure you could maintain the same precision if we double the next order?"

Galen's eyes brightened. "Of course. All work is our best work in this shop."

Galen glanced toward me, and I held his gaze. His eyes narrowed beneath the forge's fiery glow.

"Great, we'll send the order through the temple," Ren said, doing a double-take when she saw me. She raised her eyebrows and smiled, but said nothing as she walked out.

Galen watched me with the corner of his eye. "Can I help you?" Galen asked in fluent Chaeten, his voice gruff.

My throat tightened. I felt ridiculous and out of place under Galen's stern gaze. "I heard your forge is hiring?"

Galen's eyes narrowed, his hand gripping the front counter. "Who told you that?"

"The woman across the street, the one who makes the lentil curry."

"Juna," Galen said, his face a mask. "That's her name."

Shame burned in my cheeks. *Why didn't I ask her name?* "I'm strong, a hard worker, and I know a little about Chaeten tech. And—" I faltered, unsure how much to reveal, or even how much was true. I'd wanted to be an engineer like Oren not so long ago, so I knew a bit here and there. Most of the classes we took in school prepared us for the mine. Maybe some of that transferred. As soon as we all learned to read, we had chemistry and math problems about isolating metal from ore, purifying the best alloys.

But would it be safe to tell him I came from a mining colony in the Bend? Asher told me to tell no one. *Did that include his dad?*

His gaze bored into me, searching for something. I'm not sure what. The forge machine whirred. I listened to the rhythmic clang of metal.

"Which unit sent you?" Galen said, voice abrupt.

"I don't understand."

He crossed his broad arms across his chest, pacing the room. "A Chaeten stranger walks into my shop. But there's no such thing as strangers, or coincidences, when we are the only shop left for kilometers working orders for the North Barrack. You are no stranger, *na?*"

I just stared, bewildered.

"Tell your unit we are toeing the line for the empire and you will find nothing in this shop you won't find in our empire paperwork."

"I don't know what that means," I pleaded.

"Even so." He shifted his stance. "I watch my trade secrets too carefully to hire a strange boy. I won't put a sword into the hand of someone who might kill me in my sleep."

His words struck like a hammer blow. Every clang in the shop rang through my chest. My hope, so bright only minutes ago, sputtered and died.

And that's when I saw Asher walking over. His smile wilted to dust at whatever he saw on my face.

But I didn't wait around. Humiliated, I picked up my pack and strode out the door.

Cool damp wind slammed against my face as I emerged from the forge, its warmth already missed. I strode toward the market, trying to regroup my thoughts.

There would be better days, just not today.

"Jesse!" Asher called, as confident and warm as if he'd said my name thousands of times. He chased me halfway down the street in his thin black tunic, his tan arms bare for the heat of the forge.

I hesitated, torn between the comfort of his presence and the need to lick my wounds in private. "You look cold."

He stopped short, a grin struggling to find purchase on his soot-stained face. "I'm sorry for what my dad said." He shivered. "I didn't want to miss you."

The unabashed absurdity of that last statement warmed me from the inside out.

"Thanks, Asher," I said, unable to mask just how starved I was for even a word of kindness. "I can't blame your dad, though. He doesn't know me, and there are a lot of dangerous people wandering around Noé these days, right?"

Asher scoffed, shoving his hands into his pockets. "Not you, though. I'll tell him that. He'll trust my *dahn*."

That word again. "What's a dahn?"

He rubbed his hands together in the shivering cold. "Given talent. Power," he said in Chaeten. At my confused look, he said: "Magic—born, not trained."

"Oh." I blinked. Only elite Z'har could use Asri magic, or the queen. I thought it was illegal for everyone else. But Asher didn't seem to be talking about the sort of magic that could destroy minds or tech. This must be something else. "So your *dahn* is knowing who's an asshole and who isn't?"

His face fell. "You wouldn't be the first to be suspicious that this is a real thing."

"No, I—" I put a hand on his shoulder when I couldn't get the words out fast enough. "I've just never met anyone with a *dahn* before. I just wish I had someone like that around."

He grinned at me then, looking back toward the forge as he hugged his bare arms to his chest. "I better get back. Will you be in the market tomorrow?"

"Today, at least." I should at least try to sell what I came here for.

"Right, well, I'm going to try to finish up quick before you run out of strawberries."

I set down my pack and fished out a basket for him. "No need."

"I don't have any coin on me. Walk me back to the forge and I'll grab some?"

"Not a chance." I laughed. "It's fine, really. Please tell your dad they aren't poisoned."

I felt that heartache thing at the sound of Asher's laugh, certain I'd never hear that sound again.

CHAPTER 8

The Worst Way I Know to Make Friends

The wind blew damp and chilled that night, and Galen's words gnawed at my mind. *"I wouldn't put a sword in the hand of someone who might kill me in my sleep."* They didn't cut deep enough to make me hate him, but the sting kept me from getting much rest. I surrendered and rose while it was still dark.

The ritual of packing up and moving on wasn't as comforting as it used to be, when I'd planned to travel no farther than the North Barrack. Even though it was less than a day's travel, there was no point now. I'd run into those soldiers in Nunbiren. Why lay out my entire story to them, if they are just going to lie to me about what's really going on? Yet hopping on a ship to another island felt like running away, when now more than ever I wanted a path that would lead me to putting a sword through the Red Demon's heart.

East would do, to Noé's capital in Uyr Elderven. I knew there were other Chaeten settlements on the east side of Noé on my map, and it seems there'd been no attacks in that direction. Hoisting my bag, I slipped into the pre-dawn gloom, the forest whispering amid the pale green of early spring.

I stalked like a shadow, a refined habit by now, my path taking me closer to the clearing where I'd seen Asher and Galen train yesterday. Dawn still hadn't broken the horizon before I sketched together a plan. Well, maybe not a plan: a stupid last-resort for someone with nothing else to lose.

The frosted ground packed firm under my boots, and I was grateful I didn't have to worry much about tracks. I got my knife and rope out of my bag before hiding it behind a log, layering on the usual brush and dried leaves. Then I found my tree: an ancient oak with thick branches overhanging the training area. Using my rope and knife, I shimmied up high above the clearing and waited. I shifted close to the trunk, hiding as much of my body as I could.

My skin warmed to the glow of the rising sun before I heard them. There was a chance I could prove myself, but this was the riskiest part of the plan. When they were on the far side of the clearing coming my way, they'd be most likely to spot me, not when I was right above. Iden was the brother who'd taught me to ambush, teaching me that people—namely, our siblings—don't look straight up in a forest as often as you'd think.

No one called out a warning as the militia entered the clearing. I heard a thud as the bag of weapons dropped under me, a five meter drop to the ground, maybe six. I waited until their chattering voices were all assembled beneath me; then I shifted my weight to look.

Asher laughed at a girl next to him, dark-skinned with fitted blue armor and auburn braids wound tight to her head. She gave him a wry smile, turning back to the broad-chested boy behind them with long brown hair: their camaraderie feeling so familiar and foreign all at once.

Dawn stained the mist-shrouded clearing with a pale gold as Galen called the militia to order. They spread out with an arrangement of weapons as he walked to the center of the clearing, every exhale seeming to carry the heat of his forge and the weight of command.

"Meragc," Galen boomed, then nodded up at a tall muscular Asri man, sporting short dark hair and pale skin. "Remind us why we are here."

A low murmur rippled through the group.

"Weapon testing is important for your forge's quality control, *na?*" Meragc said in sarcastic Chaeten. I recognized his dark hair as the man I saw sparring with Asher before, and I could now make out his bright blue and yellow-ringed eyes.

Galen snorted, a sound like molten metal hissing against water. "I didn't say the Z'har were asking. You're saying you want a pep talk, Meragc?"

A few cheers, including Asher. The girl in the blue armor huffed beside him. A woman clapped, one with long dusky blond braids tied behind her head.

Galen gestured for silence. "What language does the Goddess speak? And her Z'har? Not Chaeten. Not Asri."

"Power!" Meragc and the others called back the word in unison. With that, Galen unsheathed his sword and practiced a series of quick thrusts and turns, clean and powerful. I drank in every move. The man knew what he was doing.

"We can speak that language too, but it is not enough. We live by the code of our ancestors. We live by *Niire Mai*. There can be no clean justice from an explosion from the void, not a—"

Between my vocabulary limitations and a gust of wind, I couldn't catch the rest, but the small crowd groaned in disgust, then cheered.

"We believe what, Ruan?" Galen said.

Ruan, the dark-skinned girl beside Asher, stepped forward. She looked about my age, even if that blue armor was the suit of a mature warrior. "If the demon must die, look them in the eye!"

Galen worked the crowd, his dark eyes sparkling. "Let's repeat that together."

"If the demon must die, look them in the eye!" They chanted it a couple more times, louder each time.

I knew what demon sprang to mind for me, but I also knew that a century ago, the Attiq-ka went to war over their belief that no Chaeten was human. To those Asri that fought with them, all it took to label me a demon was the rabbit I had for dinner last night. Asher couldn't possibly believe that, so I focused on the demon I knew. I wanted to look the Red Demon in the eye like Galen said. I wanted her helpless at my feet, repentant. I needed her to feel every bit of pain she ever inflicted before I finished her, and I wanted both the strength and the patience to deliver it. If the intensity of that desire made me a demon, a *sa*, by Asri standards: fine. She deserved that.

"Atalia, show us the fourth form, the best you remember," Galen said, his booming voice echoing between the trees.

Atalia, the woman with the dusky gold braids, appeared ten or fifteen years my senior, pale-skinned with dark, Asri-ringed eyes. She spun her sword before she began, letting it glint in her hands. She repeated the form's movements, halting near the end and following it up with a grunt. Galen repeated the form with a smooth combination of sweeps and upper body attacks added to the end. Atalia mirrored, picking up the remaining movements on the second try.

"Good. Pair off with Ruan and show her. Meragc, work with Plato and I'll show Ash and Tamon. After you have it down, work out the best attack to meet that, the mirror to the form. Last, we'll finish with an open-form spar."

Ruan's gaze scanned up to my perch as she walked across the field with Atalia. I held my breath, knowing better than to move, to make myself easier to see.

She looked away.

The clearing erupted in a whirlwind of movement as each pair practiced the form together. As I lay on my branch to watch, a mix of emotions churned within me. Admiration for their skill, envy for their friendships, a twinge of fear for the real possibility that I was about to get my dumb ass killed. They clearly had—in each other—a reason to live. I didn't have many reasons left.

My fingers tightened around the rough bark of the oak. I'd gotten the measure of them, so it was time to get this over with. But I couldn't help from doing Galen's assignment in my head, the part where I decided how best to parry and challenge the sequence of moves he demonstrated. I stalled a few minutes more as dawn continued its climb.

I couldn't delay any longer. Galen moved into position, sword in hand, below the place where I perched like a spider. I took a deep breath, then launched.

That fall was every bit of six meters, but my modded Chaeten bones were hard to break. The world seemed to slow as the sun glinted off Galen's polished blade. I closed my fingers around the hilt just as my body met his, twisting midair like a predator to keep from crushing myself. I rolled on impact, the blade flashing above my head. Galen yelped in alarm, staying down as I pulled into a crouch.

I scrambled away, swinging as the others dove for me, adrenaline pumping through my veins. A startled shout rose behind me, and before I could blink, a pair of hands clamped onto my shoulders, pinning me to the earth. I twisted and fought to maintain my blade.

I'd learned to outwrestle all my older brothers. It was a bit of an obsession for years, with Mal the undefeated champion for far too long. I'd bested Iden by the time I started school. At twelve, I got my first win on Oren, taking Mal just as I turned fourteen. I escaped Meragc's grip, dodging back.

But three attackers at once with no holds barred was new. A dark arm found its way around my throat, Ruan. I lacked the leverage to roll her off as broad-chested Plato fell onto me too. I grew dizzy, fighting for my next breath with Plato's face near mine. Handsome guy.

Just as my vision started to tunnel from lack of oxygen, I found my opening, relaxing into Ruan's grip, then shifting, throwing her off balance. I took a breath, struggling free—

A voice boomed, "Let him go!" Asher.

I was already up, sword still in hand. Heavier than sticks back home, but I'd like to think I held it in a way to prove I wasn't completely useless.

I blinked, the air thick with sweat and steel. Galen stood above me, his face a hard facade. Behind him, Ruan, Meragc and Plato stood with weapons ready.

"There's a knife on your belt." Galen's voice rumbled through my chest. "You could have killed me."

"Yeah? You said you couldn't hire someone who might kill you in your sleep. I could have killed you wide-awake, in front of your friends here. But I didn't, did I?" I laughed, a breathy, ragged sound.

Heavy silence descended. The militia exchanged uneasy glances, some with amusement, others with trepidation. I analyzed Asher's face, etched with a mixture of bewilderment and what I hoped was respect.

"No, you didn't." Galen stared at me, his gaze boring into my soul.

I let the sword fall and crossed my arms in front of my chest to show deference.

"I told you, Dad," Asher said.

"Who the fuck is this guy?" Ruan mumbled, sheathing her blade.

"Please trust me. Give me a job. And—" I almost forgot to show my countermove, the best attack for form four. I swept, pretended to parry, to thrust the invisible blade in the gap. "Let me train with you."

I didn't know what to do with the silence. I scanned the militia's faces, trying not to let my desperation show. Those movements were smoother in my head, but I hoped the incredulous gazes I got from most of them meant it wasn't terrible.

"Why would a Chaeten-ka boy want to train alongside Asri?" Galen rubbed his side where my knee had pummeled him.

Ka. Human, not a demon in his eyes, so that was a start. I knew what I wanted to say, but I just couldn't get it out in front of everyone. "Why not?" I held my head high.

Galen uncrossed his arms. "Well, that's certainly the worst way I've ever seen a boy try to make friends."

"Did it work?"

Galen grimaced and stepped closer. "Pick up the blade."

I did, eyes wide. A glimpse of Asher's grin kept my arm steady.

"You have good balance, but your grip is wrong. And you should lead with the tip of the blade next time." Galen made a slow arc. I tried to copy it.

"May I?" Galen gestured.

I tried to surrender the hilt, but he gripped my arm, signaling for me to keep it. Galen led my arm back in a low rotation, guiding my center of motion to the tip, not halfway on the blade where I thought it felt strongest. He adjusted my grip on the hilt on the way back.

Galen nodded, then clapped my back when I'd done it right. "You're young. Where are your parents?"

I shook my head.

"Raised in one of those Chaeten academies then? Never met your mother?"

"No," I whispered. "She's just dead."

He inhaled. "Father?"

"Dead a year. My siblings died a little over two months ago." I looked around at the faces in the militia. "South Bend. I'm from Crofton."

No more lies. I'd just run if that frightened them. The small group shifted, staring back until I looked away.

Galen gestured up to the trees. "I'm surprised you can stand after that drop, boy."

"A solid roll," Meragc said.

"We'll try you today at the forge. Tomorrow, in lieu of a form, I want you to teach us that jump of yours." He rubbed his side. "Even if my bruises disagree, Ash is convinced you aren't trouble."

I stared at his extended hand, then at the incredulous faces around me. This was madness, and I savored every bit of it, grinning wide.

Laughing, I grasped his hand.

CHAPTER 9

A New Beginning

As I started my first day of work, I realized the demands of the forest had taken their toll. My mind had excitement to spare, but I'd thinned out, losing strength in my arms. Sweat stung my eyes as I hauled another bucket of pelleted charcoal into the smoldering furnace.

Galen stood a few paces away, holding a red-hot rod between thick mitts. He vised it into place with deft hands, unconcerned by the heat, giving the rod his undivided attention as each thud of the auto-hammer shook the floor. Asher whirled between the two of us, checking controls on the Chaeten fabricator, the machine that took the bars Galen was done with and produced what appeared to be a complete blade. What came out only needed hilting, engraving, and a final polish. What I found astounding was that Galen spent more time prepping the bars going into the fabricator than the remainder of the process.

"Why not reprogram the fabricator to do the whole thing?" I asked Galen. I'd been holding in the question for hours, not wanting to be a nuisance. That's how the Chaeten built just about everything, including swords.

He angled the bar under the forging press once more before looking up to answer my question. "The metal remembers. That's why the first touch—and the last—must be human."

I didn't understand what he meant by that. And when Galen didn't explain further, I kept my hands busy shoveling another load of fuel from the other end of the workroom until the furnace roared.

"Wipe your hands, then pull down the blade on the wall behind the counter, boy," Galen said, vising another raw steel rod. "The one with the green and gold hilt."

I found it where he said, taking time to admire it on the way back. The grip showed enough minor scuffs between grooves of the design to indicate it was an antique. Yet as I removed it from the scabbard with a click, I held up a polished blade that caught the firelight with a gleam.

"This sword," Galen said, running his finger down the fuller, "has walked beside an Attiq-ka for millennia in my family, and I share his name. The immortal Galen died in the Tower. He will no longer reincarnate down our line."

With awe, I watched as the blade glowed blue behind his touch.

"Istaran adheres to *Niire Mai*—only used to take a life to save another—or kill a demon. It remembers every time it takes blood. Istaran remembers who holds it, and can track anyone who injures or kills its master."

Galen offered me the sword. Carefully, I took it, the cool weight of the metal feeling strange on my skin. I wondered how many Chaeten lives it took in the war. The engravings on the sword came alive in my grip, the pale blue glow snaking from the hilt in mazes down the blade.

I almost dropped it, but set it down on the table instead.

"Interesting." Galen's black eyes twinkled with something inscrutable. Asher and his father shared a look.

"What was that?" I knew that cyan light was the sign of Asri magic at work.

Galen turned to rummage through a large wooden cabinet, shaking his head as if to uproot a thought. "Nothing dangerous." He turned and gave me a squinting glare. "Or illegal. Istaran decided you were worthy of its trust."

"Worthy how?" I stared at the hilted blade.

He huffed. "Wish I knew. Old magic, *na*." He produced a similar-looking blade from the cabinets. "I carry on what rituals I know, including a few I can't claim to fully understand—knowledge the Attiq-ka took with them. But they limit what is allowed, even for their soldiers. The empire won't let me make Oria-synched blades like Istaran, even for them."

He passed me a fresh blade, hilt first. It felt just as light as Istaran, every bit as sharp, but it didn't glow, or otherwise creep me out.

"That's a sword we made here. It will last—sharp—and I guess that's good enough. I do the first fold of carbon steel by hand as my grandfather did, using a grade to offer the blade durability and strength. I take a nickel-titanium alloy next, to give the blade enough flexibility not to shatter. The Chaeten machines—" He gestured behind him, to the large thrumming fabricator. "—Are programmed to do what my ancestors taught me, but work faster, using electromagnetic pulses to build a matrix of the two materials."

"So you don't just melt them together?" I had no idea it was so complicated.

"Try your hand at the cold steel. You'll get a feel for it." He nodded at a raw bar on the counter.

I picked up the first rod, heavy and unyielding in my grip. My fingers traced the rough edges, imagining the heat that would soon mold it, the shape it would take once I knew what in the cold void I was doing.

He handed me another piece of metal. Brighter, shinier, light. "Try bending that."

I did. Although it appeared strong, it gave in to my grip, springing right back when I released it.

"Good," Galen said. "If you increase a material's strength and hardness, it's going to be brittle, breakable. It's sharp until it shatters. But if you want a metal that's going to give way and not break on impact, it's less sharp." He assessed me for a moment, looming over me with arms crossed. "*Ka* are no different, I suppose."

I met his gaze, not sure what I'd find there, but it was nothing cruel. He looked away.

"If you melt them together, you'd get a mediocre sword. But an engineered matrix of two alloys allows the properties of both, durable and true." He handed me the replica sword again, the one he copied from Istaran.

"That's incredible," I said, and meant it.

The rest of the day, I worked alongside Asher, doing the first fold for the steel bars. We'd heat them, flatten out imperfections with the forging press, heat them again, keep going. When it seemed long enough to be a sword, we'd bend it over and flatten twice more before we passed the work to the fabricator. Sweat dripped from my brow as I cranked the vise handle, feeling the raw heat of the metal beside it. I brought the forging press down, the clang echoing in my ears, a primal rhythm that resonated deep to my bones. It was too loud to talk much, but I was fine with that.

They'd offered me lunch, but I waved them off, insisting on eating some of the supplies in my pack instead. I wasn't a charity case. I was the guy who would finish aligning these bars in record time.

Galen ducked between the shop and workroom, then directed Asher upstairs by late afternoon. I kept the fastest pace I could to finish the work, determined to prove to Galen he did not make a mistake hiring me. My body could complain later, when I was back in my leaf and stick shelter that night. My hungry belly could complain later too.

"I said you can stop now, boy," Galen said.

From the look on his face, he'd said that before, but then his eyes turned to my work. Beside me sat a stack of neatly aligned bars, their surfaces smooth and shimmering under the fabricator's light. Galen assessed them in appreciation before nodding at me. I felt a flicker of pride at that, warm as the furnace room.

"The shop is closed; Ash has dinner ready upstairs," Galen said.

"Okay." I wiped my face down with a rag beside me. "Do you want me to restock the charcoal before I go?"

He frowned. "Go where, boy? Come up for dinner once you've cleaned up."

I loosed a breath, not looking forward to the long walk back to my camp in the cold dark. But I didn't want to be rude. After I washed my hands and face, I made myself load up two baskets of firewood for the kitchen upstairs, and carried them both up the stairs in one go.

Music played in the kitchen, a fragile string melody. I couldn't see the source, but the Asri always like their tech to be as invisible as possible when they bother with it at all. The walls in the loft apartment glowed with a soft emanating light, a simple and sparse design compared to the house I grew up in. Simple pottery in dark colors, a steel pot atop an open flame hearth, a granite tray over that fire for flat bread. I lingered in the doorway, an intruder on a foreign life.

Asher flipped bread on the fire, his curly hair falling wet on his shoulders from a fresh shower. My clothes, the same as I'd been wearing for months, hung smudged with soot and wet from sweat. I probably smelled more awful than I knew. Maybe I shouldn't impose.

Asher turned back from the fire, beaming. "Jesse, garlic on your bread or plain?"

The aroma of that bread and whatever stewed on the hearth pierced my defenses. My stomach rumbling was the ultimate betrayal, echoing louder than my pride. I shrugged off my worn boots by the shoe rack in the stairwell, shuffling over the threshold.

"Garlic, please." I sat down, perched on the edge of a sturdy polished table, my spine stiff.

Galen leaned over the table, passing me a steaming mug before sitting down. His eyes, weathered and sparkling, met mine. "I was just telling Ash how much you got done. We'll have a good rest at the end of the week at this rate."

I took a sip of spiced tea—not a flavor I was used to. The herbs were soothing, almost icy on my tongue, but more hearty than a mint.

Asher set a steaming bowl in front of me. "Sweet potato and black bean stew," he announced with a flourish. "Secret family recipe, so feel honored."

Galen grunted, a sound that could have been amusement or disapproval. But his eyes held a flicker of warmth, and when I stole a glance at my plate beside my bowl, he was layering an extra slice of the flatbread on it. I felt a wave of gratitude for such a simple gesture.

Taking a bite, the earthy flavors lulled me into a comfortable complacency I hadn't felt in months.

"*Taam*, if we're ahead, can we build the bunk tomorrow?" Asher gestured to the loft. "We only got a spare bedroll in the meantime," Asher said, looking at me.

I frowned, not understanding. Galen chuckled, the bench creaking under him. "Best ensure the boy gets a bath first before you show him his bed, or he'll pass out reeking." He laughed again as Asher smiled, then turned to me. "Why didn't you wash up before dinner? Ash already laid out some fresh clothes for you in the bath house."

"I can use your bath house?" My heart skipped. A full dip in the icy river still hadn't been worth the hypothermia.

Galen looked bewildered at whatever he saw in my face.

"You're working with us," Asher explained. "This is home."

A lump formed in my throat when he met my gaze. "Chaeten jobs don't work like that. I... I didn't know."

"You thought," Galen growled, "after a day like that, we'd send a dirty, half-starved boy back to the frozen wild?"

"How long have you been living in the woods?" Asher asked.

"Since the week before Solstice."

The thin music in the air changed from string to flute.

My confidence built, and I cleared my throat. "Have you heard of the Red Demon? Have you seen her around here?"

Galen's gaze sharpened; Asher's grin faded. They both put down their spoons.

"He's not working for the Z'har, *Taam*," Asher said.

"*Ae*, Istaran trusts him, so will I." Galen let out a breath.

"I don't understand," I said.

"Major Mahakal doesn't like people spreading ... rumors about her," Asher said, and when Galen coughed at the word "rumors," he added, "Talking about her at all, really."

Galen grunted, taking another bite of his stew. "When I first met you, I thought you might be looking for trouble. Z'har hire beggars and desperate people to spy around towns, reporting back things that no one will say to a priest or a soldier's face. They check in on any empire contractors from time to time, making sure we are following the law."

"Oh." I thought back to how Galen reacted when I entered his shop. "Well, I'm not a Z'har spy."

"No." Galen chuckled. "Most of them are academy born, unable to do a hard day's work if their life depended on it. Clearly not you."

I sat up straighter at the praise. "So you've heard of the Red Demon?"

Galen and Asher shared a look.

"Major Mahakal's unit is looking for a Chaeten-sa, one with scars on her face," Asher said. "But the weird thing is, the temple doesn't have posters up or anything, like with other criminals. They've pulled people aside and asked about her though. That's who you mean, right? The scarred woman?"

I described her as well as I could, the long straight hair that seemed to drink red light, the worn-out armor, how fast she could move. Then

I slipped into telling them about Mal outside the mine, and when I saw their faces, it looked like they both actually cared.

"Is that what happened to your mother, then?" Galen asked.

So I told them about the rest of my family and my town. I tried to keep it factual, brief, but the memories still clawed at my throat on the way out.

When I finished with Iden's fate, a heavy silence hung across the table. Asher looked as wounded as I felt.

"I'm very sorry for what you've survived, boy." Galen spoke with finality, his voice rough but kind.

The pity his gaze exuded was more than I could bear. I looked away. "It's going to happen again, to someone else, unless I stop her."

"*You*? Stop her?" Asher said, more confused than disapproving.

Galen took that in with a nod. "I've discussed her with the elders from other towns. More rumors than not, as there aren't many who've gotten as close as you." He paused for a moment, his dark and gold-flecked eyes boring into mine. "She's attacked Asri too. Not whole towns like the Chaeten in the Bend, but she's in the crossroads and wilds, picking off people as far as Baren Golkhi. Until now, I didn't know Mahakal wanted her for what's happening in the Bend. Never would have thought a Chaeten-sa would kill her own."

I looked at him, bewildered.

Galen sighed. "You should tell Major Mahakal everything you told me. He's your best chance to do something about it all."

"*Taam*," Asher said, in warning.

I drew out a long breath, thinking it through. "Why? Mahakal seemed more concerned with keeping the worst of what's happening secret." I gave Asher a side glance.

Galen shifted on the bench. "There's no politics but dirty politics. The empire wants people to believe they have the situation under control, because that gives them the best chance of making that true."

"If you are up every morning preparing to defend yourselves, you know no one's safe," I said.

Galen gave a tight, slow nod. "Queen Azara's empire does less for the people of our town than the Attiq-ka council used to. She can only wield so much power on the edges of the empire, and I don't resent her for that. Queen Azara did what she could and asked for little back—her priests enhanced the khels on our walls. No ghost can enter this town, neither a malicious ruren-sa nor the rest." Galen took another bite. "We only need to concern ourselves with whoever is riling the ghosts up, and presumably they have bodies we can fight."

Asher nodded in agreement, his face tight.

"Ghosts? What about the bioweapon, virus, whatever it is?" I asked.

He frowned. "No Asri has contracted SBO yet anywhere in Noé, to my knowledge, just Chaeten. Until now, I had no Chaeten in my town to worry about besides the barrack soldiers, and well, you'd be dead by now if you could catch it at all."

I drummed my fingers on the table. "What do you think will happen when I tell Major Mahakal what I told you?"

Galen leaned back on the stool and scratched his curly black hair. "With a story like yours, the sole survivor of Crofton, chances are he'd want to make sure others could question you too. He'll take you to his commander, and no one in the Barrack will tell me who *that* is, but I suspect he reports directly to the General himself. Seems we'll be losing a worker soon."

"Don't do it." Asher said.

I whipped my gaze to him.

He crumpled, looking between his father and me. "They won't let you say no if you don't want to go away."

I smiled. "You'd miss me already, Ash?"

"Well, yeah," he said, his brown and gold eyes wide.

That stark honesty took me aback. For a moment, I wasn't sure what to say.

"Could your militia kill the Red Demon?" I asked Galen. "With Istaran?"

Galen finished the last of his stew and put down his spoon with a clank. "With any blade. A Chaeten-sa is a difficult kill, not impossible. She'll move faster, heal and mute her pain as she goes. But it's still blood in her heart and muscle connecting her head to her shoulders. Outnumbered, she will die like anyone else." Galen made a gesture from his heart. "We won't go roaming the wild looking for her, but if she attacked this town, we'd face her without mercy. It is no sin to kill a demon."

I nodded, and those words fanned an ember of hope to flame.

CHAPTER 10

Mahakal

Two days later, I sought Mahakal out at the temple, a tall, ornate structure that had likely been at the center of town since its inception. Inside, the air tasted smoky—the scent of the incense burning in little metal grates was altogether foreign to me, but soothing.

Candles flickered shadows across the stark Asri marble walls and the frescoes high above. Along the alcove that led to offices and private rooms, however, the temple gave the Chaeten a voice, vibrant art depicting war heroes and half-remembered history from our lost planet. I paused at a painting of the day my ancestor's planet died, a bright corona around the once shining globe. On one side, the planet was stark and black as the surrounding void. On the other, the webs of golden lights held out long enough for vessels to escape. I made myself keep moving, feeling watched. Maybe I *was* being watched. I turned to see two acolytes drifting through the sanctuary toward me, slithering with seductive grace. What sheer fabric they wore let me see everything the man and woman were not wearing underneath. *Voids.* Their eyes gleamed in unison with a practiced welcome at my tall, muscled form. But I was no soldier from the nearby barrack looking to buy some time with them. Once they were close enough to see my face through the smoke, their smiles vanished, replaced by what might be pity. *Sorry. Too young to fuck either of you, even if I could afford the donation.* Shame flamed hot in my cheeks when the man turned back, catching me leering at his muscled back and ass. I looked away. Across the sanctuary was an open door, and then I saw who I came for, and that set both my heads straight. Inside, Major Mahakal leaned against an intricate marble pillar, whispering with two red-armored soldiers. He crossed muscular arms and frowned, his black and silver tunic stark against the white room, with a sash mimicking the green and violet sheen of his raven. Two other high-ranking Z'har sat near him at a table, their faces torn with thin scars, their conversation punctuated with grim nods. As I approached, their voices trailed off, replaced by a mute chorus of three hard stares.

"Major Mahakal." I forced my feet forward.

An assessing frown creased his brow. "Friend, find a priest for your questions." Captain Havoc took a step forward to direct me away. Major Mahakal raised a hand in quiet, his green eyes squinting at me.

"Did you know the Red Demon attacked Crofton?" The words tumbled out in a rush. Mahakal scarcely adjusted his posture, but I felt a wave of emotion shift in the little room. "She's responsible for the Crofton Mine collapse, and I think all the deaths in that town."

Major Mahakal smiled, and although I found the intensity of his grin a bit terrifying, it felt like he was listening. "You've seen this firsthand?"

I squinted my eyes shut, clenching and unclenching a fist. To admit that I had would mean I'd come from below the Bend, that I escaped the quarantine efforts. "Yes."

"I see," he said, his voice deep and honeyed.

"Major," Captain Havoc said, and the silent conversation that took place between him, Mahakal and the other Asri officer made all the hairs on my neck stand up. I'd said goodbye to Ash and Galen just in case, and Asher had hugged me so tight. Mahakal cleared his throat, and his strange pale eyes bore into me. This time, there was a hint of warmth in his voice. "Would you join me for lunch? There's a little restaurant across the street with a few decent Chaeten dishes. I think we both might be more comfortable hearing your story there."

I managed to hide my shock. "Yes. Thank you, Major Mahakal."

I followed Mahakal, his gait too fluid to be anything but unsettling. I tamped down my bigotry when the word "inhuman" sprang to mind, hating myself a little for thinking like that. He served the queen. Across the bustling street, a sign with a vibrant splash of gold and violet stood out among the weathered white-stone buildings. RYU'S HARMONY TAVERN. Inside, I perused colorful Chaeten-style murals depicting Asri life: families harvesting painted rice paddies, children chasing butterflies across violet-blue skies, the mycelial webs of the Oria bionetwork reaching deep into the earth. On another wall, the gleaming city of Thebos, that even I could tell must have come from an illustration rather than someone who'd seen it first-hand. Still, I appreciated the attempt to make it seem like we all belonged in the same world, even though they couldn't make us fit on the same wall. Ginger and spices met my nose, and the familiar scent of Asri flatbread. Cushions occupied the space around low Asri tables, topped with spring wildflowers. On the opposite side of the room were a couple of wooden booths with mismatched chairs. I supposed that was the nod to the Chaeten way of doing things. Mahakal led me to an empty booth.

A kind-faced old man with a neatly trimmed auburn beard approached. His green and blue ringed eyes crinkled at the corners when he smiled, that smile flickering when he looked at me. "Welcome back, Major! And how lovely to meet your new ... recruit."

"Thank you, Ryu," Mahakal said. "Two of whatever your Chaeten special is today, please."

"Ah! Today we've had some river-caught trout, spring greens—"

"That will be excellent Ryu, thank you," Mahakal cut him off with an apologetic smile. Ryu stood firm on exchanging pleasantries, though. He wasn't satisfied until he had my name along with my drink order, my opinions on the weather, and my plans for the upcoming Rain Festival. Mahakal turned to me with a wry smile as soon as Ryu turned away. "If any man could talk his way out of a battle, it's Ryu. His skills are underutilized in a place like this."

"Yeah, he's nice," I said, although my mind lingered in a colder and darker place, where the ground rumbled from mining equipment and Mal lay twitching in the snow. I looked up to see Mahakal studying me, and I wilted under his gaze—how similar his features were to the first Chaeten-sa I'd met. To my surprise, Mahakal reached across the table and gave my shoulder a familiar pat, strong and measured. "Don't be so tense, friend. I can tell you've been living rough for a while. But it seems your luck turned around?"

I nodded. "Elder Galen Eirini gave me a job at his forge. He's the one who told me I should talk to you."

"Ah. I'm glad you've found some stability after your hardship. I hope you can trust that I want to help you in any way I can."

I blinked. Voids, he was nothing like the Red Demon. I studied his earnest, intelligent gaze. "Thank you, but I'm not looking for charity. I just wanted to tell you what I know, to do the right thing."

"I recognize that." Mahakal leaned closer, his voice dropping to a whisper. "You saw her first. That's why I terrify you, isn't it? Or is it because you don't want to be the only Chaeten in a refugee camp?"

I froze, then considered running out the door. But Ryu arrived with the drinks then, and Mahakal smiled as he brought a frothy beer to his lips. My breath hitched.

"Please don't be afraid." He set down his glass. "If you told a half-witted priest where you are from—yes, he'd ship you off for breaking past the quarantine line. But I'll run a blood test in the temple to confirm what I suspect, that you aren't capable of catching or spreading the South Bend Outbreak: SBO. If you are putting innocent people at risk, well then—" His eyes were on fire.

"I never got sick." A deep breath calmed my racing heart.

"I trust you. And I'm going to need you to trust me back, Jesse." Mahakal met my gaze, his jaw hard. "If I don't have the whole truth, I may not be able to find her. Every fact helps, no matter how small. Hold nothing back. Nothing."

I frowned. "Okay."

He studied my expression, unsatisfied. "There's a reason I named myself Mahakal when I came of age," the Major said, his tone reflective. "I was off to war, and I needed a symbol the Attiq-ka and their Asri loyalists could understand. They like mythology from forgotten worlds—the more obscure, the better." He waved his hand in a loop to show what he thought of that. "My name and my raven stand for justice. To those that do evil, I bring death, swift or slow, depending on the crime. Someone with Chaeten code killing their own kind en masse deserves the worst side of me, as do the Asri mages my elite soldiers hunt," he finished with a solemn nod.

"Justice sounds good." I felt I could match the intensity he radiated. The world bent around me with an unspoken promise, vengeance simmering in the blaze of Mahakal's eyes.

"But I also represent peace." The Major leaned forward. "The righteous, I'll reward within my sphere of influence, give them power to do more. To the innocent who have suffered, I'll protect them; give them boons where I can. You are someone that deserves my favor." Hope sprouted in me like the first flowers in the morning training grounds. I took in a sharp breath. "Let's create justice together," Mahakal whispered.

I told him every detail I remembered. He let me speak, eating little when Ryu laid out plates of smoked trout, interrupting to ask exactly where I'd seen her last, and picking apart every detail I knew about the Crofton mine. Questions on the number of diggers and the trucks idling outside kept me focused on the facts, and kept me from falling apart as I relived every horrible detail. "Someone else mentioned ghosts, ruren-sa like in the war," I said. "You think it's SBO instead?"

He huffed, then took an angry bite. "Most people repeating these rumors mean no harm, but it's still ignorance. Some Asri like to pin everything they don't understand on the dead by default. Not to say I haven't fought off some ghosts through the years, but the simplest explanation is usually correct."

"What do you mean?"

He tilted his chin at me, assessing. "Normally I would only share this with those pledged to serve the empire and keep its secrets, so consider this a boon. Will you promise me you will keep this conversation private, just between us?"

"Yes, of course, Major."

He picked some trout away from the bone, savoring it. "Fact one: Our Queen and General inherited Chaeten bioweapon labs built before the war. These labs created viruses to kill crowds. Fact two: there's recently been a leak in one of those labs which I've connected to Asri rebels. Fact three: Any ghost I encountered in the war was more or less indiscriminate in its violence. They would attack Chaeten and Asri alike when riled, and they didn't stay in one place—nothing like the targeted attack we see in Crofton. Fact four: No Asri dead." He leaned across the table. "So where does that leave us, Jesse?"

My every muscle tensed. "But if that was a disease that could kill people instantly, how am I the only one in town who got away?"

"You weren't. The Red Demon picked off all the immune survivors—except you, apparently."

I blinked. *Right.* She'd stabbed some people in the square before I even got there. "What if I just never got infected?"

"This bioweapon, SBO, can survive in the air for days. You and your brother were infected the moment you got back to town. You were both immune." I clenched my eyes tight. "I honestly don't know how you outmaneuvered her, mentally if not physically." He sighed, taking a bite. "She'd have to know you'd tell someone everything."

I shrunk into myself. I hadn't outmaneuvered her. She'd let me get away—I must not have explained that part quite right. But I didn't correct him, forcing my back straight. "Why?" I said in a small voice, having lost what little appetite I came with. "Why would she work with Asri rebels if she fought for Queen Azara?"

He took another sip of wine. "She never fought for the queen, and her mother was Asri, an Attiq-ka to be specific." My mouth fell open. I didn't know the two types of immortals had any children together. Even the queen, despite carrying the soul and memories of an Attiq-ka, was born Chaeten. "Again, repeat none of this. Not just for the empire, but for your own safety," he said. "We've tracked and killed a good number of surviving Attiq-ka by now, save the queen's mentor Marles, who supported her from the beginning. The rest would hunt you for even the rumor that such a demon came from one of them."

"How did this even happen?" I raked my hands through my curly hair. "And... The Red Demon looks so much like you—" I cut myself off, realizing I'd never seen an Attiq-ka. Maybe the way she moved and that otherworldly intensity was something all the immortals had in common. Chaeten-sa code had to come from somewhere.

He gave a sly smile at that, looking away and back. "Just because she has red hair and cat green eyes? We're all coded for complete phenotypic dominance." When I looked confused, he added, "All our mutts look like us."

It took me a moment for my brain to catch up. "Mutts?"

"How old are you, friend?" He drove his hand down his face, looking around the room. I followed his gaze to one of the servers, a black-haired Asri girl a few years older than me with a brilliant smile.

"Fourteen," I said to my lap.

"Okay, censored version, then. Stop me if you already learned this in school. Our Academy tried coding our spec line for peace first; war was the backup plan. They built us to be appealing mates to Attiq-ka, and they coded our minds to find anyone willing to touch us appealing." He groaned, looking off toward the girl. "Some of our brilliant leaders thought if we merged their immortal line with ours, the Attiq-ka would have to recognize us as equals. We'd just fuck like bunnies until there was peace across the Nara."

"Okay," I said, wondering what the uncensored version was.

He raked his eyes up and down the girl with black hair, who rushed past our table on her way to the kitchen. Major Mahakal straightened his tunic as she passed. "None of us are fathering half-breeds these days, but things were different just before the war, and during."

"So you don't—" I stuttered, deciding that was none of my business.

He laughed loud and long, leaning back in his booth. "It's just the silphium mod, friend." He stared at me in bewilderment. "I certainly haven't stopped living since I met Ryu's great grandmother."

"Oh." I eyed the table, then looked up to find Ryu. *Ohh.* His seastorm ringed eyes and gray-flecked auburn hair looked Asri to me, kneeling by the low table to serve his guests. But I could make out the resemblance now, if I looked for it.

"It's for the best," he said. "I expect they're sparing you kids from the worst of Chaeten-sa horrors in your school books, but those were dark days. For every one of us that survived childhood and was strong enough to meet an Attiq-ka's magic blade to blade, I'd say five died, maybe fifteen, depending on how young you started counting." He sighed, looking into the distance. "So any children I brought into the world are so heavily modded, there's little to connect us. I refused to let any of them suffer like I did."

I leaned back in my chair, deciding I respected Mahakal for that. "So Ryu's mortal?"

"Yes, coded for a happy, fruitful life. I let him keep spec lines the empire is propagating and replaced the rest. Coding for fearlessness and resilience has ... fun side effects. I expect if your parents gave you so many siblings, you're carrying that mod too. You'll figure it out soon enough." If there wasn't a mine under Nunbiren, I was about to crawl under the table and start digging one. Mahakal laughed. "Forgive me. I didn't mean to make you uncomfortable there, friend. The point is, the Asri can leave their future to fate if they wish, but from one Chaeten to another, I think our people place a higher value on learning from our mistakes." He stared until I met his eyes. "Believe me when I tell you the Red Demon is one of our worst mistakes."

CHAPTER 11

Brother

A weight eased from my heart after sharing my story with Mahakal. To his credit, he left to travel south the next day to seek his justice. For weeks afterward, I'd visit the temple daily to check the posted bulletins for news. When I saw nothing about the Red Demon, I reminded myself that if her identity wasn't public knowledge, her death might not be either.

In the meantime, I settled into a familiar rhythm with Galen and Asher. Nunbiren was in a good place to heal, to grow stronger, and to develop new skills. Weeks spilled into months with no news. Folding at the forging press kept me from thinking too hard, as did learning how to use and maintain the fabricator at the heart of the forge. I excelled in the morning training. Galen was eager to teach me everything—how to bend steel to my will and to create poetry from small movements with every weapon we birthed from fire. I strove to move beyond the predictable rhythms and movements to mastery, giving everything I did my whole heart.

I found comfort in my new life. Each night Galen and Asher had fresh questions for me, and even the ones that ended in silence brought me closer to them both. They'd lost someone too: Asher's mom died a few years back from cancer. In the case of all our dead, there were no answers, just acknowledgement of a grief shared. Every time I freed a secret that made me feel fragile or lost, I felt stronger. Each time I felt alone, they drew me closer.

Asher took a little over a week to start calling me brother. Galen was more reserved, but beyond his exacting and commanding presence, he was a patient and kind man, a natural leader. In some ways, I trusted his gruff attitude more: being slow to trust meant I had full faith in his judgments. I don't think it was just Asher's influence when things shifted a couple months later, over a dinner with the last of the strawberries for the year, greens blended into the spicy lentil stew.

"You figure you still need a father, boy?" he asked, setting down tea for us both.

I hesitated, the stew in front of me forgotten. Studying the wrinkles in his face, and his black and gold eyes, I nodded, finding a certainty in something I hadn't considered a moment ago.

Galen's smile crinkled the corners of his weathered face, bright as the forge fire. "Very well, son," he'd declared, with Asher grinning beside me, slapping me on the back. From that day on, I was "son" and not "boy," and a few days later, recognized by the elders and ancestors in a ceremony to name me part of the Eirini family.

The night of my adoption, I'd realized he used the Asri word, "*Taam*," not the word I'd called my dad. Maybe that's why it didn't feel like I was replacing anyone I'd lost, just stepping into a new life.

Nunbiren became home.

Months passed into seasons, and Mahakal did not return to town, but each season painted fresh memories. Ruan, Ash and I swam in the forest under starlit skies, laughter mingling with the bite of fall. In the winter, I started sparring with Plato on my days off. He was a guy who just kept going, steel clashing to sweat, as difficult to exhaust as I was. Meragc and Atalia got married the following summer, and I held their first child a year later, Nestor, a curious little boy wrapped in the brightest colored blanket I could find to gift him. Those Asri brought drab colors into their nurseries too, but I had not forgotten where I came from.

There were cozy winter nights in the rooms of the forge, when Ash was learning to play the mandolin, and my taam and I both had to make the best of it. Laughter echoed through the walls as I'd offer my best singing voice and worst possible lyrics for his songs. Galen would shake his head and pretend I wasn't funny, but of course I was.

It all took a while to catch up to me.

The second time I attended the Harvest Festival, I knew what to expect. The sky painted the night with a thousand flickering dreams. Paper lanterns brought some of those nebulae down to the Nara, bobbing their lights on lines throughout the market, their warm colors dancing on celebrants' faces. I clutched a steaming mug of cider, watching the celebration unfold in the square, letting the spiced warmth spread through me.

Ash never missed the ceremony in the woods; he always wanted me with him to meet the ancestors. Mazes of blue lines throbbed brighter and fainter in the ground, a network of mycelium connecting the magic of the core of the world to us. At the edge of the forest, the trees glistened with cyan magic light, rustling in the wind in a way they didn't any other time. It terrified me the first time I saw the trees like that. The Asri magic in the ground made me uneasy enough without the trees drinking it up.

The empire didn't even try to pretend it could control the magic of the Oria bionetwork, even as it tried to keep us safe from everything else. That fungus covered the whole world over, and the Asri believed the souls of their dead will still merge with it when they die, and it would preserve their soul and memories. At Harvest Festival, they'd sit in the shining glade, chatting with the glowing ground, even though some of them—like me—heard nothing in return.

I believed my parents' warnings. They said Oria can kill you if it feels threatened, and the long dead Attiq-ka and Asri that compose it might mark any Chaeten a threat. But Ash and Galen and the rest didn't fear it at all, and they didn't expect me to fear it either. "*No murderers dwell in Oria*," Galen explained. A soul has to be accepted as righteous to return there, where they may rest until reincarnation. The wicked become demons, their ghosts fragmenting as ruren-sa, roaming the wilds until they fade to dust.

In my sixteen years, I had seen no evidence of either ancestors or ghosts reaching out to me. No Chaeten expected anything beyond their death. Yet I couldn't get through any major Asri ceremony without thinking of the family I lost. That year, I endeavored to do a better job hiding unease for the sake of the people around me.

Laughter floated in the air, mingling with the hum of the bionetwork thrumming beneath our feet. At Harvest, Oria's low drone is more discernible, like a distant waterfall. Families clustered in the forest muttering to the dirt, their faces reflecting joy, claiming they heard whispers, laughter in the wind.

"Thank you Mona Terana, I am happy to see you too," Asher said, as a burst of wind rustled the glowing branches. The crackle of the leaves stopped as he paused to listen, his closed eyes reflecting the lights.

"My grandfather is just here to complain, I think. He says they've been waiting for me all night," Meragc said to me, laughing.

I forced a smile. Something in his tone and the cool weather made me think of Iden, of the voices he heard on his last night alive. *Didn't he say the same, that they were waiting for him all night?* Maybe the whispers in the trees were just the wind. But my stomach tightened all the same.

Meragc pointed to something in the trees, then spun around. "I can hear you clearly. Glad you're well, old man."

"Well, there's a whole crowd keeping tabs on me," Asher said, laughing, "Hello, family!" he waved.

I started shutting down, unable to really listen. Iden had seen a crowd too. Maybe these same spirits, so kind to my friends, were the ones that drove Iden mad.

"One at a time please, you're all too loud," Meragc said.

"Maybe how loud they get is proportional to how much whiskey is in your cider, Meragc," I said, grateful for the dark. I was closing my eyes tight, keeping the dark memory at arm's length.

"You really can't see anything at all?" Asher asked. "Or hear them?"

I heard the rustle of falling leaves in the dark, the distant waterfall sound. Imagination would run wild with that if I let it, but I knew better. My brother survived SBO only to open a door to voices in the wind, and something, probably Oria, drove him insane on a whispering night like this. I couldn't save him. I could only keep my own doors locked.

"No, but I'm fine with that." I winced, realizing I let a little more bitterness in my tone than I intended.

Asher's smile faded among the dancing lights.

I patted him on the shoulder. "Sorry Ash. I'll meet you back home, okay?" I saluted back to Meragc, his tall frame hunched in the dark. "See you at dawn."

He waved his glass. "Nope, I'm sleeping in!"

Walking the streets back, the lantern lights bobbed bright against the inky blackness. A pang of sadness tightened my throat. My new family welcomed me into their world, but I wasn't sure that world could ever fully be mine.

I sank onto a bench outside the forge with my thoughts, not quite ready to make my way inside.

Footsteps. Asher's familiar gait broke the quiet, his boots clicking in a steady rhythm against the stones. He landed beside me on the stone bench, and I watched the sky until his stare felt too heavy.

"What's wrong, Brother?"

I shrugged, the gesture small and ineffective.

He nudged me with his shoulder. "Your ancestors staying silent?" The reflection of the lanterns lit the gold at the center of his brown eyes. "The fact that mine were so bent on killing yours for a while?"

When I didn't smile with him, he whispered, "Iden."

"Yeah." I stared up at the star-dusted void, flickering with the chill of fall.

He sighed, looking up at the stars with me, his leg warm against mine.

"I'm just being a shit," I said. "All of you are so happy on nights like this, and I try to be happy too, and that's what gets to me. I feel bad for being happy when, well—" I gave a vague gesture off to the south, thinking about my Chaeten mother and siblings, and all the dead.

"Wouldn't your Chaeten family want you to be happy?"

I ran my hands through my hair, a little longer now. "At what point am I slacking off by not avenging them? I have no idea what's happening in the Bend, or if Mahakal did anything at all."

Asher grimaced. "They'd tell us good news, *na*?"

A gust of wind swept through the square, rustling the leaves on the lone tree and momentarily dimming the lantern's glow. Asher followed it with his eyes, shadows drifting across his face.

"You're right, it is weird. The empire evacuated everyone by now. There should be no one left down there to kill. Yet the roads south of the Bend are still closed."

I looked back at the lanterns down the street, hearing the echoes of laughter from the market, my chest hollow. "I could head through the woods again. Go back and check it out."

"But if you ran into the Red Demon, do you think you'd be strong enough to kill her?"

My gut twisted. "No." And once that was out, I began to unravel. That's what I feared most of all, not being strong enough when that moment came, watching her take more lives.

Voids, I had a way to go.

Asher gripped my shoulder, anchoring me through my swirling thoughts. "You're already the strongest fighter in the militia. You've probably learned more in two years than the Z'har soldiers learn after a decade in the barracks."

His words were a balm, goatshit though that statement was.

"I think she's on your path. When the time comes to face her, you'll be strong enough. Until then, stay and get stronger with me."

"What if that's impossible?" The question sank in the pit of my stomach. "If Mahakal hasn't killed her yet, how could I?"

He traced the cobbles with his foot. "I'll ask Oria when you feel ready. I've told my mom all about you. My grandparents, voids, anyone who will listen, about the awesome brother they didn't get to meet. They'll help us."

"They'll know you're exaggerating."

Asher's grip felt warm on my shoulder. "Taam tells them all the same things."

Nothing I could think to say could dim that.

"We'll face her together, just like we face everything else. Meragc, and Atalia, and Ruan, and Plato and—"

The night air blew cool between us. I met Asher's gaze.

I swallowed. "How do you say 'You sure are a sappy piece of shit' in Asri? I guess I'm still not fluent. Nothing sounds right."

"You'd say: 'Thank you. I appreciate you, Brother.' Or does your cold Chaeten heart not have that emotional range to make sense of that?"

"Voids, my brothers would have eaten you alive, all this talk of emotional ranges ... and hearts." I laughed out the last word.

"Eat *me* alive?" He huffed. "Even for a metaphor, that's horrendous. There's no history behind that, right? Were any of those poor rabbits and deer alive when you tore into them?"

I shook my head. "No, fuck you, we—"

But he was laughing at me. It was a laugh that could shake loose the stars from the sky and must have left his abs begging for mercy. I let it carry me away too.

I leaned back on the bench beside him, and when my chest stopped heaving, I said, "They'd have liked you though, really."

And I wished I could convince myself they'd be listening, so I could tell them all about the brother they never met.

The next day, I practiced the Red Demon's move to double sheath her swords after stilling from a run, thinking about killing her the whole time. And I trained twice as hard for each day that followed. Years took root underneath my feet, and I grew stronger, learning to think with every limb. It only takes a moment to die; I would make use of any moment I got.

CHAPTER 12

Ashes

A dusty sunbeam cut through the shop window as Ash worked the final Asri-style engraving on an officer's sword. He was much better than I was at those minuscule mazes around the hilt and down the blade. I set up materials to do some first-folding, the second-favorite part of my day, as training in the clearing at dawn remained the undefeated first. Six years and counting since my first day at the forge, and I still wasn't tired of the routine.

It was a slow day, so I set the forging press aside and tried hammering by hand on the anvil to grow my muscles.

Asher looked up. "Why are you leading with your right hand?"

I followed the swing through before I answered, feeling the clang in my bones. "Because it's a little weaker than the left."

"Brother, you're left-handed."

"With a little work, I'll fix that." I swung another blow.

"You're crazy. Perhaps you should grip with your elbows next to really push your limits." He mimicked the motion.

I smiled. "Show me that again?"

Galen walked in a moment later with a stack of orders, and we leaned back into our work.

Business was booming, and we'd built a great reputation, cornering a lot of empire contracts that used to come from the shops and factories in the Bend. We now only took the work we liked best. The Bend remained closed. By now, that felt normal.

"We get the North Barrack order in yet?" I set down the hammer and took a sip of water. They remained our biggest client by far, sending an order every week.

"The usual, plus some crossbow bolts." Galen shrugged. "But put the Governor's house at the top of tomorrow's list. They just need some hinges and bolts right now, but they'll be tacking on some fabrication for the back gate." He spread his papers out and leaned over the table to study them. "I need one of you boys to look after the shop this afternoon, so I can collect the specs."

"Jesse should do it, since it's pickup day. Flirting with the soldiers is good for business," Asher said.

"Fighting with new opponents is good for training, and business," I clarified.

Asher's smile said he wasn't buying it.

I rolled my eyes, as his running joke did not deserve any further dignity.

It was usually a lower ranked soldier or fresh recruit sent to pick up orders. The North Barrack did not trust anyone to ship their weapons but themselves, so they'd test quality with their own sensors before loading up. Each week the soldier came, I'd ask him—or her—whomever, to show me their best moves with their weapon of choice. If they were in a good mood and up to the challenge, I'd show them mine, and we'd spar out back.

Sometimes I'd learn a new move, or just face someone a little less predictable than the rest of the morning training group, whom I could read several moves in advance now. Sure, I'd flirt a bit, but only once did that clash of swords lead to—well—a clash of swords. I was dumb enough to brag a bit to Ash, giving his uptight Asri mind the vaguest details, and he'd still never let me hear the end of it, even though I never saw that guy ever again.

Fuuuck, I hope I don't see Kane today. Or ever, with Ash around.

Galen leveled a stare at Asher as he folded the orders and invoices into their appropriate cubbies. "Maybe you can learn a thing or two from your brother, Asher. Even if you tell the elders you want to be arranged, you'll be hard-pressed getting a girl to accept you if you can't talk to her. Elder Austren has some potential matches in her village, if you'll be ready this year."

Asher's engraving tools clanged on the table. I lanced a sly grin at Ash, but knew to clear my face before Galen turned my way, lest I be the next person he threatened to unleash the town elders on.

Galen straightened his sky-blue tunic and arranged the folds of his black robe embroidered with gold. He'd cleaned himself up and changed out of the black tunics he usually wore around the forge. "How do I look?"

"Good enough to meet the governor." I'd yet to meet the man, but I knew he had arrived a few days back.

"Why not greet him in the century robe?" Asher asked.

The century robe had been passed down through Galen's family for, well … I don't know how long, but I knew the original Attiq-ka owner wasn't coming back to claim it. Along with the sword Istaran, the robe had survived at least three of the original Galen's lifetimes.

Galen grimaced. "I doubt Governor Solonstrong will demand formality if he called me to measure a fence. He's a practical man, from what I've heard."

"Then why'd he name himself 'Solonstrong?' Pretty cocky choice," Asher said.

"The queen was born in the Solon Academy. There's something very practical about that, *na*?" Galen's dark eyes twinkled.

"So, he's a kiss up." I inspected my last iron bar to ensure the fold was straight.

"He's a politician. And both my sons should remember it's a good thing for the town to be big enough to be granted a governor."

He'd groused about Nunbiren deserving a governor for years now, telling us how good it would be to see the houses in town full again, with more trade and more business for us to open forges of our own.

He ran his fingers through his hair and saluted. The bells on the door clanged as he left.

Ash got back to his engraving. The afternoon sun lowered its slant through the dusty window, casting shadows across the worn stone floor as I got back to my hammering.

When I heard the soft chime of the shop bell, I yelled that I was on my way, washing my hands before heading over.

Sunlight sliced through the smokey air of the shop, giving the young woman before me a golden aura. She stared at me agape with Chaeten eyes. Maybe it was my matching eyes that startled her, maybe it was my smudged and dirty tunic from the hard work next door. Our regulars were used to my face, but I'd never seen her before, and this was no barrack soldier picking up an order. She wore an emerald sundress that complimented chestnut skin, with styled raven-black hair shining across her shoulders. In her hands, she held a small, strange metal box with a display panel.

"Can you repair electronics here?" She nodded to the Chaeten fabricator in the workshop and stood tall. "I heard you might be my best chance."

"Ash," I called out, a smile in my voice.

The girl froze, every muscle tense. I wasn't sure why.

"Asher is your best bet for any delicate work." I patted the counter for her to place the box there.

"Asher?" she said, just as he walked up. "Ooooh." She laughed, her voice tinkling like sunlight on a stream. "I'm Ashmira. My friends call me Ash too, so for a second—" She put a hand on her mouth and got a hold of herself. "Anyway, nice to meet you. What's your name?"

"Jesse Eirini." I crossed my arms, smiling. "Are you used to your reputation preceding you? I'm afraid I'm out of the loop. Good reputation or bad?"

"My brilliance is greatly exaggerated, I expect."

I raised an eyebrow. "Well, I'm fond of Ashes. Already found one good one."

"Jesse and the Ashes might work as the name for a musical troupe. Do you play anything?"

"First-Ash plays mandolin, and I can manage drums." I turned to Asher as he arrived beside me. He stared at her, mouth slightly ajar. I kicked him under the booth so he'd get his shit together and interact with a human like a human, or at the very least, a customer.

"Anyway, what do you got there?" I gestured to the metal box about the size of a large coffee mug. There was a little door on it, and those panels looked very complex. The more I stared at the thing, the more I wondered why she'd bring it to us.

She leaned in on the desk, her voice just above a whisper. "A code sequencer."

I said "No fucking way" while Asher squeaked out something that sounded like "What?"

A code sequencer could not only read genetics from a sample, it could be used to build mods. This machine belonged in an empire academy or an expensive doctor's office, not our forge at the edge of the empire. Voids, we had to get a permit at the temple for my coffee machine.

"I have so many questions," I whispered, leaning in. "Starting with 'How'd you get something like that?' and ending with 'Why are you coming to a blacksmith instead of a Chaeten engineer to fix it?'"

She looked to Asher, her head high. "Was there a biotechnology lab I missed in town? Maybe behind the stables?"

"The temple priests are probably your best bet," Asher offered.

"Unless she lacks a permit," I wondered aloud, and watched her eyes widen. "Which she does."

She snatched the machine from the counter.

"We won't tell anyone," Asher rushed to add, eying me in warning. "I'll take a look now."

This surprised me. If our taam was here, he'd have already sent her away. But the look my brother gave me meant she passed the dahn-check. He trusted her.

She sighed in relief. "I didn't steal it. It was broken. My Academy in Thebos threw it out. A Z'har there said I could keep it."

A Z'har that didn't have the access to transfer the permit, I noted, but didn't say aloud.

"I think there's just a bad circuit in the power supply. The drive tested clean, software intact." She studied our faces. "I'm stumped so far. But I heard you keep a full-scale fabricator working here, so—" She looked at one of the swords in the display case. Then she leaned in, her face pinched. "Did you engrave that mazework or did the machine?"

Asher followed her gaze. "Hand-engraved; my work."

She stared at him, assessing. "It's exquisite." She ran her fingers over the display case.

Asher ducked down and pulled it out of the casing, holding it atop thick velvet. "You like swords?"

She leaned in, running a finger over the hilt in Asher's hands, her emerald eyes sparkling with admiration. "Not a fan of the typical use case, but I can certainly appreciate your steady hand."

Asher the steady-handed fumbled the blade as she drew alongside him, his tanned cheeks flushing. Ashmira reached out to steady the wrapped sword, brushing his arm. "The artistic detail is, well, it's stunning. Rewiring a circuit should be nothing compared to this. I have faith in you."

I looked at my brother with a mischievous smile, but he was all business.

Asher set down the sword and turned his attention to the code sequencer, turning it over in his hands. "Let me get a screwdriver for the casing."

Ashmira continued to run her finger down the sword once Asher left. "You'd think someone would be too afraid of damaging the art to use it."

"It's durable," I said. "But yeah, maybe you're right. Those Asri rebels will get too caught up trying to read the script mid-battle that they'll trip up." I pantomimed being impaled, then motioned to my opponent to give me a moment to appreciate the artwork on the fuller before he drove the blade into my chest.

She laughed as Asher came back with the screwdriver in time to roll his eyes. "Excuse this brute."

I chuckled, the sound rumbling deep in my chest. "So what brings you to Nunbiren?"

She let out a breath. "My parents sponsored me at an elite academy in Thebos before I was grown, and I've since failed to secure a post there on my own. I'm taking a gap year with the governor until I figure out what's next."

"I see." I'd heard the governor came with about a couple dozen empire workers: staff and their families.

"What do you do for him?" Asher asked.

"Provided bragging rights until recently. I'm his daughter," she said to the ground.

I searched her face, unsure why that would make her uncomfortable. "Well, it will be great to have another Chaeten around. I could count on one hand the Chaeten I've met in this shop who aren't a soldier just passing through."

"I'm expecting an adjustment from Thebos in that regard, yes," she said, still smiling to the ground.

Meanwhile, Asher had removed the sequencer's casing and was squinting at the parts. Most of the machine was empty space: a cavity to rotate a disk in the middle, plus a few smaller holes that appeared color-coded for some sort of chemical reagents. Ash produced his magnifying lenses to get a good look at the circuitry, motioning for me to look too. It was tight work, intricate compared to the engineering we'd learned to keep our fabricator going.

"Can you give us a couple days?" Asher asked. "No charge if we don't figure it out."

I raised my eyebrows at that. Our taam liked to follow the rules, and keeping an unlicensed code sequencer in our shop to repair for free was drifting further still from those rules.

She considered, green eyes darting. "Yes, thank you. I'm loath to part with it, but you and your husband seem trustworthy."

"Husband?" Asher asked at the same time I snorted and said, "Eww, no."

I laughed at Asher's flustered expression. "We're brothers," I explained to Ashmira.

"Brothers?" She hesitated, burying her head in her hands. "That was an ignorant assumption. I'm so sorry."

Crossing my arms, I studied her, a warmth radiating in my chest. I'd gotten quite a range of reactions from people who'd met Ash and I for the first time—from incredulity to the statement we looked nothing alike. Most typically, it led into a barrage of curious questions. This was the first time where someone just accepted it at face value.

I respected Ashmira for that, a lot.

So I decided if she was gracious enough not to pry into my business, I would not pry into why she was walking around with a code sequencer.

CHAPTER 13

The Governor's House

My mom used to like the phrase, "Why do one thing when you can do two?" This was a maxim I took to heart while training that day, taking on two opponents at once to keep my reflexes fresh.

The late spring air tasted crisp as I pulled each sharp breath. Sweat stung my eyes while I parried Asher's downward thrust before twisting to meet Ruan's side-strike. Steel sang to steel, the clang ringing through the clearing. Asher, a hair taller and leaner than me, moved with deceptive grace, his brown and gold eyes glinting in challenge. But I knew his every move: the subtle shift of weight before a feint, the flick of his wrist before a brutal strike.

Ruan, a blue-armored tempest of spite, attacked again from my left, carving past my parries. Her movements were more unpredictable than Asher's and more aggressive: she'd gotten far more dents and slashes on me throughout the years. I twisted, deflecting the flat of her sword as I ducked, the dagger swooshing by my ear.

The rhythm of the fight settled in, and they knew if they didn't down me fast, my stamina would outlast them both. They didn't hold back: parry, thrust, riposte. Asher feigned left, then lunged right, aiming for my ribs. I reacted just fast enough, stepping back and spinning until Ruan met my counterattack. The training swords clanged as I forced her blade upward, driving her off-balance. Asher tried to take advantage of my forward momentum, but I swung down hard to meet him, pushing him and Ruan back. Asher recovered, a grin splitting his face.

Ruan groaned, and threw a dagger from the ground, aimed for my exposed flank. Ash had met me low, but I rolled to the side, the tip of Ruan's training dagger whistling by my head as I took a shot at the back of Asher's knees.

"Point!" I yelled. "Hamstring."

Ruan came at me as Ash stepped back.

The morning dew soaked my pants as I came up, my left hand a blur as I snatched a handful of dirt, thinking to fling it into her face. I repressed the instinct rather than blind my friend, and that was all it took for Ruan to prepare a strike I knew I couldn't block. "Point," she said, sword to my chest as I pressed my unsharpened blade to her throat.

"And point." I dug in the steel until she flinched. "Killed you right back, at least!"

She glared, ready to press in, but I ducked back with a disarming strike, sending her sword clattering to the ground.

"Now that we're all dead, wanna go again?" I said, chest heaving.

Ruan scoffed at me, a mix of frustration and grudging respect in her eyes. She turned, hobbling toward her bag under the tree. "Insatiable bastard."

I laughed, going for my water bottle as the three of us sat to catch our breath, the silence filling with the chirping of birds awakening the forest.

"I gotta get to work, but good fight." Asher yawned, standing to stretch.

"Yeah, good fight. I'll come too," I said, accepting his hand up.

Ruan stalked away, gathering her daggers. Asher yawned again as he clipped his sword to his belt, and I wondered how late he'd stayed up tinkering with the code sequencer.

Galen strode over from his match at the far side of the clearing. From the satisfaction in his stride, I expected he'd won his match with Meragc. But he squinted at us, circumspect.

"What is it, Taam?" I said.

He wiped his brow with his hand. "The Governor's daughter sent a message last night on her father's letterhead, requesting that both of you call on her this afternoon."

"Both of us?" Asher echoed my thoughts.

I expected she wanted an update on her machine.

Galen shrugged, his own brow furrowed. "Seems I'm just as confused as you two. Regardless, clean up and make a good impression."

The afternoon sun soaked warmth into the skin of our necks as we made our way toward the governor's mansion. I wore a silky forest green shirt and some pants I hadn't stained yet. Asher, for reasons understood only to himself, donned Galen's formal century robe. I'd helped him tie the last fold off to get the right fit, but I still wasn't sure I had it right. That silver embroidery and void-black fabric also didn't pair well with the slightly wrinkled linen pants that peeked out from underneath. He moved with a self-conscious shuffle, the garment whispering against the cobblestone with each step.

"Does Taam know you borrowed that?" It should have been him tying it off.

Asher's cheeks flushed as he straightened the stiff garment around his shoulders. "I asked if I could borrow a robe. He didn't ask which one."

"For all we know, the governor wants us to check up on the new fence." A chuckle escaped me. The image of Asher, resplendent in Galen's robe, kneeling in the dirt, was quite the picture.

"It's also my first meeting with the governor. Why do one thing when you can do two?" Asher said.

"Don't use my mom's words against me. Besides, you think the governor is going to introduce us to the queen? You getting married on the way?"

Asher grimaced. "Just giving a governor's summons the best respect I can, I guess. Technically, he's nobility," he trailed off, half stifling a yawn.

"Fine." My playful smile faltered. The dark circles under his eyes were more pronounced, and he was still leaning over the half-assembled code-sequencer in our shared loft late into the night. He'd taken it out to work on only when Taam wasn't around. He shifted the weight of the bag on his shoulder, and I peeked in at the little machine. "You got it working?"

He stiffened. "Almost. Just a few tweaks to go."

"What tweaks?"

He tightened his jaw and shrugged.

There it was again, that wall he'd put up whenever I tried to troubleshoot. I couldn't understand it. I'd always pulled my weight on any other complex job, but the only part of the burden he let me shoulder here was keeping the secret from Galen.

Before I could voice my thoughts, we arrived. The three-story governor's mansion was the largest building in town and showed a lot of improvements since I'd last walked down this street. Fresh whitewash shone on the stone walls, the windows accented in deep indigo and burnt orange, the colors on his Solonstrong crest. The renovation maintained the original slate roofing tiles, but replaced the broken ones with ceramic in a rainbow of colors that somehow all fit together, shimmering like scales in the midday sun.

Two guards, clad in Chaeten leather beneath indigo and orange shirts, stood flanking the grand oak doors. I expected that was the Solonstrong crest over their heart: two swords clashing and melting into one. A mediocre final product if you melt two alloys together—Galen told me that on my first day at the forge. Asher straightened his posture to offer an Asri salute, his century robe swooshing. A guard gave a curt nod and waved us past.

"It's gorgeous here," I muttered to Ash.

Chaeten touches were present in tech, sleek metallic accents and electric lights snaking along the walls. The glowing central display in the entrance hall illuminated the time in bold lights, the video showing a deep forest scene overlaid with music.

A young Chaeten woman greeted us, and it seemed she'd cemented her loyalty by modding her skin a little blue and her eyes a deep orange to go along with her clothes. I tried not to stare.

"Welcome. I'm the head butler, Ursinia. Jesse and Asher Eirini, I presume?" she said.

I nodded.

"Excellent. Please follow me," she said, with a sweep of her hand.

We followed her through a wide hallway. Bright walls hung with vibrant paintings, abstract except for a map that seemed to show the first Chaeten Academies on the Nara. The air thrummed with a comforting rumble, like the sound of the climate control system in my old primary school. Beyond the hallway, the butler led us through double doors to a lush and broad garden, the beds freshly mulched and planted with spring flowers blooming in riotous colors on the edges of green. Garlands and unlit lights strung from the corner of the house to the trees at the edge of the yard.

Nestled in a sunken alcove in the center of the yard was a small group of young men and women about our age, mostly Chaeten-attired, lounging around some patio furniture. I scanned their faces and turned backs, finding Ashmira's cascading dark hair braided over her chestnut-skinned neck. She turned, smiled and made a beeline toward us.

"There you both are!" Ashmira's grin radiated warm as the spring sun. Then her brows widened as she took in Asher's century robe. Asher drew the lumpy bag from his shoulder to his chest.

"Is that…?"

Asher puffed out his chest a fraction and nodded. "It's powering on now, but I'm not sure the software is doing what it should yet. Maybe we could take a look together?"

Ashmira's smile widened. She gestured back toward the doorway.

Inside, she spread open double doors, and then turned into another room beyond the first to a parlor. Plush purple carpets stretched across the polished floor, a bit out of place next to the aged stone beams of the original construction. Wooden furniture, meticulously carved and polished to a gleam, sat tucked in the corner near the unlit fireplace. There were so many clean pillows on top I wasn't sure if I was supposed to sit on it until she gestured.

I sat, and she, to my surprise, nestled just beside me, motioning for Ash to take the other side. Ash shifted down on the edge of a nearby velvet chair. Ashmira's gaze remained glued to the bag on the table.

"I can't wait!" Her voice simmered in excitement.

Asher unwrapped and set the machine down with a flourish. He flipped a series of switches, and a low whirring sound filled the room. The white lights on the device flickered to life, pulsing slow and repetitive. "That's all I can get the display to do." Ashmira grinned at the machine a moment, then got off the couch and threw her arms around my brother in a tight hug. Asher stiffened momentarily before chuckling into her shoulder. He closed his eyes as a faint blush crept up his neck.

I raised my eyebrow at this. Ash would hug everyone hello if he thought he could get away with it. Chaeten though, are usually more reserved with strangers—unless they want to fuck them.

"You were right to check the power supply first," he admitted, scratching the back of his neck. "Just a fried circuit. Do you have a manual so I can figure out what to do next?"

Ashmira stepped back, her smile undimmed. "It's fine! I know what those blinks mean. It just needs a quick recalibration. I knew you could do it." Her praise seemed to fluster Asher more.

She turned to me then, her eyes gleaming with gratitude. "And you, Jesse. I'm sure you helped too."

"All Ash." I shrugged with a smile.

She reached into a side drawer, pulling out a pouch of coin. The sum she offered was more than double our rate for a two-day-job. My eyebrows shot up.

Asher shifted in his seat, mumbled something under his breath about no charge.

"I insist you be paid for your time." She handed him the money. He looked down as if he found it insulting.

"What is it?"

"It was a lot of fun to work on." Asher's eyes flashed with something I could not make sense of. "Will you let me watch you calibrate?"

"I'd love that." Ashmira smiled, uncrossing her legs. She wore a loose-fitting purple something that looked like a dress until the bottom separated into pant legs. It looked like the sort of thing that would be fashionable.

"What are you doing the rest of today?" Asher gestured to the device on the short table. "Can we start now?"

"I have a few minutes before dance lessons." She leaned forward. "You got a knife handy?"

Ash nodded to me. "Jesse's always armed."

Frowning, I dug into my pants for a pocket-knife. "Why?"

"I need a drop of blood to calibrate. I wasn't going to order collection tubes until I knew I could get it working." She reached for the knife. "May I please?"

I handed it over, but could not fix my face. "Does your dad know you have this thing?"

"He does, yes." She shrugged as she pricked her finger with the tip of the knife. "He's kin—my father—but it's odd to think of him as 'Dad' like a child might say." She closed the door, then went to dig around in a cabinet. "I hadn't seen the governor in years until a few months ago."

Asher watched her every move, taking a deep, sullen breath. "When did he send you away?"

She seemed struck by the question, pausing with a vial in her hand. "I think he pledged me to the Academy when I was four, but I knew it was coming. My mother had been reading all about how early pledges make for stronger, more successful adults. I'm closer to my Academy Mother and friends than my kin."

I watched Asher's heart break for her, but I knew better. People rarely miss things they don't know are missing. This wasn't even that uncommon. Apart from frontier villages like mine, most Chaeten ship their kids off to academies about six or seven, only seeing them on holidays and festivals from thereon out.

"Do you still speak with your mom?" Asher asked.

"Dead, I expect." She set down an arrangement of vials on the table. "I last heard from her when I was eight. Governor Solonstrong hasn't mentioned her since, and by now, I'm hesitant to bring it up."

"Well, if you'd like, Ashmira, I can invite you to our Dead Moms club. It's my turn to bring snacks next week," I said.

Asher stared at me, agape.

Ashmira smiled. "I'd love that, assuming the point of that meeting is to do anything except talk about the dead."

I leaned in. "Swimming? This weekend?"

She poured a clear liquid into one of the code sequencer's compartments with a squint. "I'd love to."

Asher just stared at me, confused. Voids, no, he looked betrayed.

"Are you in, Ash?" I said, never intending to leave him out.

They both looked up.

"Well, this will just get confusing," she said, snapping the lid back down on the sequencer. "Perhaps you two should call me Mira."

"My heart was set on Second-Ash, but I can live with Mira," I said.

She huffed. "Is he always like this?" Mira asked Asher.

A blush crept up Asher's neck under Mira's gaze. He wrestled for a response.

Her smile grew wider the more he floundered to get words out of his face. She put a hand on his knee, which made it worse.

"He is harmless," Asher finally said, a hesitant smile tugging at his lips. "Unless you get a sword in his hands. Glad you're taking him swimming."

My chest tightened, unsure if that was true.

Suddenly, the machine on the table let out a pleasant ding. Light pulsed as the display came to life, churning out a string of Chaeten chemistry terminology that was far beyond my limited education.

"What's happening?" I asked.

Mira's expression snapped and held to the device, a smile blooming on her face. She whipped out a small tablet from her pocket, its screen mirroring the symbols scrolling on the sequencer. Her eyes darted between the two, a triumphant grin splitting her face.

"It's perfect! It's actually perfect!" she exclaimed, her joy radiant. Before I could react, Asher was on his feet, a relieved laugh escaping his lips. He pulled Mira into a hug this time, his arms engulfing her.

She blinked, then hugged him back, holding tight. The gesture seemed innocent enough coming from Ash, but something about it felt—new. The way they fit together, that look on his face.

Asher broke the hug, a faint blush dusting his cheeks as he stepped back.

"Oh, it's almost time for my dance lessons," Mira said, glancing at the time on the wall. With some effort, Mira pulled her eyes away from the machine, tucking it in a drawer with a pat. She gestured toward the garden door. "Are you both free? You could join if you like."

"Yes," Asher said, and I echoed.

"Excellent. Do you two prefer to lead or follow?"

CHAPTER 14

Dance Lessons

"I prefer to lead," said Asher, already heading out the door.

"Whatever," I said.

She grimaced, pausing by the door leading back out to the garden. "Excellent, we're low on leads, I expect. But don't feel pressured if you'd rather go home. But since the rumor around town is that you are both good at swordplay, I expect you'll be able to pick it up quickly."

"You asked around town about us?" Asher said.

"And we have rumors," I added with a smile.

Sunlight dappled through the vibrant blooms that lined the garden path. Chatter drifted on the warm air, and we saw the same small crowd as before. I counted six: five Chaeten young people staring back with curious expressions, and one older Chaeten woman standing with an intimidating posture. I sensed little affinity with the colorful, refined crowd from the inner empire. Even if I had my Chaeten father's best clothes on my back, I wasn't sure I'd fit into their world, or cared to. Mira turned back, biting her lip. "Can I partner with you, Ash?"

Asher, his cheeks dusted with a blush, managed a hesitant smile.

The middle-aged woman turned our way, sporting a short bob of hair highlighted in blue and white. She wore an asymmetrical sky-colored dress that seemed to shimmer in the sunlight.

"Jesse and Asher Eirini, this is Luzan, my tutor," Mira said, her voice laced with respect. "As far as I'm aware, the best dancer in Noé."

Luzan offered a smile that at first crinkled her eyes until it started twitching a bit at the century robe.

"It is wonderful to meet you both," she said in a melodious tone that translated "wonderful" to "diverting," at best. "Oh my, aren't you impeccable?" She reached for the hem of Asher's robe.

"Thank you." Asher ran his hand through the waves of his brown and sun-highlighted hair. "Sorry if I'm overdressed."

"Oh nonsense. It's simply gorgeous." She patted his arm with a tight-lipped smile, giving the fabric an appreciative feel.

I shrugged at Mira. I was the most underdressed person here, I suspected, but I didn't care. She didn't seem to care either.

"Well, I suppose time is slipping by." She nodded and took a few steps back. With a wave of her hand, Luzan gestured toward the group. "Pair off, please."

The crowd murmured. Two dark-haired young women sprang up together from the patio furniture, and a man and a woman beside them. A pink-haired girl caught my gaze and meandered over in my direction as Asher reached for Ashmira's hand.

"Today, we delve into the art of the Aetel waltz."

My stomach fluttered. I'd picked up a bit of Asri dancing from festivals, but I didn't know a speck in the void about what dancing looked like in the culture I was born into. And if I was supposed to lead…

The girl with pink hair waved as she took a spot across from me, offering me an apprehensive smile. "Can I be your partner?"

"Sure, but expect me to be quite bad at this."

A mischievous glint sparkled in Mira's eyes as she grabbed her friend's shoulder and met my gaze. "Don't worry, Jesse. Lila is a natural."

"Hello Lila," I said, smiling.

"Leaders to my right, please. Followers to my left." Luzan motioned for silence after she assessed our rows.

"Alright everyone, most of you are likely familiar with the traditional waltz or free-form line dances. The Aetel waltz will fall somewhere in between. Leads, let's begin by offering your right hand to your partner."

Fabric rustled through the garden as we complied, and I studied Luzan's modeled form and posture before I extended my hand. Lila mirrored the gesture, her hand warm and delicate in mine.

"Now, place your other hand on your partner's back, about shoulder height. The top of the frame should remain poised, a bit more rigid than free form." She modeled a range of movement, a bow, a turn, her upper spine and neck remaining straight. "Remember, this dance is all about connection and flow. Followers, move with your partner, feel their rhythm. Leaders—feel back."

A brown-haired young woman leaned in to whisper to her partner, a broad-shouldered Chaeten man with a short-cropped cut in red and violet. He chuckled, glancing at me with an eyebrow raised. I grinned at them both until they looked back to Luzan.

Luzan clapped her hands once, the sharp sound cutting through the nervous chatter. Music drifted through the garden from panels lining the house.

"Alright, let's begin. Basic waltz step: leads, one step forward with your left foot, close with their right. Followers, the reverse."

The first few steps felt awkward, my feet stumbling into the rhythm while Lila nailed it every time. But Lila was patient with me, her movements fluid and light until I got it down. The music swelled, a gentle melody with a touch of Chaeten modernism underneath. I must have heard this song before a very long time ago—a part of my life reconnected through that music.

Luzan's words echoed in my head: connection and flow. I forgot perfection and tried to feel it out. Luzan walked around, straightening Asher's back, re-angling Mira's arm. The pair shared a smile that eased like the dawn on both of their faces. When she got to me, she watched for several steps before nodding with a raised eyebrow.

Luzan's cleared throat announced a change. "Now, for the improvisation! We will do the first three steps of the traditional waltz and finish with a five-beat improv." She clapped out a beat and moved, ducking and spinning. "Lead your partners in any direction you choose; express yourselves! Remember, as long as you make it back to the start position on time, the move is correct."

I winced. A playful smile tugged at the corner of Lila's lips.

"Want me to lead the first time?" she whispered.

"Sure."

With a gentle tug, Lila pulled me in a quick circle, then leaned back, her hand still clasped in mine. After a few iterations, I countered with a spin of my own, mirroring the playful glint in her eyes. Laughter bubbled up inside me, the tension of the unfamiliar dance fading away. This was ... fun.

Across the garden, Asher and Mira fumbled, then Ash dipped to recover with a flourish. Their laughter echoed amid the music as they entered the next traditional steps with easy synchronicity. Mira seemed to anticipate each turn and spin, their bodies moving as one. A pang of joy tugged at my chest until that distraction almost had me stepping on some poor tulips. Lila glided away; I met her for the next measure.

My heart soared under the gentle spring sun, breathing in the floral wind. I spun Lila with playful abandon.

That's when I saw a familiar Chaeten-sa enter the garden. Mahakal, his raven fluttering from the roof to land on his shoulder.

His presence hit like a physical blow. I could feel the sickening weight of guilt. I let go of Lila and closed my hand in a fist. Six years Mahakal had been gone—no word, no confirmation of the Red Demon's death, no closure for the gaping hole in my soul. And here I was, twirling under the sun while she still breathed, a carefree interloper in my own stolen life.

I couldn't dance another step. I whispered an apology to Lila and walked toward Major Mahakal without looking back.

Mahakal cocked his head as he stared, arms crossed, his flame red hair catching fire in the sunlight. He appeared as young-looking as when I'd first encountered him, but something was different. His eyes, once that feline yellow-green like the Red Demon, were gone. Okay, not gone, just void black, iris and all, like the bird who bobbed her head beside him. His fresh-modded eyes matched the dark, iridescent Chaeten leather he wore to the neck, where the actual raven perched above the winged lapel on his arm. I guess he thought his raven motif wasn't subtle enough before deciding to extend it into his skull.

Beside him stood a man I recognized at once as Governor Solonstrong. Although this was the first time I'd met him, his chestnut brown face resembled Mira's, as did his pine-colored eyes. He leaned into Mahakal's tall shoulder to whisper as I crossed the garden, his attention fixed on his daughter, his eyes squinting into a laughing smile. Mahakal's lips barely curled as he flicked his gaze to me.

I offered a polite salute to them both. "Good afternoon Major Mahakal, Governor Solonstrong."

"Do I know you?" Major Mahakal said, one eyebrow raised. "You're certainly handsome enough to remember."

I exhaled, wondering if his memory actually sucked or if he didn't want to go into the details in front of the governor. "Jesse Eirini. We ate together at Ryu's Tavern when you were last in town."

His face flushed. "Ah." He turned away from the governor with an apologetic smile, then gestured down the garden path. A gentle wind combed the fresh grass, caressing away my sweat.

He dismissed his bird to the air, then led me under a willow at the far edge of the garden, as far as possible from the dancers. Vibrant blooms gave way to manicured hedges. The willow branches cast long shadows across his golden-brown face and black eyes.

"Did you kill her yet?" I asked.

"The Red Demon?" A flicker of frustration marred his features as he shook his head. "She's been a shadow flitting through the outskirts of the empire for almost a century. The weeks-old intel you gave me that day was helpful in other ways, but she remains at large."

"Fuck." I no longer cared if I was being polite. "So where is she now, Major? Still in the Bend?"

"A wisp of smoke. No recent sightings." He sighed, and the ice in his weird black eyes melted. "However, your information did lead me to dig deeper into the Crofton mine collapse."

I remembered the ground rumbling under my feet, the dusty air. Mal. "What did you find?"

Mahakal studied me for a long moment, his void-black eyes unreadable. "Asri magic. She manipulated it to control the machines, and we were able to find out how. The empire must not allow devastation of that magnitude to happen again. We've learned from it and tightened security on other operations since."

"Explains a lot." I leaned into the tree. Trucks were illegal in Noé now. Even the military had switched to horses.

A ghost of a smile played on Mahakal's lips. "I wish I could say more. Although by now I think you are old enough to join the army and find out quite a bit for yourself, friend." He reached out and grasped my shoulder. He angled his face toward mine, and I could smell mint and anise on his breath. "Don't I owe you a boon?"

"You don't owe me anything." I held his gaze. "I just want her dead."

"You're welcome to seek your vengeance by my side—well, under me." He leaned in closer, his face hovering over my hair before he pulled back, the scent of leather and well-worn armor invading my senses. "You're immune to SBO, and any vaccines remain experimental. I'd love a man like you in my battalion, perhaps my personal squad, if you are ready to be a man."

I felt a little uncomfortable as his hand lingered on my shoulder, and I looked toward the dancers, the prism of their vibrant clothing under the sun. Stepping out of the shadows, I caught Mira's eye across the garden, her brow furrowed in worry before she whirled out of my line of sight. Then it was Asher, fumbling his steps when he saw me, questioning.

To follow Mahakal, I'd need to leave Asher behind; Galen too. Pledges were a life commitment. I might never see my new family again.

"Thank you Major. I know that's a generous offer, but I'd like to sleep on this if you'll let me. My taam would need a little time to replace me in the shop if I join you."

"Your taam?" There was a hint of laughter in his voice.

Lila squinted at me from across the garden, now paired with Luzan, but my heart was pounding as I looked back to Mahakal.

"Thank you for updating me, Major Mahakal." I bowed, stiff and formal. "I'll give you my answer soon."

His gaze left no shade under that tree. "I will not be in the area long. See that you don't keep me waiting."

CHAPTER 15

Warning

I was a much better swordsman than a staff fighter, which is why I practiced with a staff that morning. The engraved wood and steel met Asher's training blade with a satisfying crack. Sweat slicked my palms, the cool morning air sweet in my lungs.

On the edge of the clearing, a flicker of blue dress and brown skin caught my eye. Mira. My focus wavered for a split second, a fatal mistake. Asher's sword found its mark with a solid whack on my shoulder.

Pain hitched my breath. "Ow!" I rubbed the sore spot.

Asher, his chest heaving, grinned at me. "Point."

Mira waved, taking a seat at the bottom of a tree.

Asher turned and waved back. "You're late, and you aren't even dressed!" he called out, his voice echoing through the clearing. We both walked closer.

Mira crossed her arms under a navy blue shawl, amusement dancing in her eyes. "I said I'd come. I didn't say I'd get bruised up! Show off a little more, will you?"

"Of course," Asher said.

A flicker of intensity ignited in Asher's gold-ringed eyes. He unsheathed his sword again, the polished metal gleaming in the dawn. "Ready, Brother?"

I welcomed every bit of his confidence as I took my stance. With a nod, he swung into an attack.

Asher tended to fight with measured tactics, defensive until he saw a wide opening and room for a strong finish. Today, his movements were a tornado of controlled severity, his blade curling with fierce precision. Strands of his brown and highlighted hair clung to the sweat on his forehead.

But he was just one man. Instinct kicked in as I felt my way around my least favorite weapon, and I meandered my way from defense to offense. The engraved and reinforced staff met Asher's blade, faster each time. Every move I made, Asher countered with calculated fury. I kept him at bay with the extended reach of my weapon, prodding him to overextend and falter.

A strange thrill shot through me as I deflected a vicious thrust. He evaded mine. Adrenaline surged when his blade struck my armor—hard enough to bruise. I flicked my eyes to Mira, who stood open-mouthed, captivated by the display. Her eyes darted between us, following the dance. I couldn't help but feel a spark of appreciation for Asher's renewed focus that day: my best match with him yet.

Sound joined motion. My muscles screamed in protest with each heavy blow, my breath coming in ragged gasps. But as usual, Asher's movements slowed before I ran out of stamina.

Then he screwed up: I capitalized on his overextended lunge. With a swift flick of my wrist, I used the staff to disarm him, sending the sword clattering to the ground several feet away. Asher stumbled back, his face distorting. I lunged forward, thrusting my staff harmlessly at his chest.

"Point," I announced, panting.

Asher lowered his hands, chest straining out his breaths. "Good fight, Brother." A humorless grimace split his face.

Mira clapped, her face radiant. "That was incredible, both of you!" She rushed over to us. "Jesse, you were amazing! And Asher, well, you looked positively feral out there."

A faint blush crept up Asher's cheeks, but he schooled his expression. "I'll strive for amazing over feral next time."

I wasn't sure what to do with that, or the frown I caught before he cleared it.

Galen yelled out the end of our practice. As we walked out of the clearing and down the road home, Mira sidled up next to me.

"Jesse, why did you approach the Chaeten-sa major? Do you know him?"

Asher looked between us, wiping his brow. "For the record, he gave my dahn the creeps yesterday."

"Your dahn?" Mira said, wary.

"Not the magic that would demand a pledge to a temple," I said. Even though no Attiq-ka were reincarnating anymore, the empire kept a strict eye on some of the power that ran in Asri families. The temple didn't even bother to register Ash.

"I just know when someone means well, and when they don't," Asher said with a shrug.

"Ah," Mira said, and I could see her sifting through questions as Asher wilted under her gaze. "That sounds like it could be a powerful advantage."

Asher smiled and looked away.

After studying Asher in silence, Mira turned to me. "Anyway, I suggest you listen to your brother. I know Mahakal is a war hero, so I will be careful with what I say here. He's propositioned everyone I've brought with me from the capital. Some more than once. Lila told me never to leave her alone with him ever again."

My stomach clenched at the memory of Mahakal's grip on my shoulder, his unsettling gaze. I could find attraction for almost any soldier, but not him. After my first encounter with a Chaeten-sa, I guessed there was a primal gut repulsion there I'd never be able to talk myself out of.

I nodded, trying to keep my face blank. "Sounds about right. But he only asked me to join his unit."

Mira shifted uncomfortably beside me. "I know it's not my business, but you looked … troubled, darting away mid-dance like that. Lila was worried for you too."

I couldn't hold her gaze.

"What are you going to tell him?" Asher said, and the two of us shared a look.

"Nothing, yet. I'm still thinking it through." Even though I already thought of Mira as a friend, it didn't mean I should burden her with things I'd gotten much better at hiding over the years. I'd packed away so many memories from my old life that it didn't always feel like mine. Yet sometimes jagged bits of terror and confusion would float to the surface, flashing into my dreams each night.

"You approached him first," Mira said. "Why?"

"I haven't seen him in years now."

But she saw through my light tone. "You lost someone in the Bend? Kin?"

I huffed. "Yep."

Mira traced a hand on my arm, comforting. "It's okay," she said, her voice soft. "I won't press more if this is difficult to talk about." Her voice held a depth of empathy that I warmed to.

I looked into her eyes, her concern eroding my defenses. But I changed the subject as Ash started walking ahead. We caught up to him.

We reached the forge. Asher didn't look back at us as he opened the door with a creak.

"I'll go make breakfast while you talk," he said, his voice devoid of its usual warmth. He glanced pointedly at Mira, then back at me. "Tell her everything, Jesse. She passed the dahn check with flying colors." I watched him swallow.

"Nonsense Ash, we'll help you with breakfast," I followed him when he tried to outpace me up the stairs.

We talked about the dance lessons, which we'd committed to doing weekly. I ladled out a grain porridge to which Ash scooped out nuts and berries, and Galen, seeing that we had a girl in the kitchen, took a bowl fast and made himself busy downstairs. I knew he'd pry later, especially after Asher invited her to join us for breakfast anytime she wished.

Chapter 16

Settled

The fabricator roared along to Galen's rhythmic hammering, working alongside me to fasten hilts to finished blades. Sweat trickled down my back as we worked, despite the open windows letting in a cool spring breeze. The barracks had recently expanded their weekly order, adding a massive number of swords to what should be a sizable stockpile.

"Think the barracks are expecting trouble?" Asher wiped his brow with a handkerchief, his eyes narrowing as he engraved mazework down the shaft of an arrow.

I paused, considering. "Maybe. Not that they'd tell us anything."

Galen boomed a laugh beside me, the sound momentarily drowning out the clang of metal. "*Ae*, true! But I'll take the business." He washed his face with a thick rag, his weathered face creased with a smile. "Soon it seems you boys will have your own families to support. Maybe it's time to stop working with your taam. There's little room in this shop for you to train apprentices, and someday your children. We could repurpose Tamon's grandfather's old restaurant next door. It has the ventilation system built already—"

"Taam," Asher whispered over Galen, his voice strained. He cast a worried glance at me, and I smiled as I hammered another hilt together. Galen had peppered comments like this our way for days, clearly excited by the fact that we'd invited someone outside the militia over to share a meal. By Chaeten standards, this meant nothing. To an Asri elder, he probably expected one of us to request a marriage blessing within a few weeks. The Asri move fast and marry young, even if that was no future I envisioned for myself anytime soon.

There were many things I'd learned to appreciate about life among the Asri, but their take on relationships was something I never thought I'd wrap my head around. To do things by Galen's standards, we'd both approach a town elder sometime within the next few years and ask them to match us off. We'd give the elder basic hard criteria regarding personality, body type, occupation—or gender, in Ash's case. They'd work with elders in other villages and do the rest.

Some Asri had a person in mind and just asked for the elder's blessing, but most walked in blind. A date or a dance was enough for an Asri to reject someone from their short list. A few weeks at most was the typical length of a successful courtship. I found all that insane.

Crazier still, everything moved forward only if the elders agreed. If you suggested a match to an elder and they thought you misaligned on long-term goals or something else, they'd refuse the match, and tell you why. But if you got their blessing, you went before the ancestors of Oria next, committing to a life of mutual monogamy, with the ideal being multiple lives.

Then there was their take on sex. It wasn't polite to talk about it, ever. Plato and I had fucked for a month in our bonus weekend practices. He never told a soul we were ever more than friends, insisting I do the same.

I'd been the one to lose interest first. I always fell short on whatever the Asri have going on in their heads. Plato was a sweet guy, but silence with him felt empty when we weren't sparring or fucking, and he wanted more than I could give. He'd still have married me if I gave him any hope, so I'd cut it off.

I'd always said something non-committal whenever Galen asked me when I'd be ready for the elders. I knew he believed I'd mature and see things his way in time. He gave me a thin metaphor about a child who might need a few snacks before dinner but at some point would learn to sit down, waiting for the host before dipping his fingers in the dessert. I would do anything to fend off a similar lecture.

"You're slowing down, old man," I told Galen. "It would be cruel if we started our own shop and left you all this work, *na*?"

The Asri accent sold it. He laughed and shook his head at me.

"Well, as an old man, I suppose I should rest my arthritic bones and draw up an order for more steel." With that, he hung up his hammer, grabbed some papers, and hustled up the stairs.

I tried to catch Asher's eye as he bent forward again under his lamp, the light filtering through the highlights in his curled hair as he squinted at the etching pen.

"We're behind, Brother," Ash said. "If you start the first folds on the next batch, I'll switch gears in a few minutes."

I sighed, picking up the metal with my tongs and bringing it to the fire. "Ash," I said in a low voice as the metal settled in the coals. "Don't tell Taam, but—" I set down my tongs with a clatter that echoed in the sudden quiet of the forge.

He looked at me sidelong, gripping the edge of the desk.

"Mahakal. Don't mention Mahakal until I figure it out."

A frown creased Asher's brow as he let out a breath. "Not what I was expecting you to say."

"What were you expecting?"

Asher's face sharpened. "Doesn't matter. What exactly did Mahakal offer you?"

I told him everything.

He crossed his arms. "I said he failed my dahn check. Why even consider it?"

I bristled. "He invited me to his unit, not his bed. Okay, well—he's interested, but I don't think it's connected. It's my SBO immunity he wants."

Ash reddened, and he looked back at his engraving. "I don't trust him—when it comes to you."

"I know," I said. "But I think he'd always throw off your dahn the minute he saw me as a soldier. For that, he has to see me as a tool, a game piece he may need to sacrifice in battle. That's his job."

Asher sighed up at the ceiling. "I guess that makes sense."

I leaned back on Ash's table. "He has to think like that to be effective."

"Effective," Asher's jaw clenched. "He hasn't caught the Red Demon, remember? Isn't that still what you want? He can't promise you that."

"Valid." I rubbed the stubble on my face. "But he's doing more than me. He's trying, and if she's seen again, he can help. And otherwise I'm just sparring, folding metal, fucking dancing—" The metal was glowing red in the fire. I took my tongs to go pick it out.

"You're still training. We'll take her on together whenever you feel ready. That's been our plan all along, right?" Despite speaking low, his words tore through me as I began folding.

"I'm restless, I guess." I went to reheat my blade. "Nothing seems right."

"Then nothing is right," Asher said. "When you see your path, walk it, but if you're this cut up about it, this isn't it."

"It's the same feeling I get staying still, Ash. Or whenever Galen—" I let the forging press drown my thoughts. I marveled at how every decision Asher ever made seemed to fall in a straight line, while my thoughts always tumbled over each other. "I don't think I can ever be happy or have a normal life until I know she's dead."

CHAPTER 17

Swimming

We'd been rained out the first time Mira and I tried to go swimming, but today was perfect. The late spring sun melted into a blue-violet sky with just a few puffy clouds as we emerged from the trail by the old dam. A small waterfall tumbled over moss-covered rocks in the forest, roaring alongside the chorus of unseen birds. The spray of the water cooled our foreheads, and the shimmering surface of the pool beckoned.

"Breathtaking," Mira marveled at the beauty of the spot, the ancient granite ruins cupping the water in labyrinthine designs. "I feel privileged that you've shared this with me."

A grin spread across my face. "I know, right? Ash has been coming here since he was a kid. He takes it for granted." I walked along the edge of the pool, searching for my favorite rock.

Mira perched herself beside me, biting her lip. "Where is he?"

I sighed in the misty air. "I don't know. He said he needed to wrap some things up around the house." I removed my shirt, feeling the spray on my skin.

She ran her hands down her face. "Well, I hope you make him feel a little guilty when you get home. It's hard to be Jesse and the Ashes with just the two of us."

"Still a valid meeting of the Dead Moms Club."

With a wink, she turned her back to me and slipped out of her pink sundress to a matching swimsuit. My cheeks warmed a little as she turned around in the two-piece bathing suit, showing off quite a bit more skin than what any of the Asri wear in the water. I slipped off my pants and shoes and tossed them under a tree.

"Well, if he was here he'd probably just be picking your brain about the code sequencer, rather than doing normal stuff, like this—" I picked her up and threw us both in the deep water.

Her eyes lit up as her shriek morphed into a laugh. She swam just out of arm's reach before her counterattack, wrestling me under the water and climbing onto my shoulders. I found my footing, holding her in place.

We splashed and floated in the green-edged water, the spray curling over the carved masonry of a lost world. Mira was an easy person to laugh with. Asher had missed such a beautiful day.

An hour later, we dried off. I'd promised her it wasn't necessary to pack lunch, that nature would provide. I caught a fish with my hands, dressed it alongside some small greens and mushrooms, and found a broad leaf to wrap it for roasting. Mira picked some berries when I showed her the best spot. As I bent to bring a fire to life to cook it all on the banks, she looked at me like I was a miracle worker, not a man who, at one point, lived on the edge of survival in these woods.

"How did you learn all that?" she said, with the smoking flames reflected in her eyes.

I tossed more tinder onto the budding flame. "I grew up on the South tip of the Noé Bend. No major cities, only the tech we couldn't live without. I learned to do a lot of things."

She bit her lip with unasked questions, the curiosity back in full force. "How old were you when you left?"

Okay. Here we go. I answered some of what she really wanted to know, focusing on the facts rather than how it left gashes in my heart. Fourteen. Siblings and Mom died. I didn't.

The fire crackled as she listened with sad eyes, the murmur of her apologies blending with the whispering waterfall behind us. We split the wine-colored berries as the fish cooked.

"How about you, my Thebos-raised scholar?"

She raised her eyebrow.

"What do you miss that you want back? You said you came here to figure stuff out."

A wistful smile touched Mira's lips. "I miss my friends, my professors," she said after a moment. "Varuna was a small, withdrawn academy, so I became very close with the people there."

I frowned. She made it sound like being able to grow close to anyone in the long term was not a common thing.

"But most of all, I missed the amazing lab I worked in. It felt like a place where anything was possible. My professors were brilliant, some of the best minds in the empire. I got to be witness to groundbreaking discoveries in Mod Technology, altering code to cure diseases and enhance the body. I got to watch people change their lives with the treatments we developed there. That's the sort of thing that's worth my whole life."

"Can you do that somewhere else?"

"I hope so," she trailed off, her gaze flickering toward the distant trees. "I'm enjoying my time here. Even so, this can't be home for long. My father would never allow it. I'm a race horse he bets on, and I've lost my first race."

"Honestly, that sounds awful," I said, feeling brave.

"Yeah, my father loves me in his way, but not like how I know Galen sees you. Or how you and Asher—" She didn't finish the sentence. She didn't need to.

"He's not family," I said, using the Asri word.

She leaned back against the rock, watching the fire. "No."

I unwrapped the fish, prodding the middle with a stick.

"I started a lab in my father's greenhouse," she said. "There's not been much research on code lines out of Noé, something to explain why only the Chaeten have succumbed here."

I could sense just as much caring in her delivery of that as curiosity.

"My plan is to write to my old tutors and see if I can collect some samples for them, test some of their research questions. Only fair, as I got the machine from them." She smiled.

"Mira, could you do anything with a sample from a Chaeten who survived the virus?" My heart pounded. "I was right there during the attack in Crofton. I was exposed."

Her head popped up. She shuffled imperceptibly back.

I swallowed. "Major Mahakal knows it all. He said I'm immune. That's what I was talking to him about before, and why he wants me."

She drew her legs under her with furrowed brows. "What do you mean by immune?"

I told her everything Mahakal didn't forbid me to repeat, everything except the Red Demon. But I told her my brothers died by a rebel sword, not the virus.

"My Academy studied a few samples from the South Bend Out-break, from the dead, but we couldn't find much." She licked her lips. "And I've never met anyone who survived exposure. You could help a lot of people. Jesse, this could be ground-breaking."

"How much blood do you need?"

"Just a drop," she said. "Assuming I can get a clean sequence on the first try."

Excitement bubbled in her voice as she continued on about all the people I could help, but I couldn't help but notice a flicker of sadness as well. My heart responded to that complexity; I felt she understood the things I found too painful to share. I studied the rays of sunshine filtering through the trees between us, and her smiling face. This was a better day, one I could be happy with, the things I once dreamed about alone in these forests.

Mira surprised me by reaching out and pulling me into a hug. The warmth of her body pressed into mine, still a little wet where her swimsuit met my chest, the scent of wildflowers and sunshine filling my senses. As she pulled away, she leaned in and planted a soft kiss on my cheek.

Quick preface here: although by that point in my life I was sure I found women just as satisfying to look at as men, I wasn't sure if I'd enjoy following through, especially since—so far—that never ended well. Once at fifteen, after a satisfying spar in the backyard of Ruan's parent's house, I misread the moment, and tried to kiss Ruan. In response, she kneed me right in the balls, apologized, then invited me to a very awkward dinner with her parents. I'd only kissed one other girl in the years since, and the experience was only a marginal improvement. Men liked me back. So far, no women.

In the swell of the moment, I forgot those fears, and I turned my head to meet Mira's mouth. I kissed her.

A spark jumped between us—she kissed back. Her lips were soft at first, a tentative exploration that made me shiver in the heat. But then her kiss deepened, her lips parting as her hand reached up to cup my cheek. Her touch sent a jolt through me.

Together we tasted of berries and woodsmoke, a sweetness mingling with the earthy tang of the forest. The sound of the waterfall faded away, replaced by the triumphant drumming of my heart. I tightened my arms around her, pulling her closer. I felt the press of her body against mine, with only the thin layer of her swimsuit between us.

A twig snapped behind us. Footsteps.

She pulled away first, gasping for breath. Mira's cheeks were flushed, eyes wide—maybe a flicker of fear, or perhaps a reflection of the racing pulse in both our chests.

Then there, standing a few paces back with an unreadable expression on his face, was Asher. His brow furrowed, his gaze darting between me and Mira.

The birds sang on, oblivious to my awkwardness. Mira cleared her throat, a forced smile tugging at her lips.

I wasn't certain what, if anything, Ash had seen. And I wasn't entirely sure why I felt like I'd betrayed him. *Okay, that was a lie. I did.* The warm wind on my skin felt like ice on my back, and I went to put on my shirt rather than face him.

"Looks like Jesse's keeping dirty secrets," Ash said with a tight smile. "Taam would have a lot to say if he heard you were eating a fish out here."

I breathed out a sigh as I shrugged on my pants.

"I'm so glad you can join us, Asher," Mira said with a smile. "Truly," she added with a little extra force. His face was unreadable as he studied her. Ash hesitated, then took a seat against a rock. He fished out some cold bottles of cider from his bag and met my gaze as he handed it to me.

"It's okay, Brother," he said with a laugh. "I'm not telling Taam about your fish."

He'd have nothing to tell, anyway. I was no longer hungry, and apparently, neither was Mira.

Chapter 18

Sister

Hand-to-hand combat day, and I was cocky enough to take on four. Ash and Galen stayed out of it, leaving me pitted against Meragc, Ruan, Plato and a younger boy named Horeshio who'd been coming to morning training since last fall.

I got my ass handed to me the first time, nursed my bruises, then scored on three out of four the second time.

Asher stepped in that last round when poor Horeshio had enough, and just as Ash was attempting to land an elbow strike, a flash of pink dress caught my eye. Mira, her black hair shining in the dawn. She'd been coming every day for almost two weeks now.

Asher got his elbow shot in, sending me stumbling back. He grinned, wiping sweat from his brow.

"Mira's here to leer. That's our signal to wrap up," Galen boomed across the clearing, giving her a teasing grin.

Mira waved back. "And how are you this morning, Elder Eirini?"

I grimaced. No one ever called him that. But he puffed his chest out and saluted all the same.

Last week, when she started arriving in the middle of the sessions, Galen had insisted there were no spectators in his militia. Although Mira tried some forms with us for a few days, she always wanted no part of the violent sparring, and threw out very Asri-sounding reasons as to why. Since then, she'd made a point of arriving precisely one hour after sunrise to walk us back along the forest path, bringing a dish of cut fruit or duck eggs to contribute to breakfast.

I picked up my bag and hustled toward her before Galen had a chance to say anything awkward. Asher took his time, chatting with Ruan.

Dogwood petals fell around Mira, fluttering in the space between us. We hadn't been alone to talk since, well—voids, I didn't know what happened after we went swimming. I was afraid to bring it up and have everything fall apart, and that alone was the sign that it already had. That kiss didn't sit well, and I was no stranger to that feeling, even if I didn't understand why I felt it almost every time, with anyone. Time to be brave, and end it before there was anything to end.

"Hey," I said, my voice a hoarse whisper.

"Hi Jesse," she said, her voice crisp as the rainy morning breeze. She rummaged through the purse across her body and pulled out a small vial. She unscrewed it, revealing a needle on the cap. "Do you mind if I collect that blood sample now?"

"Go ahead."

"I'll need your hand."

My hand? I'll let the elders know. That would be the worst possible thing I could say out loud. I held out my palm, trying to clear my head as she unwrapped a cloth that smelled like alcohol.

She scrubbed at my callused finger for what felt like forever.

"Jesse," she said. "Are you ready?"

The concern in her eyes, the gentle touch of her hand gripping my arm, sent a different kind of spark through me. I wanted to keep this much in my life; her in my life.

"Didn't you just see Ash elbow me in the gut? I don't need a warning, just go ahead and—"

She pricked me, smirking.

"Yeah, do that," I mumbled.

"All done." She sealed the vial with a click. "Thanks, Jesse."

"No problem." My words caught in my throat. I needed to talk this out before I confused myself further.

"We should talk." She looked over my shoulder, and I turned. Ash met our gaze, then pretended he didn't, keeping his distance on the far side of the clearing. Galen was already walking ahead of us up the road.

"Yeah," I said.

"Jesse." She met my gaze with what appeared to be some effort. "You're incredible. You're kind, funny, brave. You did nothing wrong…" She took a shaky breath.

My heart flapped in my chest like a trapped bird, waiting for the "but."

"But what I realized," she continued, her voice gaining strength, "is that I really admire that bond you have with Asher. The brotherly connection. I've had friendships, but nothing quite like what you both share. I haven't known you very long, sure, but…"

The words trailed off, what was left unsaid heavy in the air. Relief washed over me, and I felt like I understood. My own thoughts settled.

"If I'm ever dumb enough to let an elder marry me off," I began.

She froze.

Not a good start. I winced. "Family is there for you, no matter what," I tried again. "Ash will have a couch for me when I get divorced, much to Galen's shame. We've already worked out the details. Or more likely, I'll refuse to get married in the first place, much to Galen's shame. I just have to figure out what will shame him least, and stick to that. But I'll need Ash's couch either way. Anyway—" *Fuck.* I was rambling.

She just stared, considering.

Asher looked away when I caught his eye across the clearing. "I seriously doubt he's going to have the same problems I do."

"I agree." A wistful smile graced Mira's lips. "So what does a girl who has known you for such a brief period of time need to do to get a couch from you? Or is that inappropriate?"

A smile tugged at my own lips. "Yeah, you got a brother, if that's what you mean." I realized the full depth of that didn't terrify me. I shifted my stance. "Ash adopted me in his head after a week, and well, I think I feel the same about you as I do for him."

She lit up at that, and we both looked at Ash, who was still pretending not to be side-eying us as he packed the last of his things.

"But I don't have a couch. I need to get my shit together," I said.

Her smile widened. "Maybe in a year, I'll have a little apartment in Thebos or Ea Shadohe. Same offer. And I mean it. A decade from now. Twenty. I'll be there for you too. Family."

I closed my eyes with the warmth of her words. And it meant so much more than the hurricane of emotions I felt after kissing her. This was the foundation that survived all that. "My home will always be open to you too, Sister."

She hugged me then, holding me tight, with her head to my heart. It felt right for her to be there, safe.

I caught a glimpse of Asher's back as he strode fast down the path home, alone.

CHAPTER 19

A Man Who Knows His Place

The summer sun beat down on my sweaty brow as I walked through the garden to Mira's greenhouse lab. Opening the rickety door of the frosted glass structure for the first time, I was grateful to find it was climate controlled inside.

It was clear that Mira was working off a low budget, despite her father investing plenty of coin into modernizing the governor's house. Her lab was a cluttered haven of two tables, a shelf, a tablet, lots of books and stacks of papers, and her little code sequencer running with a low, electronic thrum. Ash and Mira sat huddled over the tablet, their brows furrowed in exhausted concentration.

Research was not going well.

"Hey Ashes," I said, the sound echoing off the glass walls. "Who wants mint lemonade?"

Mira glanced up, her frustration tugged away by a smile.

Voids, had she even slept? Asher didn't look much better. He'd been staying up reading some of Mira's Mod-Tech books in an effort to help her figure out what she was doing wrong. He'd retested every circuit, coming up empty. That was all he cared to share with me regarding anything to do with Mira.

"Still getting error messages?" I asked, knowing if she wasn't, she would have told me before the door creaked closed behind me.

"Drowning in them." Mira rubbed the exhaustion out of her eyes. "Same as the last sample. I've isolated some segments of code that don't throw it, but there are far too many that do. It can't be right. None of this can be right."

My stomach churned. "What would it mean if it was right?"

Mira snorted. "It means you should be dead. We've already tried pulling your sample three times, same result."

I let out a shaky breath. "So it's real, whatever it is."

"Trust me, it can't be. Asher? Back me up."

Asher peeled his eyes away from her. "From what I've read, yeah. The database she connects to can translate code at any level: gene groups, interactions, modulators, even break it down to individual proteins. At some point, this is all Mira's expertise," he said with a blooming smile, "but even I understand you shouldn't have lethal sequences in your code. One instance you might survive, not fifty-three."

I picked up a vial of clear liquid and studied it. Mira snatched it from my hands and placed it back.

"Maybe the database is wrong?" I said.

"It's not. The database is the system of record. All scientific labs can connect to the same one and much of these code sequences, like your lethal one, predates the empire. There's been more than enough time to correct a human error." She drummed her fingers. "I could model the sequence, but I'd need more equipment. And besides—I know it doesn't interact with the SBO virus. The problem is, nothing in your code does."

"Okay fine. Have you run any other samples besides mine and yours to see if your machine is just buggy?"

"No." She placed the vial back, then met my brother's gaze. "Ash, may I borrow your blood?"

"If I can be your dance partner again tomorrow, you may bleed me dry," Asher said, eyes twinkling.

"That might interfere with future dancing," she laughed, and gathered the supplies. "Or dinner tonight."

"I won't wear the century robe this time, I promise."

"Yes please, even if I'll admit you're stunning in it," Mira said.

"You think so?" Ash said, flustered.

Warm electric lights shone around the polished mahogany table, empty apart from arranged plates, glasses and silver. Soft flutes and string music trilled from the speakers embedded in the walls.

Governor Solonstrong was not a man of imposing stature, but he was a person who stood with his shoulder's back as if he expected all eyes to be on him. His black hair was meticulously styled and glossy, and he kept the chin of his handsome brown face high. Mira sat next to him sipping some coffee, her fresh braid shimmering as she, no doubt, was still thinking through the issues at the lab. Next to her, Asher, stiff and uncomfortable in the best blue shirt he owned, fidgeted with his napkin.

"I'm grateful you've taken an interest in meeting my friends, Father," Mira said. He'd been explaining the progress of his winery on the Island of Ment, where he hoped to retire one day. Asher and I had very little to contribute to that conversation.

"Of course. It's important that I meet those who work closely with our elders," he said, giving Asher a cursory glance before settling on me. "And to meet those who build such a high percentage of the North Barrack's weapons. I know that both of you have been quite busy lately as the empire plans to reopen the Bend."

"What?" I said.

Two servers walked in just then, their movements precise as they shifted silver platters from their trays onto the center of the table. They laid out a steaming bowl of saffron rice and thick brown noodles, colorful curries studded with vibrant vegetables, a roasted duck, and an assortment of flatbreads arranged in a pretty pattern. The scent of spices filled the air, a mix of Chaeten and Asri culinary influences far more exotic than the staples in our home above the forge. We didn't have someone who'd walk around and fill our glasses with wine at home, either.

Asher leaned toward Mira and whispered, "Which ones are vegetarian?"

Governor Solonstrong answered for her. "Ah. There's duck fat in the noodles and the red curry, and best avoid the duck as well."

Asher grimaced politely. "Thank you, Governor."

When the governor passed me the duck, I passed it on to Mira, who paused, then set it back in the center after a glance to Ash. The governor frowned.

"You'd mentioned something about the South Bend reopening, Governor?" I asked.

Governor Solonstrong nodded as he sawed through a chunk of crispy meat. "The hope is to open up the Bend in two months: resettling it with a mix of refugees and fresh recruits from the inner empire. I understand Major Mahakal has extended an invitation for you to join his unit toward that purpose?"

It took me a moment to process that. The governor watched me over a glass of wine.

"Yes, Governor. I'm still thinking it over."

"It would be quite an honor to work alongside a Ghost War veteran. I understand he wants you in his personal squad. Many would kill for such a post."

I ladled some vegetable curry atop the rice on my plate with all eyes on me, deciding what to say.

"I can just as easily do my part for the Bend and the empire by keeping weapons and tools sharp," I said. "Asher and Galen hold me to high standards, although Ash has the steadier hand for some of the more intricate work." I nodded to my brother, who grinned.

The Governor's features softened as my words sunk in. "A commendable sentiment, young man. You aren't afraid of hard work, even menial work, and I respect a man who knows his place." He took a moment to chew his meat. "Humility is a virtue often overlooked these days."

"Thank you," I said, uncertain what else to say.

Governor Solonstrong cleared his throat. "The way I see it, nobility *is* humility, at its core." He chuckled. "Take me, for instance. After years serving Queen Azara in Ea Shadohe, at the heart of the empire, I admit I felt humbled when offered this position. But it was a necessary lesson. Sometimes, we must trust our immortal leaders have a plan, even if the details are unclear to us. After seeing how life is in the wild frontier, I understand now how vital it is that we reopen the Bend, to return our queen's light to the far corners of the empire. It is a far more important role than the work I did before, in the capital."

"How is it safe to open the Bend if there's no mod yet to prevent SBO infection?" Mira's voice was soft, but the challenge was unmistakable.

The Governor waved his fork at her. "Just because the immortals don't share the plan with us, it doesn't mean it doesn't exist. After five years since the last attack, I think we can assume that there are no more rebels with living samples."

"Then why hasn't the empire announced that?" Asher asked. "If those soldiers go in and drop dead, what's the next move? You should be fully aware of contingency plans, at least."

The governor narrowed his eyes at the challenge. "Yes, we should plan for emergencies, but it is impossible to plan for each and every crisis." He waved his wine glass. "The empire is focused on curtailing Asri rebels and their attacks on tech in Noé, so that will be my focus too, to show I have learned from my mistakes. We must have faith our reincarnated queen knows what she is doing more than a young blacksmith, no? As wonderful as your creations are—stunning."

I looked to Ash, who frowned at his plate. Mira had good reasons to feel distant from her father. It was stupid to assume that the rebels who unleashed the virus that caused the South Bend Outbreak wouldn't have another sample, for one. To an Attiq-ka immortal, waiting five years was nothing in their quest to kill Chaeten and our queen. Besides, the Red Demon was still out there, and I was willing to bet that Solonstrong knew next to nothing about her.

The governor sipped his wine. "Now, my unsolicited advice to young Jesse here is to take Major Mahakal's offer. Your reputation precedes you, young man. Ashmira tells me you can overcome several opponents at once from our local militia, and have never lost a match to anyone from the barracks. Do I have that right?"

"Sorry, no, Governor," I said, face burning. "I lost to both Major Ryder and Lieutenant Suluku." I'd lost fighting both the pair at once at a festival after they snuck me my first taste of whiskey, but I already didn't like where this was going.

"With formal training, you would be perfect," he rumbled. "It's a waste to have you pouring metal when you could be putting those talents to use defending the empire. And while I respect your humility, it is my role here to ensure the gifts of people under my care do not go to waste. Do you understand me, Jesse Eirini? If you have a reason to turn Mahakal down, fine, I'll recommend you to the barrack in Uyr Elderven. You can accompany Ashmira when she takes her post there."

Ash turned to her with a start. "You're leaving, Mira?"

Her gaze hardened to something glass-shattering when she turned to face her father. "I did not say I'd be accepting that post, Father. I'm leaning toward no."

My heart thumped in my chest, but I schooled my expression.

His pointed look lingered on Mira. "I have read every report from my brilliant daughter's schooling through the years." He turned a whimsical smile to me. "I have a couple framed in my office, in fact, but it seems she needs to take a lesson from you."

He turned to Mira, his tone hardening to a point. "Humility, dear daughter. If you care at all for my advice, do not chase honors Queen Azara has taken away from us both. Be grateful for the post you were offered in Uyr Elderven, and if you cannot, secure another before it expires. The longer you stay here with me, the more your reputation will degrade. I invited you here to heal from your disappointment, to give you space to plan a strategic move. I'm less certain this nonsense in the greenhouse is bringing you any closer to that."

The governor glared at Ash as well.

Mira sat with her back stiff. "Thank you father, I will reflect on your advice." Her smile faded in a blink as the governor turned away.

"Excellent," he said in a neutral tone. "And what beautiful dancing you all have been doing. Every one of you—"

I tried to catch Asher's tired eyes as the conversation switched to lighter topics, and I made all the usual jokes to keep that banter light, but Ash just stared at his plate with only a few bites torn out of his flatbread. Mira squeezed his knee under the table and only got a wilted smile for her effort.

On the walk home, I told Ash he was lucky to be the only one who escaped the meal without the governor's "unsolicited advice." But instead of a chuckle or even a smile, he just shook his head at me.

"You alright, Ash?"

"Yeah. Just not ready to laugh this one off." A long exhale. "No sense talking about it."

There was that silent treatment again. I'd hoped he'd open up if I was quiet back. His fists clenched and unclenched on the walk, while cicadas woke to the night.

CHAPTER 20

No

I'd been over to the North Barrack a few times before—in day-light—during very different circumstances. The path out of the compound wound through a copse of maple trees, their leaves waving in the rosy sunset. A raven cawed from the trees as I led Meragc's borrowed horse through the gate. Laughter spilled from an open window. I took a deep breath to ease the knot of tension in my chest. I'd delayed this enough.

Mahakal met me in his office. Electric lights cast my sweaty reflection in a window that would—in the daytime—overlook the training yard. The air inside Mahakal's office tasted sterile, like sharpened steel and clean Chaeten efficiency. A black settee faced a sturdy desk, and he'd flicked all the screens to black before I entered. The Major's smile dimmed when he saw I had none.

As I sat, Mahakal moved to a cabinet, uncorking a half-empty bottle of wine.

"It's quite late, friend." Mahakal's voice was so much friendlier than those whiteless eyes. "Not that I mind." He set down a glass for me. "You're welcome to rest the night—"

"No." My voice came out loud, sharp.

Major Mahakal froze, then set the wine bottle on his desk. He turned to me with unbridled concern.

"No thank you," I said again, my mouth dry. "Thank you, really. But…"

Mahakal waited, pushing the red hair from his striking eyes.

I shook my head, the movement jerky and raw. "This has been a difficult decision, but I won't be joining your unit. Thanks again for the honor of your offer. That's all I came to say—I'll just head home."

I planned words on the ride that felt all wrong now. He wouldn't understand how I felt his unit wasn't my path, or that I had an Asri family that remade themselves around me to fit my jagged pieces.

"I thought you'd feel drawn back to the Bend," Mahakal said, his voice soft.

"It's not home anymore. There's no one there left to defend. My people are here."

Mahakal watched me, his features weaving a tapestry of emotions I couldn't decipher beyond a twitch in his eyes.

"You know there are things I'm not cleared to tell you," Mahakal said. "But believe me when I say the rebels are still among us. My unit is your chance at justice, vengeance—your best chance."

"I agree." Heat rose in my chest, the phantom itch for violence still tempting. "I think it's time for me to let go of all that. You can't promise me the Red Demon. I'd pledge my life in a heartbeat if you could. There's no point in me pledging my life in your unit in exchange for vengeance I may never see. So I'm going to move on, do what I need to do to stop obsessing about this. I have a job I'm good at, good people around me."

Mahakal sighed, a long, weary sound. "Right." Disappointment flickered in his eyes before he stood up to his full height. "When we first spoke, I told you I wanted to protect you, to offer you a boon for all you suffered. I will ask you just one more time before I wash my hands of this. Join my unit. Even if I can't guarantee you the Red Demon, I have plans for you. I will ensure you rise to the life you deserve."

"I don't want that." I hated the quaver in my voice.

Mahakal crossed his arms, studying me in silence. Finally, he nod-ded. "Go in peace, friend." The Major offered me a small smile and a firm grip that threatened to swallow me whole.

CHAPTER 21

The Gift

When no work order came from the North Barrack the following week, we welcomed the break. Asher was able to spend every day in Mira's lab, and I trained longer and harder in the mornings, focusing on teaching a few new kids a few years younger than me. Those few years were huge, as I'd now shed the last misgivings about considering myself a man.

In the afternoons, I took time to cut some firewood for the winter, dropping some to Atalia and Meragc since they let me borrow their horse cart for the hauling. Then I'd meet up with Mira and Ash, and walk home, and listen to Ash tell me about that day's failed diagnostic attempt.

I love how the air shift in a Noé summer—the smooth green aroma that promises growth and renewal, and all the warmth my skin can soak up. I love how bright the once stark and cool world becomes, and in such moments, it's easy to feel like all my nightmares are behind me. Back then, whenever the nightmares quite literally did not go away, I shuttered my thoughts away at first light, walking the dawn path to beat or swing that darkness out in the clearing. That was good enough.

When no work order arrived after two weeks, Galen began to worry. The Barrack had ordered weekly shipments for years, except for oc-casional breaks around the festivals. He inquired and got non-committal answers. We cleaned the shop, organized the equipment—and waited.

I was taking a long lunch and rinsing some lentils and collards for dinner when I heard the shop door open with a ring. Wiping my hands on a towel, I hurried down the stairs.

When I saw the tall, broad-shouldered man in the red military uniform, my heart skipped for three reasons. First, he'd be bringing that barrack order. Second, it was Kane, a man with Asri eyes the color of molten gold and stormy seas and muscles everywhere, my favorite one-time sparring partner. Yes, *that* one-time sparring partner. One look was enough to remember all the things he could do with that body, sparring or not, and just how that body felt against mine. Voids, he was hot. Thirdly—if I could remember what I was counting and why—I had the shop and house to myself, and the bathhouse too, the safest place to spend a wonderful afternoon.

"Jesse, how have you been?" he asked in that deep voice, a smile playing on his lips as he looked me up and down. "You look well."

"You don't." I sidled up beside him with a *tsk*, moving some of the hair from his sweaty face. "Looks like you had a long ride. Care for a cold drink upstairs? A hot meal?" My eyes dipped down to the hot meal I envisioned for myself, then back up. His smile glazed over.

Kane groaned, pressing his body into mine. "I was supposed to make the delivery and come right back, but I suppose I can come up with an excuse." He nodded to the hefty package wrapped in coarse burlap on the counter. "Seems you've gotten the Major's attention."

The warmth tightening my pants chilled instantly. Attached to the parcel was a hand-inked note with the words: "To Galen's son: I look forward to working with you soon. Regards, Mahakal."

I set it down on the counter without opening it. Kane watched me with a smirk.

"Did Major Ryder send an order with you? There was nothing sent through the temple."

Kane's smile flickered. "Sorry, just this. But you don't have to open it right now."

He tried to lace a kiss on my neck, but I ducked away, unwrapping the twine on the burlap package with irritated swiftness. A sword, Chaeten steel of good quality, the blade dull. A small green LED blinked in slow rhythm on the grip, but when I touched it, nothing happened.

"What in the black void is this?" I turned the weapon over in my hands, the polished grip feeling cold against my skin. "Our shop makes better."

Kane shrugged with a hint of unease that mirrored my own. "Maybe he'll activate it for you when you start?" He smiled at my lips, then leaned in to whisper in my ear. "I'm so glad you're pledging. I'm shipping out with Mahakal too. I'd love your bunk next to mine."

My breath hitched. "I'm in no mood right now, Kane. I told Mahakal no." The metallic tang of anger rose in my throat, but it wasn't Kane's fault.

He just looked confused. "He's immortal, Jesse. Whether you mean fucking him or joining the unit, either way, missed opportunity."

I could no longer mask my disgust. "Get the fuck out of here, Kane." I stormed back upstairs, relaxing a bit when the door dinged closed.

He didn't take the stupid sword back with him, so I brought it upstairs to stare at the audacity of it, wanting to hurl it into the wall to confirm that dull piece of shit couldn't dent granite. I made tea instead. The door chime sang again. Slow footsteps plodded up the stairs.

Galen ambled by the window, framed in the pollen-dusted sunlight. Despair hung on my taam's face where his smile lines usually cut parallel to Asher's. Dread seeped the warmth from that summer day.

"What's wrong?"

He didn't speak, just shook his head and shuffled toward the worn bench. The weight he carried didn't seem to ease as he sat, staring in dull silence across the small kitchen.

I grabbed a mug, the clay warm where it hung by the kettle, and poured him a cup of the catnip and mint tea I'd been brewing, the bubbling whisper frantic. His hand shook beside the cup.

"Taam, what's wrong?"

A low breath. "The barrack is done with us. For good. The governor sat me down with Major Ryder to give me the news."

My stomach clenched. The North Barrack was, by far, our top client. *Without them...* "Why?" I asked, the question laced with the panic that had been rising in me since before Galen stepped into the door.

"They've built a forge in the Bend, planning to use tech they only want Z'har knowing about. Offered me a job there if I pledge."

"Pledge?" Disbelief warred with shadows. "They want you to become Z'har?"

A grimace twisted Galen's lips. "I told them I prefer my freedom. While I have no trouble seeing myself as a servant to the people, I won't be a slave, told where to sleep and when to rise." He cast a curious glance at the wrapped weapon on the table. "What's that?"

I unfurled the cloth. "Delivery from Mahakal. It's shit, as far as I can tell."

Galen picked up the blade, studying the tech-infused hilt. "It's probably work from the new forge, although I don't understand what he's trying to say."

"An insult? A power play? Does it matter which?" I spat. "And why was the governor getting involved in all this?" Then I remembered what Governor Solonstrong said at dinner. He felt it was his job to ensure my talents didn't go to waste, that he'd do anything to ensure they didn't.

My mouth went dry. He'd done just that.

Galen shook his head, his features numb, then took a deep meditative breath. "I'll see if Oria will listen, although I'm not sure I've ever been that good at hearing them speak." Another deep breath. "Ash has his mother's ears though."

"I'll fetch him," I said, wrapping the weapon to carry with me. Maybe he or Mira could make sense of it.

CHAPTER 22

Galen's Son

I jogged to the greenhouse lab, fuming in the afternoon heat as I passed the market booths and white-washed homes on the way. The air felt stifling until I burst through that door into the climate-controlled greenhouse, the wrapped sword still clutched in my hand.

Mira looked up from Asher's shoulder with red, wet eyes. Their startled glances locked with mine. They separated. Ash slumped against the frosted glass wall without so much as a hello.

"What happened?" My question echoed. I set down the blade on the table.

"Jesse," Mira started, her voice barely a whisper. "My father has given me an ultimatum. I have to leave in a week."

My brow furrowed. "Leave? Where?"

"I'll be taking that post in Uyr Elderven," she said, a bitter edge creeping into her tone. "The post is at the central hospital—implementing mods and following orders rather than researching—but at least it's somewhat related to what I love. And I'll be helping people again. That's more than I'm doing now."

Asher stared down at the table as if it held the answers we were desperate for.

"It's for the best. I've made no progress at all. And..." she trailed off, her voice cracking. "I expected more from myself."

I stepped closer to hug her. Asher remained a silent statue, his despair seeping toward me like smoke.

"It's not your fault. You said it yourself, you could do more with other machines," I said, holding her.

Mira wiped a stray tear. "I analyzed enough, Jesse. Honestly, there's nothing to explain your immunity. That much I should find. And when I ran Asher's code…" she trailed off, a hesitant glance thrown toward Asher's still form. "There were no anomalies like yours. He'll probably outlive us all by a decade, though. I'm glad."

A bittersweet smile flickered across both her and Asher's faces before vanishing as quickly as it appeared. Asher pushed away from the table and walked over to the window, turning his back on us. "I tried to tell her not to blame herself. If anyone messed anything up, it's me."

I didn't understand what he meant by that. "Both of you need to quit the self-blame. Voids." A knot of tension tightened at my temple. Mira's frustration, Asher's dejection, the growing sense of helplessness for what I came here to tell them. *Oh right.*

My anger rekindled. "Mira, we lost the barrack as a client, and I think your father has something to do with it."

Asher walked back toward us, his gaze scanning the cluttered workbench, and then the wrapped sword on the ground. A flicker of a storm rekindled in his eyes. "We heard the news."

I exchanged a worried glance with Mira.

"Why do you think my father interfered?" she asked.

"He threatened me at dinner," I growled. "When he said he'd do what he needed to make sure I didn't waste my gifts."

Asher snorted. Both Mira and I looked up to see him unwrap the sword.

"Yeah, there's that thing too," I said, hand on my head. "A shitty gift from Mahakal that doesn't even work. He writes that note like he can't even remember my name."

Asher read the note aloud, "To Galen's Son, I look forward to working with you." He let out a dark laugh.

I held my breath. "What is it, Ash?"

"Not everything is about you, Brother."

With that, he opened the door and strode out with the sword in hand, leaving the burlap wrapping behind. In his grip, the sword hummed to life, a light blooming down the hilt.

"Ash?" Mira said, voice quavering.

A row of peach trees stood blooming by the greenhouse, and Asher swung at one of the fruits, shoulder muscles tightening as he followed through to dissect it in half, stone and all.

My mouth fell open. "That was dull as shit for me. How did you get it to work?"

He sliced again, eyes intense. "Standard issue in Mahakal's unit, I'm told." He flipped it, and as soon as the blade was in the air, the glow stopped, and I saw a shimmer of movement at the edge of the blade as it dulled. "Neat tech, isn't it? The blade sharpens at my touch and only mine, reforming itself in battle to keep its edge."

I blinked, dumbfounded.

"I'm the one whose name doesn't matter—Galen's son. He probably doesn't remember my name. But—" He ran a finger down the fuller and turned the grip over in his hands. "At least I have a cool sword now, right?"

I stared at the blade in Asher's hand, my mind reeling. "Mira," I finally managed, "Did you know?"

Mira nodded, her face pale. "He volunteered a few days ago."

"I don't understand." I inhaled, my breath stinging.

Ash picked up the scabbard and sheathed his sword. He laced it on his belt without answering.

"Ash?" Mira whispered.

He looked up at her voice; his anger softened.

"I think you should explain," Mira said.

Asher squeezed his eyes tight. "I'm in no mood, Mira." And with that, he started walking toward the street in bold strides.

I could see red in my vision watching him go. "I need a sword, Mira."

"What?"

I darted toward the mansion's back door. Flinging the door open, I ran down the hall with the awful purple carpet to the guards' storeroom. Inside, I met one of the guards dressing for a shift, a muscular brown-haired woman, scanning me agape from head to toe. Beside her, weapons.

"I need to borrow this," I blurted out, swiping the best of the lot.

Mira tried to block my path, her arms wide in flowy pink sleeves. "You're not going to hurt him, are you?"

I darted under her, too caught up in the storm of emotions churning within me to respond. I glanced back at the front door, a flicker of guilt breaking free before I started running. Ash was already too far up the road for me to see.

"Jesse!" Mira's cry fell under the sound of my pounding boots.

I started catching up to Ash on his way home, but he veered off, picking up into a run into the woods as he passed Ruan's house.

My lungs were heaving as I reached the training clearing, the sky bathed in the first fires of sunset. He kept his back to me as he came to a halt, his hand resting on the grip of his sword.

"Ash!" I called out, my voice raspy from the run.

He whirled around, his face a mask of fury. He gripped the haft with a tight fist.

"Leave me alone, Jesse. I don't want to talk." His tone was neutral, but I could see his rage straining its leash. He never wanted to talk anymore. He was shutting me out yet again.

"Spar?" I couldn't understand his anger, but I was tired of it. I let my anger rise to meet him where he was at, drawing the borrowed blade in one fluid motion.

His eyes widened, hardened. We both knew how stupid it was to fight with battle-ready blades and no armor. In retrospect, I was a cocky idiot to assume I wouldn't hurt him. I considered no other possibility.

With a nod, he was on me. The clash of steel shattered the tense silence. Sparks flew as our blades met in a flurry, leaving a groove in mine from the force of his first strike.

Voids. It *was* a good blade.

"Remember what you told me when Mahakal asked me to join his battalion?" I yelled between parries. "You asked why in the black void I even considered it."

Asher countered with a brutal swipe, forcing me to backpedal. "I'm not you."

"Yeah, and that means you're more likely to die out there," I said, launching a series of quick attacks that put him on the defensive.

"Because I'm weak? Because you're the better man?" he roared, regaining his footing and landing a blow that sent a jolt up my arm.

I'd been thinking about the SBO immunity, but I was too busy reeling away from that steel to say so.

"I've been in your shadow for years now. Everyone notices you first."

I just laughed, swinging. "No."

"The governor!"

I parried, my blade sparking, shredding.

"The major!"

My blade broke against his, and I barely twisted away.

"Mira." His blow landed, cutting me to the bone across the chest.

I folded.

Asher froze, his blazing eyes going distant when I didn't rise. "Sometimes ... sometimes I do want to cut you a little."

My hands soaked red. I tried to push past the pain, pulling my shirt open to study the wound. It was the first time I'd seen the white of my bones. "I can tell," I wheezed out. "I yield, by the way. Point yours."

He dropped the blade, kneeling in the dirt beside me. Before I knew what was happening, he had ripped the shirt off my back and was winding strips of it tight around my chest. He then removed his own shirt to do the same.

Pain pulsed above my heart, stinging sharp with each ragged breath.

Asher knelt beside me, the dying light of the sunset reflecting the worry on his face. "I'm sorry. Voids, I'm sorry."

A tremor ran through his hands as he ripped the last of his shirt to close my wound, and I found it hard to sit up to make that easy. "I need to get you to a healer, fast."

With a grunt of effort, he helped me to my feet. Once up, I couldn't convince my back to fully straighten. But I kept my head afloat, leaning most of my weight on Asher as we stumbled through the darkening woods, dripping a trail of blood between the trees.

"About a week ago, I asked Mira if she'd go to the elders with me," Asher said, just above a whisper.

My head lolled up, disbelief as sharp as the throbbing in my chest. "What? Fuck."

Asher looked away. "She—she turned me down."

"Ash," I rasped, my voice weak. "She was always leaving. You knew that."

He stopped walking to regain a stronger grip on my arm. "I know," he admitted. "But I knew I loved her the moment I met her."

My heartbeat fluttered. I was speechless.

"Her research is important... Sure, I can support that. I could open a forge anywhere and follow her around. She didn't want me to—in her words—give up my whole life for her."

A bitter chuckle escaped my lips until I cringed from the pain of even a little laughter. "Loving like that—the minute you saw her. That'll scare any Chaeten, Ash."

His breathing picked up beside my ear, and I wondered if he was crying. "She said she loves me, that's what hurts the most. I'm not like either of you, though. To her, research is first. To you—killing someone is first. For me, the people I love are first. You don't want my help with the Red Demon anymore. She doesn't need me at all. So what good is that love?"

I wanted to stand up, to look at him, but I couldn't find the strength. "Maybe she just needs more time."

"There is no time. The post she's taking, it's not a civilian one. It requires a pledge after a few months, and Z'har can't marry. So—" His voice broke, and a sob wracked his body. My vision blurred, a mixture of pain and a rising sense of dread.

"No Ash, there's not... She... She can't—" My words failed me as my vision spun, and the world tilted on its axis. "Ash," I managed, my voice a hoarse whisper. "I love you, Brother."

The words slurred out, a long breath of cool evening air. Then, the darkness rushed in as I fell onto the mossy path.

Ghost's Warning

I can barely remember saying goodbye. It was probably the herbs the healer gave me for those gashes across my heart. Or maybe I knew better than to hold that memory too tight after all the pain I'd seared into my mind from Iden and Mal, whose blood still sprayed my skin in my dreams. I remember Mira's disappointed face as she sat beside my bed, incessant throbbing when the wounds got infected, and nothing worked. I remember anger I could not let out, perhaps because I wasn't sure who I should be mad at. Mira kissed my forehead wearing her travel cloak on the day they left. Ash saluted and walked her out. I felt abandoned, wishing they could just stay, but I had enough of my wits not to say that.

It took two months for those wounds to heal, leaving an angry pink scar over my heart. Galen hated to see it during practice, hated the reminder that his boys would be stupid enough to spar with new tech and no armor. That's all we'd say. We didn't want to trouble him further.

The only part of Nunbiren that still felt constant was my taam, although he was not the same man he used to be. Galen took a step back from morning training once I healed up, using his mornings to pray and light a candle in the temple for Ash's safety, or speak with the ancestors in the woods. As far as I know, he got no sign or direction from these rituals. But it kept him calm, if not happier.

Taam was quieter, kinder, and never once in the next couple months did he suggest I go to the elders, plan my future for me, or rail about the new forge in the Bend. His acceptance of our situation scared me the most, but I kept my doubts to myself.

"A Galen has lived in this town for two thousand years," he said one day, leaning in the near empty shop. We'd tried to expand into some woodworking, but it wasn't catching on. "I can't be the first to leave. And Amenirdis, the immortal Galen's wife, might still be reborn. She'd know to come here for Istaran and the robe."

"I understand," I said, filing down the engraving on a chair I suspected no one would buy. And I did understand why he needed to believe that. For his sake, I did my best to believe it too.

We'd check the temple regularly for news about the Bend. The soldiers were doing well, escorting settlers willing to take the risk of further Asri rebel attacks. The volunteers came from the crowded cities and academies from all over the empire. Red-robed priests came to town sometimes to recruit for certain trades, and by the end of summer, the town began to thin.

Ash wrote a couple times, but he was not allowed to share where he was, or anything about the classified work he was doing. He ignored my questions and said he was fine. I came to resent those letters more than look forward to them.

I turned twenty-one on a rainy day in early fall. Galen made me an ugly mess of a chocolate cake that still tasted divine. That was the day I missed Ash the most. I wondered what had changed so drastically for him to not write for a month. He wasn't a casualty. I checked.

Six weeks later, I woke to Galen telling me to arm myself, Istaran strapped across his back. There was a stranger at the gate; signs of Attiq-ka magic. The night guard had called the elders and the governor, and Galen assembled the militia.

Dawn bled across the horizon by the time we got to the front gate. There she was, a little girl of eight or nine, standing hunched in the road with tangled black hair that brushed her shoulders. I squinted and could not make out the face she wouldn't lift to meet us.

Governor Solonstrong arrived. He greeted Galen with a smile, then grumbled about being woken up for something like this, whatever it was.

"She just looks like she needs help." I too couldn't see a reason to be afraid of a child.

The black-haired night guard, Austin, just shook his head. "Watch." He turned, cupping his hands to her. "Hello!"

She didn't move.

"*Syo na,*" Galen called out between muscled hands. "I'm Elder Galen Eirini. Who are you, child?"

She cocked her head at him, her lips forming the shape of his name in silence. Her eyes, wide and hollow, stared straight ahead. I had to make sure I wasn't imagining this: her skin glowed, only for a moment. She fucking glowed like the faint blue of Oria.

"I have a message for you, Elder," she said in Asri, her accent strange to me. It was difficult to untangle her voice from the sounds of the wind.

"I'm Governor Solonstrong, girl. State your business."

She paused, disgust on her face. At the Governor's strong Chaeten accent or his tone, I'm not sure. She dropped her head again, silent when we called again.

"Taam, who is she? What is she?" I asked. The governor whipped toward us both, the same question evident on his face.

Galen didn't look away from her, jaw clenched, but he spoke so only I or the Governor could hear. "Attiq-ka, probably, with that glow. But she's not well."

"Or just another illegally trained rebel," the Governor said. "There's more every year, the magic sickens them, and—"

"Don't disrespect her, governor," Galen's voice rumbled low. "We need to know who and what we're dealing with. A trained rebel could still do a lot of damage. And if she's not born with that power..." Galen shook his head at the thought.

The girl came closer, swaying like a wisp of smoke and veering away as she stepped closer to the gate. "I have a message for you, Elders."

"And we will listen." Galen offered her a deep Asri salute. He looked to the governor, who stood straight, offering no salute or sign of respect.

The girl raised an eyebrow.

"You look unwell, Elder. Have you eaten?" Galen said. All Attiq-ka are elders, if not more.

"Don't offer her anything," the Governor hissed under his breath.

The girl looked at the governor, then let her head roam, eyes dull and skin pulsing blue. "I need no food. And you won't listen, will you? This warning is for my people. Not this demon governor."

She lowered her head again, refusing to speak for the next fifteen minutes no matter what Galen or the Governor yelled down.

"That magic is illegal. She's a rebel," Solonstrong said. "This smells like a trap."

"We agree on that last bit," Galen said. "But I'd wager that's a ghost. There's a war in that child's mind. Look at her little hands shaking. She does not seem to be fully in control of her own body."

Part of me wondered if this was just one crazy child bringing a town to its knees by just standing there. I'd never before seen those blue veins pulsing under golden brown skin, but I knew that was a sign of illegal Attiq-ka magic. The priests didn't tell us much, but no Attiq-ka in my history books or wanted posters looked disheveled and slumped like that. The queen certainly didn't, although her Attiq-ka mind was born into a Chaeten body. Maybe Galen was right, or maybe this was magic gone wrong, like the governor said.

A crowd gathered behind us. Meragc's house was just inside the wall by the gate, and I saw him on the roof of his house trying to see over, his four-year-old son Nestor fussing at his heels. Atalia, recently appointed Elder, came to join us atop the wall.

Finally, in a voice devoid of emotion, the little Asri girl spoke again. "I bring a warning from the Pathfinder."

Galen and Atalia exchanged a worried glance, then looked to the red-faced governor. They'd made him promise, by this point, to let the elders do all the talking, but Solonstrong didn't seem to find this an easy task. I knew the Pathfinder was a title from when Attiq-ka ruled the Nara: a seat on their council. There was no Pathfinder anymore.

"What is the warning, Elder?" Galen asked.

The girl's lips barely moved as she repeated, her voice flat, "Flee south to the Bend, or east as far as Uyr Elderven. Do not go west, or east past Baren Golkhi. Your khels will fail and the *ruren-sa* will take you. Leave today. Move fast and do not linger."

Ruren-sa translated to "ghost demons." Ice pricked the back of my neck at that. I didn't know which type of khels that Z'har priests placed on the temple, but the magical barrier on our town wall kept ghosts from coming in. The girl stared, calm and passive like she was drugged, experiencing none of the urgency she demanded of us.

"Thank you, Elder. Why should we avoid north and west?"

"It's a trap," Solonstrong said, low enough where only I and the people beside him could hear.

"Flee south to the Bend, or east as far as Uyr Elderven. Do not go west, or east past Baren Golkhi. Your khels will fail and the ruren-sa will take you. Leave today. Move fast and do not linger," the girl repeated, in the same tone as before.

Frustration and desperation flickered in the governor's eyes. "We need to bring her inside for questioning."

Galen and Atalia said nothing. I'm not even sure they heard the governor with so much we all had to think about right then.

The governor leaned over to his guards below. "Seize the rebel. Bring her here!"

Austin, the stocky black-haired guard, looked up. "The ghost?"

"Now!" Solonstrong ordered.

Austin hustled to the button on the wall. Falma covered her brown hair with a helmet and took a place beside him, the same guard whose sword I'd broken on Ash's. I'd made her a better one since, which she unsheathed now.

The gate creaked open. The child rolled her head up. I held my breath.

"No!" Galen yelled. "Do not open that gate!"

"Continue! Seize her," Governor Solonstrong countermanded. The guards strode out in unison, grabbing the child's thin arm in rough grips as she tried to run away with stilting steps. The child stiffened, wailing in their arms. Guards held her shoulders on either side as they dragged her. Falma looked up at Solonstrong, questioning, as she and Austin dragged the child forward.

"Niire Mai!" Galen's scream vibrated in my chest.

Never harm, he said, but I didn't see how they were harming her.

"The law is above your superstitions!" the Governor growled.

Just inside the gate, the girl stiffened, her body convulsing as if struck by lightning. "No—No, Elders," she grated out.

"You are killing a child!" Galen rumbled, his words carrying over the restless crowd as he ran down to the stairs. "Take her outside! She has not harmed us!"

The guards paused after one more step, but neither appeared shocked. A low, guttural sound escaped the girl's throat as her eyes rolled back and stilled.

Austin let go. The child crumbled in Falma's arms, who lowered her to the ground, unmoving.

The crowd closed in. Atalia was the first to check the child's neck for a pulse, taking a sharp breath in as Galen and I joined her, the Governor behind.

"They killed her," Atalia said.

"How?" Solonstrong blinked down at her body.

"Because that was an Attiq-ka ghost you dragged through the khel, you black voided simpleton," Galen said, and I heard the ring of Istaran flying from its sheath before I forced my face away from the girl. Galen held it glowing to the governor's neck as Atalia drew her blade on Falma.

I drew my blade too, shaking as I took position across from Austin. Around us on the walls, all Asri glared and shouted, supporting their elders.

"You—you cannot threaten a governor," Solonstrong protested.

"Tell the queen we need a new governor then," Galen said, pressing the blade closer as Solonstrong stepped back. "Because if I thought for one moment you understood what you just did, you'd be bleeding out already. It is no sin to kill a demon."

More in the crowd drew weapons, pressing in, jeering.

"Get out of our town, Solonstrong," Galen said.

Atalia had already disarmed Falma. She pressed her knee into the guard's back, her sword to her neck, poised to strike. I was so shocked I'd stopped watching Austin. He tried to run, but there was Meragc, running to intercept him, slashing at his leg. Ruan came alongside, aiming at Austin's neck, slicing with a spray.

I looked back at Atalia. Falma bled out beside the ghost girl, a clean blow through the skull.

My head reeled, unable to process what was happening.

"They both knew," Atalia called to the crowd. "These guards knew this girl held a ghost in her mind. They have paid for their crimes." I took a few steps to the body of the girl by Atalia, her skin having lost all trace of the blue magic, the bright veins. She slept there in dirty clothes and hair, but otherwise, like any child might sleep.

"Go or die, Solonstrong!" Ruan roared. "You killed both that child and the Attiq-ka!"

"Kill him!" the crowd jeered, pressing around me. I stood straight, grateful for my height that I could see. The governor protested as a dozen swords prodded him back.

The gate rumbled open. Voices chanted as the crowd shoved Mira's father out onto the open road.

CHAPTER 24

Battle Plans

I reassured myself of two things. One: Solonstrong could walk to the North Barrack by the afternoon, if he kept a good pace. I wouldn't have to tell Mira I had a hand in killing her father. Two: whether retribution came our way via a horde of ghosts or a unit of Z'har soldiers led by Solonstrong, my instinct was to run, and take my taam with me. But Galen was methodical as usual, gathering the entire militia in his shop for a calm discussion. I could see his decision already in the tightness of his jaw. The events of that morning caught me off guard. I would not be unprepared for this battle too.

"I could have helped the girl if the governor did not interfere," Atalia told Ola and Vann, the two youngest in the militia. She swept aside Ola's unbrushed hair from her shoulder and stroked her cheek in reassurance.

Just then, Galen's massive hand slammed onto the counter, stealing the breath from my anxious lungs and silencing the nervous chatter echoing throughout the shop. "Alright, let's get our heads clear and quick. Where is Elder Varen?"

Varen, a geriatric healer who worked out of the temple, was the only Elder who I'd never seen at a militia practice.

"Varen is at the temple exchanging messages with the barrack," Meragc said. "I'll connect with him afterward."

"Good, *na*." Galen's gaze lingered on each of our worried faces. Ruan, her fiery auburn braids across her breast, gripped the hilt of her dagger a little tighter. Plato, usually the most stoic among us, wore a concerned crease between his brows.

Galen cleared his throat. "Let's recap facts. A ghost who claimed to bring a warning from the Pathfinder approached our gate. Our former governor forced that child's body across our khels, killing both their minds: child and Attiq-ka ghost. We punished those responsible."

"The ghost could have fled," Meragc said.

"To what host? Spirits cannot survive long without a mind," Atalia said.

I blinked. "How do you know all this?" I'd been with the Asri almost seven years, and that day I felt as lost as the day I arrived.

Galen raised his hands in silence. "I figure there are two ways to look at this. Either that ghost *is* a messenger for a deceased Pathfinder or not. Let's say she is, even if it's suspicious that she wouldn't name the specific Pathfinder whom she served. Maybe she lost that memory, and means well." He paused, letting the weight of his words settle. "In that case, how can we trust if the ghost is correct about the threat? Or the escape path? All she gave us was a vague warning that ruren-sa will overwhelm our khels and that, of all places, we should head to the Bend."

Ruan scoffed. "The khel is fine. We just watched it do exactly what it was built for."

A chorus of agreement rose from several others.

"Maybe there's Chaeten tech we don't know about. Some of them still want us dead," Vann said, knowing better than to meet my gaze with that shit.

"And which Chaeten faction is teaming up with Asri ghosts, Vann?" I challenged. A murmur rippled through the room, most taking my side.

Galen held up his hand for silence. "We don't know the specifics; but I think we have enough evidence to conclude that was a fragmented soul, if she has any left of one at all."

"Do you think the ghost is *ruren-sa*?" Ruan asked.

Our little crowd of a dozen murmured again. Galen's dark eyes flickered. "*Ae*, what I'm leaning toward."

Acid in my throat. In the ghost war, those spirits killed two out of three people alive on the planet, mostly Asri, but Chaeten too.

"But thanks to Solonstrong, we can't be sure." Galen wrinkled his face in agitated thought. "If the ghost left willingly to spare the girl and leave her mind intact, I would assume good intentions and judgment, even from a broken soul. But a ruren-sa would not have been able to disentangle its broken mind from a host. Such a demon might try to lure us all past the protection of the khels for easy picking. Maybe the Bend resettlement kicked up a few angry spirits, now out here for some trouble."

"How could a ruren-sa coordinate a trap alone, though? Broken minds would need living help for a strategy like that," I said. For the sake of not picking a fight with Vann, I was careful not to mention that Asri rebels were my prime suspects.

Galen gave a grim nod of his dark head. "A good point, and a terrifying one. In that scenario, the safest move would be to stay within our khels and work with the empire to kill off these ghosts with tech or *chout*. And..." He raised a finger, a spark of defiance in his eyes. "This militia, we're trained. We can fight the living. If rebels come, we can defend our walls."

He shifted his weight, his gaze meeting mine. A shiver ran down my spine.

"I think we should trust the warning and move on," Atalia said, her voice more calm than the one in my head. "There are better lies to get us out of town. Voids, ghosts could pick off our militia in training any morning if they were roaming these woods."

Galen gave her a curt nod. "A small meal for a swarm, though. I don't think any intelligent mind can be certain here."

He scanned the faces around the room, his gaze lingering on each member of the militia. "I will respect any decision each of you make for yourself, either a broken mind who got a dire warning right or a cunning demon toying with us. In my case, either option leads me to the same choice."

Galen let his words hang in the air for a moment. "My roots grow too deep in the soil where I was born, the soil where Oria knows my name. I will make my stand and die on my land, be it tomorrow or decades from now."

Meragc cleared his throat. "I trust the khel, Galen. I trust my eyes. No ghost is getting past that gate. And if there are rebels out there, those are people we can fight. I will stay." There were nods of agreement around the room. Atalia sighed beside her husband, then gestured her acceptance.

One by one, everyone voiced their agreement. The teenagers Olan and Vann, nodded in tears, orphans that no one could countermand. Horeshio, the other teen recruit, fell in line with them, gripping their shoulders.

Plato, who I knew had recently been itching to go to the Bend, gave a curt nod, adding, "I didn't train with you all just to run away." He looked at me just as long as Galen.

My resolve solidified, even if uncertainty raked at the corners of my mind. If they were certain, and if my taam would stay and fight, I knew where I belonged.

"I will stand with you, brothers, sisters, Taam," I said, gesturing to my mind and heart in an Asri salute.

"I am proud to fight beside you, son." Pride flickered in Galen's eyes as they settled on me. "Plato, find out who else in Nunbiren will stand with us. I'll arm them. Ruan, coordinate the watches on the walls, two on each of the four gates, closed by nightfall," Galen said.

"What about an external watch?" I said. "Whether it's SBO or ghosts, I'm immune. I can climb the tallest tree on the forest edge and run patrol from there."

"I'll rotate with you," Plato said.

"Sure," I said. He could climb as well as me.

Plato's blue and gray eyes twinkled; his throat bobbed.

Galen frowned, drumming his hand on the table. "Jesse, I won't argue with your immunity, but I will argue with Plato." Galen turned to him. "You should stay behind my khels."

"Fine, makes sense. I'll take provisions and camp the night," I said.

"I'll run you some night-vision goggles from the temple, Jesse," Meragc stroked his dark beard.

Relief washed over me. With those goggles and a tall enough perch, I could see any threat coming from tens of kilometers away.

"I'll make my stand at the temple," Meragc said. "And see what tech we can disperse to those in town who aren't trained with weapons."

"We should move Nestor and the other children to the temple at night, since it has extra khels—same for those too old to fight. I'll take point on that," Atalia said, tugging her golden hair behind her head.

The clock on the forge fabricator ticked off the hour.

"I will speak to the ancestors next," Galen said, pouring himself a glass of water. "If the governor brought an Attiq-ka to the dust, I should let the rest of Oria know we have avenged the death."

"Meragc, what tech do we have that's safe to use around Attiq-ka magic? I'll need to be in contact."

Atalia's hand brushed against mine, her blue blade humming as she raised it a finger's breadth from her scabbard. "Have you gotten over your fear of Oria-threaded weapons?" she asked, her voice a low murmur.

"Not a fear, just... I don't have a license to carry one," I said. Half of that was a lie, and from the look on Atalia's face, I wasn't fooling her.

"Yeah, only the elders do, but fuck that," Ruan said. All around me, my Asri friends drew their weapons, illuminating the shop in a faint blue glow. I froze, feeling a hum of energy, like standing beside the nuclear generator in the mine on a field trip years ago. Any other sword felt like death I could control, not one that would rather kill me.

They all had one.

I'd heard countless lectures through the years of how holding Istaran should give me the peace of my adopted ancestors, supporting me with each swing. Asher had told me I'd get a mental boost from all the minds that had connected to an Oria-threaded weapon blade, a clarity of purpose. Nope, just anxiety—every fucking time.

Plato laid a supportive hand on my shoulder. "I can lend you a blade."

Galen grunted. "Thank you, Plato. But the blade Asher left behind knows him. It should respond to him best."

I nodded, suspecting that I failed to hide the panic in my chest." Voids, Galen, I better tell him," Ruan blurted, and I turned to see she was watching me.

"Tell me? Tell me what?"

She took a deep breath, her blue and green eyes not leaving mine. "If you carry an Oria-threaded sword and sync it to me, I won't just get a vague sense if you're alive or dead like the rest of us. I'll feel or see everything you do from your guard post—every sensation."

Ruan stood with every muscle tense. Looking around, it seemed I and the youngest recruits were the only ones who didn't know about her dahn. I suppose she still harbored a little fear that a Chaeten would disapprove or turn her in, because this was definitely a gift the empire wouldn't want her free to use as she chose. The priests would probably make her pledge somewhere if they knew.

I smiled at her, throwing as much reassurance as I could into it. "That's amazing, Ruan. Just look away when I need to take a piss up there, will you?"

She relaxed as I got a few chuckles from the rest of the group.

"I'll fetch Ash's sword," I said. Panic ambushed me the moment I was alone, my steps creaking up the familiar stairs to the loft. Planning battle was one thing, but looking at the cozy little kitchen and fire that was already one brother short, my heart pounded. I buried my fear deep as a grave, the little voice that everything was falling apart.

The latch clicked on the engraved wooden box under Asher's bunk. The blade roused its soft glow in my hands, as I touched the engraving Ash had spent so much time and love making perfect only to leave behind. Voids, I wished he was here. I wonder if he could have looked that ghost girl in the eyes—if he could have given me the certainty we lacked. I carried the weapon down the stairs; a whispering pulse of energy trailed up my arm.

I paused on the last step, looking out at a scene. We practiced this ritual many times in our familiar clearing, each time with wooden blades. The priests would have banned the militia if we'd done it any other way. The empire strictly forbade this magic outside of war, or elite academies, for fear the practice would corrupt in the wrong hands.

A dozen Asri clustered below me with their blue pulsing blades, whispering forehead to forehead as they touched their weapons. And as unattuned as I'd always been to Asri magic, even I couldn't miss the hum of energy, a faint indistinct sound that made my heart beat cold.

"Son," Galen said, gesturing for me after he and Meragc split away.

I stepped closer, crossing Ash's blade over my heart as Galen did the same with Istaran. Then he pulled my head to his in his powerful grip, our blades still crossed between us, singing in a low hum.

"Do you remember the words?" he asked.

I nodded, not telling him it was my Chaeten dad who first whispered them to me, warning us in a bedtime story about the decimation of my people. Those stories used to keep me awake, where I'd imagined myself impaled on a blue blade like this, now held over my heart in reverence.

We whispered in unison, breath to breath. "My heart and mind are with you always, my blood and ally, to defend what is worth my death. May you feel each fear and glory, and may our communion guide our hands, as our ancestors guide us in our wisdom."

And while I understood the power in the clap of his hand on my back, I did not understand the tears my taam kept fenced within his eyes as he pulled away.

To this day, I wish I did.

CHAPTER 25

Taam

Cool wind blew from my perch in the highest redwood, but I had a clear view of town. The silence of the forest pressed in close on my senses, with only the rustle of the leaves and the occasional hoot of a nearby owl. Several hours after nightfall, I scanned the dark expanse below with the night-vision goggles. Nunbiren glowed to the south—a constellation of electric torches lit along the walls.

I kept my go-bag clipped to the tree, made of hardy century fabric unlike the leather I'd carried into the forest years ago. But as I dug out my canteen, my hand brushed a sliver of gold bracelet tied to a loop just inside the first small pocket. The inscription there, barely visible anymore, was a name—Amelia, my mom. The memento, warm in my hands, brought me closer to my old life than I'd felt in years.

I wanted so much to have Iden beside me in that tree, the constant shadow of my childhood. His grin was harder to win, but it glowed so much brighter than mine when he shared it. On hunts, he always had a plan. He'd have one now.

The exodus of people heading east or south had slowed to a trickle, having peaked that afternoon with most families choosing to head for the Bend. Plenty had stayed—more than I thought—guarded by sentries patrolling the outer edges of the village. I could make out Atalia, then Ruan through the goggles by the gate. The air crackled as I adjusted the controls to scan the green-tinted forest.

Nothing.

Yet.

I did a full scan in all directions, then settled in for a nap at the long hour, with nineteen extra minutes to give the Nara the same twenty-four hours in their day as the planet the Asri ancestors came from long ago.

Ruan had told me to hold Asher's blade to my chest when I slept, so that those on guard could find their way into my dreams and rouse me the moment there was a threat. She'd wake me at the guard change, so I could scan again. I secured both myself and the blade to the branch with rope and let the sway of the branch and low creak of the trees lull my eyes closed.

I dreamed as I did on so many nights: Iden's eyes, wide with terror as he begged me to run. Mal, who I'd now outlived by a year, his bearded face contorted in a silent scream. Behind his blond head, the usual flash of red hair and a glint of metal, the splash of blood I always felt on my skin, the dread of that never lessening.

I ran the snow-blanketed forest, cold and eerie in a way the land around Nunbiren could never be. The undergrowth snagged at my clothes as I ran, the sound of my ragged breaths echoing in my ears. "Asher!" I called, my voice rough with desperation. My eyes scanned the dense trees, searching for any sign of my brother's sun-lightened curls, his familiar gait. I braced myself to find him like the rest, lying motionless and silent in the snow.

Just then, a flicker of red hair caught my eye, a fleeting glimpse through the skeletal branches ahead. My heart galloped. Was it? No.

Adrenaline jolted me awake. The black horizon stared back, painted with the silver strokes of a crescent moon. Asher's blade pulsed with a faint warmth in my hand, a gentle hum vibrating against my palm. Ruan was checking in.

"I'm okay," I whispered into the bonded blade, my voice thickened with sleep. "Just a shitty dream."

A reassuring warmth laced with fiery irritation flowed back through the connection. I smiled as I reached out for the familiar presence of my friends, my taam. They were all safe, for now. And it was official, Asri weapons no longer freaked me out.

Squinting through the goggles, I scanned the forest below in sectors. The goggles rendered everything in green, gray, and red. The cool sway of grass and branch, anything cold that moved: green. The mice that flitted across the clearing: red, any heat enhanced and brought to the forefront. Anything else, the goggles ignored, the trees black pillars on the view.

The emerald glow revealed a sleeping Nunbiren, patrols intact. Our guards strode with crisp steps along the lit wall. That was Plato on the north watchtower. Crickets thrummed as I checked the road.

Exhaustion gnawed at my mind, but I vowed to check the full perimeter before I let myself sleep again. I allowed my eyelids to drop for a fleeting moment, before a sliver of red caught my peripheral vision, something in the dense foliage to the east.

My heart lurched against my ribs, the frantic beat of a trapped bird. Was it…? It could have been anything in the darkness, a wild animal moving quickly. But it felt like the memory of my dream, the terror of the Red Demon.

Steadying my breath, I scanned the trees to make sure. I tightened my grip on Asher's blade, and a tremor ran through the metal: a low, unsettling hum. This was something I'd never felt from the blade yet. This was a vibration of raw, primal fear. I sent a bit of that fear right back.

The town fell dark, the electric lights on the wall black as the void. "Ruan?" I whispered.

The blade stirred, waves of emotions confused and fearful. Then the unmistakable sound of clashing steel reached me, a scream shattering the silence. I scanned outside the perimeter of town, seeing no one. Another yell, sharp and desperate, followed by another, then a chorus of them. My blood ran cold, and so did the blade in my hand.

Attack. Under attack.

I grabbed supplies and settled my rope on the tree to slide down. As I shuddered against the bark, the sword continued to vibrate in its sheath, riling my terror. I forgot strategy; all I knew was I needed to get back to Taam, to defend my home.

I threw myself down the last few meters, the ground rushing up to meet me in a blur. I rolled with the impact, adrenaline masking the sting of the brush. I scrambled to my feet and plunged out of the undergrowth, the clatter of my boots swallowed by the blur of the path as I tore home.

A blue maze, the mycelium of Oria, glowed under each step as I bit forward. It wasn't usually awake like this. The ground beneath my feet crackled with magic, a bite strong enough now where even I could sense it: anger, fear, death. Asher's blade pulsed a frenzied rhythm against my palm.

I felt Plato freeze; his heart stop. My throat tightened, a strangled cry escaping me as I ran on. I imagined him crumpled on the ground, his face locked in fear.

Another pulse, another loss. Horeshio. Vann. Their heartbeats slowed and stilled through the Oria-threaded blade.

The moonlight against Nunbiren's old white walls was the only light at the gate. Tears stung my eyes as I sprinted, my chest burning for air. Ruan, that was Ruan's blue armor and her braids. She was locked in a fierce duel on the wall with...

With Ola. The bright-faced teenage spitfire who I'd taught to duck like that.

"Ruan! Stop!" I roared. Their steel continued to clash, unhearing.

It was too late. With a final swing, Ruan disarmed Ola. The girl's surrender died on her lips as Ruan's blade found its mark up and under the armor on her chest, silencing her forever. A wave of nausea washed over me as I watched Ruan push Ola off her blade, hurling her body off the wall.

"Ruan!" I called again. She ran for the stairs. I ran to meet her by the stairwell door.

Juna, the old woman who sold lentil curry by the forge, stepped outside, armed only with a kitchen knife. I turned to her; yelled for her to get back inside and hide.

I felt Ruan through the sword before she charged past me, a blue blur. Before Juna could scream, Ruan's blade danced again, slicing the old woman's throat with brutal efficiency. I didn't know what to do. It was all I could do to hold the shaking weapon in my hand. Ruan pushed past the woman into the house, and a primal sound escaped my throat as I made to follow, then heard the echoing scream of Juna's granddaughter.

Asher's blade pulsed anew as another figure ran past me, a silhouette whose features I redrew in every nightmare—that long red hair, that broken-down armor, her eerie inhuman pace. The Red Demon burned bright against the cold inferno raging in my heart.

I chased after her.

The demon was a blur of moon-shining steel as she vaulted over a body and away, charging fast down the main street of Nunbiren. The embers of rage ignited in my chest.

Atalia was a proficient warrior, but the Red Demon scythed her down without so much as a parry. She sliced, effortless, killing with a shiver.

With a choked roar, I scrambled after the demon, legs churning, lungs burning. I ran down a smoky dark street as she turned a corner, past the bakery starting to smolder, flames licking the walls. My boots pounded a frantic rhythm over slick cobblestones—blood from the baker in the street. The sounds of screams and conflict through every cracked window. Asher's blade thrummed in my hand as my people died around me.

Each corner I rounded, each alley I sprinted down, I'd see a flash at most before I lost her somewhere near the center of town. The demon, despite all that agility, must be hiding like a coward. Frustration gnawed frantic at my chest, holding back my despair. But then, as I burst into the market square, I wasn't alone.

Galen. My taam. He stood hunched over an armored body, his sword, Istaran, slick with crimson in his muscled hand. Relief washed over me in waves. Galen was alive. He'd gotten her.

"Taam!" I bellowed, my voice hoarse with exertion. He turned slowly, his movements stiff and unnatural. And that wasn't the Red Demon at his feet. It was Tamon, our neighbor who always brought us apples from his trees each fall.

Tears carved glistening tracks through Galen's once stoic face.

"You?" His voice was a rasp, weak over the roar of flames now licking up the bakery roof.

"Taam," I said. He was speaking, still with me. That was good. Heart aching, I took a tentative step forward, my hand outstretched. "Taam, I saw the Red Demon. She's close. You have to help me find her; end this."

He didn't respond, his stare smoldering as hot as the smoke in the bakery. He stepped closer. A shiver of unease snaked down my back. His eyes were glazed over—no warmth, none of the familiar twinkle I knew and loved.

"Die, demon!" The words erupted from him, guttural. He attacked, carving a bloody arc through the air as he swung. Silver, only a whisper of blue. Istaran wasn't glowing for him anymore.

Hot pain lanced through my arm, ripping me from my stupor. I stumbled back. Galen, my taam, was trying to kill me.

"Taam?"

He attacked with a feral intensity, his movements frantic, devoid of his usual controlled precision. I held back, defending. Each clang of our blades shattered my world a little more.

"Taam, it's me, Jesse!" My throat tore raw in ashen air. "I'm your son. What is wrong with you?"

He lunged again, a snarl twisting his features. I parried the blow, the impact sending tremors through my entire body. I croaked out his name one more useless time. This couldn't be happening.

With a desperate lunge, I disarmed him. Istaran clattered to the cobblestones.

He froze.

"Taam?" I said.

His fists unclenched, resigned. He looked at me, curious as if just now recognizing me. Just as I lunged forward to embrace him—

The Red Demon. She materialized from between the shadowed market stalls, washed in the silver light of the moon and stars. One of her curved blades sliced through the air, burying itself deep in Galen's chest. She used her shorter blade to carve him off.

Galen's eyes widened, a flicker of open recognition when he locked eyes with me one last time. At least, that's what I chose to believe, that I got to say goodbye. His eyes went blank as his spirit left him. My Taam crumpled to the ground at the demon's feet.

A primal scream tore from my throat, imbued with such unrepentant pain and fury that it seemed to split the night sky. The Red Demon, for the first time, seemed to hesitate. Her yellow-green eyes, chillingly familiar, cocked at mine for a heartbeat before she turned and fled.

"You will face me!" My voice cracked as I charged toward her. She turned the dark corner, and when I followed—nothing, shadows.

I listened for her footsteps: silence.

"Face me, coward!" I screamed, and the words echoed.

"Die Demon!" I called again, then froze, unable to breathe, unable to escape the fact that I'd just repeated the last words my taam ever said to me.

The last words he would ever say.

CHAPTER 26

Istaran

To Galen, I was a demon.

I knew he wasn't himself, but in his final moments, I was no longer his son. I was not even human. Ghosts—it had to be ruren-sa in his mind. We were all so stupid. And now, the Red Demon was about to get away again. No—I couldn't let that happen.

I grew dizzy, chest heaving in quick breaths and sobs, unable to keep my mind from splintering in the silent street. I needed to keep it together, just as Iden said long ago. I needed to take Asher's sword and…

Istaran.

Galen once told me the sword could track anyone that killed its master. Istaran could track the Red Demon. That cleared my head: a plan. I could end this, act now and feel later. Turning back in the moonlight, I bolted toward the market.

I found Istaran gleaming under the stars. Sheathing Asher's blade against my back first, I picked it up. Istaran pulsed in my hand as the engraving lit blue, syncing to my heartbeat, just as it did the first time Galen let me hold it in his shop so many years ago. Cleaning it on the curtain of a market stall, I rushed to my taam's body for the scabbard, shaking as I slipped it off his belt. I touched his cooling forehead before I forced my feet back up with a sob. I needed to go after her.

But how? Galen had never explained how to make the magic work, and touching it did not seem to be enough. *Okay. Fine.* Maybe I had to make myself the new master.

I pricked the tip with my finger and ran the blood down the fuller.

"I pledge myself to you, to protect you as you protect me. But help me find the one who killed Galen—Galen Eirini, your last master." I choked out the words, hoping I got them close enough, hoping the sword could read the desires of my heart.

The glow brightened, twisted, then did the same thing Asher's borrowed sword did, pulsing with my heartbeat, with no other bonds or connections I could feel. Frustration gnawed. I sheathed it and grabbed Asher's sword to search for the souls of my friends, the remaining militia. Maybe someone could help, maybe someone else had escaped. A tremor threatened to engulf me. Then—a faint sensation pulsed through the sword's hilt. Meragc, and a pulse of Ruan. Meragc had sworn to protect the elderly and children huddled in the temple. I could feel his terror, but he lived.

"I'm coming," I told him. My heart lurched. Maybe Meragc was safe. He'd locked himself in behind the temple's khels, with those secondary levels of protection. I sprinted toward the stone spires, my legs pumping against the worn cobblestones. The familiar street lay quiet, the dead fallen in the street.

The sword pulsed and sputtered against my skin as I felt Meragc's heart breaking, failing. With heaving breaths, I burst through the temple doors, bracing myself.

In the main sanctuary, I could taste the steel tang of blood in the air. The candles flickered their prayers in the windows as the young and old lay dead in heaps in front of the pillars. Faces I knew, all innocent, dead by the sword.

"Anyone?"

Only candles stuttered back.

White marble pillars, once gleaming, stood stained with dark streaks as I forced myself to find Meragc. The ornate woven rug that cushioned the stone floor sloshed under my feet. I saw no red robes of Z'har priest or acolytes among the dead. They'd all heeded the warning and left for the Bend.

There he was.

Meragc, his once-proud form slumped against the central dais. A crimson stain bloomed down his slit throat, while his boy Nestor lay dead beside him, spine twisted. To this day I can't unsee that.

I fell to my knees, pounding the wet stone with my fists, their blood still warm on my skin. But I couldn't succumb to grief. Not yet. Istaran renewed its glow in my hand as I forced myself to rise. I jogged out of the sanctuary, refusing to look at any more faces staring back, my ears ringing.

Under the stars and cold void, I held the blade in my hand and begged, voice rasping. "Please. My taam—Galen Eirini's been killed. Please show me how to find his killer, the Red Demon."

Silence. The mute engraving on Istaran flashed its mazes for the moon.

I latched my eyes tight, forcing myself to stay still, to think.

The grove—the place in the woods where Oria pulsed strongest with the memories of the Asri during festivals, the place where Galen had retreated almost daily since Asher's departure. I started running. I'd never heard a voided thing there, but I had no better idea. Istaran pulsed in my hands, strong. I took that as a good sign.

Clouds wrapped over the silver moon, but my night vision kept my feet steady as I tore through the rustling leaves. The twig under my foot reminded me of the snap of his ribs; the low rumble of the distant gorges reminded me of the huff of his laugh. They fueled my resolve as I pushed my body faster, the air thick with the scent of autumn and damp earth.

I broke into the clearing. The ancient redwood stretched its branches high above me. Moonlight dappled the ground where generations of Asri had knelt eons before me, seeking solace or guidance. My fingers trembled as I brushed aside the leaves, revealing the pulsing blue network of Oria beneath.

"Oria, Ancestors, I'm Galen's son," I said into the still night, my voice hoarse with desperation, my palm to the ground. "The Red Demon murdered him, the whole town. Help me find her."

Silence. No whispers on the wind, no comforting presence, no ethereal visions. Just the fungal aroma and the relentless blue glow of the Oria network. A deafening silence, a rejection that echoed in my hollow soul.

Die Demon.

"I'm Galen's son! Jesse! The town held a ceremony so you'd know my name, remember? Asher said—" My voice broke. "I'm Jesse Eirini. Help me."

Nothing. I calmed my breaths, listening in every way I knew how—trying to push aside the hot fury threatening to surge. I removed Istaran from the scabbard and laid it on the ground. *Die Demon.*

"Please," I begged, sobbing. "Please, I'm Galen's son. I'm doing all I can. Please let that be enough."

Nothing. I put my head to the glowing ground, rocking.

"You want blood?" I sliced my finger, dropping it on Istaran, sprinkling the ground. "Some fucking magic words?"

It was not enough. *I* was not enough.

"Taam, if you're in there—" I choked out. "Please be in there."

Nothing.

A scream tore from my throat. I slammed Istaran into the soft earth, the blade embedding itself in the ground with a thud before toppling.

A flash of icy light, a pause.

I held my breath. Then I grabbed Istaran again and plunged it into the ground.

Tendrils of lacy, bioluminescent mycelium erupted from the base of the sword, quickly weaving themselves toward me, pulsing as the wind picked up in the trees.

"Galen? Taam?" I whispered.

The wind breathed warm on my neck. The ground beneath me roared with light.

"Galen." The lights pulsed faster with their blue etchings, stretching like a westward wave across the clearing.

I reached out for Istaran with a trembling hand, hesitating before I pulled it from the ground. A warm breeze washed over me when I touched the blade, like the first time my taam told me he was proud. Tears streamed down my face, hot and unchecked, as I grasped the sword and stood, feeling strong.

The lights waved at my feet, laying out a path to the edge of the clearing. I followed it, and a new path spread its glowing tendrils in front of my feet. When it pulsed faster on a deer path, I started running. The cool night air whipped through my hair as I sprinted deeper into the woods. My breath picked up, my chest finding a steady rhythm as I ran through the blurred world of black and white and cyan pulsing bright under the leaves. Five minutes, ten: the path twisted and turned a little south. At a half hour in, I began to flag, but the lights flashed brighter, urgent. I licked my dry lips and kept going on through the dark night as fast as I could make my body move.

Upstream from the dam, I fell beside the river and drank, allowing my chest to ease. Then the lights pushed me again. I jogged as the ground grew rocky under my feet, and gorges rose on either side. I no longer recognized the landscape.

Dawn crawled behind my back, painting the sky with streaks of pink and orange as I finally reached the crest of a hill. Below, the lights of Oria twirled and circled by the bank of a gurgling river. The finish line: empty.

I slid down the clay-soiled gorge, Istaran warm and bright in my hands. No one, but the lights pulsed at the base of a log. Sword ready, I hopped over. Just a bag under some leaves, leather. A cold, abandoned campfire lay doused nearby. Beside it lay a bedroll, unfurled.

Still catching my breath, I inched closer, every muscle taut with tension. The air hung heavy with woodsmoke, dampened by the mist from a bubbling stream.

I reached out of a tentative hand for the bag, the worn leather cool and damp beneath my fingers. My heartbeat raced and rebelled as I lifted the flap and loosed the drawstring. Inside, nestled amongst crumpled clothing and some dried herbs, lay a worn leather journal, its cover embossed with swirling Asri script, a name carved at the bottom: Faruhar.

I was about to open it when I heard a rustle at the top of the gorge, sending a flock of crows scattering into the sky. My gaze snapped upward, landing on a tall figure silhouetted against the dawn.

The Red Demon.

CHAPTER 27

Face Off

There she was, at the tree line—her dark figure against the rising sun.

Only when she started running for her camp, for me, could I make out the expression on her face—smiling.

In all the many ways I imagined this faceoff through the years, this was never how it started. Her mouth curved in joy as she jumped down the slanted gorge, air under her feet and dawn in her hair. I'm not sure if she was oblivious to me or uncaring, but I watched her grab a red-leafed branch and twist down to the next, graceful and light while I stood there, scabbard in hand. The demon who murdered my taam before my eyes had the carefree demeanor of a kid scampering around a summer festival.

I hated her all the more for that.

She rolled and ground to a stop. The dawn lit the maze of little scars over her face, young and unchanged by time since the day we met. She said nothing, staring me down with her yellow-green predator eyes. The Red Demon exhaled unnaturally slow, unwinded.

Time compressed around me. My mind stilled and sharpened to a point. All my life—all my somedays and tomorrows—were right now, in this moment where she was two paces away, her neck exposed for my kill.

I drew Istaran from the scabbard with a shing. "Please draw your sword," I said, cold and clear.

With a frown, she slid a canvas bag of something from her back and hurled it at the base of a tree. Then she unbuckled her belt, her twin sheaths with it, and tossed the weapons in the dirt at her feet.

My mouth fell open. "I—I will not accept your surrender."

"I'm not surrendering," she said. A husky, smoky voice. A knife dropped from a clip on her waist in one fluid movement.

I blinked. "Pick up your sword," I demanded.

"Even a knife is too much if you don't know how to use that thing." She nodded to Istaran in my hand, then up to my Chaeten eyes. Her playful tone did nothing to dampen my hatred.

"I know enough to give you the death you deserve."

"Ah." She shook her head, rolling her eyes. "You're not smart, are you?" She moved to sheath her knife.

With the snap of a twig, I struck with every ounce of my rage, knocking her blade up from her hands. The knife hung in the air while I kicked her squarely in the chest to land under it.

She fell back on her heel and blinked at me before ducking away, a surprised smile on her scarred face.

"Face me," I said through my teeth.

"Happy to."

I swung Istaran. She dodged, propelling herself past me for the dagger, holding it between us when I turned for her. I gave her space, circling, assessing how she moved.

"That blade smells wrong on you, Chaeten."

I was proud to draw blood at that comment, running steel down her arm and finishing with a fresh nick in her chest armor before she deflected. She raised her eyebrows at me, nodding. The Red Demon dropped to reach for her boot, and I angled for her neck. She rolled away, coming back with a second dagger.

Then she attacked.

She was a difficult read, but after years of training against several opponents at once, I had the reflexes to match one fast demon and make sure she didn't draw blood. I'd read a bluff, but not the countermoves. The Red Demon would turn in anything but the direction that made the most sense to me. I wasn't even sure which of her hands were dominant: she led one way, then another.

She wasn't even properly armored, fighting me with those daggers. She left flirtations of open flesh: neck, arms, and upper lungs exposed. The Red Demon moved in a blur, then baited me with a false stumble and exposed chest, drawing me in. I fell for it, meeting a sequence of movements so precise and controlled I'm not even sure how she disarmed me. She gashed my chest armor away from the neck, slicing down my ribs as she tore the ties open. She grinned down at my confusion as Istaran fell across the forest floor. Dropping both her daggers into the dirt, she beckoned my bleeding body on with her fists.

Still a fucking game to her.

She landed a blow on my ribs that shot through me, then another to my shoulder as I flung her back with a hard cut to the chin. She rallied, only to be flung back again. Her fists were powerful, beautifully fast, but not as strong as mine. *Oh fuck, maybe that's because she was guarding the force of her attacks, feeling me out. Yeah, that.* Panting, I kept up, blow for blow, my strength against her speed. I bit back pain at a grazing punch to the gut, but landed a kick to her hip that had her tumbling hard into the rocky ground.

That was it. I lunged before she could get up, only to find both of her legs wrapped around my body, twisting me, spinning me with more force than I thought possible. I landed against a fallen tree, my ribs giving way under a shard of branch, cracking. Breath heaved out of me, my body hungry for air no matter how I panted.

Panicked, I looked around. Her dagger wasn't far away, and unlike her, I was not above using any weapon I could reach to stay alive. My chest burned as I picked up the cold black hilt, swiping up as I did. I landed a thin cut across her chin, just missing her neck. She met me with a flurry, leading with punches and kicks. I rolled and twisted and used every stone on the riverbed I could find with my free hand, feeling their weight and trajectory as if they were familiar tools, aiming them at every soft part of her body. The rocky shore was thick with dust as we dove at each other.

My movements slowed, breaths burning and shallow, but I would hate her with every heartbeat I had left. I coughed on the dust, but held my feet as she swung one fist, then the next. She kicked me back into the bark, grabbing my shoulder as I went down, dislocating it with a crack to take back her dagger. I gripped the tree with the other hand, seeing stars of pain.

"Enough?" she said in her husky voice. She'd taken a step back, waiting.

Never. She died or I did.

I pretended to drop, to nod and catch my breath. A stick lay at my feet. With my remaining good arm, I speared it at her eye.

She ducked faster than I thought anyone could move. "Guess not."

I twisted to the side, putting the tree between us, but she met me on the other side. Ready, I landed a punch square in the jaw as she wobbled in front of me. I moved to grab her, but she twisted out, curled back in, taking me by the neck and driving her boot down against the side of my knee.

I heard the crack of my kneecap. And before she let me drop, pain shot up my other leg so bright it blurred my vision red.

She broke both my legs. Just like that.

I crumpled to the ground, panting out the pain, feeling her cold dagger at my throat. I'd nicked her with that blade first, and now she cut a shallow burning line across my throat, her blood meeting mine.

My mind cleared. It was over. With a wave of whatever peace we all get at the end, the pain washed away. My mind held strong even as my weak body quivered and twitched. I would look the demon in the eyes, prepared to make no sound and die a man without regrets.

I closed my wet eyes and smiled. "Kill me."

The blade under my neck only shivered, holding its place.

"No," she said in that torn up voice.

My heart ran and stuttered. "Do it."

The stream rippled, birds silent.

"I won't," she said.

"Change your fucking mind." I almost laughed the words out.

She released the knife from my throat and I felt her grip my arm, my shoulder. With a thud and another wave of pain, she popped my arm back into the joint.

I groaned and shuddered, falling into the dirt when she let me go.

She stood there, watching as I caught my breath.

"Kill me. You've taken everything else, everyone else. My life is yours."

She stood up and walked away without a word. I found a rock at my feet, pelting it at her back from my tangled heap with my last good limb. She whirled on me.

"Kill me!" The words burned my throat.

The sting of my landed blow didn't register. Her eyes, which I hoped to kindle into rage, shone cool, hesitant.

Doubt gnawed at me. Was she toying with me? Extending my suffering? This would be an agonizing, disgraceful death unless she made it quick. I snarled, reaching for anything else I could throw. My hand met only dirt. My vision swam in pain, balance whirling even as I sat.

"Don't," she rasped. Her voice cracked, strained—but with what emotion, who fucking knew.

A dark chuckle escaped me, and I almost passed out from the pain just from that. "At least toss me a dagger so I can see myself out."

"You'd just throw it at my eye."

"Thought about it." My words slurred, the world dissolving into the colors of dawn. "If I say I yield, will you kill me, then?"

She didn't reply. Instead, she took a hesitant step forward, then stopped. Her gaze flickered between me and the riverbank.

Then, with a swiftness that defied her earlier hesitation, she knelt beside me. Her hand brushed against my arm, gentle. "Why am I your death wish?"

The defiance that should have fueled a quick response quavered in pain, and the list of her crimes remained stubbornly lodged in my throat.

"End this, please," I said, the words thick with blood and despair.

She listened. I could see it on her face. Her breath on my face, her wide winged eyes, were the thought I grasped before darkness engulfed me, pulling me home.

CHAPTER 28

Lullaby

I rose to the sky beside my body, but I lingered. It felt like the wind carried me, and I alternated between hefts and shivers of movement. I felt warm, timeless, laying on a cloud to die all over again. But when I heard the sounds of night, I was home.

Sleeping in a cot by Mom's kitchen fire was the best part of being sick. Mom hummed as she worked. I lay warm and comfortable under my favorite quilt, surrounded by the aroma of her cooking, the gentle touches, and everything that meant love. The noise of my siblings or the kids my mom would watch played and laughed, drifting in and out of my dreams. Mom would remind everyone to whisper while I slept, or to play outside. The little jerks would climb all over me, never listening for long. I never minded; they knew that.

There was a tree just outside the window with deep-grooved branches that would wind up to the roof, and Oren was teaching Bella how to climb it. I kept listening to my mom's lilting voice between pauses, the high notes at the end of each whisper, the shared lullaby on so many nights when Dad was working late.

Through my closed eyes, I heard her chopping the vegetables into my favorite stew. Gamey rabbit with a hint of spices in the boiling pot.

Were they all here? I'd missed them all so much, and if I could open my heavy eyes, I'd be home.

I didn't recognize the stone ceiling—if you could call it a ceiling. The stones were jagged, and ... glowing? Not the Oria glow, but a creamy, ethereal white permeated the stones of the cavern, giving the misty corners of the room a gentle, otherworldly light where the orange flickers from the fire couldn't reach.

I fell back, listening to Mom's humming, listening to the children play.

It took a long time until I had the strength to open my eyes again, but my mom's lullaby anchored me. She kept singing when the other voices faded away. My fingers brushed the wall beside me, finding stone and not the wood of home, cool to my touch. I felt too weak to sit up just yet and see the fire, but I needed to see her.

My dry mouth rasped out a sound as my chest muscles protested. I tried to say her name. Every part of me throbbed with pain, and I'm not sure she heard me. *Why did it hurt so much?*

I fell in and out of those waves, my mind rising slowly from the ocean of dreams, cresting the surface again. It was her—her song. I focused on that song to numb the pain, open my eyes.

But it was this strange small cabin again, and the nightmare at the corner of my mind crashed in, overtaking me with a bone-cracking blow. Everyone was dead. Mom, my siblings, the militia, Galen. With a shudder, I saw Galen die, the Red Demon's strike following through. All dead.

Ash. My eyes were too dry to cry when I thought of him, although I wanted to. Still alive, but just as lost. Mira too. They were all I had left—and I wasn't sure I did.

Who was singing? It should be possible to twist my head just a little more to see. I could just make her out beside the hearth, thinner than my memories, kneeling over a small iron pot bubbling with a fragrant brew. Whispering the lullaby, she brushed a lock of long red hair behind her back and—

Fuck.

FUCK.

The Red Demon, the fucking Red Demon, moved from the fire to settle on a woven mat. I watched, dry lips parted, as she drew her legs into a cross and picked up a needle and thread, unfurling a shirt. *My* shirt. Her long, fiery hair flowed straight and freshly brushed as she pushed the needle in. Feline pale green eyes glowed in their mesmerizing strangeness by the fire. Her deft fingers moved in quick motions through the fabric, her eyes squinting to a crescent in concentration.

Her gaze locked on mine with predatory stillness. The Red Demon looked at and then past me—just as she had before she killed Galen—just as she had so many years ago, so rigid I wasn't sure she breathed.

I forgot to breathe too.

Her gaze tracked to the door where both her swords leaned against the stone wall. She flitted her eyes back to me with a frown. Rising, she stalked to the table between us, lifting a ceramic pitcher. The Red Demon poured a glass of water, then prowled toward me.

I lifted my head, failed to sit up. My ribs throbbed under wrapped bandages, chest bare above the blanket. With effort, I twisted sideways to prop myself up with a pillow, my body protesting all the while.

The Red Demon knelt beside me, offering the glass of water with a measured hand.

I did not take it. Her yellow-green eyes bore into mine.

"Still want to die?" The Red Demon's voice was a gentle raspy, sound. Wind through a creaking branch at night.

I paused, my gut sinking with so many dark memories, and the woman in front of me, responsible for it all.

With effort, I sat up straight to face her. The blanket fell to my lap as I heaved up to lean on the irregular stone wall. I looked down at my bandaged body, the wrapped cloth tinged pink and green from plantain leaves and congealing blood. My mother used plantain in my bandages too. Between that and the smell of meat in Chaeten spices—yeah, it still smelled like my childhood home. The Red Demon had been nursing me; mothering me.

My legs throbbed, swollen; I peeked under the blanket to find them splinted and wrapped. Voids, I was naked apart from the bandages. Searching for my pants, I found them hanging clean but shredded on a rack by the fireplace. I brought the blanket tighter over myself.

"Just take the glass or let me hold it for you," she said.

My resolve crumbled, and I reached out, clutching the proffered water. I took a messy, trembling sip, the cool liquid soothing my parched throat under her scrutiny.

"Thank—" I stopped myself from thanking her, my voice hoarse and painful.

She huffed, watching me with rapt attention as I swallowed, refilling my glass.

"Why?"

The Red Demon shrugged, her eyes softening as I drank again. "I'm Faruhar. What's your name, Chaeten?"

The name echoed in my mind, and I remembered the scrawl of writing on that leather journal. With another sip, I felt life returning to my body. I expected my hatred for her to return in full force as I stared her down. She deserved to die. *She still deserved to die.*

"How long has it been since I—" I winced at the effort of holding myself to a sitting position. "—challenged you?"

Her face wrinkled at the question, and she stepped away, bending over to pick up a notebook on the table—the leather-bound journal. "Since you tried to kill me?" She flipped a page. "Three days, I think."

Days. The plantain bandages around my body were fresh. The long grasses that made up my bed felt dry against my skin, but if I'd been out for days... Well, I could imagine why I was lying on straw like cattle, and why the straw did not smell like cattle. I flushed with embarrassment, then chugged the remaining water.

"Another?"

I shook my head, finding that it hurt a little. "Why?"

Faruhar took back the glass, setting it beside the ceramic pitcher with the swirling Asri design. "Why what?"

I slowly gestured with my hand to the room; to me.

She squinted in concentration. "You fought well. Kept breathing. You refused to die." Faruhar cocked her head at me, assessing until I looked away. "You are very stubborn—and very strange."

The fireplace crackled in the dimly lit room. I could smell the stew bubbling on the fire. My stomach rumbled.

"Again, why?" I said, but she waited for the rest. "Why do anything for me at all?"

"I respect stubborn. Even if you are too stubborn to tell me your name. I suppose I won't remember it anyway."

I looked up, but the Red Demon was not smiling. "Jesse."

"Have you chosen your second name, Jesse?"

I clenched my jaw. "You killed the man who gave me one. You don't deserve that name."

She shook her head. "You named yourself after an Asri family?"

I huffed, looking away.

"Okay Jesse, will you try to kill me the minute I turn my back, or when I sleep?"

At first, it sounded like a straightforward question. It wasn't. The cold stone rubbed against my back.

"You won. That wouldn't be ... honorable." I had to use the Asri word. I couldn't remember a Chaeten word that felt right.

"Honorable." Faruhar huffed, mirthless. "The honorable *ka* kill more than anyone. It is no sin to slay a demon, *na?*" she said in Asri. "Hasn't your family told you the same?"

My stomach churned, but I got the words out. "You deserve to die for what you've done."

Faruhar slumped back to the iron pot by the fire, stirring the stew in the uneasy silence. "Aren't you a demon too?"

I stuttered at the question. I struggled to find words, meaning in any of this.

"Quarter-blood maybe, One-eighth Chaeten-sa in your code? It would explain how you can fight like that."

"No, I—" I said, but faltered. My hungry, exhausted brain was useless, straining to watch her fluid movements ladle out a bowl of hearty stew and walk back toward me. Her maze of scars was as detailed as a century robe up close, and I got lost tracing them with my eyes. I found it difficult to look at this woman with her long unbound hair, beautiful on anyone else. Yet this woman in her simple linen tunic had gutted Galen like a yearling fawn.

Faruhar frowned as I reached out for the bowl, holding it to her hip. "You still want to kill me. I'm not blind to that."

"You won. Someone else will have to do that now." It felt so empty to realize that, to have that taken away.

Her silence felt like that of a multitude.

"Do you have any people who can help you while you recover?"

"You killed them all." I thought of Asher, Mira, but I wouldn't give her the names of the last two people she could take away from me. I could stay alive for them, though. With a sigh, I reached for that bowl of soup.

She held it tight in her hands. "I will need to sleep soon. Promise me you won't try to slip a dagger to my throat or otherwise try to kill me. I'd rather not wake up to you dead."

"That's confident of you."

"Yes." I wasn't sure what to make of her face, other than it was softer than what I expected—solemn.

My stomach rumbled. Clamping my eyes tight, I fell back on my pillow. "I promise." The words tasted acidic. "You've taken the rest from me, but you can't take my honor. If I say I'm not going to try to kill you again, I won't."

I reached for the bowl again.

She knelt beside me with the stew, clinking the spoon against the Asri ceramic as she raised it, angling it toward my mouth.

Wincing, I sat up straighter, gesturing to take the bowl myself. I grabbed the spoon and ate with equal parts relish and guilt, pursing my eyes shut. It had been years since I ate wild game. Ash and Galen would be mortified. My mind whirled at the explosion of flavor, so like my mother's venison stew I couldn't bear it. When I'd drained my bowl, she was ready with more.

The thank-you died on my tongue again.

"Who did I take from you?" There was no mockery or guile in the question I could find. She appeared earnest.

"You want their names or a count?" I studied her, searching for any reaction or guilt, but her expression remained blank: bewildered, which angered me more. "Cause I've lost count. Lost some names too, if we go far enough back. But there was no one you took from me who wasn't a good person. My taam Galen—he was ... everything." My voice broke.

Faruhar's brow furrowed.

"Why did you kill him?" I asked, simmering with anger.

Faruhar hesitated, her eyes clouding. "I don't know."

"You don't know. What the fuck does that even mean?"

In response, she turned away, then walked to the other side of the small cabin. She stoked the fire, scrubbed her hands with aggressive force. When she saw I was taking slow bites myself, she served up a bowl for herself, sitting back on the mat in the far corner of the room.

I finished the last of my stew in uneasy silence. I flexed my uninjured arm, eager to stretch and move again, and felt less pain than I did before. With a few quick breaths, I shifted my splinted legs sideways and off the grassy floor. My ribs protested as I sat forward. With a determined push, I heaved my body up, leveraging uneven stones on the wall for grip.

"Idiot," she hissed at me, rising up from her mat.

One leg protested with a vengeance. I gritted my teeth and fell back, my face contorting with pain at the impact back onto the straw. Eyes closed, I took heavy breaths.

Faruhar leaned over me with furrowed brows. "Don't be stupid. You can't mend broken bones in two days. There's just Azaprofin in your stew."

"What's that?" I asked between breaths that did not want to slow.

She nodded back to the chopping board of leafy vegetables, then back to the fire. "A painkiller in those greens. Your splints should be tight enough to allow you to move with help, but you'll rebreak those legs if you fall on them. Ask for help if you need it."

I leaned heavy against the wall, the reality of my vulnerability a crumbling landslide. "Is there a bathroom in this place?"

She rose from her spot by the fire and grabbed a bucket, her lithe figure casting shadows in the dim light. I looked away, mortified.

"Is there?" I looked up to the jagged ceiling. "I'm going to need to sit for this."

Her eyes flickered. She stooped down to my level, wearing a grave expression. "We could head down a level to a broken part of the Underground. It's pitch black down there, and doesn't smell like the deadly fungus grew back just yet. That being said, I'm not sure the plumbing works since Oria would normally power that."

I groaned.

"From the look on your face, you'd rather die."

She wasn't wrong.

"Then let's get you up the stairs then. I'm hoping the rain has let up at least."

"Stairs? You're joking," I said, but her face said otherwise.

"We'll just take it one step at a time. Let me help you get on your feet." She extended both hands toward me.

I accepted her help in a daze, allowing her to support and steady me as I rose to my feet. The underground cabin seemed to sway around me. I had to cling to the Red Demon until my head steadied. The blanket fell away, leaving me wearing nothing but those stained bandages.

"How many steps?" I grit my teeth, finding I needed her to support a lot of my weight even on the flat ground.

"I don't remember." Faruhar adjusted my arm over her shoulder. "And I don't think I can carry you and a lantern. We'll just need to figure it out in the dark and hope the wild dogs have given up on your trail of blood."

My heart skipped and stuttered, but maybe that was just the blood loss or the lung I'm pretty sure I punctured. I still wasn't breathing right.

She opened the cabin door with a creak. It was pitch dark beyond, like she said. I took a first step up into the narrow passage, and touched cold, smooth walls. She opened another door. One jaw-clenching step more on flat ground, and I found a stone railing. I shifted my weight off of Faruhar, to the stone.

And then my eyes adjusted to the dim light, and I saw the toilet. A fucking toilet, sink and soap in front with a folded towel on the wall.

I shifted to glare at her, but she was busy lighting the lantern by the sink.

"Should I stick around to wipe your ass, or do you think you got that?"

My mouth bumped open with a hoard of tangled thoughts. "I'm good."

I caught the spark of a smirk as she closed the door.

CHAPTER 29

What I Am

Once back to my pallet, exhaustion kicked in fast, either from the Red Demon's herbs or my body's limitations, I don't know. She changed my bandages as I drifted to sleep, leaving me to meditate on the fact that her hands were as deft and gentle with my bandages as they were efficient at piercing Mal's chest.

I woke to a glass of water on a stool beside me, and a lumpy loaf of mushroom-grain flatbread. As I reached for the water, I heard mumbling, the sound of the Red Demon whispering in her sleep. I turned to watch. Sometimes it was groans, sometimes indistinguishable speech. All of it sounded ... afraid.

I didn't know Chaeten-sa could feel that. I thought they modded that out.

"Please," she said between words I could not make out.

I sat up, gripping the blanket around me. Stale air in the cave chilled my skin, the fire long out. The bed across the cabin room lay untouched, the worn sheets neatly folded. The Red Demon slept huddled on the mat by the fire, weapon in hand.

"No. No. No!" she mumbled, her chest heaving fast under loose, shining hair. Her fists gripped the dusty rug underneath her.

I cleared the small stool beside me of its water and bread. Then, I tried to rise, leaning all my weight on the stool so as not to bend my legs. I gripped the cool stone wall with my other hand, inching up. My knees and chest throbbed, though less than yesterday. I could manage the pain through clenched teeth as I stood.

Across the dim chamber, the Red Demon lay sleeping on a floor mat, her lean, scarred body lost under all that hair, her knees curved to her chest like a newborn child. I felt a mix of emotions at the sight. The weaker part of me would apparently forgive that vulnerable woman for a meal and a fucking glass of water. The rest of me recognized how easy it would be to kill her right now, honor or not.

I took a step closer, my head throbbing.

She breathed fast, eyes closed and tight. One of her swords lay sheathed on the ground between us. I could pick it up, give her the justice she deserved. I'd be saving lives.

"It is no sin to kill a demon," Galen would say. Maybe Taam would say how that feeling of hating myself made no sense at all. I should kill her, regardless of what I said yesterday; get this over with.

But I knew what Ash would say: if I had to talk myself into it, not the path. Walk the path.

Fucking fine.

Another uneasy step toward her, and I leaned heavily on a side table. On it, some jars, herbs, a pen, and that stained leather journal I'd found at her camp.

I flipped open well-worn pages filled with scrawling text. On the first page, I read, "My name is Faruhar." Then something crossed out in heavy ink. Below it, "Look after Bria." Then, scratched out but still legible, "Be near people, be helpful to them. You'll remember more." Angrier text lay below it and to the side. "They will die when you sleep. Do not stay near people."

Her swords lay beside her, in easy reach.

I flipped the pages: blank pages in the middle but at the end, angry lines, page after page of tallies, broken up by descriptions: "The man who gave me tea at the cottage, the priest with the candles." The last entry read: "The man in the market." Beside it, scrawled on the side, it read: "Galen, Jesse's taam."

I shivered, realizing what the tallies meant—the names.

Flipping back to the front, on the last lines before the gap of blank white: my name, a tally of four lines, and above it "Days in the cave." The writing was a mess of Asri cursive; the Red Demon had terrible handwriting. I had to bring the journal close to my face, squinting in the dim light before I was sure of anything.

A burst of motion. In a heartbeat, she was up and beside me, her weapon drawn, the blade angled straight at my throat.

I froze, dropping the notebook onto the table, my heart crashing wild between my bandaged ribs. Her cold steel stung the sensitive flesh of my throat. I met her eyes, planning to look her in her eyes as she killed me.

The blade twitched against me with a tremor that ran through her entire body. "I know you." Her voice cracked—brittle, faint. She didn't move the blade as she mumbled again. "I'm sorry."

The tension bled out of me, replaced by a cold confusion as I kept breathing. I searched her face for my fate. But all I saw were wide eyes as frantic as mine.

"No." She lowered her weapon with a clatter, the despair in her voice echoing in the stone room. "I know you. J-Jesse." She clutched her head as if to hold it in place. "Do you know my name?"

I blinked. "What?"

"The journal," she said, her voice low and feral.

I tried to hand it over, almost losing my balance, holding tight against that table to remain standing. She took my arm, steadying me before grabbing her book.

"You're hurt. Sit down," she said in a rush, breathing fast. Her scarred arm gestured to the chair. "You're real, right? You look the same."

Not knowing what to say, I let her ease me into a chair until she withdrew her shaking hand.

After studying me to, perhaps, ensure my ass couldn't fall out of a chair, she turned for the journal, picking it up with reverence. Her breathing calmed as she read the cover. "Faruhar."

I swallowed, all my thoughts, hatred included, flickered and gutted. *This savage murderer, the demon I feared for so long, didn't remember her own name?*

"Faruhar," I repeated. "You told me that yesterday."

A minute passed, two, as she flipped pages, wild and fast, the only sound echoing in the room. Her eyes closed wet when she thudded the leather book closed. "What else do you know? You told me to draw my sword; you fought well." She paused, blinking. "You said I took everything from you. What did I do? I didn't write that down."

A choked sound came out of my open mouth.

"Please. Tell me. There's so much fading under the surface. If you tell me, I can bring it back." She gripped her head.

"You really don't remember?"

Faruhar, the Red Demon, the destroyer of Nunbiren: she rocked back and forth, her body shaking with silent sobs.

"No," she rasped, the word a desperate plea that scraped against the raw grief clinging to me like second skin. "No. No. No... What did I do to you?"

I pictured Galen, swinging his blade at me with all his mighty strength. The sound of her last slash bled into the silence of my mind, tightening the knot in my gut.

"You—you killed a lot of people—my taam." Voids, I hated the taste of those words.

She nodded, eyes distant. "Where?"

"A town called Nunbiren. All dead."

"Why did I kill them?"

"I don't know," I stuttered out. "A ghost girl warned us about the attack. We were stupid enough to stay. We expected rebels and got you. When you showed up, my friends started killing each other."

She flinched violently, her shoulders hunching as if under an invisible blow. Her breaths came in ragged gasps, her eyes squeezed shut so tight they threatened to disappear altogether.

"I remember Nunbiren. You said your father was Galen. I wrote him down," she said, the word a hollow whisper. "Who else? Tell me their names." She pulled out her book.

"You want to write them down?"

Tears welled in her winged, yellow-green eyes. "I need to remember what I am."

My breaths stuttered, but I forced them out.

"Atalia." I lashed out every name I knew, slain by her sword or the ghosts she brought with her. Meragc, Nestor, Vann, Ola, Plato ... Juna, her granddaughter Terana upstairs. She winced with each name.

She stared at me with wide eyes. "I don't remember them all. Some are gone. Who else?"

When I'd named everyone I knew was dead in Nunbiren, I kept going. I listed any death I'd learned through Galen, counting everyone the elders credited as her kill in Noé. Ten dead on the road by Blind Tree. Thirty in Farris. She wouldn't write the number if she couldn't find a matching record. Instead, she tallied in slow strokes, one by one.

"Anyone else?" She eyed me with hunger, gripping the bones of her arms as if they'd strike again.

I cleared my throat. "Seven years ago, you destroyed a lot of Chaeten towns in the Bend. I don't know who helped you. The empire evacuated any survivors within a year."

"Why would I do that?" Her voice cracked.

I shook my head, heart pounding.

She closed her eyes tight. "In Nunbiren, I didn't think they were real. You're sure?" Her chest heaved and shuddered in silence before she looked back at me.

I swallowed, nodding.

"Tell me about Crofton."

I clenched my fists, knuckles whitening as I fought the urge to lash out at just how strange this all was. "You got my brother Iden with a sword. I think you sent ghosts for him; broke his mind," I said. "My brother Mal too. He was messed up, but getting better when you killed him. And before that, a whole town of people who just fell dead. They told me rebels spread the SBO virus, but it was you. You let me just run away…"

"There was a boy like you, dead by the river." She paused. "Same hair and eyes. I already wrote him down."

"Iden," I growled. "Did writing that down make it all okay?"

The monster I swore to kill crumpled to her knees, burying her face in her hands. "No," she sobbed, the word raw and desperate. "I thought he was a ghost. He wasn't real. What did I miss?" Hollow despair echoed in her empty eyes. "I don't always get it right. I know what I am."

"What does that even mean!?"

"I know what I am." She began rocking. "But I can't let Bria die."

"Who?"

She only shook her head, continuing a slow rock of her body with her knees to her chest. We sat in a tense silence for a long moment, the only sound her ragged gasps and the steady drip of water from a tap on the far side of the cabin.

This broken woman was a fucking mess. Terrifying as she may be in a fight, she had a mind like wormy duck shit. I thought she'd been leading the center of some vast rebel conspiracy. At best, she was a weapon.

There'd be a hand. Someone in control.

Her breathing calmed. Her face steeled. She wiped her tears away with what appeared like disgust. "If I can get you to the fire, can you start it?"

"Yeah," I said, exhaling. She helped me over.

"I'm going to get some firewood. Breakfast." Her eyes trailed over my bandages in cold assessment before she left.

Faruhar came back to the cave in a much better mood, humming as she added ingredients for more venison stew to the pot. She washed her hands, then rummaged through old jars on the shelf, sniffing them and making faces. "I couldn't find more plantain for your wounds. Hoping I can find something useful in here, but it's all old."

"Is this where you live?"

"No." She pulled up a few dried flowers from a clay jar with her tweezers, squinting. After sniffing it, she grabbed another jar instead. She accepted whatever she found in that one, pulling it onto the side table.

"So who lives here?"

"No one, anymore." She sprinkled some herbs into a cup. "Asri rebels used to use it until the empire got to them, killed off tunnels in this area. It will take a while for Oria to grow back. Bria helped me find it."

"Who?"

She clenched her jaw. "My sister." She stirred, added a pinch of something white and powdery, tasted and adjusted. At last, she was satisfied.

"Drink." She brought me a hot cup to where I sat in a chair, my legs propped awkwardly on a low crate.

I sniffed the pungent brew, closing my eyes tight.

"Keep healing. You'll have plenty of time to die when I'm not looking."

I tipped the cup to my lips, taking a slow, bitter sip.

"Down it fast. It gets slimy as it gets cold."

The next sip was more difficult than the last, the sour taste building. I slumped halfway through, but got the work done.

"Good. Let's check your wounds."

She placed a warm hand over my heart, pressing, listening to the rhythm. I studied the scars on her chin, trying to find the line I cut, healed over among the rest. Maybe it was the herbs that had me transfixed by the design of those thin scars over her skin—that had me not wanting to claw back her hand from my body.

She stepped back, her fingers brushing against the edge of the loose fabric over my broken ribs. I tensed, but her touch was light, hesitant.

"Relax," she said. "You have honor, remember? Even if I'm close enough for you to strangle."

I exhaled, torn somewhere between suspicion and vulnerability. Faruhar turned to kneel behind me, her long hair tickling my skin as she untied a clasp on the linen. I leaned forward to accommodate her as she unwrapped the bandage with a gentle rustle. The warmth of her breath stirred the hairs on my arm, the studs on her chest armor chilled the skin on my back as she leaned in. The room seemed to shrink as the last of the fabric came off in her hands, the only sounds her breathing and the erratic thump of my heart.

I awaited her verdict.

"You're healing too fast for a *sedo*, even if you mostly smell like one." Her finger hovered over the broken skin above my lungs, then my bruised and once dislocated shoulder.

Sedo, it literally meant dying in archaic Asri, what the Attiq-ka called mortals. I did not know how to respond to that, but I inhaled, hoping to find something to insult in return. Earth, sweat, and perhaps something more floral in the mix. Nothing I could hate.

She reached into a pouch at her waist and pulled out a small vial, opening the jar to reveal something white and half-translucent. Faruhar dipped two fingers into the jar and brought them to my shoulder and down my ribs. I shivered at the touch. Then, she brought up some clean bandages, stained but hand-washed, guiding my hands to hold the fabric firm to my chest as she began wrapping. Her touch lingered a moment, tracing Asher's scar across my heart, tying the bandage tight.

"There," she said finally, stepping back. "If those splints hold, I'd say a few more days, a week until you can care for yourself again."

"What?" It had taken me about two months to heal from far less.

"Will you accept my help that long?"

I stuttered. "Yes." I guess that healing speed didn't seem odd to her. Even with the best medicine, it should be.

"Great, my sister wants me to hurry this up. I'll restock what I can and take off as soon as I know you won't die."

Taking a deep breath, I forced myself to speak. "Is your sister the one who tells you who to kill?"

Faruhar picked up the dirty bandages. "She's none of your business."

I huffed, the force painful on my wrapped chest. "Anyone who had a hand in killing the people I love is my business. Who do you work with?"

She shook her head out with a nervous laugh, removing the blanket on my legs, starting to unwind the fabric around my splinted leg.

"Don't you fucking say you don't remember. You must know that much." I crossed my arms, glaring. "Who is Bria?"

"If you still want to die, keep talking about her. Maybe we can work something out." She met my gaze with defiance until her eyes flicked down to my bare groin.

Nope, no bandages there. I stared back, unshaken until she looked away. Embarrassed, I hope.

She hustled across the room, grabbing a handful of fabric and throwing it hard at my lap.

"Ow!" I unfurled the unfamiliar fabric to see an oversized set of drawstring pants, worn and moth-eaten, but clean. But unlike what I had on when I challenged her, these were loose enough to fit over the splints on my legs.

"What do you mean 'ow'? It's just flax," she said.

"So are riding crops, and I'd prefer those off my groin."

She snorted. "As masochistic as you were when you fought me, that's a surprise."

My mouth fell open at the bemused twinkle in her eyes. "There's something really wrong with you."

That crushed her smirk. "I know."

My hand covered my heated face.

"I'm terrible at talking to people. I'm sorry." Her words tumbled out. "Just keep reminding me how much you hate me, and I'll remember to say as little as possible." She let out a nervous chuckle and wiped the hair out of her eyes. "I'm going to go look for some more herbs. See if you can get your pants on without breaking a bone. Then stir that stew, please."

She gathered her weapons and moved toward the door. I got a twinge of a headache just looking at her. The fear, anger and hate I once thought limitless sputtered in the space between us, replaced by a sharp sense of who-the-fuck-knows-what.

"Thank you," I said, failing to keep those words caged.

CHAPTER 30

Field Station

This was not the body I remembered. Here I was, five days after a punctured lung, breathing fine. And although my legs throbbed under my splint, I knew a broken leg should take at least a couple months to mend. Yet that dawn, I woke with my muscles itching for their daily exercise.

The doorknob rumbled, and I could hear Faruhar murmuring to herself. I'd noticed her talking to herself from time to time, but I still couldn't say that was the strangest thing about her. She walked in with a canvas bag slung over her shoulder, then shrugged out of a damp cloak.

"Did you sleep at all?" I asked.

She'd insisted on sleeping on the floor by the fire and giving me the bed. I'd hated her enough not to argue, but I also hated that she'd offered, since that made it more difficult to hate her.

"Just up early," she said, hanging up her cloak.

She caught my stare and a flicker of *something* crossed her face—*annoyance? Discomfort? Confusion. Ah.*

"You're Faruhar and I'm Jesse. Neither of us are killing each other today," I said. "Did you find your journal?"

She sighed. "I looked through it when I woke up. You just smell different."

"That bad, huh?" A smile ticked up on the corner of my mouth before I could stop it. I'd washed myself with a wet rag, but hadn't risked a full shower in my state.

"Sweat and wood smoke—nothing bad." She threw her bag on the table and studied me again. "But you also smell restless."

"I didn't know restless was a smell."

"It is. Why do you smell that way?"

I closed my eyes tight. Even though I was stuck here, I had thought some things through last night. If I wanted to know who she worked with, and who was responsible for these deaths, I could not treat every conversation like an interrogation. If I opened up a little about safe things, made small talk without giving her anything she could use against me, maybe I'd get closer.

"Just ... anxious to bury Galen; my friends," I said, his name catching a little in my throat. "If soldiers sweep in, they may burn them like they did for Chaeten in the Bend. Asri would find that disrespectful."

She leaned across the table, pulling out a gutted rabbit and some mushrooms. "The soldiers haven't moved in yet."

I held my breath. The barrack was so close that this couldn't be right. "How do you know that?"

"My sister looked around. Too many ruren-sa."

I gripped the edge of the bed. "So your sister is out there foraging with you in the forest?"

"Yeah." She pulled down some herbs from the shelf. "Waiting for me to be done with you. I told her I wanted to keep a man from dying. She said more people died because I stayed. And more keep dying every day until I join her."

"So, she's threatening you?" I needed more information, someone to kill.

She looked at me out of the corner of her eye. "She already doesn't like you, don't make it worse."

"Why doesn't she like me?"

"Might have been that time you tried to kill me." She pushed her hair out of her face.

Faruhar hummed as she washed the herbs in the sink, then laid them out to dry. We'd reached a dead end in the conversation—unless I thought of something.

"I have a brother. Someone I'm pretty sure you haven't killed," I said, adding the word 'yet' in my head. I wouldn't give her his name, but... "I miss him."

She cocked her head at me. "You said you had no kin to help you."

"He can't help me," I said. "He's a soldier. I don't even know where he is stationed right now."

"If he's fighting for the empire, you can look that up." She pulled out twine from a cabinet.

"I thought about that. If I walk to another town's temple and tell them everything I've seen, they'll either quarantine or arrest me until they sort this all out. I'm Chaeten; Asri are dead." I sighed.

She went to her larger leather bag and started digging. "There's a military field station a couple of kilometers from here. They'll have a terminal. Bria can help us get in."

My heart skipped a beat. I'd get to meet the sister, and find Ash. It seemed too good to be true.

"Wouldn't we need ... Z'har credentials?"

She stopped rummaging and met my gaze, amusement simmering in her cat green eyes. "Yeah." She produced a key card from the bag, several key-cards to choose from, in fact.

"How did you get all those?"

"The dead don't need them."

I clenched my jaw. "I guess I know better than to ask how they died," I said, out loud, like an idiot.

"Good," she said, her voice clipped. "Get yourself ready while I hang these herbs."

I stared at her. "Get ready, how?"

"Take off the splint and leave the knee wrapped. Your legs are well enough to stand on." She raised an eyebrow when I stared open-mouthed. "You didn't know?"

I knew, but I'd been trying to hide my fast healing as best I could, pretending the bones ached more than they did, hoping to have more time to untangle her secrets. "I didn't know."

There were, indeed, many stairs to get out to the surface, and no railing. But Faruhar found me a sturdy enough stick to suffice as a cane, and we took one irregular step at a time together on the ancient stonework. I studied those stairs, the mossy engraving on the dark walls once there was sufficient light to grow it—anything but her arm on mine as we walked.

We ventured out into the drizzle, and I broke away. But the forest path was slick underfoot, and my leg throbbed with each step. Faruhar stayed close, offering a steady arm whenever I stumbled, and I felt her gaze on me even when the terrain was easy.

There was no sign of her sister, but I decided I'd let her be the one to bring that up.

About an hour later, we reached the field station, a small concrete box of a building half-hidden by overgrown brush. Lichen clung to the walls, and the solar generator on the roof sat at a precarious angle.

"Are you sure it's still functional?" I asked.

"No." She pulled out the first keycard from her bag and held it against a black square by the door. "If it's not, we'll try another. There are other little booths in the woods for emergencies, further away."

The first metallic card did nothing. Tossing it on the ground, she tried the second. A little LED flashed green beside the door.

With a push, the door creaked open, revealing a dark interior until we stepped inside.

The air inside tasted stale and moldy. A single light with a yellowed glow lit us overhead in a small room about the size of the bathhouse back home. A dusty terminal sat over a counter, with two sturdy metal chairs in front. The screen flickered on with monochrome white text above the image of an oak tree with two intertwining branches: Queen Azara's Introgression Tree.

Fuck, I could get arrested for this, couldn't I?

Then displays lit up around the room—maps, news headlines.

"I'll be just outside." Her voice echoed in the cramped space. "You're safe in here."

I nodded. The door closed behind her before I moved a finger. I didn't need her looking over my shoulder, learning where to go to kill my last brother.

The buttons felt familiar in my hands, even though it had been a while. I'd loved the terminal I sometimes got to use in my school at Crofton. Perhaps being told I couldn't take them home made them seem more magical.

I saw a headline: "Asri rebels overtake tech in Syren, Meyit. Citizens demand tighter restrictions." Underneath, a photo of a crying child behind the burnt remains of a truck. Directly beside it, an article about the last episode of a serial called "Crossed Wires," described as "an unlikely love story between a Chaeten Z'har scholar and a scrappy member of an Asri-street gang." In the last episode, the Asri main character Arana had been beaten by her father when she failed to follow through on an attack on the Chaeten boy's temple. I could click a button to watch, but I kept looking for the program to find Ash.

I found it: Central Citizenship. At the temple, priests could use it to show where everyone in the empire lived, among other things. First, I typed in my last name, "Eirini." clicked the box for "living" and narrowed down other filters. A wave of relief washed over me when I saw Asher's name listed alongside mine, and photos taken by the priests during the last Rain Festival.

Most of Ash's profile was locked away. A security prompt materialized on the screen, demanding a passcode when I tried to click further.

"Great," I muttered, glancing back at the empty doorway.

I picked my walking stick off the floor, hoping she wasn't far away.

"You need help?" her husky voice startled me. Faruhar stood in the doorway, leaning against the frame.

"Voids, you move fast," I said. "And so quiet it's creepy."

"That *almost* wasn't an insult," she said, one eyebrow raised. "What do you need?"

I sighed, gesturing to the screen. "I think this is a dead end."

She leaned over my shoulder, eyes roving. "Right," she muttered, "Bria can ask around. Stay here."

She strode out the doorway, and out into the rustling forest, closing the metal door behind her to leave me in the dim yellow room. I was not above listening at the door. Rising to my unsteady feet, I limped with quiet steps, placing my ear against cold steel.

The hollow ringing of the metal door, and the steady click of the solar generator—nothing else. I wondered if it was time to get back to my seat. Maybe this thing was so insulated I wouldn't even hear her steps.

And voids, that creepy quiet mode of hers, I might not hear her with no door at all.

"You're not being reasonable," Faruhar said, angry, voice muffled through the door.

No response, at least none I could make out. Faruhar's voice dropped lower, almost inaudible.

"I'd do it for you, without question," Faruhar hissed again.

My heart thumped in my chest. When no angry voice responded, doubt sprouted in my mind. *Was she ... talking to herself? Or was her sister just quiet?*

I was grateful Faruhar took angry steps back rather than creepy quiet ones. I tried to look bored, slouching on the wall when the metal door hissed open.

Faruhar slipped back in, her face unreadable. She strode with purpose toward the terminal.

"Are you able to get in?" I asked.

"Don't talk, or this will fall right out of my brain." She placed a hand on the keyboard, and I held my breath as her fingers tapped out a series of random characters.

The screen flickered, then the red security prompt vanished, replaced by a welcoming blue login. *How in the dark void...*

"There you go," Faruhar said, her voice gruff. "Take your time. I have some things I need to do out there. Knock when you want to come out." Before I could ask what that meant, she turned and headed back toward the door.

I delved into Asher's profile, which was a lot more detailed than I expected. There was a link to show his medical records and past injuries, mods, who his parents were ... his whole code sequence. I checked 'known addresses' and only saw our house in Nunbiren. Under Service History, I found he was slated to arrive at some forest outpost in central Noé. I zoomed in on a map, trying to memorize every detail of the terrain in the middle of the forest, along with the coordinates. Clicking away, I saw notes from commanders, a psychological assessment, and a log of his personal message. A cold sweat pricked my skin. The sheer volume of information was staggering, all meticulously documented by the empire.

That made me curious. I clicked on my name and braced myself. The screen displayed a list of details, most of which aligned with what I knew: my age, birthplace in Crofton, my biological parents' names. I clicked on their pictures, and relished a look at their faces after so many years, realizing that if I shaved off my current stubble, I'd look so much like my dad.

Then I saw my father's occupation as "medical lab technician" with the employer as "Crofton Mine." He'd been a mechanic who worked on the rigs. He'd shown me his work station one day. Yet as I clicked through to his employment reviews, there was nothing about mechanical engineering. He worked in a lab. There were order histories of chemicals and work correspondence I didn't understand. It felt like a betrayal. I loved my dad, a man with a quiet strength who worked hard and taught me to do the same. *Why did he lie about his job?*

I glanced at the door, a million questions swirling in my head. But for now, I had no one I trusted enough to talk this out with. And I had one more search to try.

No hits on Red Demon in that database, and the only two Faruhars recorded looked nothing like her: Asri who died centuries ago.

A knock at the door: not like a tap-tap-tap, just one. I rose on my cane to go investigate, squinting as my eyes readjusted to the burst of late afternoon light. Taking a deep breath of crisp, pine-scented air, I pushed off into the forest, wincing at the throb in my leg.

"Faruhar?" I called out, my voice resounding through the trees. Birds chirped, insects buzzed. A woodpecker drummed in the distance.

She couldn't have gotten far. I closed the door behind me with a click, and started limping down the leaf-strewn path, hoping to track her.

I rounded a bend in the path, and I heard movement in the brush beside me.

"Not creepy quiet this time, but you could still call back," I said.

The figure emerged, then another. In a clearing dappled with sunlight and shadow, stood a pack of wild dogs.

Chapter 31

Wild Dogs

The Nara didn't have dogs before we Chaeten got here. The Asri found the idea of a meat-eating pet repellent, but we Chaeten loved our pups. When we went to war, outnumbered, we modded them to kill. These feral dogs that roamed the woods descended from those war dogs, and my ancestors did not re-engineer these creatures for their looks.

As a child, Mom never allowed me in the woods alone until she was sure I could defend myself. Dogs would take toddlers or young children who wandered too far, but they shied from a good knife. Most armed adults had no fear of them; the deer were easier prey. But I was unarmed, alone, limping. My breath hitched in my dry throat. I was afraid to turn my back to them to find more behind.

The pack stood furred in a range of matted, earthy colors, scarred and growling low. Overgrown muscles strained against taut skin that could barely contain their bulk, each movement showcasing honed predatory power. Their eyes, gleaming cold, fixed on me with more intelligence than I remembered. Wide, long jaws, sharp teeth and claws.

Eight. I counted eight.

"Faruhar!" I called out, hating how vulnerable I felt. "I need your help!"

A low growl rumbled from the largest of the pack. On his hind legs, that tan beast would stand as tall as me, and those teeth—voids, if they got anywhere near my throat I was done. I had a walking stick; that was it. The dogs took a collective step forward, muscles coiling beneath mottled fur.

"Faruhar! Please!"

Ears pricked, tails held high. I knew what that meant.

The pack lunged. I gripped a tree branch for balance as terror took hold, and swung my stick-cane straight at the nearest dog's eye with all my might, connecting with a thwack on the skull. The beast yelped and stumbled back, but three others were already upon me, and one sunk its teeth into my bad leg.

Adrenaline surged through my veins, and I lashed out with the cane again, the wood splintering under the force. I barely deflected a snapping jaw, leaving a hot streak of slobber and pain across my arm. But now I had two sharp pieces of that wooden cane. I got one through a dog's throat before it found mine.

A black mass of muscle grabbed my arm and pulled me across the ground as others tried to gut me. I roared, kicking back despite the pain; a primal sound ripped from my throat.

"Faruhar!"

A searing pain erupted in my calf as teeth sunk into flesh. I kicked out with my best leg, connecting with canine ribs, forcing a temporary release. I stabbed another off and rolled atop a furry body, flinging the stick and snapping its neck with my hands.

Taking down one in the pack should be enough to drive the creatures away. *Why weren't they running?*

A searing pain in my shoulder, a whirlwind of jaws and teeth. Guttural growls, mine and theirs as I twisted at any head that came within reach, between ragged gasps for breath.

My last half of the walking stick got stuck between a furred ribcage as I felt the hot breath of a dog against my neck, then a blur of red and brown-studded leather slammed into the pack.

Faruhar had three dogs dead in seconds, both swords flashing in the dappled sunlight. The last two put their tails between their legs to flee at full speed. She tucked her swords and ran them down, her eyes glinting as she sliced with her curved blades. The first mottled beast fell with a thud, her sword buried deep into the matted fur before it even had time to yelp. She went after the last, almost out of sight when it crumpled, twitching to the ground.

I leaned against a tree, adrenaline washing away. Faruhar scanned the clearing as she jogged back, then locked eyes with me. At best, I saw a flicker of relief before she scowled at my wounds.

"I told you not to come out, idiot," she snapped, rushing to my side.

Standing slumped against a nearby tree, the fight drained from me like water over a broken dam. Or maybe that broken dam was the blood running from my leg, arm, and shoulder.

"Where were you?" I slid down the bark to the ground.

She scowled. "Well, look around."

All I saw was dog carcasses strewn around me and leaves drifting to the forest floor.

"Even if these *ruren-sa* aren't able to get into your mind, it doesn't mean they can't get into a wild dog. You're lucky there's no people around for them to claim." She winced as her eyes landed on my leg, bloodied and torn.

I blinked. *Ruren-sa.* Ghost demons. "Ghosts? In dogs?"

"Just—shut up and take off your pants."

My mouth stuttered open.

She rolled her eyes. "To wrap your wounds before you bleed out."

I heaved down my pants to the cold earth, grateful that the lack of leg splints meant I had been able to get a pair of underwear on this morning. She yanked off my shoes and wasn't gentle about it.

"Tell me how these ruren-sa work, please."

"Not now," she growled, taking those oversized linen pants and ripping them into strips.

"Faruhar..." I trailed off, unable to voice the fear. "How do the ghosts do what they do?"

She sighed. "What don't you know? The bastards are everywhere. Ask them."

I looked around the forest again. No birds, no chirping insects, which was a little odd. Nothing.

"I can't see them. I can't hear them."

She stared me down, tightening the fabric around my thigh. "Then that's all the more reason to get you back to the cave." Her eyes flashed. "Bria, shut up!" she said, turning to empty air.

The breath whooshed out of my lungs. "Your sister is a ghost?"

"Stop bleeding! Maybe if you weren't talking so much you could concentrate on that!"

I sighed, watching her work.

She swore, looking at my torn leg dripping through the bandage, then stared at me as she ripped more of my pants into strips. "These ruren-sa are riled up, swarming. They each want a human mind to hold their pieces together. When there isn't much left of them, a wild dog is enough to keep them from fading to dust." She cursed again under her breath, continuing to wind the bandage.

I thought back to Galen, his final words. "What happens if a ghost gets into someone's mind? Is their host alive too?" I needed to hear it, even if I thought I knew.

"With these ghosts? No. They claim the mind as soon as they are in, make the host kill until they can't anymore. If you're fast, you can destroy the ruren-sa when you kill the body they stole. If the death is slow, they can sometimes wriggle out in time and find someone else. Bria wants me to kill them all, every time."

My breathing came fast, heart pounding. She looked up from where she'd finished the last of my shredded pants around my wounded leg.

"That's why you killed Galen." I felt gutted, trying to shake that feeling off. "He was dead already."

She didn't look up.

I felt the ground sway beneath me, and I gripped Faruhar's arm to steady myself. "You're trying to help?"

Two dead towns. A destroyed mine. Mal, after he seemed to come to his senses, more or less. I still couldn't trust her.

She turned her attention to my forearm, still trickling in dark red gushes where the jaws clenched in. "Fuck."

"What?" I said, feeling light-headed. *Iden... She'd spared him until he'd lost his mind.*

She began unzipping her leather chest armor.

"You're weakening; cold. And that arm needs wrapping too."

I blinked, taking time to process what she said. She lifted the leather armor over her chest and long hair, and all my dwindling mental capacity turned my attention to where she was ready to pull up her undershirt.

With a glare, she turned around, and I saw her scars extended across her back, thin over tan skin and muscle.

"It could have been my shirt," I said, trying to be practical.

"It would be no one's shirt if you did what you were told."

"Okay," I said. She bent over to grab her armor from the ground, glaring at me as she shrugged it on. The sharp movement of her neck, the feline shade of her eyes: I needed that. A reminder that she wasn't human, not—

Two dead towns I'd seen with my own eyes, I reminded myself, even if some of the deaths weren't what I thought. She had a hand spreading SBO. There were all the other names in the book. The deaths Galen told me about.

"Tie that shirt around the wound with your good arm, idiot. Don't rip it," she said, zipping up the armor on her chest.

I obeyed, although she untied and rewound it all with a frown the minute I was done.

"On your feet. We're going," she said.

I hauled myself up, using the tree for support. My vision swam, and I crested past a wave of nausea. She was there to hold me, dragging me into my first step, and carrying most of my weight back to the cabin.

CHAPTER 32

Farewell

I'd done my best to wake first in the cavern apartment, suspecting that if I didn't, Faruhar might stab me in my sleep before finding her book. That morning, she rose first.

"Jesse?" she whispered, her voice uncertain.

I sat up in the bed I'd yet to offer to share. In two days, the last of my wounds from the dog attacks had scarred over. Faruhar looked up at me from her bedroll on the floor, rubbing her neck.

"Faruhar," I said, "What do you remember?"

She blinked in concentration. "Jesse. You hate me but won't kill me. You have honor. I took everyone from you but I don't know their names. Can you tell me their names?" The same panic rose in her voice.

"You wrote them down," I said with as much gentleness as I could, unable to say, "it's okay." I shifted, drawing my legs to the floor with no pain. "We haven't corrected the book yet, but I gave you too many names. I'll set that right before you go."

She took that in with a grave nod. She read every name and confirmed every detail I knew before starting the day, watching her pack her things. There were so many names I could never clear for her. I needed that reminder too.

We said our farewells outside, the crisp autumn air invigorating my lungs, making me want to run and train at dawn like I used to. This still wasn't the body I remembered. No matter what was in the salve that Faruhar worked into gashes as deep as my fingertips, I had to recognize the change in how fast I could heal, and wonder. I could barely make out the scar, and I expected it to fade by tomorrow.

Faruhar didn't seem to give my fast healing much thought at all. She'd spent most of the prior two days outside, coming back at lengthening intervals, bringing medicine or food.

It was essential I kept busy, grinding herbs and preparing meals for us both. Not only had I been ravenous while healing, but it kept my thoughts from swimming in circles. When she was home, I'd catch her watching me, and I'd find my eyes drifting to her unless I forced them away.

For all I knew, I'd restocked these herbs for rebels, the ones who dropped SBO or broke the khels on Nunbiren. Maybe an Attiq-ka rebel used their magic to make Faruhar forget her part in this. Maybe they made her do all of this.

Outside, Faruhar first clipped on her swords and slung her pack, assessing me one last time. Those didn't look like a killer's eyes to me anymore, despite the facts. That gaze looked soft, like concern. It was harder to make the pieces fit each day. But since she'd given me no information at all about her allies, I'd need to let this convoluted battle rage somewhere she couldn't see it.

"Thank you," I muttered, the words gruff. "You are a better person than I thought you were." I wasn't sure what else I could say that was true.

Her smile fluttered and took wing. And fuck me—but that smile was the most beautiful thing I'd ever seen. *One dead town I'd seen with my own eyes*, I reminded myself. I was no longer sure it was two towns, but Crofton was enough.

"Please be careful," she said. "Bria wanted me to tell you that you'll be safe in the South Bend, or east to Uyr Elderven, but there are swarms further east past Baren Golkhi. She says you should regain your strength before you leave here. There are ruren-sa all over these woods."

"I'll rest a while longer," I lied. Asher's military company camped far to the east, and I'd be leaving today. A pang twisted in my gut as she gave me a clap on my shoulder, and I gave her an Asri salute.

"Farewell, Jesse." Her face tightened.

"Goodbye Far," I said.

She cocked her head at that. "Far?"

I shrugged, trying not to smile. "Try to remember me if we meet again."

Her eyes went distant before her gaze fluttered down to roost on me. "I always remember the people I trust."

She took quick steps away through the brush before I could respond, then broke into a run when the trail cleared. I watched her go as far as I could, with her last words taking root in my mind.

Within minutes, I'd packed up all I needed, tying up a few extra supplies into my century-fabric go-bag. Wearing my old clothes that Far had mended for me, I strapped Istaran at my side, planning to be in Nunbiren as soon as possible to bury my taam and friends.

Scarlet and orange fallen leaves and brittle twigs crunched underfoot. Sunlight filtered through the leaves still hanging on, dappling mosaics on the path. I drank in the crisp air, feeling strong, restless. There wasn't a hint of pain left anywhere in my body, and my legs wanted so much to run. So I did.

Five minutes, ten, fifteen, and my lungs met each breath with relish like never before. My body anticipated every curve, every log in my path, reacting to jump and dodge each hurdle. The stamina shocked me the longer I kept going, even as I savored the freedom of this new strength. I pushed on, trying to wear myself down and find the edge where I'd be panting at my limit.

Thirst found me first, then ravenous hunger by the time I reached the old dam around noon. But I only felt tired when I sat down, looking out on the sparkling water I swam with Mira, so much colder than the day I was dumb enough to kiss her.

I walked the rest of the way to Nunbiren, but only because I did not want to miss any clues; I wondered if there were ghosts around I couldn't see. But it was just my familiar forest with its towering trees and tangled undergrowth. The thought of Galen and my friends decaying on the cold ground spurred me onward. I had to brace myself for what I'd see, what I'd feel.

The Asri believe that to join their ancestors in Oria, their bodies have to return to the earth before their souls fade. They bury the dead as fast as they can—same day or next. Some souls fade more quickly than others, and sometimes they fracture into ghosts regardless. Beyond that, I don't know how it works exactly, but I believed Galen was home. Maybe it was Istaran, maybe a drop of blood was enough for Oria to cradle his memories. But I would bury as many of the rest as I could, just in case it wasn't too late.

The clouds were clearing over a misty afternoon when I stumbled out of the woods near the town walls. I met a lingering smoke in the air, acrid, the unsettling birdless silence like when the wild dogs attacked. My heart kept time as I forced my feet closer. At first, I saw nothing to explain the smoky taste of the air. The skyline was intact, but it all made sense when I saw the mound just inside the gate.

It looked much like the Chaeten town I stumbled on years ago. The bodies lay burned: only a few pale bone fragments lingered in the gray ash. I was too late. Overcome, I fell to my knees in the dusty street.

I stayed that way for a while, saying what funerary words I could remember, repeating each name and asking Oria to accept them. It wouldn't work, but I needed to do it anyway.

Then I walked home, passing looted houses on every street, open doors and broken furniture. I was surprised to find the forge door locked and undisturbed. Fishing out my key, I walked in, embraced by familiar walls, unfamiliar silence.

I could not bear to stay there long, to light a fire and sit in this empty shell of a home. I changed my clothes, shaved my face, and resupplied. To keep it together, I pretended Ash and Galen were just on an errand, and they would be home for dinner soon. When I'd had enough of that pretense, I gathered the things I wouldn't want looters to find, planning to hide the bag in the woods. I would make sure Asher had a chance to wear his century robe again.

By the time I'd reached the edge of town, I was crying like an idiot, grateful no one was there to see me.

Then I saw the four graves, freshly dug with loose heaps of fragrant sod. And as I drew closer to read the script on the hasty wooden grave markers, I realized I knew that messy scrawl of handwriting from a familiar leather journal.

"The girl in the pink nightgown." "The man by the carpenter shop." "Atalia Takashi." "Galen Eirini." I traced each knife-stricken word, each copied from Faruhar's journal, realizing that I hadn't fallen apart, not really, until just then.

CHAPTER 33

The Deal

I t didn't surprise me that the coordinates I had for Ash were in the middle of nowhere, deep in the forests of eastern Noé, not the South Bend. If Mahakal hunted rebels who resented the joint society of the empire, they'd be on the edges of it, in the hollows of the wild.

I was much better prepared than when I'd wandered the woods so many years ago. Since then, I'd stocked my go-bag with all the essentials I'd need if I ever got the chance to hunt the Red Demon. I had a military-grade compass, my favorite solstice gift ever from Galen, where I plugged in the coordinates I'd memorized from the field station. My Chaeten-fleece pants and shirt regulated heat on the coldest nights. I had the best armor that a civilian could buy. These twenty days in the field should be livable.

I did not plan for my recent surge in energy. It took me about thirteen days to jog most of the way, feeling like I just came from morning practice, albeit much hungrier. I could eat a whole rabbit in one meal now, and still wake up hungry in the morning.

When I arrived at the coordinates, I spotted disturbed ground and the cold remnants of campfires. I'd just missed them. Dozens of soldiers and at least a few horses left a clear trail.

The Fall Festival passed a few days ago. I imagined Asher walking around these woods, communing with Oria in this patch of trees, thinking of me. If anyone could hear Galen, it would be Ash, and I'd hoped he'd been able to sense that I was alive, looking for him.

Six days of tracking later, the long shadows of dusk cast through the trees as I found what must be Mahakal's camp. A neat square of tents and tarps lay nested atop a hill, with lichen-thick ruins of gray stone. I kept hidden, scoping them out with goggles to make sure I had found some of Mahakal's troops and not the rebels they were chasing. The camp bustled with activity, smoke curling from cook fires and clusters of huddled men gesturing at shared screens or scurrying between tents. Red military uniforms, the raven on the shoulder of an officer.

Taking a deep breath, I hid my bag of supplies, then circled from a new direction to enter camp. I refused to leave Istaran, but I snapped its comforting light into its scabbard so as not to spook them.

"Hello! *Syo na!*"

Tension crackled in the air as the soldiers turned to me. I scanned the faces, hoping to glimpse Asher, but no one seemed familiar. Doubt gnawed. Mahakal had several hundred soldiers under his command; those tents might hold a hundred at most. He might not be here.

Commotion erupted near the entrance. Soldiers ran to join the guards, digging into bags as they moved into position. Several at the front pulled out gray helmets with mesh that covered their mouth and nose.

"You! Stay where you are," a broad-shouldered soldier yelled my way, one of the few wearing an officer's uniform. I recognized the scars over his lips, the golden skin.

"Is that you, Havoc?" I called out. He'd been a captain when I first arrived in Nunbiren, and from the looks of his uniform, no one promoted him in those many years.

From the look on his face, he did not remember me.

I raised my hands, doing as they asked. "My name is Jesse Eirini. I'm here for Asher Eirini. Our father's dead. I just want to speak to him and I'll be on my way."

He paled instantly, looking like he saw a ghost. A soldier ran up beside Havoc, passing him a helmet. Havoc whispered to the soldier before slipping it on.

"Ash? Are you there?!" I shouted, but my voice got lost in the sudden flurry of activity. Two soldiers, their eyes wide behind the visors of their helmets, converged on me with huge crossbows.

"Stand down. Place your weapon on the ground," a woman with a ponytail said. "You're being placed under quarantine."

Frustration bubbled up inside me. "Quarantine from what? I'm immune to SBO. Ask Mahakal, or my broth—"

Ponytail held up her hand. "Don't make me shoot you. Eirini told us about his brother, although he failed to mention he'd be stupid enough to wander into a classified military camp uninvited."

Scar-arms chuckled under his helmet. "Stand down. Basic quarantine protocol."

My insides twisted. Protocol. I decided I hated that word, reeking of blind obedience. I would have always made a terrible soldier.

Still, I released my grip on Istaran and slowly placed it on the ground. Scar-arms directed my steps away. I felt I'd betrayed my sword when Ponytail picked it up. "I'll be expecting that back."

"Put this on," Ponytail said, tossing me what looked like a cheaper version of her own helmet: no tech, but snug around the neck with a mesh filter to cover my face. "Now empty all your pockets."

"Why?"

"So we can search you, friend," Ponytail said, with enough stress on the word "friend" to make it clear she thought I was anything but, that my presence here could only mean the worst intentions.

I did as she asked. "Where's Ash? Or Mahakal?"

"This way," Scar-arms said, his voice muffled through his helmet, gesturing toward an isolated building on the camp's edge that a soldier had just finished roping off. The ancient little building had four walls and no windows, the arched stone roof still standing. Perhaps a granary or an old storage shed, centuries ago. Once I was in, they bolted the heavy door shut behind them, leaving me with a single flickering lantern, a bedroll, and a camp toilet.

"We'll inform the Major you're here," Ponytail said through the door. "Stay inside, don't make a scene, and we won't have any issues. Try to leave before the Major clears you, and you can expect a crossbow bolt. You can take that helmet off now."

"Can I at least talk to Ash like this, with the helmet?"

"No," said Ponytail, as the sound of her footsteps in the leaves grew fainter.

The weight of the silence pressed down in the coming night. I lay awake smelling musty air from the cold stones, grateful at least for my layer of Chaeten fleece. In the morning, a soldier opened the door long enough to pass through a metal tray of bland food and a canteen, offering no news. I exercised as best as I could in the dark, still finding myself with unexplained pent-up energy. I tried not to let my mind wander too far into dangerous places.

Three food trays and a bucket of soapy water later, the door opened and a familiar figure filled the entry. Mahakal, no helmet, a lantern flickering over his grim features and unsettling black eyes. He held Istaran in his hands.

"Jesse," he said, his voice low and full. "Let me start by saying I'm very sorry for your loss." He sat on a stone across from me in the little building, rubbing his eyes. "I'd love to hear how and why you wandered into my camp without proper clearance."

"Where's Asher?" I couldn't hide my panic. "What loss are you sorry for?"

"Eirini's fine," Mahakal said with a gentle sigh. "A hard-working, resilient man—the heart of his squad." Mahakal cocked his head. "I meant Nunbiren, and Elder Galen Eirini. It's quite a loss."

I whispered a thank you as he studied me.

"I'm uncertain what I find more remarkable." He leaned forward on his knees. "The fact that you're the sole survivor of yet another bioterrorism attack, or the fact that you were able to find my battalion in the field. How'd you do it?"

"You think it was another virus?"

"Yes." He leaned back. "Although I'll be asking the questions. I need answers, friend."

I ran my hand through uncombed hair, tasting the earthy air of the small stone room. "Aren't you worried you'll catch whatever you think I have?"

He exhaled. "No, we've sequenced the new strain already. I cannot carry the new SBO variant, even if my soldiers can." He dug for something in his pocket. "If you will not be forthright about how you found us, let's start with whether you experienced any new symptoms, physical or mental? This variant of SBO can have a longer half-life. It is ... unpredictable."

I thought of the healing, the increase in stamina. *That couldn't be what he meant, right?* "Nothing."

"Good." He passed me a small vial with a needle, similar to what Mira used to test my code. "We'll run a blood test to be sure, of course."

I frowned, but opened the vial with a click, and pricked a drop of blood to place inside. I tossed the vial; Mahakal's thick arms flexed to catch it.

"Why are you here, Jesse?" he said, voice colder than before.

"For my brother. He needs to know what happened."

"*He* needs to know?" Mahakal huffed. "*I* need to know."

"He lost his family. All his friends. I just want a few minutes with him."

"This is war. We all have losses." The ice in his voice was undeniable. "But a good soldier pushes through. Here I was, hoping you'd come to join the fight, or at least offer information to help the empire. You expected we'd grant a social visit, with two towns destroyed in northwest Noé?" He took a moment to gather himself. The anger in his face vanished into the calm demeanor I remembered. "Tell me what you saw in that town, friend. We need to end this."

Two towns. I frowned. "There was a ghost girl. She came to warn us."

Mahakal nodded. "I'm clear on that from those that heeded her warning. Tell me about the attack."

I told him what little I saw, or rather what I didn't see. "...and then Galen attacked me like he didn't recognize me. He called me a demon." I paused when I got to Galen's death, to Faruhar. She couldn't be completely innocent. Maybe I should tell Mahakal everything, so we could sort it out. My heart pounded.

"It must trouble you to know the man harbored those secret thoughts, that the virus brought that into the light." Mahakal rubbed dark circles under his eyes. "The variant will increase irritability and violence while making him betray his darkest fears, not redefine core beliefs."

I frowned, unable to believe that. "It wasn't him. It was a ruren-sa. I was right there."

"I'm willing to incorporate new information, but we already isolated and sequenced the virus. Did you see anyone suspicious who might have infected the town?"

I choked out a sound, my heart pounding. "Well, I saw ... her. The Red Demon." It felt wrong as soon as I said it. The wrong path.

He paused, his gaze flickering between me and Istaran at his feet. "The Red Demon?"

I nodded, seeing dark anger cloud his face again.

"Of course. If I'm immune, perhaps so is she. Who better to infect the town? And this means she's now had a chance to kill you twice, and here you are." Mahakal's black eyes twinkled in the lantern light. "And you would have challenged her. You're no coward."

"I did." My heart lurched. *Faruhar.* I remembered her hands gentle on my wounded chest, the writing scrawled on Galen's tombstone. "She got away in the end."

"How did you survive her?"

I squeezed my eyes tight. "She disarmed me. She let me live."

"Did she speak to you? Enough of this caging around. I don't have time for vagaries when people are dying." He seared me with those void-black eyes.

"Yes, I spoke to her. It was … confusing. She's not a mastermind." I took a deep breath. "I don't think she's sane."

Mahakal's eyes narrowed for a moment, then he nodded. "She's sane enough to kill, and be told who to kill."

I always remember those I trust, she'd said. *She trusted me.* The world vanished behind my lids. *She shouldn't trust me.*

"She mentioned a sister," I said. "An Asri ghost named Bria. Do you recognize that name?"

"A ghost? Were you able to sense this 'Bria?' Did she let you see her?"

I hesitated. It was at that moment I remembered what Bria said, where it was safe and where the ghosts were moving. The phrasing was exactly the same as what the ghost girl said at the attack on Nunbiren. I *had* met Bria. She'd been the one to warn us.

Fuck.

Faruhar must have been close enough that day for Bria to survive.

I could tell Mahakal about the other names in Faruhar's book, the contradictions. But he wasn't looking for complexity, to send her to the queen for a fair trial with all the facts. He was looking for a way to find her and kill her.

I kept my face blank. "No, I couldn't sense Bria at all. I'm not even certain she's real. I wish I had more to tell you. What little the Red Demon said just doesn't add up."

Mahakal crossed his ankle over his knee, stroking his smooth face. "There are some things I cannot share, but I'll tell you what the empire is confident enough to report. A Chaeten gang attacked Nunbiren. They want retribution for SBO, and they are feeling emboldened as we settle more Chaeten into the bend. These terrorists cut the power. They dropped a modified SBO variant, then later looted the dead wearing stealth cloaks. They also cut power to the North Barrack, so we did not learn of the attack until too late."

My heart roared in my chest. I couldn't look at him. Would rebels have burned the bodies? Would Faruhar have time to coordinate with Chaeten thieves while she was in the underground cabin with me? It didn't make sense. Mahakal was the one who told me that the simplest explanation was most likely correct. This was not simple.

"Didn't you say the Red Demon was working with *Asri* rebels in the Bend?" I asked.

His jaw twitched. "The Red Demon is a mercenary. She has no loyalties I can determine. This gang probably offered her a better price."

"They can't have offered much. She's still wearing those leather rags for armor," I said, before I thought better.

Mahakal leaned back against the wall, his eyes boring into me. "You're right Jesse, not all the pieces fit. For example, why weren't you one of the many men, women and children she's slaughtered without a thought?"

I sighed, throwing up my hands. "No idea. She said I was strange and stubborn. That she respects stubborn."

A slow smile spread across Mahakal's face, giving way to a mirthless laugh. "Interesting. You do have a way of turning heads. Even the Red Demon is infatuated with you, it seems."

My stomach clenched, bristling at the gleam in his eyes. "No... I..." I felt my face flushing, thinking about her smile as she said goodbye.

Fuck, if anything, I was the one with clouded judgment.

Mahakal's smile bloomed into a smirk. "You've given me quite a bit to think about, Jesse." He turned back to eye the door, then stooped to pick up the sword, the engraved scabbard glittering. "Galen's inheritance, I imagine. What's its name?"

"My inheritance now. Istaran."

Mahakal unsheathed it a few inches. The metal lay still and dark in his hands. "This is now illegal tech. Galen Eirini could justify holding onto it to do his best work, but the days of putting such powerful tech in civilian hands are over. I'll need to confiscate this to ensure the empire stays safe. I'm terribly sorry."

A battle raged within me as I met his gaze. "It's an ancestral sword. It's been in our family for thousands of years."

Mahakal laughed out loud. "Your family?"

I scowled. He laughed again, rising to a stand. "Oh how I regret not sending you to be raised with your own. I should have sponsored you the day I met you, ensured you'd been finished in a proper Academy, not raised half-wild."

He stepped closer, too close, his voice just above a whisper. "Your mind should feed on the fire of the stars our people have conquered. It is we who sail the void, parent galaxies, choose our own names and destinies. We do not choose names for our father's dead dreams, for ancient primitives. It pains me to see someone like you, so finely coded—" He took another step, raking his eyes down my body. "You're a stunning, remarkable man Jesse, but what comes out of that feral mouth of yours can be such a turnoff."

I swallowed. He certainly didn't look "turned off" to me. "What do you want from me, Major?"

He gave me a rakish smile, lifting my chin. "It's just as well you refused to join my battalion. I'm gentle with those under my command. But you need someone to teach you a lesson, Jesse. I have no desire to be gentle with you." He said the last part at a low growl.

I froze as he drew his face closer to mine, my heart beating in my ears at the strength of his grip. He smelled musky, minty—wrong. But I buried my fear. I'd play this out.

I smirked. "Who said I wanted you to be gentle?" I leaned my head into his shoulder to offer a biting kiss, tracing my hand down his chest as he took in a sharp breath, his teeth in my hair as he shivered. He was distracted enough that I could twist Istaran out of its sheath with one fluid motion.

He stepped back, wide-eyed as I held the shining blade to his neck.

"Are you threatening me?" he asked, voice cool.

I pressed in, the glowing blade pulsing in my hand. "I'm teaching you a lesson."

He tried to move, to disarm me, but I ducked away, cutting him across the arm.

He inhaled. "Well, the Red Demon wasn't wrong about your stubbornness. But I don't share her penchant for treason."

I rolled my eyes, heart pounding all the while. "You'll heal quick. And you don't like gentle, remember?" But he wasn't wrong. I was committing treason. And if I didn't play this right, he'd kill me.

There was only one move left.

"I once told you I'd pledge if you could help me kill her. We have a fresh trail now. I failed to kill her on my own, but I still want the same thing. My price is my sword, though." Still holding Istaran in front, I smiled.

He blinked at me.

"Okay, Fine—we want the same thing, except one." I dropped a lingering glance at his groin. "I'll pledge myself to you, for life, if you can promise none of your commands involve fucking you. Is that good enough?"

He crossed his arms with deliberation, my sword still trained on him.

I sighed, realizing he was not going to agree to anything at swordpoint. I handed him the hilt, heart hammering in my ears, watching the blue light fade as he wrapped his muscled hand around the grip. He sheathed it.

I heard running footsteps outside. "Major Mahakal! We need you in command," a soldier said.

"Tell Havoc I'll be there in a few minutes, Navarro." Mahakal's eyes did not leave me.

"Redsky was just killed at her post, Major," Navarro said.

Mahakal swore under his breath. He turned to go, remembering me as an afterthought. "You'll stay here in quarantine until we're confident about your bloodwork." He clipped Istaran to his belt. "I'll find an appropriate use for you afterward."

CHAPTER 34

Soldier

Two more soapy buckets and six more meal trays passed before I was allowed to leave the stale air of the quarantine building. Those were a rough two days: I didn't sleep well, I couldn't keep much food down, and I wasn't sure what was wrong with me other than feeling worn out. I'd about given up when I heard a voice on the other side of the bolted door, telling me the medics cleared my bloodwork.

They let me step outside. My eyes watered, adjusting to a sunny winter afternoon. I scanned the military camp—more bustling than I remembered. There, beside the soldier glaring at me, was a face I loved.

"Ash," I said, a lump in my throat.

He looked rough. Gone was the boy who smiled his way through every practice and the man who hummed his mandolin music as he engraved at his desk. His sun-kissed curls were shorn close to his head, with dirt worn into new lines on his tan face. Yet, when our eyes met, a smile bloomed on his face.

Before I could take another breath, Ash sprinted across the uneven ground with a whoop, his smile exploding into a full-blown grin. Our embrace was fierce, exchanging relief and worry. I felt his calloused hands on my neck as he brought his forehead to mine.

"Jesse. Brother," he breathed, pulling back but not letting go entirely. "You're alive. Voids, I ... thought I lost you too."

I squeezed his shoulder, mirroring the unspoken worry in his voice. "I won't leave you alone. Ever."

Asher chuckled as he pulled away. "You look sick. Too pale."

"Born that way, asshole," I laughed. "Let's get my pale ass some sun."

We weaved through the throngs of soldiers, and he filled me in the last few months in whispers. His squad had just gotten back from an attack on a rebel safehouse. He described a cluster of desperate underground rebels, cursing Queen Azara while their skin glowed blue with illegal magic. He felt madness tearing at his mind before they flicked on the magic blockers to take the rebels down.

His head dropped. "Those were clean deaths. But last week, I tracked an Attiq-ka. The machine gives them seizures if they use their magic, but she used her magic knowing she'd die anyway. She wiped out half my squad. It felt like—hammers in my head, loud screaming, until I got a crossbow bolt into her."

I recognized the tremor in his voice, the forced nonchalance. Haunted eyes. "You alright, Ash?"

He hesitated, then gave a curt nod. "That was one of the easier deaths to live with. My first kill was just a scared kid, maybe fifteen. Dangerous, but voids—" He swallowed. "I killed that kid before he killed me first." He paused. "I'm sorry I didn't write home often. I didn't know what to say."

A heavy silence descended between us. I wanted to press him, to share the weight he carried, but I knew there was only so much I could take from his shoulders. I'd yet to kill anyone.

"You're a good man, Ash. Taking out dangerous rebels while I've been chasing shadows."

"Chasing shadows?"

I shrugged, nodding to all the people around. There was no way I could explain everything right here. I needed to get him alone.

We reached the armory tent. Asher rummaged through the gear, pulling out a pair of black pants and a long-sleeved shirt like his, the fabric hugging tight up the neck.

"Top quality Chaeten leather," Asher said, holding it up. "Deflects a lot of damage; already saved my life twice. You'd never know by looking at it, right?"

I ran my fingers across the material, surprised by how soft and thin it felt on the inside of the shirt. "Yeah."

"Did the Chaeten gang have tech like this in Nunbiren?" Ash said, whispering to ensure the soldiers just outside the tent couldn't hear.

A flicker of unease sparked in my gut. "I didn't see any Chaeten rebels during the attack."

"What about the unit that caught them looting?"

"What unit?" I asked.

"The report didn't specify—classified." Asher gestured to the shirt. "Put this on under your uniform. Make sure it fits."

I peeled off my dirty layers to put it on. Asher helped me into the secondary armor, the pieces conforming to my body like a second skin. He strapped on a utility belt loaded with pouches and daggers.

My thoughts whirled as I followed him out of the armory. Wind licked my face as the rest of me stayed warm under the Chaeten leather.

"Jesse, how did Taam die?" Ash whispered.

My heart sank in my chest. "A demon in his mind, after the khels fell." I clenched my fist. "We should have done what the ghost girl said and left. I should have trusted my instincts."

He paused, his gaze flickering away for a moment. "What ghost girl?"

I frowned. "Mahakal said he knew about that. I thought he'd have told the whole unit."

Asher pulled me aside when a cluster of soldiers walked by, and I could see his panic rising. "Tell me everything, from the beginning."

I recounted everything I thought I could unravel quickly: what the ghost said, Solonstrong, Ruan killing Ola as if she didn't even know her. Asher's face contorted into a variety of expressions as I spoke, but he didn't interrupt.

"That's very different from what my squad leader told me," Asher said. "Something is not adding up."

"Ash, there's so much more we need to talk about—alone, as soon as possible," I said. Even now, his ravaged expression and roving eyes were getting stares from passing soldiers.

Before I could say more, a harsh voice sliced the air. "Eirini! What in the voids are you doing with Biohazard?"

Captain Havoc approached, his scarred lips pursed in irritation. His gaze flicked between me and Asher, another furrow appearing on his forehead with each passing second.

"Captain, Sir," Asher said, his voice tight. "The med tent cleared my brother. I volunteered to help him with his gear."

Havoc snorted. "Someone in the med tent, not your commanding officer, allowed you to leave your post to do *their* job?"

Asher opened his mouth to protest, but Havoc cut him off with a sharp gesture. "Back to squad leader Navarro, and expect some extra duties tonight. And you... Biohazard." Havoc turned his steely gaze on me. "Unless you've passed basic and pledged in that shed, you aren't free to wander. Let's put you to work in the meantime. You'll be reporting to me."

A flicker of concern crossed Asher's face. He saluted Havoc, then turned to me. "See you later, Brother. Clean that pond water out of your canteen, *na?*"

Pond water. His code word for someone throwing off his dahn. I gave him an Asri salute farewell, burying the jolt his warning sent through me. *Havoc. I shouldn't trust Havoc.* I jerked my head to confirm I had that right, but Asher was already marching off.

Havoc barked another order to follow, and I did, crossing the camp in bold strides. A knot of unease tightened in my stomach.

"All right, soldier," Havoc snapped, pulling me from my thoughts. "I need you to relieve a guard on the edge of the camp."

I blinked. It all felt rushed. I hadn't showered since getting out of quarantine. No one showed me where my quarters were, or even briefed me on basic procedures yet. But I knew enough not to appear defiant when given orders. "Yes sir, Captain Havoc."

Havoc tossed me a ration bar and gestured toward a group of soldiers clustered near the camp's edge. He pointed toward a tall woman, and I recognized the brown ponytail peeking out from her helmet. That was the same soldier who'd been rude to me when I first got into camp.

"That's Riverhawk," Havoc said, his voice clipped. "She'll be making sure you're more help than trouble." He strode off without another word.

I approached Riverhawk, who shook my hand. She stood straight and lean, Chaeten, giving me a guarded look with those sharp green eyes, but no sneer. "Havoc said your name is Biohazard until you earn something better. He thinks it's confusing to have two Eirinis around."

The soldier beside her laughed, a petite, tawny-faced man with a contagious smile and sharp gray eyes. "Havoc is easily confused. He wouldn't know whether to go down or out a latrine unless Mahakal was holding the door, off the record, of course."

Riverhawk snorted. "Yep."

"I'm Victor Eight," the man said, shaking my hand.

"Eight?"

"How many times I almost died before I joined up," he said. "Eventful childhood. Still Eight."

"You've held that count in the military?" I whistled.

"So far." He grinned. "Nice to meet you, man."

"Give Biohazard your headset, Eight," Riverhawk said. "He's your relief."

Eight shrugged off a small device in his ear, cleaning it off with his shirt before he handed it over.

"Connects you to the command tent with a tap. And this—" She pulled out a black visor. "That will give you enhanced motion and heat detection for the perimeter."

"Wouldn't you want me trained before you put me on patrol?" I asked.

Riverhawk's smile was humorless. "Do you need to be trained to tell the difference between a rabbit and a guy with a sword?"

"Well, I walked right in, didn't I?"

Eight laughed. "Yeah, on her watch."

She frowned. "You looked about as threatening as the rabbit, but you're one of the reasons we doubled perimeter guards."

I grimaced. "Sorry."

"You gonna warn him about the other reason?" Eight asked.

Riverhawk sighed, and the two shared a sullen look. "Stay sharp. We've lost two soldiers in the last two days. Redsky and Liu were both picked off running patrols outside of camp." She bent down to a crate beside her and removed a crossbow, one with small shining darts and a barrel. "Mahakal said you should be a decent shot?"

I nodded, admiring the light weapon. "What's the range?"

"Two hundred meters. Watch the recoil. The mitigation system can only do so much." She lowered her visor, saluted to Eight, and motioned for me to follow her.

I'll never tire of the scent of the Noé wild.

The forest beyond the camp stretched out below, a vast expanse of ancient trees between the old gorges, cloaked in the hues of late autumn twilight. Camp was on one of three hills in this area, and we'd be watching the other, a patchy beard of oak and cedar with brown leaves still clinging.

Riverhawk took her watch about a hundred meters away, and I did my best to stay sharp, to not let my mind wander.

I tore open my ration bar and took a bite, forcing down the bland mix of grains and powdered protein. It tasted vaguely metallic, and I decided any complaints I heard about military food were justified.

The sun set the sky on fire, red and purple and gold. As I looked out at the darkening forest, a movement caught my eye on the treeline. It was just a flicker, a splash of color against dying leaves. But something about it felt wrong. I squinted, adjusting the visor, and for a fleeting moment, I could have sworn I saw...

Fuck.

I knew that mane of red hair anywhere, cascading in the wind over her worn leather armor, a battered crossbow clutched in her hand. Faruhar ducked behind a tree.

My breath hitched in my throat. *What the fuck was she doing here?* Two soldiers picked off by arrows, that's what. I tried to untangle the knot of conflicting emotions in my chest.

The metallic taste in my mouth intensified, a bitter tang that spread like a slow-burning fire through my throat. Panic clawed at me as my head throbbed.

"Riverhawk," I rasped through the comm, my voice tight. A wave of dizziness washed over me. I pointed to the treeline as she walked over, my hand shaking. The nausea intensified.

Riverhawk rushed over, face lined with concern. "You all right? You don't look all right."

"Just—a minute," I said, clutching my stomach. The forest seemed to press in on me, the rustling leaves whispering with malevolence.

"Hey!" Riverhawk gripped my arm. "Biohazard, what's happening?"

Before I could respond, I swayed, doubling over to empty the contents of my stomach onto the forest floor.

She took a step back.

"Looks like Havoc gave you the right name. Fuck."

I rubbed my temples, reminding myself these soldiers didn't deserve to die. *Command. I was supposed to call Command.* I touched my headset, my gaze darting back to the treeline. But the Red Demon was gone.

Stay that way.

"This is Command, Perimeter Guard."

Riverhawk shot me a questioning glance, then touched her own headset. "Biohazard needs to be relieved. He's pretty sick."

"SBO symptoms?" the soldier in our ears said.

My stomach chose that time to heave again, and I'm sure Command heard it all. I wiped my mouth after, disgusted with myself.

"Just puking all over the forest, Ma'am," Riverhawk said.

"Copy that," Command said. "Continue patrol until you're relieved."

Riverhawk gave my back a sympathetic pat. "Rough first day, huh?"

"Tree line," I said, even if I couldn't bring myself to say her name.

She clipped her headset back on and turned away with a nod: all business. "Clear. What did you see?"

Maybe I hallucinated her. My focus came in and out in waves.

I heard running footsteps and looked up to see Havoc, his face a mask of thunder. "Riverhawk," he barked, "head back to camp. I'm relieving you."

"Don't you mean him?" she said, gesturing her head at me.

Havoc glared in response. "Major wants a word with you. I'll deal with him."

Confused, I watched Riverhawk salute, then jog back to the camp. Havoc sauntered toward me, his face odd... Angry. *Why was he so angry?* I rose to my feet from where I sat at the base of the tree. I'd forgotten to salute. Maybe that was it.

It wasn't. He pulled out a dagger, sizing me up.

My heart hammered. Was he...

A sickening thud. A bolt protruded from Havoc's eye. His mouth widened in surprise, his hand tightening around the hilt of the knife pointed at me. He crumpled to the ground. Another arrow followed, glancing off the Chaeten leather on his chest.

He'd been about to kill me. Asher's dahn was right.

CHAPTER 35

Battle on the Third Hill

I looked up, following the path of the arrow that lay lodged in Havoc's brain. I saw nothing: the visor's heat detection was useless with so many trees to block the scope.

The dizziness faded enough for me to stand. I had to clear my head, get to Ash, tell him everything. We needed to walk the narrow path to survival together.

I waited as long as I could, counting to sixty, one hundred twenty, one eighty. I kept my body low in the brush as I peeked out at the ridge.

"We're under attack. Havoc is down," I said to Command. "Shot right beside me."

"Roger that," said Command. "Did you see the attacker?"

"Just a flash of movement through the scope. Didn't get a clear view." I heard a scream from farther up the forest: the perimeter guard in a nearby sector.

Fuck, she was still killing.

"There's a second man down. Stay low, backup is on the way," Command said.

More footsteps behind me, then nothing. I looked back to see three soldiers, dropped low to the ground with their crossbows out. I recognized Eight, Scar-arms (whatever his name was), but not the third helmeted soldier.

"We'll cover your retreat, Biohazard. We're pulling back patrols," Scar-arms said, flicking up the visor to speak. "Stay low."

Turning back, I saw a flicker of her through the visor, her scarred skin and green eyes peeking out behind a tree. *Why was she still here?* I couldn't aim at her when she saved my life again, even if she appeared to. She assessed her shot before her arrow flew, whizzing past me.

Scar-arms, right in the eye.

"Fuck," Eight said, breathing hard a body's length behind me. "She's fast. I can't aim that fast." He called Command. "Capri is down, caught with his visor up."

"And Jesse Eirini?" I heard in my headset.

"Biohazard's alive," Eight said. "The Red Demon can match our range."

"You got visual?" Command said.

"That's why I said Red Demon, Ma'am."

"Stay covered, Eight. We're sending Mahakal's squad."

When I peeked over the hill again, I saw no sign of her, no heat on the visor.

Before long, a squad of ten soldiers approached from behind us. Clad in full battle armor: Chaeten leather, black helmets and chest plate. They came from behind us, covering our retreat with their bodies so we could turn back to camp. I stood, my legs shaking a bit with each step.

We reached Mahakal, his face grim. He levied a hard, calculating stare at me with those creepy black eyes.

"Jesse," he said, his voice tight. "Keep up, or go back to quarantine."

I dragged my hands down my face, my heart pounding. After Havoc, I decided I was safest in a group, with witnesses. My breathing heaved as I trailed Mahakal's quick strides across camp.

Mahakal's personal squad circled us, prowling like a pack of lions with their full gear and raven wings on the arms of their uniforms. We reached the other side of the camp and beyond and kept walking down the valley.

"Sir?" a soldier asked. "We're going out at night?"

"We're the ambush, Huan, not her," Mahakal rumbled.

"What's the plan, sir?" Huan asked.

"She's alone; we have the numbers to take her down. We're joining Navarro's unit on the third hill, in case she makes a move. Ren and Ovid's units are circling to take her from the back of the second," Mahakal said, gesturing to the hill where she'd attacked from. "Foul's squad will cover the front. The rest hold camp on hill one."

"Her last position?" Huan asked.

Mahakal held up a hand. "Quiet comms only from here. Command, fill in my squad," he whispered into his own headset. A low hum filled my ears, then static as the surrounding soldiers nodded, listening. They could hear instructions I couldn't. Frustration bubbled up, and I tried to speak. "Sir, my comm—"

Mahakal again motioned for silence.

The ground leveled and rose under the procession of our boots, with my headset only buzzing in my ear. We reached the ridge, the wide trees leaving ample places to hide and wait. The wind brushed cold at the summit of the hill, whistling through the surrounding branches.

I saw a familiar outline, a gait I could recognize anywhere. Asher dropped to a crouch beside an oak, scanning the ridgeline with his crossbow. Looking up to me, I thought I imagined his smile through that helmet.

With a relieved breath, I saluted mind and heart, then took a step toward him, until Mahakal grabbed my elbow to stay.

I leaned into him. "Orders, sir? My comms are—" His gloved hand clamped over my mouth before I could finish.

"Quiet," Mahakal said, his voice low and urgent. He didn't move away, even when he removed his hand from my mouth.

Confusion clawed at me; Fear.

Mahakal's black eyes locked onto mine in the pale moonlight. "Stay still," he whispered. Then, a cold glint of metal pressed against my throat. Istaran, humming blue only where it touched the skin of my throat.

He nodded to a member of his squad, who dropped to his bag, retrieving rope. The soldier motioned for my hands as I jerked them away.

Istaran pressed against my exhale. "You don't need to be afraid, Jesse," he whispered. "Just ... act afraid."

The soldier pointed to a tree, a small one in the underbrush I could have put my arms around. Mahakal's grip tightened further, Istaran's point digging into my skin as he prodded me toward it. The adrenaline from the attack, the confusion of his threat, and the remnants of my illness, it all muddied my head.

"You're bait, Jesse," he said through his teeth. As the soldier secured me, he put his finger to his comm, his eyes roving the valleys before he turned back to whisper in my ear. "Time to scream. Howl at the moon, wild dog. Convince the mutt."

Panic gnawed at me, a cold serpent coiling my ribs. Mahakal's hand clamped around my neck, muffling the questions hammering in my head. *Did he think it was that simple? Faruhar would scamper up from low ground at the sound of my voice? Voids, she probably didn't even remember who I was.*

When I laughed at the absurdity of it all, Mahakal drew blood on my neck. I jerked my head back into the bark, feeling terror for the first time. I remembered the look in Havoc's eye before he drew, a look so much like Mahakal's right now.

"This is as real as you need it to be, even if I have to gut you with your elder's sword," Mahakal growled. "Scream like the traitor you are!"

My scream burned like shame up my throat, a raw, desperate plea that echoed through the dark trees. As my voice faded, the forest echoed silent, too silent: not an owl or chirping insect. Then, surrounding the hill as far as I could see, blue light webbed on the low ground between hills, clusters of Oria like fallen stars on the forest floor. I took in a sharp intake of breath, unsure what that meant.

"That's impossible. Scan with other frequencies then," Mahakal hissed into his comm, his voice raw with anger.

"Ghosts don't have magic," Huan said to his comm. Mahakal's black eyes glittered as he gave a signal for Huan to shut up, gesturing to me.

All other soldiers listened to their comms, the only sound in the forest the rustling of the soldiers in their gear. Ash turned back to me, tense, but I could not make out his face through the helmet.

Mahakal growled, a sound deep in his chest. "Then hold your position. Full aerial assault. Target each one," he whispered into his comm.

Static crackled in my ear again. Mahakal's gaze darted around the perimeter, the soldiers frozen in various states of apprehension. The blue glow pulsed again, seeming to mock their confusion. Resolve hardened Mahakal's face.

A distant rumble echoed through the trees before the night sky erupted. Orange streaks of light tore through the darkness, slamming into the forest floor with an explosion. The ground trembled beneath me, and ripples of warm shockwaves rustled my hair. Mahakal watched the valley with grim satisfaction as his surrounding soldiers roved their eyes in all directions. Two soldiers guarding the flank were the first to lift their visors, looking up.

Two arrows fell from above in less than a second, piercing through eyes to skulls as the explosions crashed around us. The other soldiers began pulling off their chest armor and helmets, swatting at their skin.

Ash removed his helmet too. *No. Why? What was happening?*

Over the sounds and lights of the explosions, she dropped gracefully from the trees. The Red Demon's swords sliced through eyes and between gaps in Chaeten leather: two kidneys sliced in one brutal blow, a head pierced, red hair flying. My breath hitched in my throat. Three, then six more soldiers down as the last of the mycelial lights winked out. Mahakal was still on his comm, eyes on the rumbling valley.

"It's her!"

"Ash!" I cried.

Mahakal turned smirking, then froze as he saw the dead.

Faruhar ducked, slicing as the crossbolts flew. She launched off bent shoulders to pivot off a branch and keep killing with both swords. I strained at the ropes, my voice lost in the fray.

Before a soldier could put his helmet back on, Faruhar's blade pierced under his chin through to his brain. She grabbed and speared a soldier in front of her chest, giving the dead the arrow meant for her. Faruhar kept killing, silent and precise. When Mahakal and the remaining soldiers tried to circle her, she leapt for the trees, scaling the bark with flashing swords, and knives built into the inner side of her boots. An arrow glanced off her armor. She pulled another from her leg, stashing it in a quiver before turning out of view.

Mahakal snaked away from me with a roar, throwing down his crossbow and unleashing his own blade, Istaran sheathed at his belt.

Desperate, I scanned for my brother in the darkness. "Ash!"

"Command, we—" Another man down as she dropped beside him from above, slicing.

Her movements were a blur as she danced through their ranks, her blades piercing each narrow mark.

Mahakal swore into his comm, losing her behind a tree.

"Jesse!" Asher's voice rang out, and then he was beside me.

She turned at my name, angling her head in a question. A crossbow bolt hit her in the shoulder just as she'd speared a screaming woman to a tree. She ducked away.

Then, she charged Ash.

Terror flooded my veins as my brother raised his blade to meet her. "Not him, Far!"

The Red Demon, mid-strike, whipped toward me, her crimson hair flying like a banner of war. Our eyes met, a flash too quick to be certain of in the dark, but voids, I hoped it was recognition. She sliced men to either side, backing away from Asher.

Asher's chest heaved, staring wide-eyed at me. "Far?" He looked between me and the Red Demon, lost.

"Cut me loose, Ash," I said.

He did.

Bodies lay in heaps around us, and whoever remained alive stayed low. I grabbed a crossbow from one of the fallen, keeping close beside Asher.

I saw two soldiers creeping on the edge of the ridge with crossbows, trying to get behind her. She had no helmet, and her worn armor wasn't worth much at this range. My heart pounded.

Mahakal gashed at Faruhar, his sharp blade tearing into a tree. I studied Istaran, dark on his belt.

"Fight me, you fucking mutt!" he roared at her.

"You." I saw pure hate in her as she circled him. "I know what you did to my mother."

His laugh echoed through the forest. Mahakal drew his own blade as she sliced, catching his belt. Istaran fell to the ground.

I'd never seen Mahakal fight, but I had heard the rumors. None of them did him justice. Even with my nightvision, I could barely track his movement. The remaining soldiers on the ridge aimed their crossbows, ready for their shot, but the two forms blurred together between clanging steel.

I dove for Istaran, the blade glowing blue as soon as I touched the grip. I caught Asher's gaze, silent but so alive, screaming at me with his eyes.

Mahakal landed a blow on Faruhar, a deep slash under her arm. She cried out, her thick blood leaving her in pulses. She froze; that earned her a crossbow to the leg. Another flew as she groaned into another sequence of attacks, glancing off Mahakal's armor. She was slowing. He was not.

I reminded myself of the names in her journal I didn't know. I reminded myself Mal seemed to get better before she killed him. They weren't all ruren-sa; she told me herself.

Havoc. That was the third time she saved my life.

"Your mother was much more fun," Mahakal shouted. "More fear, less fire, but we'll work on that."

"You fucking bastard!" Jagged pain laced her voice as she charged.

"She screamed for me." Mahakal laughed as he deflected, sending her reeling. "I loved her scream. Did she scream when you killed her? Can you make the same sound for me?"

She roared at him, throwing a sloppy attack with her injured arm that the other limb couldn't compensate for. Mahakal sliced her up the leg as she stumbled.

My heart pounded. The air was thick with the iron tang of blood. I stood there, frozen, but not in confusion. The path was clear, the wrong thing took convincing. I waited for my opening.

She cried out again, her eyes on me as Istaran pulsed in my hand.

I attacked.

One moment I was staring at Mahakal's smug face, the next I'd twisted behind him to cut across his lower back. I sliced the weak spot between the Chaeten leather shirt and pants with enough force to cut his kidneys, just as I saw Faruhar do. Mahakal dropped to his knees.

"Go, Faruhar!" I bellowed, throwing the churn of everything wild in me into my voice. "Go!"

Mahakal turned over from the ground, his eyes wide and panicked, darting to the few soldiers flanking. "All forces to the third hill. Now!" he said to his comm.

Faruhar had another man dead before his finger twitched on the crossbow, bleeding though she was.

She cut down another on the ridge with his hand on his comm. Istaran pulsed as I moved to finish Mahakal. I'd never killed a man; my first would be Chaeten-sa.

Asher planted his body in front of me. "Jesse, brother." He aimed a trembling crossbow at my face.

"Out of the way, Ash!" I growled.

"SBO aggression, Eirini!" Mahakal rasped, desperation replacing his earlier arrogance. "Do your duty."

"Is SBO even a real thing or is that another lie you're pulling out of your ass?" My sword hung in the air, but I doubted I could disarm Ash before his bolt took me down. "Is the queen in on all this?"

Mahakal just laughed. "He's insane."

"Ash, please trust me." I gripped Istaran tighter.

Asher took a step back, his crossbow still trained on me.

"Such a waste," Mahakal said, laughing at me.

"You need to go, Jesse. Bria said they are coming to kill you too," Faruhar rasped behind me.

"Why are you still here, Far?!" I demanded, leering at the blooming trail of blood on her torso. "Run!"

"Jesse," Asher said, emotion heavy in his voice, looking between her and me. "I don't understand."

"Use your dahn. Look at her and look at him!" I gestured to Mahakal, my sword shaking in my hand.

"We need to go, Jesse," Faruhar said. "Now!"

A streak of silver whizzed past my ear. The crossbow bolt buried itself in the oak ahead of me. My breath hitched, the world snapping back into focus as Mahakal rose to a stand. Another bolt, launched in quick succession, found my back as I began to run. I reached back, finding I'd been saved by Chaeten leather.

Faruhar cursed, running down the hill, darting between trees and around the broken earth from the aerial assault. I plowed through the grotesque shadows in the moonlight, the frosty air filling my nostrils as soldiers pursued.

"Ash!" I yelled, hoping he was right behind me.

CHAPTER 36

Ruins

I clipped Istaran to my belt to hide its light as the towering trees loomed over me in judgment, their bare branches grasping. Footsteps pounded behind us. "Ash! That better be you back there!"

"They can hear you." Faruhar breathed hard through her injuries, but kept pace beside me.

"They can track our heat signatures too. This would be a great time for that sister of yours to help out," I said as a crossbow bolt whizzed between us.

"She's resting."

"Her friends can destroy whole towns!"

"Bria doesn't kill," Faruhar said between heaving breaths. "She's mad enough at you without you calling her a demon."

The footsteps behind me drew closer. The world blurred as I spun around, my blood pounding in my ears, drowning everything out except Asher, his face moonlit with fear as he chased after us.

"Slow down!" Asher wheezed, trying to catch up.

"I need better ideas than that, Ash," I turned back around, beaming.

Time wore on. Asher's panting breaths grew ragged.

I slowed, letting him sidle up next to me. "Give me your bag, and keep running."

Ash slid it off, slowing for the exchange. I pulled him along once I had settled into the weight.

"Not tired?" he pushed out.

"He is. There's poison in his sweat," Faruhar said between gasps of air. "At least two kinds."

That ration bar. I'd felt ill that last day in quarantine too. "I didn't think Mahakal would go that far."

"So confused," Asher panted.

"Last poison dose must have been a few hours ago. I've been getting better," I said.

We pushed past our exhaustion and fear. When the bolts stopped coming, we slowed to a jog. While we had the lead, she would twist to run backward in mud, throw a rock to gash into a tree down a deer path, leave subtle signs to mislead.

Finally, as the moon climbed higher in the inky sky, she led us inside a crumbling stone structure, its once tall walls half-swallowed by the forest, with no roof between us and the stars.

"I'm hoping they'll think I have friends to ambush; wait until dawn," Faruhar rasped between breaths. "Bria will warn us if they come closer." She gestured to the air beside her, where I saw no one.

"Who's Bria?" Asher asked.

"Her ghost sister. One who doesn't kill," I said, as if that wasn't the extent of my knowledge on the subject. I turned to Faruhar. "That was her with the shiny lights, right? Confusing the soldiers before your attack?"

She nodded, eyes closed against the wall.

Asher frowned. "I'll get some water from that river."

Faruhar breathed ragged and deep, leaning against a degraded fresco, her armor stained dark red. "Far, can I help you to the water to drink?"

She blinked, listening. "Bria thinks you should fill my canteen. This was my camp last night." She gestured toward the far wall, arm shaking.

"Sure." I dove to find her bag hidden behind some rubble, buried in leaves.

Faruhar hesitated. "Thank you—Jesse."

"How'd you remember?"

"Your brother said your name in battle; it clicked," she said through lidded eyes.

I couldn't help but smile. I dug around in her bag until I found a canteen.

Asher knelt beside the gurgling stream that snaked through the clearing. He glared at me as I washed out the canteen, drinking deep, refilling again. I moved to go back to Far, but he grabbed me by the arm.

"What the fuck, Brother," Asher said.

"Can you be more specific? My brain's a mess right now."

"What the fuck seems most appropriate. That's the fucking Red Demon back there."

"Her name's Faruhar." I groaned, holding my head. "I was so wrong, Ash. She killed people in Nunbiren, but I can't blame her. Crofton too, except maybe Mal. But I'm going to assume—"

"Who'd she kill in Nunbiren?"

I took a deep breath. "Taam, after his demon got in. Atalia, same reason. There was no virus in Nunbiren, just ghosts that made everyone kill each other. All she's trying to do is make them stop."

Asher looked toward the ruins, face tight.

"As far as I can tell, the empire is useless." I gripped the tree beside me. "There were no Chaeten rebels either. Mahakal is just helping cover up the ghost attacks, making up stories that make the empire look good. When he questioned me in quarantine, he was seeing what I knew; seeing if he could still cover it up or if he'd need to kill me and cover that up too. I'd hoped I could buy myself enough time to tell you everything—get you out of here."

"Fuck," Asher said, his fingers tight on the back of his head. "Fuck. She killed Taam?"

"Are you even listening?"

"It's just a lot," Asher said.

"I got more. So will she, if she remembers anything—"

"Show me the sword. Show me Istaran." Asher gripped his knees tight.

I blinked, confused.

"Just hold it," he said, his voice panicked.

I unsheathed the blade at my hip, and it glowed in my hands.

Asher jittered his leg, anxious. "He told me his mods block the magic. But I saw it glow when he put that to your throat. He's lying. The ancestors just don't trust him. They still trust you."

"Why not let me kill him for that alone?"

Asher shook his head, dropping back on his knees beside the stream. "I never liked the guy. Just convinced myself we needed a demon to take out demons." He shivered. "I don't really want to work with any of them, Jesse." He gestured back to the ruins.

"Faruhar saved my ass three times now," I said. "Havoc tried to kill me, by the way. Your dahn was right. It should be right about her too."

He shook his head at me and sighed. "She confuses the fuck out of my dahn, to be honest." The moonlight cast shadows on his features. "It's like ... seeing two people with one face. For a moment or two, what you're telling me makes sense. She doesn't want to hurt you. Otherwise it's like—visual static, and not good. Hurts to look too close."

"Voids, really?" I looked back at the ruins. "I owe her a life, a couple to spare." She had so much blood on her armor, that shallow breathing. I got up to go, canteen in hand.

"She probably took twenty lives to buy yours," Asher called after me. "Good men and women, with families that love them!"

Faruhar sat propped up against the crumbling wall, her blood blending into hints of red fresco; a sewing kit lay on her lap. Her armor lay discarded beside her, with a wide crimson stain blooming down the side of her torn linen shirt.

I knelt beside her, and she took the canteen in shaking hands, her lips pale.

"Hold still. I'll take a look," I murmured as I pulled the wet fabric aside. The wound cut deep; a jagged gash of flesh. No signs of healing.

"Couldn't see to sew it up," she said, voice hoarse.

"I got you." I settled in. She poured a little water from her canteen over the wound, then drank again.

Asher's footsteps rustled behind me. He paused, taking in the scene. "I got a lighter to heat that needle." He dug around in his cargo pants. "Then I'll check the woods for some plantain." Between practice and the forge, this was not the first time we'd mended flesh.

I nodded my thanks to him as the needle glowed red in the flame. I looked back to see the fire reflected in Faruhar's lidded, exhausted gaze. A shiver wracked her body, tremoring the arm I held steady. I flicked the needle cool as Asher left.

"What were you doing with those soldiers?" she asked, voice cold.

"Finding my brother, like I told you. It took me a while to figure out who Mahakal really is." Pain twinged my chest. "I'm not smart. I don't know if you remember, but that's one of the first things you ever said to me."

She gave me a weak smile. I threaded the needle.

"You ready?" I held the needlepoint to her cool skin.

A raspy laugh escaped her lips. "I can block pain. Just keep the blood in."

I got to work. I'd never stitched up a wound this deep. It wasn't properly cleaned, but I'd hoped Faruhar's enhanced healing abilities would make up the difference. "Why were *you* there, Faruhar? Did you follow me?"

She grimaced, a flicker of defiance crossing her features. "I was following a lead."

"A lead?" I pulled the string taut.

"A rumor from the other ghosts, a risk, but good enough for me, even if Bria didn't want me to try. She doesn't like it when I get close to Mahakal." Faruhar's voice raked the frigid air. "Then I saw you and I couldn't just go. You looked so afraid. I thought—"

"You thought you could take on two military squads on your own?" I finished for her, a mix of exasperation and something deeper twisting in my gut. "You almost died."

"You sound just like Bria," she murmured, with a hint of a smile between pursed lips. "She thanks you for that one."

"Hi Bria," I said to the open air. "Sorry I tried to kill your sister. Truce?"

Faruhar just sighed.

"How'd you get to that tree without anyone seeing you?"

She huffed. "I was in that tree before Mahakal showed up. When they did, well, no one ever looks straight up in the forest as much as you'd think," she explained, her voice growing fainter.

"My brother Iden taught me the same thing." I smiled, then remembered she'd killed him. "You could have waited until it was safe, until we cleared out."

"Mahakal—" Her eyes fluttered closed, her head lolling against the stone.

Panic surged through me. "Far? Stay awake for me." I fumbled for her canteen, forcing a few sips of water past her parched lips and checking her pulse. Faint.

A crackle of leaves announced Asher's return to the ruins. His face grim, he clutched a handful of round, green leaves. "Got the plantain," he said, jaw locked as he looked at Faruhar. "Voids, will that make a difference?"

"Ash, help me," I begged.

I set to work on the gash on Faruhar's leg while Asher knelt beside me, bruising and crushing the leaves before applying them under her arm. I awaited each rasp of her lungs.

"Far, what else do you need to heal?" I'd just finished the last stitch on her leg.

Little warmth lingered beneath my fingertips. She didn't answer.

"Far? How do I heal you?" I repeated, urgent.

She opened fluttering, unfocused eyes. "I need to make blood," she whispered. "Water. Meat. Time."

"Okay." I held the canteen to her lips for her to drain.

When she was done, I went for the jerky I saw in her bag.

Asher stiffened when he saw it. He'd just as soon eat a person. To his credit, he kept his mouth shut, offering to fill the water bottle as I cut the strips into thinner slices to make them easier to chew. She was barely breathing.

"I'm going to gather some wood for a fire," Asher said when he came back. "We'll hide it in the morning."

I nodded, analyzing every movement as she insisted on feeding herself with a trembling hand, even as her eyes kept drifting closed.

Faruhar coughed, a weak sound. "Thank you." Her eyes drooped closed again.

Asher lit the fire inside our corner of the ruin. The night deepened as the flame brought a fresco to life on the nearest wall: a herd of hoofed beasts I didn't recognize. Asher turned his back to us both on the other side of the fire, lying down to sleep. I sat beside Faruhar, watching her violent shivers until I couldn't stay silent anymore.

"You're too cold from that blood loss," I murmured.

Her eyelids fluttered open, a sliver of defiance still clinging to their depths. "Survived worse," she said, her raspy voice barely audible. But her defiance flickered and died, replaced by a glimmer of vulnerability as she closed her eyes again.

My heart hammered against my ribs. "Do you want me to..." I hesitated, the question felt heavy on my tongue. "Can I keep you warm?"

That vulnerability in her eyes deepened. Fear, maybe.

"It's fine. I don't mind," I whispered, the words leaving my lips before I could stop them.

She nodded with a sigh.

Without another word, I eased my body into the leaves, spooning my chest to her back, offering what little warmth I could. She was so cold, more than I thought possible for anyone.

"You said I deserved to die. I wrote that down," she whispered.

"I was wrong." An unwonted spark ignited in my chest. "Bria, wherever you are, make sure she crosses that one out."

"I've written that down before," she said, with a shiver that wracked us both.

I began to hum my mother's lullaby, the one Faruhar sang when I recovered in the cave. Her breathing, shallow and uneven, began to stabilize and lengthen. Her heartbeats fell in step with mine as our song became our breathing, and then the sounds of morning birds.

CHAPTER 37

Outlaw

The rhythmic rise and fall of Faruhar's breathing kept my sleep that night shallow, tethered to wakefulness. I felt relieved her body radiated heat against mine. The first rays of dawn lit the ruined atrium and crumbling archway. Just as I was drifting back to sleep, that warmth left me, and I heard the thud of a knife leaving a sheath.

I sprang up.

Faruhar stood over Asher, her eyes wide. She held one of her swords, its blade glinting in the pale winter light, angled at his throat. Her gaze darted between me and Asher, who had crawled back with a gasp, his back to the wall.

"Who are you?" she demanded of Asher, her voice hoarse, her stance ready.

Ice shivered up my spine, but I pushed panic back down with a breath. I forgot about the journal; I should have left it in sight.

"Faruhar, you're safe." I made slow movements to stand between them. "I'm Jesse. That's Asher, my brother. You can trust him."

She frowned, her gaze dissecting Asher, who watched back with raw terror.

"Jesse?" he stammered, looking at me.

The sight of Asher's face sent a jolt through me. Faruhar narrowed her eyes as I moved closer to my brother, unarmed. Her sword lowered a fraction, but her grip remained tight.

"Jesse?" she echoed, her voice uncertain. "Where…? Who tore my armor? I was injured."

"Major Mahakal injured you," I said. "Last night you attacked his camp. You got us out; Asher too." I gestured back to my brother with pleading eyes.

"Mahakal." That word sparked a dark fire to life. Her nostrils flared before her eyes refocused. "Sorry Asher; Jesse."

Asher's mouth fell open, his muscles relaxing only after she sheathed her sword.

I couldn't decipher the scurry of emotions contorting her face. "Thank you," she said in her whispery rasp. "For saving me."

"Same," I said, exhaling.

A few birds trilled across the frosted forest. She went to her bag in the corner, removed the journal, flipping through pages at a rush.

"She can't remember?" Asher whispered, keeping his back pinned to the wall.

"Who are you looking for?" I asked Faruhar.

"Mahakal," she said. "I hate him. I need to remember why. Bria doesn't want to talk about it, but she told me once."

"Told you what?" I asked.

She'd found the page she was looking for. And the leather book shook in her hand as she tried to smooth the page. "He was one of the Chaeten-sa that raped my mother."

I looked from her to Asher, his mouth open.

"How do you know that?" I asked her.

"Bria was there. Mahakal might be my father for all I know," she said. "I don't think I want to know."

The horror of that left me speechless, my hands fisted. *"I'm sorry"* didn't cut it.

We sat in silence. She seemed to remember herself with a shiver. "I need some water." She gestured outside to the stream. "You both must be tired, but we should get moving again soon."

Asher watched her go, his back still plastered to the wall. His fearful brown and gold eyes met mine. "We need to leave her. Now."

I shook my head, mind racing. "You're scared of her?"

"You're not?" he asked, but my face must have been enough of an answer. He gripped his head with his hands, biceps tense. "You're not. Fuck."

"She's evaded Mahakal and the empire for almost a century. We need her help." I ran a hand through my short curls. "I expect we'll have wanted posters up in temples soon, our code records posted in every hospital. Sorry I dragged you into this. I didn't see another way."

Asher sighed, head against the wall. "If you never showed up, I'd still be out there tracking and killing Asri rebels. Can't stop thinking about it. I've only seen them defending themselves, Jesse. They hate the empire, but their crimes against anyone else, I've taken on faith." His eyes lost focus. "Mahakal only tolerates us Asri—the queen demands we're in the unit too. He doesn't respect us. I've probably been killing innocent *ka* for him." His body trembled against the stone.

I sat down beside him, my shoulder to his. "You didn't know."

He sighed, shook his head; kept shaking. "We still don't know much. What I do know is that the Red Demon just tried to kill me."

I'm pretty sure that anything I said next to reassure Ash didn't work, but I tried to catch him up. He kept his thoughts to himself as we set to work, dousing the embers with the remains of my canteen and hiding the ashes under fallen leaves.

Faruhar returned, striding fast to put her journal in her bag. "Mahakal's battalion is on the move. Let's go."

I came up alongside her, gesturing to see her arm, eying her ripped pants. "Shouldn't we check your injuries first?"

Faruhar glanced down, pulling the gash of bloody fabric aside under her arm, her brow furrowing at the plantain dried to her skin. She brushed it off with a harsh scrub that made me cringe. "It's fine." A fresh pink scar under her arm was all that remained of the wound that almost killed her, a fresh line to add to the maze on her body.

My mouth dropped open. No wonder she thought nothing of my new healing abilities if this is what her body could do.

"Ready to go? We'll forage for some breakfast on the way," she said.

We rose. Ash grimaced, but didn't argue. With a brisk pace, we plunged back into the brown leaves between bare branches.

We fell into a rhythm. Faruhar and I carried the bags, our movements silent, a dance in harmony. I tried to out-quiet her while matching her speed. Her yellow-green eyes darted between the path ahead and the undergrowth flanking us. Now and then, she'd fall into a crouch, plucking nuts that had fallen near her route, dropping them into an open satchel. My stomach growled when she came to a full stop, a tree with wide leaves still clinging, and oblong fist-sized fruits.

"Asimina." She smiled, offering me and Ash the largest ones.

I peeled the yellow fruit with a knife as we walked, the cool, custardy flesh only taking the edge off my hunger.

"Hide the peels well," she said to Ash, who was about to toss it. "Leave no trace."

"No problem, Far." I smiled at her.

She glared, guarded. "Far. Why do you say it like that? Are we friends?"

I weighed that. "I think so," I said at the same time Asher said, "No."

Ash scowled back at my raised eyebrow, a muscle twitching in his jaw. Faruhar laughed, picking her way over a branch.

"I don't mean to be disrespectful. I'm very grateful for all you've done for my brother," Asher said. "But I've heard so many things about you before last night, about what you do with your life and—"

"It's fine, Asher." She chuckled. "You *should* be terrified of me. It's what your brother says that doesn't make any sense." Her gaze softened as she flicked her hair out of her eyes. "I don't need you to think of me a friend, but I guess I don't mind his pretending. It's fun to have someone to talk to."

"We're running for our lives, and you're having fun talking?" I asked.

She pointed out a patch of beechnuts nestled amongst the fallen leaves, their brown shells gleaming in the sun. "We're walking for our lives, currently. For me, that's an ideal day."

I knelt beside her to collect nuts, trying to make sense of that smile.

"Bria likes you, Asher," Faruhar said. "She says it's okay to tell you most things, and she'll answer what she can."

Asher cracked a nut with his pocket knife, stuffing another in his pocket. "Who's Bria? I mean, who was she when she was alive?"

Faruhar paused, listening. "She's Attiq-ka, and she knew my mother before I was born. Bria has been in my mind as long as I can remember. She kept me alive when people attempted to kill me as a child."

"As a child? Who?" Asher gave her a sidelong glance.

A bitter laugh. "I'm a halfbreed born during the Ghost War. *Everyone* wanted to kill me. Bria says I got my first scars as a baby when the town elders tried to throw me in the fire. She convinced someone to get me out."

"Fuck, that's horrible," I said, especially how she said it, with so little feeling, like that didn't matter.

Ash squinted as we walked, opened his mouth and closed it. "So, Bria's in your mind? She can talk to you in your head?" Faruhar hesitated, seeming more upset by this question than the one about being burned alive. "I don't like telling you things you could use to hurt her. But Bria said to just tell you yes. She's a ghost. Too broken to rejoin Oria, but no demon."

The path passed a fast-moving stream, the cool air carrying the scent of damp earth and running water. Faruhar hopped down the rocks to fill her canteen, motioning for us to follow.

"Jesse said you were trying to stop the ruren-sa; kill them before they hurt people," Asher said, wary.

"He makes it sound noble," she said. "I do what Bria says, because she keeps me alive, and because I want to keep *her* alive. She's the noble one; I kill. I know what I'm good at."

Screwing the lid on my canteen, I studied every flicker of light on her face, unsure if it was possible to reconcile her at all.

"Is Mahakal driving the ghost swarms, or following them?" Faruhar asked. "Bria thinks the worst, but she has no proof."

Asher frowned. "He doesn't talk about ghosts at all. Although his personal squad keeps a lot of secrets. They have a higher clearance level than the rest of us, and we don't overlap much."

Faruhar nodded. "Ruren-sa didn't swarm like this until what happened in the Bend. They prefer to be alone. When Mahakal is anywhere near a swarm, his khels are up. Bria can't hear through the khel, so she won't go close until he's on the move. He can't keep them up while traveling."

"So he can put the magic shields up in the field, like it's nothing? And turn them off?" I'd thought that was something only Asri mages could do.

She nodded.

I turned to Asher. "Good enough for me. I think someone in Mahakal's squad turned Nunbiren's khels off from the North Barrack. That's how the ghosts got in. I'm going to kill him."

Asher inhaled a breath.

Faruhar's expression frosted over. "Bria is screaming at you now, and me. She never wanted me to get anywhere near Mahakal, ever."

"Last night, too?" Asher looked between me and her.

"Yeah, she's pissed," Faruhar said with a huff. "But she's right. I can't kill him alone."

I met her gaze, my jaw set. "You don't have to do it alone. Voids, I'll kill him for both of us. I don't care." I gave Asher an expectant look. He kept his eyes on the road.

"If I can't do it alone, neither can you." Her head jumped at a sound I couldn't hear. "We need to speed up."

We rose and fell into a jog, and my body welcomed it. One kilometer, two. Asher's breath picked up into a frantic rhythm when we pushed the edge of his endurance, so we let him set our pace.

"Jesse, we should tell Mira what we know." Asher took a sharp breath. "Warn her about Mahakal, the virus—"

"Mira?" Faruhar echoed.

"Our friend. She's got a background with Modtech," Asher explained. "She couldn't map the SBO virus to Jesse's code. If there is no such thing as SBO, that would be why."

"Where is this Mira?" Faruhar asked, her long legs moving over the terrain with grace.

"Uyr Elderven." Ash caught his breath. "The research hospital."

"A Z'har? You're crazy," Faruhar huffed.

"Might not have pledged yet," Asher said. "They gave her three months."

I could hear the pain in his voice. "I always planned to head to her next, Ash. She's family. We have to warn her before that pledge."

Faruhar considered this, her face unreadable. "I'll see you both to the gates of Uyr Elderven, but you'll have to find your own way in. Although, I'd appreciate a hand along the way."

"A hand with what?"

I heard them running toward us, crashing in the underbrush and the leaves of the clearing ahead. I halted as a dozen figures spread out in front of us, carrying a mismatch of weapons and tools, their clothes dirty and eyes glazed with hate.

"Demons," she said, unsheathing her swords.

CHAPTER 38

Ruren-sa

One of the ruren-sa let out an ear-splitting yell, a dozen or so ripping across the clearing toward us. Before my mind could catch up, Faruhar was a blur of grace and death, her steel tearing into the flesh of the closest man. I froze, entranced by the flawless execution of her attack.

Ash hissed beside me, drawing his sword, and I kicked my ass into gear.

The first person I ever killed was a bearded, middle-aged man wielding a farmer's scythe. The second was an Asri woman with a stolen Chaeten blade—lower tech, its steel polished to a gleam. Ash only managed to take down one, while Faruhar danced between the rest in a single breath. Her twin swords, razor sharp, found their way to each heart and neck, felling each with efficient thuds. And when there was no one left to kill, she dropped to check her victims' pockets.

Asher's scream sliced through the clearing and I turned to see him on his knees, clutching his head in horror. I saw nothing to fight, no one to kill.

"Let her in quick," Faruhar called to him. "It's Bria."

"No, no, no." Asher shook in waves, his voice raw.

Faruhar spun on her heel and knelt beside him, her eyes blazing with a fury that chilled me—just as it had when she killed Mal. "Would you rather have her in your mind or a ruren-sa? Let her in."

My head pounded. "Ash?" I stepped closer, Istaran glowing in my hands.

Asher crumpled to the ground, his scream reverberating off barren trees.

"Fuck," she said.

The rustling of leaves at my back snapped me back to attention. A woman, her face contorted in a sneer, swung rusty garden shears at my head with all her might. I threw myself to the side just as the rusted metal snapped shut where my head had been.

Adrenaline surged through me as a fresh wave of demons ran into the clearing, too many to count. I swung Istaran, the motion grounding me in the center of the chaos. An immense man with a machete lunged at me. I parried the blow, the clang jolting my bones. I found my focus. This was no sparring session: I must kill or be killed.

My world spun around the gravity of Istaran's blade. Grunts and the squelch of flesh. Practice had never prepared me for the withdrawal of my blade from living bone. I underestimated how much force it would take, finding I needed to reverse the angle of the strike just right to avoid getting stuck. A woman with a claw hammer gave a wild swing when my blade lodged itself between ribs. I ducked, fumbling for a dagger as her hammer hummed over my head, grazing my shoulder under my Chaeten leather. I retaliated with a throw of that dagger to her chest and finished with Istaran through her neck. Her head rolled, the green in her Chaeten eyes flickering and dying.

"Ash?" I looked for him among the bodies, seeing only a man with a rusty relic of an Asri blade coming at me, workmanship that would have made Galen cry. I sliced him open and withdrew, catching Faruhar's raised eyebrow.

"You're faster than when we fought," Faruhar said beside me, felling the last in the clearing.

I saw Asher across the meadow, hunched and turned away. I bolted for him. He fixed his terrified gold-brown eyes on me, his face pale with a sheen of sweat on his brow. Then he raised his blood-wet blade at me. He didn't need to swing to gut me. My world went dark; the sun at my center collapsed in.

"Ash," I whispered. "No, Ash," I couldn't lose him too, but I had.

He lunged for me, and I froze.

In that instant, I knew I'd rather let him kill me than live through this again. Even if he was gone, I wanted none of his blood on my hands.

"Behind!" He ran past, his sword a streak of silver. As a man emerged from the clearing, Asher blooded him on the first thrust, spraying across the brown leaves as he followed through.

It took me a moment to understand, to find enough hope to take a breath. "Ash?" I ran to him.

Asher turned back, his sword slick with blood. "I'm fine," he gasped, his voice hoarse.

I stared at him, searching his face for any sign of a demon's presence, numb to the sweat stinging my eyes. I dropped Istaran as I pulled his chest to mine, my fist to his neck as I held his bloody body, breathing ragged breaths.

"Brother, I'm fine," Ash said, a chuckle in his voice.

"Fucking stay that way," I said, not willing to let go for a while.

Over the iron-rich scent of blood, the sounds of birds returned to the clearing. Faruhar gestured to the fallen figures with a jerk of her head. "Loot what you can. Quick."

We picked through the pockets, finding a meager haul: a few silver coins, a couple of daggers that didn't need sharpening, and a small bag of mixed shortgrain and mushroom flour for flatbread. Faruhar peeled off a pair of durable pants from a woman who looked about her size.

"Bria says Mahakal's search party is closing in." Asher's gaze darted to the woods. "She's coming out to you now."

Faruhar nodded. She cleaned her blades on a corpse's shirt and did that double-sheathing move that took me a full year to get right.

Asher swayed as he sheathed his own sword, almost dropping it.

I caught him before he could fall. "You okay?"

He blinked away the dazed look in his eyes. "Weirdest feeling ever when she left, like falling up to the sky. She scared the shit out of me on the way in too."

"I noticed."

With a signal from Faruhar, I picked up Asher's bag and we took off east.

"Did she ... control you?" I thought of the ghost girl, her rigid movement.

"No," Asher said. "Just ... observing: a little girl just sitting there in rags. She's younger than I thought she'd be. I felt bad for her."

Faruhar grunted. "Surprised she protected you. It's harder for me to concentrate on the fight if I have to focus on keeping ghosts out."

"That was you fighting distracted?" I said. Her form was impeccable. "Train me to move like that, please. I'll kill as many ruren-sa as you want."

"Train you?" Faruhar picked up her pace. "Mahakal's going to know we were here the moment he sees those bodies. Let's focus on that."

We ran on for a while before Faruhar cocked her head to something I couldn't hear, quick as a bird. I looked around.

"Bria says there's another unit of Mahakal's soldiers downriver, a couple dozen on horseback. They're closing in from the north while Mahakal's coming from the west with the remainder of his forces. The river is blocking us in to the east. If we don't slip south before they intersect..."

She trailed off, but the implication was clear. Mahakal would seize us in the jaws of a trap.

Faruhar broke into a run, slashing through the undergrowth and brush as she went. We settled into pace beside her.

The forest began to thin, giving way to a vast, open plain. Sparse, wild grain popped up in a rocky meadow, and a herd of deer took off past the ruins of an old farmhouse, land once settled before the Nara lost so many people in the Ghost War.

I had no problem keeping pace with Faruhar, but Asher's breathing grew ragged, his steps faltering. At some point, we had to slow further. Up ahead, a faint rumble echoed between the hills: the undeniable sound of approaching hoofbeats.

I understood the desperation on Faruhar's face as we approached a ruined barn, but I didn't see any place to hide inside, just a square of open stone. When she skidded to a halt, I panicked.

"Far?"

"Shh," she said, blinking. Asher grabbed his knees, taking deep, heaving breaths. Faruhar muttered in frantic whispers.

The sound of the horses grew louder, a whinny on the wind that made me afraid to turn my head.

"It's the only way," Faruhar said to the open air.

She took a sharp turn and ran straight into a solid section of the stone wall, disappearing from view.

"Faruhar?" I hissed, too terrified to yell. But she was already gone. I approached the gray stone, seeing only the lichen-covered rock.

"Jesse, Asher, come on!" she said, her voice unmuffled—like there was...

Nothing. My hand went through open air. With a nod to Ash, I ran into the khel.

CHAPTER 39

Underground

I lurched atop an overgrown staircase, grabbing Asher's arm so as not to tumble down mossy steps tangled with weeds. Behind me where the wall should be, I saw an arch, the meadow still visible beyond. At the bottom of the stairs stood a matching stone archway, Faruhar standing wide eyed at the cool darkness beyond it. She clutched her elbows to her body as the horse hooves thundered closer.

Was that fear? Apart from her fitful sleep, I wasn't sure I'd ever seen her afraid.

I peered down into the inky blackness. "So ... we just walked into a wall."

Faruhar frowned. "We're behind an *a's'aan khel*. They'll be able to hear us. They can't see us unless we go past the arch. We're safe enough as long as we don't go into the tunnels."

"That's an entrance to the Underground." Asher stood frozen, cool air trickling out of the void beyond.

Faruhar nodded.

"We'll be no safer if we run into Asri rebels." He gestured to our bloodstained military uniforms, then Faruhar's Chaeten-sa face.

I faced the darkness, shivering at the scent of damp earth and fungus. Dad's bedtime stories were full of Asri magic that lured Chaeten children to the Underground. Sometimes it was rebels, sometimes the glowing mycelium would make sounds of music, or laughter, and the curious Chaeten children would follow the song to their death.

The pounding hooves grew louder, reverberating through my boots. They stopped nearby—the men shouting. Faruhar's golden-green eyes sent a jolt through me.

"What happens if they find the khel?" I asked, voice hushed.

"If Mahakal knew of this entrance, he'd have already bombed it. Scanners aren't much use out in the wild. Oria is everywhere." Asher nodded to Faruhar. "They won't find us."

Faruhar clenched her jaw, her knuckles pale on her sword. "They're tracking better than expected. We're missing something. Bria?"

The men were now gathering beside the barn. I could see red uniforms in the field above the stairs, searching the field.

I risked another whisper. "Ash, how can we survive inside?"

He exhaled, raising his hands in a shrug.

Faruhar spoke low, her face close to ours. "Inside the tunnels, Oria can kill anyone. It will take no risks: poison, hallucinations, tearing a rock tunnel down on our heads if it has to. Anyone with a scrap of ill will toward it or the Attiq-ka who built it dies, as does anyone whose conscience is not clear before the ancestors." She took a deep breath. "No empire soldier survives Oria. If we go in, Mahakal won't follow, but—"

Faruhar's eyes were lethal as she looked to Asher, drawing a dagger from her belt.

"Far?" Asher said.

"Show me your shoulder, Asher." She didn't wait, pulling down the neck of his Chaeten leather shirt tight enough to choke him as she studied his shoulder blade.

"Far?" he wheezed.

Then she cut him, tracing a delicate circle from his skin and flicking it out. She peeled something shiny and metallic from the tip, showing us both.

Ash bit on his pain, inhaling. "Fuck, a tracker?"

"Tracker." She laid it on the stone, scraping her knife over it to destroy it. "Bria heard them talking about it. But it's too late. They know we're here."

Asher rubbed his shoulder. "I'm sorry, Faruhar. I didn't know."

Mahakal's voice drifted on the wind. We shared the silence, exchanging panicked glances.

Asher stepped forward, shaking his head to clear it. Then he gestured to Istaran at my hip. Blinking, I handed the hilt to Ash with a click, who grasped my arm in thanks as he took it.

The glowing blue light welcomed him, the reflection bright in his eyes. He smiled and gestured to the dark, then handed it back to me. The mazed engraving glowed in my hands as expected.

Then I understood what he was doing. The glow signified Istaran's trust. As long as it was glowing, Oria should trust us too.

Faruhar's gaze snapped to Istaran as I passed her the grip. My breath hitched with expectation. She'd saved our lives, risking it again and again. She's saved the life of everyone those demons would hunt.

Our fingers brushed as she took it with a tight grip, her knuckles white as she stared at the intricate green and gold scabbard, a prayer on her face. Silence stretched between us as she drew the blade out. Nothing: cold steel.

A soldier's voice growled from above the stairs. "We lost signal in the barn."

"I can smell the traitors," came Mahakal's reply, far too close.

Faruhar's shoulders slumped, and she let out a shaky breath as she handed back Istaran's hilt. She pointed to Asher and me, then gestured her head at the darkness. My heart plummeted. I shook my head, clenching my fists. I would not run like a coward. If she couldn't go on, I would stand with her, taking down as many as I could.

There was so much that flew past her eyes as she read my defiance.

"Hey!" A shout at the top of the stairs. *Were we seen?*

Yep. I stared up the stairs to the soldier, panicking.

Faruhar lunged for us, her grip on our arms inviolable, pulling us through the arch into the dark. I had no chance to run back. With a rumble, the mouth of the tunnel closed from the top, a stone door rolling down to trap us into the darkness of the tunnel.

"No," I whispered in the dark, drawing Istaran so I could see the fear in Faruhar's face. Then she was on the move. When Ash delayed, I pulled his arm as the walls sprouted mycelial light around us, following her with bold strides.

The world around me gradually took on depth and detail in grayscale and pulsing cyan mazes. It wasn't just one tunnel here. Carved with precision, the passageways formed a labyrinth of tunnels within rock and earth. Faruhar pulled us down a set of stairs, breathing fast as the glowing mycelium reached its lacy fingers into the walls toward us, questioning.

This wasn't the wispy Orian tendrils I knew from the forest. The etchings on the wall gave a path for the mycelium to shine, interacting with complex bionetwork circuitry, with divots and circuitry I couldn't begin to understand. Oria snaked around the tech with sentience, vibrance flowing like a river along the walls and floor. The air shifted.

Even I could feel the malice in the air, the silence just before a death blow. I wasn't sure I believed that any of us were safe.

"How long until it tries to kill us?" I asked Faruhar.

"It's already trying." She nodded her head toward a door. "Hurry up."

I jogged on behind her. Here and there, I saw signs of recent habitation: a discarded cloak, a half-eaten meal abandoned on a ledge. I looked to Ash. "A rebel left that, right?"

"I can't see as much as you," Asher said, squinting. "But assume yes. They're the only ones down here."

The entire population of the Nara lived down here twice, before the Chaeten, when nearby stars went nova and thinned the atmosphere on the small planet. And with a fungal power source that could collect energy from both the sun and the heat of the planet core, there were no power failures in the Underground.

"Just move," Faruhar rasped, pulling us along.

The blue veins of mycelium reached into stone grooves around a heavy door. A high-pitched sound rang in my ears, like the whine of the server room I saw on a childhood field trip to the mine. A panel of hypnotic blue light pulsed at the center of a wide door. Faruhar shoved me toward it, her breath ragged.

"Put your hand on that door, Jesse," she said. "Or try touching it with your sword."

I reached out, hesitant, feeling a shiver of sensation across my skin as I touched the shining blue network. Nothing; same for holding my blade against the circuitry. Just the static of a faint electric current.

"You next." Faruhar's hand trembled as she gestured to Ash.

He stepped forward, placing his hand on the panel beside mine. A wave of light pulsed outwards. For a breathless moment, nothing happened.

"Ancestors." Asher closed his eyes in concentration. "I'm Galen's son."

The ancient door groaned open, sending a tremor through the floor as it disappeared into the wall. Beyond it, a narrow passage.

A wave of bioluminescent light spilled out, washing over us in ethereal cyan and sunny yellow. Orian mushrooms grew beyond, the first I've ever seen in person, flat shelves of creamy blooms no larger than a child's hand. The air inside was heavier with the strange, fungal odor, but it wasn't unpleasant. In fact, a strange sense of calm washed over me, a feeling of sanctuary.

But before I could voice that hope, Faruhar stumbled. Asher reacted in an instant, grabbing her arm before she could fall. Her eyes grew wide, mouth parted.

"Faruhar!" I rushed to her side, holding her up. Her grip on my arm felt weak, her breathing shallow.

"The spores," she gasped. "Killing me."

Asher's brow furrowed. He covered his mouth with his sleeve.

"You'll be fine, *Asri-ka*," Faruhar said, her voice muffled as she tried to cover her face with the fabric of her own shirt. She coughed, a wet, hacking sound that tore at my heart. "Keep going. Ash, use your dahn on the walls. Find the nearest exit."

Panic clawed at my throat when she collapsed to her knees.

As if sensing my thoughts, Asher glanced toward the open doorway. "Grab her shoulder," he said, with military command. "We'll drag her."

I looked down the glowing passage, shaking my head in denial. But I slipped one arm around her waist, helping to support her weight across my shoulder. Asher took her bag, then gripped her other side. Together, we guided her through the doorway.

The passage sloped downward, leading deeper into the heart of the Underground, but there was nowhere else to go. The bioluminescent glow intensified, lacing through the carved geometrics on the walls. Faruhar had been going through the motions of steps as we carried her, but she stopped moving with a shudder, her body slumping into mine with a shallow gasp.

"Faruhar!" My voice echoed off those damp stone walls. "Bria, Oria, please, help her."

Asher shushed me, his eyes wide as he looked around.

Faruhar remained silent, her head lolling against my shoulder. A knife of fear twisted in my abdomen. Could this be it? A pulse at her neck confirmed fading life, a slow, irregular heartbeat.

"I'll carry her," I told Asher. He nodded as I hefted her into my arms. A low moan escaped Faruhar's lips.

We strode on through the passage ahead as it widened into an underground road, ruins on either side. The bioluminescent matrix emanated a frantic pattern.

"Jesse, east," she said, pointing when we reached a crossroads.

Despite the relief flooding through me to hear her voice, something wasn't right. Her voice sounded so weak. Higher pitched, childlike. She kept breathing, eyes fluttering.

"Bria?" I hissed.

A twitch of a nod.

We moved deeper, with each cavern still sloping down, not out to an exit. The rhythmic pulse of the bioluminescence glowed stronger, casting the cavern in an eerie light. We reached an open chamber. A row of mossy platforms cut out the wall by the remains of what must have once been dwellings.

"Lay her on one of those beds. Now," Faruhar said, again in that strange voice. Her arm twitched toward a platform of thick moss in the center of the wide chamber.

I didn't argue, cupping Faruhar's head as I eased her down onto the mossy stone, threaded with cyan veins of Oria.

Faruhar's eyes remained closed as the bed glowed underneath her, tendrils of light pulsing around her body. I couldn't see her breathing anymore. I shuddered, hoping it wasn't killing her faster, that Bria wasn't just offering a painless death. Asher stepped back from the mossy bed, afraid to touch it.

"You're not allowed to die." I sank beside her to check for a pulse.

She took her first deep breath in quite some time. Her eyes fluttered open. But from that gaze, cold, frightened, I knew it wasn't Faruhar that looked back out.

"Every moment I hold control," Bria said, the strange inflection more pronounced, "the more of herself she loses. You should never have brought us here." Anger flashed in her eyes before fading to a dull stare.

"I'm sorry, Bria." My voice broke.

"She never took risks like this before," Bria said, a childish pout evident in the way Faruhar's head lolled. "She let so many die for one boy to heal, and she ran straight into danger to please you yet again."

My jaw clenched. "You're asking her to kill all the ghosts in Noé, right? Alone? You're the one demanding she risk her life. You should at least respect her choices when she chooses a different flavor of danger."

Bria laughed, just as eerie as it was bright. "Her choices benefit you, Chaeten. You aren't the first to try to take advantage of her. Your intentions are clear."

"The fuck does that mean?"

"Stop fighting! Both of you!" Asher hissed.

"I'm here to help," I bit out. "How do I help her?"

Bria closed her eyes tight, her hair pooling on the moss. "I can keep her alive here. Don't move her." She sighed. "There's so much I forgot, and I need everything left for her. I can only slow the death down when we're moving again, but she's too weak. I won't be enough." There was panic in the child's voice now. "And I can't leave, can't check to find the soldiers."

I brushed the hair out of her eyes, her lips cool to the touch.

"Faruhar told me to use my dahn on the walls," Asher said. "What did she mean?"

Bria sighed with Faruhar's body. "If your mind has any discipline at all, use it. Direct the Song."

Asher frowned. "I don't know how to use any of the illegal magic."

"*Chout*, not magic. Ask your ancestors," she said.

"What can I do?" I asked.

"You're useless," Bria growled. "I'll be here long after you're dust."

"No. I—" The anger that had flared in me moments before sputtered out, replaced by a throbbing heartsickness. Because I knew I wanted to contradict that; offer a promise with no end that came far too easy. Faruhar had only promised to see us to Uyr Elderven. I had no idea if she ever wanted to see either of us after that.

I clenched my fist around my helplessness.

Faruhar closed her eyes, and drew steady breaths, until all I could hear was the distant dripping in the cavern, the high pitch of Oria's bionetwork.

Minutes passed. Asher snaked his hands over the walls, whispering. Then he paused, sitting by the stone across the chamber. He got up and walked farther away. The silence drew on in the dark, leaning beside Faruhar on her mossy bed. Her breathing remained shallow, rasping in the eerie light.

"Ash?" It had been about an hour. My voice echoed between glimmering cavern walls.

"Bria?" I said to the unconscious Faruhar, desperate for any reassurance.

Silence.

Dread pressed me down. The air shimmered. A distorted ripple spread across my vision, now swimming in red. Istaran pulsed at my hip, afraid. When the rebels let me see them, they surrounded me.

Fifteen or so, their dark robes concealing their forms. Each cloaked figure emitted a faint blue luminescence from their outstretched hand. Some carried staffs, or swords on their belt, but I knew better: the glow in their hands was the threat.

Asher struggled in the grip of two of those dark figures. "Jesse!" His movements were sluggish, face pale, in the grip of their magic.

I looked to Faruhar, then took my stance, Istaran in hand.

Chapter 40

New Faces

"Hey friends," I said, tone casual despite my drawn sword.

Heads turned to one another at that, but I didn't hear a single rustle of fabric from them. They must have shielded both the sound and sight of their approach.

One of the figures stepped forward. A woman, still in shadow. "Surrender, Chaeten," she said in my native tongue.

I lowered Istaran a fraction. "I'm not your enemy—if you haven't noticed," I said in Asri, nodding my head at my glowing blade. "If Oria doesn't want me dead, why should you?"

The woman lowered her hood. I saw olive skin and a lock of white-braided-into-dark hair. She narrowed hazel eyes. "Who are you?"

"We're Jesse and Asher Eirini, son of Galen Eirini, late elder of Nunbiren." I saluted with a smile, relishing her blink at the Asri surname. "And that's the Red Demon behind me." I swallowed.

She nodded, unperturbed as the rebels whispered. "You may call me Master Telesilla. What tech are you using to escape judgment by Oria, and to tether that sword?"

I scoffed. "Escape judgment? Because of the Chaeten eyes? Do I need to glow blue to be human enough for you bigots?"

"That's blood on your empire uniform, Chaeten. Whose do you wear?" Telesilla said.

A man stepped forward, removing his hood to show eyes like mine, but sporting long Asri braids over dark skin. "We do not deserve your disrespect," he said, voice tight with anger. "Anyone who can live by *Niire Mai* is welcome among the disciples of Reic."

"Cool," I said. "Tell your guy to leave us alone, and we'll do the same for him."

"Master Soren," Telesilla warned. The man stepped back. She gestured to another rebel. "Search their belongings, please."

The rebels dug through our bags, laying everything out in the chamber. They swore at Faruhar's venison jerky and handled her leather journal through the fabric of their cloaks.

"What's this?" a gruff voice demanded, flipping through the pages of Faruhar's scrawling illegible text.

I bristled. "None of your fucking business."

"You bound it in flesh," the rebel said. "This had a mind once."

Telesilla cut in. "Set it aside for Reic, Kagan."

"You won't be taking anything." I brandished my sword again.

Their magic hit me quick. I saw lights explode behind my eyes, felt my legs give way, my ears ringing and head pounding. I almost gashed Faruhar and myself with Istaran as I fell onto the mossy platform, tearing my cloak instead.

When my head cleared and I found strength to raise my bruised body up, the rebels jeered around me.

"Not so tough around *Chout Attiq-ka*, are you Chaeten?"

Attiq-ka discipline, they said. They didn't call it magic, but it was.

"May I have the honor of executing the Asri-sa soldier? I saw that man kill Eliona with my own eyes," a rebel accused. The crowd murmured. Angry. Asher looked sluggish, confused.

"Let the man speak first," Telesilla said.

Someone shoved Asher forward, the ground underneath him rippling with light. Asher took a few breaths, probably clearing his head of magic to come back to himself. Then he bowed his head before Telesilla, offering a deep Asri salute of heart and mind. I shuttered away my anger at the deference.

Telesilla cleared her throat. "Oria knows you. You are a soldier for Queen Azara, a member of Major Mahakal's battalion. You killed several loyal to Oria. You slaughtered the Attiq-ka elder Eliona, and injured Sategca, both members of the Council."

I frowned at that. *What council?*

"You killed Barille, Neolin, Kandalanu—our friends, innocent of malice, minds who live by the principles of *Niire Mai*. Do you deny this?"

Asher flinched through the accusations, his head hanging lower with each word. "I also live by *Niire Mai*. I do not know the names of all I killed, but it is true I killed an Attiq-ka and at least three other rebels, believing they were demons." Shame laced his words as he spoke. "I no longer serve the empire, nor Major Mahakal."

"Why did your master dismiss you?" Telesilla asked.

While Asher gathered his words, I said, "I don't think Mahakal took it well when the Red Demon and I tried to kill him."

Asher gave me a desperate look, an order to let him do the talking. "My brother and the Chaeten-sa helped me understand Mahakal is lying to the people of the empire, including his soldiers. Mahakal is now hunting the three of us. It's why we risked coming down here."

"Then we should give you right back to your master, *na?*" a voice said.

"Great idea," I interrupted. "I'm sure Mahakal would be so grateful he'd offer you all quick deaths instead of slow. He might even skip some of the raping."

Asher clenched his eyes tight. Telesilla studied me.

"What my brother means to say is we have a common enemy. I never meant to take the lives of innocent *ka*," Asher said, with genuine emotion in his voice. "Oria knows my heart in this. If you want my life as payment, take it. But my brother has never killed *ka*. He wears only the blood of demons. Please let him and the Red Demon go. She sacrificed herself to save us, to do right."

The room fell silent. And I could feel the mood shift with uncertainty.

"What's wrong with the Red Demon?" Soren, the Chaeten rebel said.

Asher loosed a breath. "Oria is killing her."

"Then Oria has already judged her; she dies," Telesilla said, in a voice that almost sounded like she gave a shit.

I imagined cutting those self-righteous smirks and patronizing frowns off their faces with a blade. But I took a deep breath, looking to Ash for strength. "Oria is making a mistake, Master Telesilla." I bit back my anger. "I will vouch for her before the ancestors, just as my taam Galen did for me. She's been out there killing the ruren-sa standing up against Mahakal to make sure innocent people don't die. There is nothing you can demand of me that I will not consider worth the price of her life. If you have a price, name it."

The rebels murmured, the glow on their skin fading. The magical equivalent of a lowered weapon, I guess.

"You wish to kill Major Mahakal, Jesse Eirini?"

I gave a firm nod.

"My dahn tells me I can trust you, Master Telesilla," Asher's voice broke as he prostrated himself cold stone. "I stand with my brother. Guide us out of here, and we'll help in any way we can."

The air crackled with tension as Asher's words hung heavy. The rebels seemed unsure, looking from face to face. This deferential humility trip of Asher's was working better than anything I could throw at them. I had to give him that.

"I can accept the two of them, but the Chaeten-sa was bred for war," one rebel grumbled, a stocky guy I would prefer not to mess with. "Her mind is not capable of living by *Niire Mai*, as Oria itself has judged."

A mumble of agreement rippled through the crowd. Soren squinted to stare at her, at me.

Asher nodded, his voice thick with regret. "Disagree if you will, but just because it's no sin to kill a demon doesn't mean you have to. You can choose mercy. Let her continue the path she is on now and Oria will judge later. She *will* continue to help us and be a powerful ally."

Telesilla seemed to deliberate. The rest looked to her.

"Asher knows the inner workings of Mahakal's unit. All of us, the Red Demon too, will keep swinging when Mahakal's tech blocks your magic. She will repay her life debt," I said, hoping that was true.

They didn't answer, just kept shifting their gazes between us. Finally, Telesilla spoke, her voice tinged with suspicion. "Your changed opinions on Mahakal I can understand, Asher Eirini. But why would you be so eager to offer information, to help kill the minds you served with?"

Asher closed his eyes tight. "No one will support him if they know the truth." He looked around the cavern, his voice gaining conviction. "We also have a friend in Uyr Elderven, a modtech expert. Maybe she can help us if we can get her the right tools. She'll figure out why some people succumb to the ghosts and others don't. The ghosts can't touch Jesse or the Red Demon." He nodded back to me.

A long silence; the rebels looked among each other.

"Let's talk, Asher Eirini." Telesilla offered Asher a hand up from where he knelt on the ground. They walked off to a shadowed alcove in the far corner, entering a room that opened to their touch. One by one, the rebels stopped sending wary looks my way and walked off to join them. I would not risk leaving Faruhar's side, even as the minutes dragged on. Faruhar's chest rose and fell—rapid and shallow breaths.

Her eyes fluttered open only when we were alone. "They will only help us if you keep your mouth shut, Chaeten," she whispered in Bria's voice.

"Bria, where have you been?" I hissed back. "If you're Attiq-ka, they'll listen to you more than us."

"I can't." Faruhar's body shivered. "Reic can't know I'm here."

"Why?"

Her lips trembled, warbling with emotion. "He can't mend me, but he'd try, even if that would break what heart I have left. He'd also want to kill Faruhar."

I tightened my jaw, deciding that the killing Faruhar part was all I needed to understand. "I'll keep your secret, Bria."

It was almost an hour later when Asher and Telesilla returned, their faces grim but determined.

Telesilla approached Faruhar, her hand glowing. I pulled back, shielding Faruhar with my body. "No."

"It's okay, Jesse Eirini," she said. "I agreed to help her."

I looked to Asher before I found the strength to accept that. Telesilla bent down, her hands illuminating the shadows of Faruhar's scars and loose hair. The glow passed into Faruhar's skin. Faruhar groaned, but did not rise. The light flickered out. Telesilla furrowed her brows and tried again. But Faruhar's breaths were deeper, her calloused hand in mine warmer.

"She's resistant," Telesilla said. "I cannot push through beyond minor healing."

"Thank you." I relished the strength in her pulse, the warmth of her skin under my hand.

Telesilla rose to Asher, taking his face in her hands. His tan skin glowed under her touch. When she removed her hands, I saw the face of a man I didn't know, still with highlighted hair cropped short, gold rings in brown eyes. But it wasn't Asher.

"That will help you get through security in Uyr Elderven unless you go near a magic blocker."

"The police only have a couple blockers in the city, though. They wouldn't want to risk killing off their own healers." Soren's eyes narrowed at my hand on Faruhar's arm. He looked up, adding, "You should be fine."

"To remove the glamor, wash your face in a river that touches Oria, or it will fade on its own in a month, six weeks at most." Telesilla moved to touch my face.

A strange tingling sensation washed over me when her hand met my cheek. When I blinked my eyes open, I touched my face, a jaw that felt smoother than I'd left it, the bones more rounded. This was no deception. She'd changed my face.

"Whoa, that's weird," I said. "Thank you, Telesilla."

"If you are in a hurry to leave, we'll lead you out away from the soldiers," Telesilla said, her voice gentle. "Asher Eirini, my network will speak with you again when you arrive in the city. Please check into The Mora Inn when you arrive."

Soren helped Asher with our bags, and I heaved Faruhar into my arms, still leery of letting anyone else touch her. We followed Telesilla out of the chamber and into another hallway inclining up. Asher chatted away, even smiled, winning them over slowly the way Ash always does. I walked in silence, feeling not only the weight of a woman whose toned muscles and high bone density made her much heavier than she looked, but the weight of our new alliance. We weren't just outlaws anymore, we were rebels too.

I studied Faruhar's every breath, her scars, evidence of her continued survival, and yet—so vulnerable in my arms. She stirred against me, and I was aware of every place our bodies touched. I tried to rein in my thoughts, clutching her tighter to my chest. *What would Galen say if he saw how I was looking at his killer right now?*

"Stop looking at her weird," she whispered in Bria's voice.

Farmhouse

Twilight lined the sky when we stepped out by a rocky outcrop, sloping down the path into a pine forest. Telesilla tried again to heal Faruhar and apply the same glamor she did to us, her face straining, only for Faruhar to stay as she was, unconscious. I'd lowered Faruhar gently onto a bed of dried leaves, keeping vigil beside her, holding her hand. Telesilla set up a khel to hide us, saluting before disappearing back toward the caverns with Soren. Remembering the last time she woke, Asher hid her swords, then went foraging nearby. Still, she didn't wake.

Faruhar murmured under her breath, little noises that did nothing to slow my pounding heart. I kept saying her name. Finally, she responded, a slow smile spreading across her face.

Her eyes fluttered. "Is that you?"

A jolt of relief shot through me at the sound of her voice. "Faruhar," I said. "You're safe." I gripped her hand. "I'm Jesse. That's—"

She blinked, her smile faltering as she took in our surroundings, stumbling back with wild eyes. Panic flickered in my gut when I realized the worn leather journal was still with the rebels. I also realized those glamors would render us strangers, even if she'd recognized me before. She dove for the dagger on my belt. I sprang back.

"You smell like him. You're not him. Where … is the one I … trust." She dove for my dagger again.

"Faruhar, listen to my voice. Please, it's me, Jesse." I evaded her grab once more. "It's *Chout Attiq-ka*, a disguise."

Faruhar squinted, considering. "Speak again, whoever you are." A low growl rumbled in her throat as she gestured at Asher, staying far back with his weapon drawn. "And who's he?"

"That's Asher, my brother. You can trust him too. Same *Chout* glamor thing going on, but his voice will sound the same."

I nodded at Ash to speak from where he stood across the clearing. "Faruhar, it's Asher, your friend," he said, earning a bewildered look from both of us.

I smiled.

"Friend?" she echoed, her voice laced with confusion. "I don't…" Her gaze drifted past Asher, searching for something—or someone. She scowled back at me. "I don't like this magic. You were never this … ugly."

My cheeks flushed, a fire that warmed my chest. "Did you just call me—not ugly?"

"Voids. Anyway." Asher released a long-suffering breath, sheathing the Asri blade Telesilla gave him to replace his empire sword. He studied Faruhar, leaning back with arms crossed. Birds chirped.

"What, Asher?" she said.

"Just making sure you no longer want to cut me open like a melon." He stood taller. "Can I hug you? You saved our lives back there, and I—I want to hug you."

Faruhar froze, eyes still wide as she nodded. Asher enveloped her in a warm embrace, and I watched as her fists unclench. Slowly, she softened in his arms, and I wondered how long it had been since someone held her like that.

I didn't even wait for Asher to pull away before I stepped forward, wrapping my arms around them both. She turned into me. Any air between Faruhar and my body crackled with a tension that wasn't entirely unwelcome, demanding I hold her tighter. When Asher pulled away, she leaned into the warmth of me, holding on just as tight, taking a deep breath at my neck. In that moment, the forest sounds faded, replaced by the frantic drumming of my heart.

I could not let go.

"Jesse," she breathed. I froze at the sound of my name in her mouth, pulling my hips away just enough to not let this get awkward, because it was about to get awkward.

"I want my swords back," she said.

An abandoned farmhouse stood not far away, one with rough but sturdy walls. With a little firewood and a wipe of a stone table, we had a sparse home for the night. We changed into new clothes provided by Telesilla, and huddled around a true meal: roasted beech nuts, flatbread, a mushroom stew and asimina for dessert. We knew we needed the rest, and I let the heat of the fire warm us to the bone as Asher and I caught her up on what she'd missed.

Her mind kept flashes without context: our first fight, threatening Asher. Mahakal. She had most of the pieces in her mind, if I was patient enough to help her reassemble. When I sat beside her at the end of her questioning, a spark of something deeper than recognition ignited in her eyes.

I had to look away. The fire in the charcoaled hearth didn't shine as bright.

Although the farmhouse was devoid of most furniture, the Asri stone construction held strong, offering us each a separate room. Faruhar surrendered her weapons; we hid them under crates in a dusty pantry before heading for bed.

Alone in my makeshift bed of straw and leaves, sleep eluded me, my mind drifting to the stolen glances from Faruhar. I reminded myself there was no name I could place on that emotion, not if she couldn't remember her name and mine. She remembers those she trusts. I needed to be that friend she trusted.

Still, I was worried about her waking up in a strange room with no one and nothing familiar to orient her except for a few notes she promised to scrawl on the wall with charcoal. Unable to shake my unease, I rose and crept down the creaking hallway. Reaching Faruhar's door, I found it ajar, a beam of moonlight casting through the shattered window. And there she stood, a silhouette scribbling away by the window sill with dark-stained fingers. I don't know why that image stole my breath.

"Faruhar?" I creaked the door open.

She turned to me, relief flooding her features. She looked down, fiddling with the hem of her loose flaxen shirt. "Jesse. I don't know if this is enough—" She gestured to the notes she left on the walls, all of them, and then all over the floor in her scrawl of handwriting.

I bit my lip. "That's gonna be a lot to clean in the morning. We don't want to leave clues behind."

"Right. Sorry." She clenched her eyes tight. "Do you mind staying? Just in case? I know your new face now, so I should trust it even without the reminders."

Her words, so quiet, softened what little resistance I had. "No problem." She sat on the wooden bed frame topped with straw. I sat down on the window seat.

"When we're near a town, can you buy me a new journal and fill it in? I don't like taking risks like this, not when—" The vulnerability in her voice was a siren call. Within a single breath, I stepped forward, the space between us closing.

"I'm not afraid of you." I reached out a hand, hesitant at first, then with a growing sense of resolve. My fingers brushed hers, and her hand trembled for a moment before relaxing in mine, her touch electric against my skin. "You're safe with me."

It took a moment for her to breathe in, to accept that.

She lay down in the straw bed, not letting go of my hand. I settled beside her, watching her every breath.

The firelight from the hearth mirrored the same intensity I felt in my own body. I felt an overwhelming urge to pull her closer, to bridge the gap, but I knew better. I was the friend she trusted.

In the morning, she tightened her hand in mine. I'm not sure I ever let go. Her smile held its place when she opened her brilliant eyes for me. "I still like your real face better."

I swallowed, forcing myself not to make any sudden moves, just in case. "You're safe, Faruhar, I'm Jesse—"

"I know."

I shared the relief that flooded her face. It overcame me too, becoming a bittersweet pang in my chest. "You do?"

"Yeah." She squeezed my hand again. "You stayed in my dreams, even the unnerving ones. It helped that you were so close." A haunted look crossed her face, and my free hand went up to brush that fear away.

A rap at the bedroom door. Asher cleared his throat.

"Come in," I said.

Asher froze in the doorway. Uncertain, he looked between us as we sat up in bed. "You good, Faruhar?"

She squinted at her notes in charcoal on the nightstand. "Asher? Yeah. We're going to Uyr Elderven. You talked Asri rebels into sparing my life, and I'm very impressed by that."

He blinked, then his brilliant smile bloomed. "Thanks. You two up for a little training before we get on the road? We'll need to stay sharp."

Training at dawn, a bit of normalcy. And, well, I needed to get some energy out just then. "Sure thing, Brother."

The clearing by the house bathed itself in the golden light of sunrise. Frost-laden grass crackled underfoot as we circled each other. Faruhar, with her two swords held in a practiced grip, looked menacing, flawless. Ash, in his Chout-disguised face, looked kinda weird.

"Fight to disarm?" she said.

"No injuries sounds good," I said.

We had no training blades. Ash and I wore our Chaeten leather, freshly washed and dried by the fire. Faruhar wore the best armor one might salvage from stripping Noé's dead.

I charged in a blur, disarming Ash in under a minute.

"Get back in here, Ash," Faruhar said, although she disarmed him seconds after he did. After a while, he stopped trying, and I focused on Far.

I surprised myself, rising to her challenge. I found I could match her speed, my reflexes honing to her every feint and parry. But voids, she was so hard to read. It took all my concentration to fend off two limbs that seemed to attack with independent thought, all lightning-fast strikes and agile dodges. I met her like a storm cloud: powerful blows she needed her full rally to deflect. The clash of steel echoed through the clearing, punctuated by the hiss of one of Faruhar's blades slicing my face.

The scent of pine mingled with the metallic tang of blood, but the nick wasn't deep enough to worry about.

"Sorry," she said.

"You will be." I winked, holding my face. "The not ugly face is under here too."

She rolled her eyes at me.

I pressed my attack, forcing her on the defensive. Simmering in frustration, I was unable to land a solid blow. Faruhar danced around all my swings as I pressed hard. She evaded me around a copse of trees.

The forest fell silent. I'd lost track of her, but I knew to look up. My gaze darted through the brush, heart pounding in my chest. Then, a whisper of movement, and a glint of steel. Faruhar came from behind me, her twin swords crossed in a clang across my face, the sharp edge cold on my throat.

"You're too loud," she murmured in my ear, her smoky voice shivering down my spine. "I want you to practice being as quiet as you can." The warmth of her body pressed against mine was too much, almost. My breath caught.

"I can be quiet if you want. I can be whatever you want," I said, not thinking about tracking and silent maneuvers through trees just then. The pressure of her blades eased, and I felt her breath rustle my hair before she turned away, face flushed.

A cough from the edge of the forest shattered the spell. Asher stood there, eyebrows raised in a way that made me think of Taam before a lecture. "I'm going to go make breakfast. You two keep doing your thing."

"Thanks Ash," I said, my voice weak as I went to go pick up my weapon.

Faruhar pushed me to my limit on multiple levels before we walked back to the farmhouse. I went to forage on my own when I couldn't take it anymore, stopping to pick some chicory root for what my dad liked to call "camper's coffee."

Far met me outside the farmhouse with raspberries. Inside, we presented our offerings to Asher, who looked down at pancakes he'd made with ground beechnuts and the last of our flour.

"What's wrong, Ash?" Faruhar eased closer.

He looked up, arms braced on the table. "Just thinking things through."

I dropped my bundle of chicory. "Like what?"

"I made a lot of promises to Telesilla. I need to keep them all."

"Like what?"

"Disabling some of Mahakal's military tech." He shrugged. "I told them I could dissect a fabricator and a code sequencer, so I should be able to figure a magic blocker out."

"Maybe you're overthinking this. Can we bash any of that tech with a sword?" I asked, cutting up my washed chicory for roasting.

Asher huffed. "Subtle as that is, the plan depends on Mahakal not knowing the tech is broken until we move in. Maybe Mira will know how to do it remotely."

Faruhar put her hand on Asher's shoulder. "You'll get it right. Bria believes in you too."

I poured the chicory root onto a firestone, turning it over with my knife. "I can't wait to see Mira again, and I know you two will—work well together again. There's no way she's staying after she hears us out."

Asher looked up, a hopeful smile creeping along his face. "Eleven days to go, I think, if we push hard."

We made it in ten. Looking back, those days were, hands down, some of the best in my life. We trained each morning, and each day I found my body capable of doing something it could never do before. I practiced leading with my right hand, right leg, doing everything backward, just as powerful and fast. We'd practice stealth on the roads and forest paths east, disappearing around corners and ambushing. Faruhar usually got the best of us, followed by Asher, but I persisted, even if Faruhar seemed to always know where I was. I relished each moment when her eyes found mine.

We ate sitting on a fallen log during the first heavy snowfall, our fire overlooking a slate gorge with a gurgling river. We'd camp in ruins, or used the tarp in Ash's bag for hasty shelters, saving our coin for the city. Looting some ruren-sa corpses helped stock our coffers, although I couldn't say the short work of their deaths was my favorite part of the journey. Faruhar would seek out ruren-sa that wouldn't take us too far out of the way, and I knew it was best we'd put their souls to rest.

Each night I'd go to bed with her hand tethered to mine, holding her close. We both slept with fewer nightmares, although I can't say I always slept well. I had some other dreams I couldn't shake when it came to Far. But I remained the friend she trusted. Faruhar would wake unafraid, remembering more each day.

On the last night before we reached Uyr Elderven, Ash was asleep on the other side of the campfire, his chest rising in a slow rhythm. Faruhar lay on my chest as we watched the stars.

"After we kill Mahakal, what's next for you?" I said.

"What do you mean?" Her husky voice reverberated through my chest.

"I mean, what do you want? Take that however you need." I forced my eyes shut tight to keep from staring, to stop wanting to trace each line of those scars.

Her hand tightened in mine as she sighed. "Not everyone gets what they want, Jesse. I came to terms with that a long time ago."

I swallowed. "I haven't."

"Why?" she asked, breathless.

"Tell me the life you want next, and when this is over, I promise I'll help you get it."

Her gaze flickered from my hand to my face, searching for something, perhaps an answer, perhaps a reflection of the turmoil within me. "What do *you* want, Jesse, when this is over?"

My chest fell with a long exhale. "Voids, good question."

"You asked me first," she said, a chuckle in her voice.

"Okay. I want to do boring things with the people I care about and not have to worry that they'll die. I want to stay in Mira's life—wherever she lands. I want to live near Ash and his family. He's too Asri to wait long on starting one." I paused, afraid to say aloud anything I wanted involving her. She'd have to say it first.

"Do you want a family?" she asked.

My heart stuttered. That had always been an easy *no*. "I don't know. Would you ever want that with someone?"

She squinted her eyes, eyebrows raised. "How would that even work?"

I turned to rest my head on my elbow, smiling. "If that's one of the things you forgot about, I guess I could add some diagrams to your journal for future reference, when the right person comes along."

"Voids, you're shameless." She covered her open mouth with her fist. "I'm aware of the ... mechanics."

"Mechanics," I chuckled. "That's a very Asri way of saying it."

"So how would you say it then?" she challenged, and those pale yellow-green eyes cornered me, cut me down.

She smiled at my heated face, eyes glittering in the dark. I closed my hungry eyes, unsure if the thoughts in my head were safe. She traced the line of my jaw with her hand. "I'll rephrase. I shouldn't live with a family of any sort. No one should trust me with a flower garden, let alone a human life."

"Your memory improves more and more each day. You just need people around you can trust, and you'll be fine."

She frowned, haunted. "Jesse. People know what I am with one look. I heal too fast for the best disguises. It's not even safe for me to enter a city."

I sighed. "What about small towns? People will accept you if you give them a chance to see who you really are. We'll work something out."

"We?" The fire crackled.

"Faruhar," I whispered as her hand traced down to my collarbone.

"You have a scar on your shoulder," she said, tracing my skin under my shirt. "From me."

With a shaky breath, I traced a line on her face left by Istaran. "Mine."

Her lidded eyes fluttered. Her mouth parted. Then she froze under my gaze.

"Goodnight, Jesse," she said, then turned her back on me to sleep.

When she reached back for my hand, I held it like a lifeline, a man lost at sea.

CHAPTER 42

Rumors

The cafe in Uyr Elderven bustled with overlapping conversations, bathed in the fragrance of good coffee, not the chicory kind. Asher fidgeted, stealing glances at the clock. "Where is she?" He ran his hand through his short hair.

Ruren-sa continued their attack since Nunbiren. In the shadow of the fourth recent attack attributed to SBO, Noé was in crisis, with many people flocking to the safety of the island capital. We'd entered Uyr Elderven with no issues. The officials were too overwhelmed with refugees and preemptive visitors to even bother scanning our faces into the system. Telesilla's *chout* glamor still held strong on our features.

"Don't worry, she'll be here." I tried to follow my own advice as my gaze kept flitting to the door. I'd helped Asher word the note we left at the hospital front desk for Mira, hoping we'd given her enough clues to accept an invitation from strangers. Ash had claimed we were old friends from Thebos, back in the days when she wanted to start a musical troupe. We'd been in the DM club together, and we underlined those letters before writing Dancing Modtechs—in this case. She could choose the time and place to meet if she wanted to say hello to her favorite waltz partners.

We'd hoped she'd choose somewhere private, but she picked this cafe instead. The place was packed—we were lucky to get the last open table.

"Any news from our *new* friend?" Asher asked.

I knew he meant Telesilla, but anything we said here could be overheard. "Yeah, a note. It said they'd find us at the inn tonight."

The cafe door opened with a ring. Mira scanned the cafe. A halo of dark, textured strands framed her face, gathered at the back over a hospital uniform. Her brow furrowed in apprehension.

Asher waved her over. "Mira, over here." His voice sounded strange, strangled.

Mira's gaze dissected us. Asher smiled.

She didn't smile back, swallowing. "I ... I don't know you."

From his grip on the table, it was all Asher could do not to get up and hug her. "We were ... dance partners from Thebos. Carob and..." he faltered, the weight of the lie a leaden weight he had to whisper his way through.

She blinked at him. "Kian?" Mira supplied. The fake name in our letter.

I leaned forward across the table. "I'm sorry our appearance comes as a shock. We've changed our mods up to something more ... natural since dance lessons."

An intake of breath, the wave of recognition at my voice.

"I know you said I could crash on your couch anytime, but we won't take you up on that today, even if all this death has been a bit ... disruptive." I laughed, trying to sound detached, an inner empire tourist inconvenienced by war. "Are you going to sit down?"

She sat with rigid solemnity, staring at Ash. I smiled when she turned back to me, hoping to put her at ease. Even if we were outlaws now, I never expected her to be ... afraid. But there she was, her hands clenched in her lap.

"Hi," Ash said, eyes unabashedly full of so many more words than that.

Mira's eyes locked to his, flaring.

"We heard about Nunbiren," I said. "Please accept our condolences. We knew you were close to some people there."

A shiver, suppressed. "Thank you," she murmured, faint.

"Have you heard from the survivors in Nunbiren?" I pressed. "We've heard some troubling rumors about the friends you mentioned in your letters, and we are relieved to hear you were safe from all this nonsense."

Mira's eyes darted between us, like a caged animal searching for an escape. But she steeled herself.

The server came; she ordered a light roast coffee; me the same, Ash a blended tea.

"How's your father? Did he survive?" I asked.

"My father? He's..." Mira faltered, her voice cracking. "He's alive. Humbled a bit, since the eviction from office; working in an administrative post across town now. They said he refused help from the barracks before the attack."

"All that is news to me," I said with a mischievous grimace. "But I trust his fate is just. A wise man once told me humility is nobility, and that we should always trust the immortals to do right. I admire a man who knows his place." I exaggerated her father's cadence along with his words.

She closed her eyes, bit away her smile.

"Nunbiren lost so many good people." She slumped in her seat. "It's been difficult for me to process. I heard that Jesse Eirini contracted SBO, that he is either now roaming the wilds in a mad murderous rage or—" She shuddered. "Dead. Honestly, I hoped for dead."

"I've heard different rumors about your friends," I said. "But I'm sure the temple here in the Noé capital knows best."

A patron bumped our table, trying to meander the crowded room.

"What have you heard about the other survivors, like your friend Asher?" Ash searched Mira's face. "I can tell you if that's the same as the rumors I've heard."

She sipped her coffee. "The temple says Asher Eirini joined the Asri rebels, that he's a traitor," she said, her words clipped. "Is that—is that what you heard?"

"Yes." Asher held his gaze steady as Mira's face split into a rainbow of shifting emotions. An entire conversation of glances flitted between them before I nudged Ash under the table.

"Yeah, those rebels are spreading terrible rumors all over," Asher said, successfully disinterested this time. "The Asri rebels say it wasn't Chaeten gangs after all, surprising as it is they missed a chance to pass blame. They are saying it was all ghosts, ruren-sa. The empire is able to predict the movements, get Z'har out, but they aren't protecting the civilians. Mahakal might even be controlling these ghosts, and he's blaming innocent people for all of this, killing them—his soldiers are killing innocent people." Asher's voice broke a little on that, and I watched the reflection on Mira's face, her nostrils flaring.

"Terrible rumors, disgraceful," I added, when a middle-aged lady sitting at the nearest table looked our way.

"I'm sure you feel like you know Ash almost as well as I do from my letters. I miss my old friend very much," Mira said to Asher. "It pains me to think what rumors he succumbed to before turning on his commanders."

"Dangerous rumors indeed, souring minds all over the rural empire," I added with a fresh dose of arrogance. "And I know you admired Major Mahakal so much, from your letters."

"Right." She twitched a smile.

"Right," I said. "The rumors place Mahakal at the center of the cover up, and paint his character in a very different manner than you've described. They're claiming Mahakal was gloating over raping an Attiq-ka, and that he also tried to sexually assault a prisoner."

Mira's face drained of color. "Who?"

"Jesse Eirini." I shrugged.

Both their eyes widened. "I didn't hear that one yet," Asher said.

I grimaced. "Don't believe a word, of course. But these rebels are saying Mahakal tried to kill Jesse Eirini after he saw the truth in Nunbiren," I whispered. "I couldn't bear to listen to the lies beyond that."

The server dropped off our drinks, and I stared at my cup.

"What do you think of all this, Mira?" Asher reached across the table, his hand hovering over hers.

Mira pulled her hand away. "What do you mean?"

I watched as Asher's heart broke all over again. "Tell me," he said.

"Those rumors…" she said, her voice quavering. "The men in these rumors are not the men I knew. I miss both my old friends very much." She took rapid breaths, blinking, earning a curious glance from that woman the next table over.

"So, are you enjoying your time at your post?" I asked, in as light of a tone as I could feign.

"Yes," she said, stiff, too quickly. "I've come to appreciate the opportunity. I've learned a lot, and am able to help more people."

A flicker of hope ignited in Asher's eyes, only to be extinguished as quickly as it appeared when she didn't feed that flame with her gaze.

"That's wonderful. Although I admit we'd hoped you'd say you missed our dance lessons," I said. "Would you ever want to come back to the DM club? I'm sure we could find a place for you near us, even if it's not a post here."

"We miss you, Mira," Asher choked out, the words heavy with unspoken longing, his unabashed sappy goatshit for all the world to see.

Mira took a shuddering breath. "Ah, I do miss our dances in Thebos." She took a sip of her coffee. "There's no going back, but I hope you two stay safe from the violence in Noé." She checked the clock on the wall. "I should keep this short, but it was lovely of you both to check in on me and make sure I was okay."

The weight of her dismissal hung heavy between us. I forced my mouth closed, nodding. Asher reddened.

"There are rumors," Asher hissed through his teeth, "that SBO doesn't exist. That the empire fabricated it all."

He said it just loud enough for a few heads to turn. I shot out a hand, gripping Asher's knee under the table.

Mira frowned, squinting. "It's very real. I've seen the antibodies. Survivors are rare, yes, but we have a sample from a soldier—"

Mira froze, then smiled over my shoulder. "Forgive me, I'm so excited about this subject, but much of what I do is classified now. But I think we can both be sure, based on what happened, that Jesse Eirini didn't have those SBO antibodies." She took a deep breath. "Poor man," she added, a half-hearted afterthought.

I leaned forward on my fists, trying to understand.

"Anyway, that's enough wallowing for one day." Mira's voice regained a brittle cheer. "Have you been to the night market yet? You need to check out some of the food stalls before you leave tomorrow. Are you staying nearby?"

I clenched my jaw. We hadn't mentioned leaving tomorrow in our note. *Was this a warning?*

"We're staying at the Mora Inn," Asher said, his voice cracking. "Do you think you'll have time to see us again?"

Mira offered a pained smile. "No. I'll be very busy before your departure tomorrow. I'm afraid this is goodbye."

Tides of despair pulled my brother away from me. I needed to keep my head above the waves. No, I needed to be his shore to swim back to. Another breath. I folded my own pain and disappointment away as I studied Mira, unable to make sense of this, unable to reconcile how she seemed to mean everything she said to me months ago. She was still family to me, but that no longer seemed to be mutual.

"Well, thank you for making time for us," I forced out, giving Asher a subtle squeeze on the shoulder when he rose beside me. "Good luck with your research, Mira. I'm glad you have found your peace with all this."

Stiff postured, Mira rose from her chair. She laid down enough coin on the table to pay for us all, turning toward the door before we could object. She waved with a polite smile from outside the window. Asher watched her until she disappeared into the crowded street.

Chapter 43

Truth and Fear

My stomach churned as I took another swig of lukewarm ale in the quiet common room of the Mora Inn. After a few such drinks, I'd learned that besides being resistant to lethal poisons, I now seemed to be resistant to the fun ones too. I added that to the list of mysteries, knowing I wouldn't have Mira to help me solve them.

None of Telesilla's people had checked in yet. I'd been nursing this beer for the last hour rather than waste more money.

My thoughts kept drifting to Faruhar, camped outside town, avoiding the city since Telesilla's glamor had failed to work for her. But Asher had volunteered to go check on Faruhar instead, mumbling he needed to clear his head with the walk, so that left me to touch base with the Underground rebels. It made sense Asher needed some solitude after how things went with Mira, and I knew better than to try to say anything to cheer him up.

We'd made sure Faruhar had her fresh journal with a century fabric cover, filled with notes on everything she or I could think of. She insisted we shouldn't worry, reminding us she'd been sleeping alone in the forest long before we came along. Still, I felt a pang when I thought about her waking cold in the snow while I got to spend the night in a warm inn.

The clink of a glass against the table pulled my attention. A dark-skinned man with Asri braids sat down in the seat opposite me, one white braid among the black, his face weathered with the harsh lines of a life spent defying authority. Soren, the Chaeten among the Disciples of Reic. Of all the rebels I'd met in Telesilla's network, I guess I disliked him the least, so I should be grateful.

"How'd you get here so fast?" I'd expected to see a new face. I thought we made good time to Uyr Elderven, leaving him and Telesilla far to the west.

"We have tunnels through the Underground that run right to the city. Functional transport. If you weren't traveling with a Chaeten-sa, you could have used them."

"Well, fuck you too, Soren," I said. His network's bigotry toward Faruhar still rankled.

He rolled his eyes. "Just stating facts. Where's your brother?"

"He's following up on something. I'll fill him in." There were a couple of people on the other side of the common room. "Can we talk openly here?"

"I've kheled off our voices." He directed a soft smile toward the woman at the front desk. "And I'd trust the *ka* here with my life even if they were listening."

"Okay," I started, steadying my thoughts. "What's the news?"

Soren took a long pull from his drink, his green eyes studying me over the rim. "General Alexander is about to get involved in Noé, in light of the recent attacks. He'll be in port within a week, so if we want to make a move, we need to act fast. If Queen Azara hadn't banned his airships, he'd be here already."

"How do you know the General isn't trying to help?"

Soren laughed. "He's killed too many of us to be helpful. Besides, there's a reason he's the Chaeten-sa in charge of the empire forces, and not Mahakal. When he's here, all Disciples of Reic will go dark."

"All right." I gripped the table. "Anything else we need to know?"

"Mahakal has at least one squad scouting the city. He's probably watching your Modtech friend."

The mention of Mira sent a fresh wave of worry and frustration crashing over me.

"Makes sense he'd follow up on the people Ash was writing to from the field," I said. "She wants to stay out of this, though. I hope he'll leave her alone."

He frowned. "You did not mention our name, correct? Nothing she could use to harm us?"

"No," I said, disturbed by the thought. *Mira wouldn't betray us. She couldn't.*

Soren gave a curt nod. "Fine. I need to talk to your brother as soon as possible about bypassing those magic blockers."

I leaned back. "Can you tell *me* how they work? Ash wasn't the only one who kept our fabricator running." Ash was definitely more well-read on physics and mechanics, but I thought it best to project confidence.

Soren's brows furrowed, but he produced a document from his cloak and slid it between us: a technical manual. "The frequency it emits corrupts the Song within the radius of impact. We can't sense it until we connect. Then, think of it like an aeroelastic flutter specific to the delta rhythm. The damage is instant and permanent." Seeing the blank look on my face, he clarified, "The machine emits a specific electromagnetic frequency that triggers neurological arrhythmias that correspond to our *chout.*"

"All right." I frowned.

Soren sighed, throwing his hands up. "Bad machine for magic. It makes our brain hurt. Seizures until sword boo-boos kill us."

"I know what electromagnetism is," I said, a generous claim. I knew enough to repeat most of what he said to Ash.

"Good. Reic would eye-twitch himself into writing a whole new textbook if he knew I had to dumb down Chout Attiq-ka as 'magic,'" Soren said with a huff.

"He must be fun at parties." I took another sip of my impotent beer.

"Where's your brother, again?" he asked, his green eyes sharp.

I shrugged.

"When will he return? If he can bypass the anti-magic machines as he claimed, we can take out the entire unit at once."

I frowned. His implication was clear. They didn't need me or Far.

"I'm sorry, Soren. We need to connect tomorrow. I'll make sure Ash looks through this, though." I leaned forward with the manual in hand. "Do you have a place we can meet outside of town?"

He scribbled down coordinates for a tea shop, passing the paper across the table. "Anything else you wanted to discuss?"

I took a deep breath. The anger simmering inside me since leaving that cafe needed an outlet, and I didn't mind dumping on Soren. "Why doesn't your network just tell the world what's going on? Send encrypted notes, pamphlets, that sort of thing to clear your names? If people knew what the empire was up to, all the military and government corruption would self-implode."

Soren snorted. "Your mind seems like a tranquil place. Maybe all the ghosts who've tried to possess you just got bored and moved on?"

When he wouldn't stop smiling, I slammed my fist on the table. "I wasted years of my life chasing after the wrong enemy. People deserve to know what's happening!"

He leaned back, frowning through an array of facial twitches before he spoke. "I know that feeling—quite well. That's still a naïve political view, though. Fear has more persuasive power than truth, particularly when the truth is complex. Word of mouth about complicated things like 'there are swarms of ghosts on the rampage that neither the Underground nor the empire knows how to fully control'—that's a complex truth. Why should they listen to us if we don't have a better solution? But the fear of those ghosts—"

I crossed my arms, glaring as he gathered his words.

"When the Asri first met our ancestors, do you think it was truth, evidence, that made them recognize us as human? Most Attiq-ka weren't like Reic, embracing us as brothers right away." Soren stared at his glowing hand, flexing and unflexing a fist. "Queen Azara united

Asri and Chaeten to fight the ruren-sa hordes before turning the violence on the Attiq-ka. Fear united our world, not truth. Nothing's changed."

"What are you suggesting we do then? Lie just to scare people?"

He took a sip, shaking his head. "A small truth is fine, one that Azara or Mahakal can't outmaneuver. But we do need to make good *ka* afraid, to focus on one demon's one sin. We make the solution simple: kill the demon. Problem solved."

Tranquil or not, I liked being in my brain better.

"I think we agree on our first small truth. 'Mahakal is bad.' Other powerful people in the empire can get behind that, taking down one corrupt Chaeten-sa. After we act on that message, we can move on to 'General Jeron Alexander is bad,' then..."

"'Kill off anyone with Chaeten-sa code' is not my message, if I haven't made that clear."

We exchanged glares.

"Very well. We agree to one mission together: Mahakal. What can we prove about him that the world should know?"

I ran my hand through my hair. "I know he tried to kill me and he's a rapist, but I don't have hard evidence."

Soren's eyes went distant. "I grew up near the palace in Ea Shadohe, friend. Even if it's difficult to hear, I assure you that all Chaeten-sa are murderers and rapists by design."

"Nope." I stared back, unshaken.

He chuckled. "Have you considered the possibility that you're just not the Red Demon's type?"

"Again, fuck off." I decided Soren was no longer the Underground rebel I hated the least. They all sucked.

CHAPTER 44

Nine

After midnight, Asher creaked open the door to our room at the inn. I sat up in bed.

"She's fine," Asher said, sitting on the bed beside mine and removing his shoes.

"Are you?" I rubbed my eyes.

"Yeah, fine." He stared at the stucco wall. "The night market has some good food, just like Mira said. I brought Faruhar a sticky rice and shiitake thing." He bit his lip. "Then I went back and wandered the night market until it closed, hoping Mira was leaving us a clue. She didn't show up."

"What else did you buy?" I said, trying to bring him back from wherever his thoughts were going.

"Coffee, don't worry." He leaned back. "Did one of the Disciples of Reic check in?"

"Yeah. Soren." I tried to catch him up, but his eyes glazed over as soon as I started talking. "You know what? Sleep on it."

He nodded, making his way to the shower first.

In the morning we settled our bill with the innkeeper, a laugh-lined, fast-moving Asri woman who reminded me of my mom in spirit even though they looked nothing alike.

"Safe travels to you friends, and here—this was delivered this morning." The innkeeper handed us a tight folded square of paper, sealed. Unfolding the note, I read the single, typed sentence: "*I want my last gift back, please. -Mira*"

Asher leaned in, his brow furrowed as he scrutinized the note.

"I don't get it," I said. "Do you?"

"It might not be her. Anyone could type a message..." he trailed off, then his eyes sparked to flame. "The code sequencer."

"What?"

He paced, frowning. "When I traveled here with her before we took our posts, she gave me the code sequencer. But it wasn't like either of us could take it where we were going next. We buried it together in the woods." He gave me a wistful smile. "It's near a moss-covered rock in the woods that looks like a sleeping fawn."

"That reminds me, I buried your century robe and sword in the training clearing outside Nunbiren. You're welcome."

"Focus, Jesse," he said, rubbing the back of his neck. "I'm still not sure what to make of this. Why would she ask for the code sequencer back? She knows where it is."

I shook my head when I came up blank. "Let's get Far first. Bria can scope the area before we check it out."

The smell of street food and horse dung carried on the chilled air as we stepped onto the cobblestone. Turning back down the street, my breath hitched when I saw two figures half a block behind us. They were out of uniform, but I recognized their gaits, the ponytail, the disproportionate heights. Riverhawk and Eight. I hadn't had my coffee yet. Adrenaline would do.

I nudged Asher, keeping my voice low. "Mahakal's spies. Behind us."

Asher looked back with a fake yawn, cursing under his breath. "We still got the *Chout* glamors up, though."

"Well, they're following us."

We quickened our pace, taking a detour through the night market, closed down, but providing enough cover between stalls. We ducked through a couple of stores and cut through an apartment building to shake our spies. By the time we got to a minor side gate, they were nowhere to be seen.

"See anyone else you recognize?" I said as we meandered through a line of travelers on the road. He'd know the faces in Mahakal's battalion best.

"No."

When the road curved, we dove into the dense woods, the canopy closing overhead and swallowing us in a cool, green embrace.

We hiked to Faruhar's camp, silent on the path. I smelled the fire, saw the smoke rising dark from the damp wood. Relief washed over me as I recognized Faruhar's vivid red hair, bright as childhood memories, and met those wing-shaped cat-green eyes that trusted me. There was a subtle shift in her posture, but since we weren't already dead, I knew not to be afraid.

"Far." My smile bloomed. "You're safe. It's me, Jesse."

She dove into my arms, taking my breath away with the force of her hug. I held her just as tight, stroking her hair.

Something between a cough and a laugh escaped Asher's lips. "It's only been one night. Voids."

"Good morning, Ash." She pulled back to give him an Asri salute, but did not let me go. *Fine with me.*

Faruhar's lips curved into a playful smirk, her eyes twinkling with amusement as she ran a finger over my face. "It's good to see your not-ugly face again," she whispered. Her words sparked a flame in me.

Then I froze, looking at Ash's face: his original unglamored face, changed from just a moment ago. *Fuck.*

A whooshing sound. Faruhar jerked away from me, but still too slow. With a sickening thud, a crossbow bolt jutted from her shoulder. Red blood bloomed as her mouth gaped open. She stumbled back as I turned.

Another bolt whizzed past my ear as I whirled around, adrenaline coursing through me. Riverhawk and Eight stood about twenty meters away, clicking the lever to reload the next bolt into the crossbow's chamber.

"Backup, now," Riverhawk screamed into her headset, ponytail swinging. She looked to Ash, charging. "Why the fuck isn't he down?! Backup!"

He?

A primal roar tore from Faruhar's throat. She lunged toward Riverhawk, her own movements a blur of fury as she ducked below their shot. Asher got to Eight, disarming him with a blade thrust and swift kick that sent the crossbow clattering across the forest floor.

"Don't kill them!" I yelled, retrieving Istaran by the campfire. I'd left it with Faruhar for safekeeping while in the city.

Riverhawk lay prone on the ground under Faruhar's blade, but she turned over to face me when I approached, defiant.

Eight, however, furrowed his brows at me, uncertain. "Biohazard?"

"Jesse is fine, asshole."

Riverhawk whipped her head toward me, wincing as that movement earned a shallow cut from Faruhar's blade. "Any engagement might rile him, Eight."

Eight shifted uncomfortably, his gaze flickering between me and Riverhawk. "Eirini should already be down from the blocker, though."

I kept my anger contained. "Is that how Mahakal tried to spin this? Not only am I supposed to be an SBO-crazed monster after testing negative, Ash is now a trained *Chout* mage you can immobilize using a magic blocker? Because if the lies aren't adding up anymore, welcome to the club."

"They attacked us. We should kill them," Faruhar said. "We need to move fast."

Riverhawk accepted that with a proud tilt of her chin. Eight swallowed, his eyes going distant.

"No," I said. "Because if they use the brains I know they both have, they'll realize someone with SBO wouldn't be doling out acts of mercy like we're about to do now. Do I look like a raving lunatic to you?"

Riverhawk's eyes narrowed.

Eight blinked. "Mahakal said Asher is using his magic to keep you under control between battles."

Ash tilted his head at me with a raised eyebrow, letting out one burst of laughter.

"He wishes." I gestured to a rugged-cased gadget about the size of a small coffee machine. Straps snaked out from the sides, designed to be worn like a backpack. "You cleared our glamors with that magic blocker, so you know your machine works. Ash isn't shaking on the ground from a seizure. Do the math from there."

"What about her?" Riverhawk asked, gesturing to Faruhar.

"We need to go," Faruhar hissed to me.

"Call off command, and you both live," I said. "Riverhawk, please."

She stared back, unreadable. With a groan, she touched the device in her ear. "They're evading south, moving fast." She winced at whatever she heard next. "Because we're injured."

I nodded to Faruhar once she released the audio. "You heard her. They need a reason why they can't pursue."

With a nod, Faruhar sliced through Eight's Achilles tendon while simultaneously stomping her knifed boot into the bone of Riverhawk's lower leg.

"Nine, scream quieter. She went easier on you," I said.

He squinted his eyes at me through the pain. "Eight."

"Ninth time you almost died." I ticked a finger up.

He chuckled into another gasp of pain.

"You have about five minutes. They're sending medics to our location," Riverhawk said through her teeth.

"You look about my size. That's enough time," Faruhar said.

"For what?" Riverhawk said.

"Your Chaeten leather, please." Faruhar ripped the crossbow bolt from her shoulder with a grunt. "Can all decent *ka* turn around while I help her out of her pants?"

"Couldn't you have broken my leg af—" Then Riverhawk screamed.

Three minutes later, we raced through the forest with a magic blocker, Faruhar's new set of armor, and two top-of-the-line crossbows.

CHAPTER 45

Fawn Rock

Mist folded between sky and ancient trees. We navigated the mossy path—emerald green, thick as a carpet—muffling the sound of our jog. And yep, the rock at the edge of that clearing did bear an uncanny resemblance to a sleeping fawn. Bria, through Faruhar, assured us we were alone. Far then melted back into the undergrowth and scaled a tree to keep a lookout for any more of Mahakal's soldiers.

Asher dug away the damp soil with his dagger to find the code sequencer, wrapped tight in weatherproof cloth. Asher flicked a switch; the monitor blinked to life. He studied the device like it could talk. "I was hoping there might be a note or something." He peeked inside with a click. "I still don't get it."

My heart ached for my brother, still clinging to hope that Mira meant something other than goodbye.

"We can't go back to the city, Ash. You want to bury it or pack it?"

"I'll give it a funeral." Asher placed it back inside the hole, his shoulder slumping. "It felt more like planting a seed the first time," he said, with the saddest laugh I ever heard.

"Someone is coming," Faruhar hissed from the trees.

"Hide it," I said, gesturing to Ash. "Let's go."

"Civilian clothes, no weapons I can see," Faruhar said. "Female."

"Hold fire," I called up. Asher and I ducked behind the trees.

A rustle in the undergrowth. Silence. She burst into the clearing with a flurry of black hair. A worn leather bag hung from her shoulder, her breathing frantic through tear-streaked cheeks.

I stepped out from my hiding place. "Mira?"

Mira dropped the bag on the moss, her eyes scanning mine before locking onto Asher's. With a start, she was across the clearing, flinging her arms around his neck and pulling his head down to hers. She backed him into a tree, kissing him.

"What did you say to me, Ash? 'Voids, it's only been one day?'" My humor landed at my feet. Not sure they even heard me.

"Jesse, give us a minute, please," Mira said, as Asher turned her head back with fierce urgency, completely oblivious to my presence.

"There's a lot I need to tell you," Mira said a few awkward minutes later. "Both of you."

That's when Far dropped from her branch above our heads, landing with the usual predatory grace. "Soldiers are tracking your friend."

I smiled. "Soldiers are tracking *our* friend."

Mira's gasp ripped through the clearing, eyes wide at Faruhar. Her hand flew to her chest, as if to keep her heart from breaking loose: an unrepentant fear reserved for nightmares made flesh. She backed away, her terror so primal it made my gut clench.

"...Four, either military or police, I'm not sure," Faruhar said, but I'd missed some of her words over all the screaming. Faruhar glanced at Mira and smiled. "Nice to meet you."

Mira gave the smallest possible nod.

"Mira, this is our *friend* Faruhar," Asher said, going to put the code sequencer in his pack. "I'll catch you up, I promise."

Faruhar gestured to me. "We can handle four."

"Go ahead of us, Ashes. We'll catch up to you." We exchanged grinning salutes before they disappeared into the dense foliage. I slung the crossbow on my back, eying the trees.

We gestured to our chosen positions. With the aid of some blades sewn into my boots to match Faruhar's design, we hurled ourselves into the trees side by side, landing silently on our branches, taking aim in easy unison. I smiled at her, heart light despite the danger.

The four armed men moved at a brisk pace, checking the ground for Mira's trail and in constant contact with the comms in their ears. Faruhar gestured to a black bird swooping high overhead: a raven.

I gestured to my legs, arms, shoulder, then down to the men. Non-lethal shots. She nodded.

The first one went down with a roar, the small bolt piercing deep into his thigh. Far had two more on the ground before they reached for their comms. The fourth ducked behind a tree while I clicked the reload, leaning into the trunk to steady myself. Then Far shot down the raven, which shrieked as it fell, flapping and dripping to the ground.

"Touch the comms and you die!" I yelled, my voice echoing through the trees. "We don't want to hurt you!"

The closest two were young, maybe teenagers, faces filled with fear and confusion. While I dropped to a lower branch, Faruhar took to the canopy, running and jumping through the dense foliage. She grappled to the next tree with her rope, making her way to the hidden man.

"The SBO carrier!" one teen soldier shouted. His hand trembled, hovering above his comm.

"Nah, I'm good! I will still kill you if you touch that comm though," I yelled back. "Hey, what do you think the least likely thing someone with SBO would say right now, apart from giving you a chance to live? Have you guys had any coffee yet this morning? I haven't. Perhaps we can sit down over some pastry and espresso, and I could talk about the lies Mahakal has told all of us. Maybe you've figured out a few already..." I kept talking, keeping most of my body behind the angling branch, sounding as casual and friendly as I could. Perhaps I sounded crazy, but not SBO-crazy.

The uninjured man angled his head from behind his tree. I ducked away before his bolt flew beside me.

Faruhar shot him in the neck, just above his Chaeten leather collar. "On his comms. We warned you." His uniform bloomed with life blood as she dropped from the trees.

A dark-featured Asri soldier scooted back, unable to stand with his injuries, fear replacing the initial aggression in his eyes. I took a shot, landing an arrow between his knees.

"It's not that I'm a terrible shot." I pushed the point home by firing a bolt through an asimina fruit hanging between the other two open-mouthed men. "See? Not trying to kill you. Mahakal is lying. I'm not infected with anything. He just wants me silenced."

"The rest of you need to toss your weapons and comms in front of you," Faruhar said. "If we see a light on the earpiece, you die. We both have excellent eyes."

I shimmied down from my branch as they complied.

A soldier with straight black hair contorted his face into a sneer as I destroyed his comm, relishing the expensive crunch. The soldier spat. My lecture had done nothing to change his mind. There was no more time for words, no chance of reasoning with him. I stared into his Chaeten green eyes, deciding what to do.

"Jesse. Time to go," Faruhar said.

I didn't look away from the black-haired soldier. He imagined my end. He'd forfeit this battle, but he wouldn't stop until my friends and I were dead. Dread froze my chest. I should kill him too; get ahead of the risk.

I felt Far's hand on my shoulder. "He did what we asked. It's enough."

As we ran away, I wasn't sure if I agreed. I swallowed the bile rising in my throat. Weeks ago, I'd looked at her the same way that soldier looked at me.

I cleared my head.

There was something about the synchronicity of our pace that made my heart flutter. We'd dodge around a tree to meet with our limbs aligned mid-motion and jumped a log in step. She bounded like a deer over the ground beside me, and I knew by her smile that she took joy in that same tacit rhythm.

In awe of her, I took a branch to the face.

We set our path in an arc, jogging and light foraging, both to throw off pursuers and give Ash and Mira a little time to themselves. When we found them, Mira was ready to give me a proper hello. She ran to me grinning, and my arms engulfed her.

When I turned back, Faruhar shot her gaze away. I meandered over to hug her too.

Her eyes warmed to mine. "Why are you hugging me?"

"Dunno. You looked like you could use one," I said, with a self-conscious chuckle.

"I see what you mean, Ash," Mira whispered.

"I heard that. What *did* you mean, Ash?" I asked.

Asher's eyes darted away, then he pointed to an enclave of rocks with an overhang. "Looks like a good spot for lunch."

Smoke swirled from the frost-damp wood that we coaxed to burn, the scent of smoke mingling with the aroma of fire-baked wild tubers. Far contributed a meaty-textured yellow mushroom we dipped in shortgrain flour before roasting, and Mira supplied a couple of wrapped fruit and nut bars we split in half.

Mira perched on a flat rock across from me, her hand possessive on Asher's leg. "All right." She cleared her throat, her eyes flitting between Faruhar and me. "I said I had a lot to tell you. Easy conversations first. About the cafe—"

"Someone was listening, huh?" I said, finishing a bite.

"Yeah, my Academy Mother was sitting at the next table over." Her voice softened at Asher. "She was relieved by my explanation that you were an old flame who wouldn't leave me alone."

I choked on a sip of water. "Accurate enough."

"Well, I omitted my true feelings on the subject." Mira patted Ash's knee as they shared a smile.

Faruhar scanned the perimeter of the clearing, barely listening. I leaned closer. "Are we clear?"

"No one for kilometers," she told me. We both turned back to Mira.

"Anyway, most of the people I worked with were trained in the newer academies, the ones Queen Azara founded. The Academy I attended established itself decades before the war." Mira bit her lip. "The difference was ... notable. Most of the leadership had a very narrow area of expertise, with no broader curiosity. They'd take anything the empire said on faith rather than apply a scientific mindset. So..." She paused, smirking at Asher and me. "Let's just say their security was also lacking a proper education. They had some equipment and resources I was able to use, off the record."

Faruhar's lips quirked up. "Good for you."

Mira gave a hesitant smile back.

"So," I leaned forward, "what did you find out?"

"Remember that segment in your code with fifty-three repetitions?" Mira asked.

"Yeah, I should be dead. I remember."

Faruhar's head whipped to me.

"I modeled the sequence," Mira said after a bite, a spark of excitement in her face. "You were right, the database is wrong. It's a marker. Not the standard one, but..."

"What did they do to him?" Faruhar said, voice a threat. "What marker?"

"He's okay," Mira said, flustered under Faruhar's gaze. "A marker is ... a tag. Think of it like a comment line in a program."

Far cocked her head, hawklike. Mira shifted backward.

"Okay. Chaeten modtech labs have a way of flagging genes they edit. It might look like code, but it won't make a protein. It just contains notes on what lab made the last change and when. There's an established format all the Chaeten labs use, but Jesse's markers don't use that format, so I missed it until I could dig deeper."

I curled up a leg to my chest, thinking that over.

"So either it's a mistake that no one has caught in centuries, or the empire has it mislabeled in the database intentionally," Mira continued. "I'd have to know who made the last edit in the table to deduce which, but I'm leaning toward the latter scenario."

"I think I know where the mod came from," I said. "My Chaeten dad told my whole family he was a miner. His records show he was a medical lab tech ... in Crofton Mine."

"How is he modded, Mira? Is he in any danger?" Faruhar's voice cut low.

Mira frowned at Faruhar, swallowed. "I didn't get a chance to model them all yet, but those I have ... are positive. Little things that would explain how he responds well to stress, is a decent athlete." She took a deep breath. "I also found near-matches to several older Chaeten mods, pre-Nara old."

"How do you figure that?" I asked.

She drummed her fingers on her knee, no doubt working out how to dumb this down for me. "The original Chaeten refugees were all given an array of mods as soon as they arrived, either because it was necessary for their survival on Nara Mnaet or because the Asri demanded it." Mira sighed up to the sky. "In the right stage of our brain development, any of us could have accepted a soul from Oria if the Tower was still standing." She met my gaze. "Anyone but Jesse. His mind cannot interact with spirits at all."

I rolled my shoulders, taking that in. "I guess that tracks. My dad's favorite bedtime stories were about Attiq-ka coming to kill us, but he mixed in some about Oria coming to kill us to keep things interesting. He probably thought this mod would protect me."

Faruhar stared. I shuffled the gravel under my feet.

"Mira, in the cafe, you said SBO is real," Asher said.

"Ah. That." Mira looked between all of us with a newfound gravity. Reaching into her bag, she pulled out several small vials filled with a clear liquid. "This is an anti-SBO mod. The empire considers this 'experimental,' and all the articles paint the leadership who've taken it as heroes for accepting the risk. Goatshit, I think. It's not experimental at all. The code is straight-forward; it only took me two hours of modeling to be sure I know what it does."

"What does it do?" I asked, squinting at the vial in her hand.

"This mod locks changes to a frequency associated with consciousness resonance. It prevents a code change and does not cause one. I've already given it to myself. I'm certain it's safe. And based on what Ash told me, I now believe SBO summons ruren-sa. This blocks them from entering a mind." Mira handed a vial to Asher.

Asher blinked, wary.

"Normally, I wouldn't be offended if you didn't trust my work. Replicating findings is important." She bit her lip, smiling at Ash. "But everyone in the military's upper ranks and higher Z'har has taken this now. They're all fine." She held out a vial to Faruhar next.

Faruhar hesitated, her gaze dissecting the vial in Mira's hand. Asher opened his vial, and with one last glance to Mira for confirmation, downed it.

"None of those captains have ghosts that already share their mind," Faruhar said. "This would kill my sister. She lives in my mind."

"What?" Mira froze.

"Bria's a nice ghost," Asher said. "She was in my mind once too."

"What?!" Mira said, and then Ash explained.

But I didn't listen. My thoughts whirled.

Faruhar's gaze burned into me as I threw my head back to the snow-laden clouds. "Mira, can you test my code again?" I asked. "Look for infections, new mods?"

"Why?"

"Since the attack on Nunbiren, my body has been weird: good weird, but weird." I hissed out a breath. "I heal faster; poisons don't affect me.

I don't get tired when I run. I keep up with Far in training. Kicked her ass recently, too."

"Not often. And none of that is weird if you're not *sedo*," Faruhar said.

My head snapped up. "I'm no immortal. My parents aged. I look just like them."

"You don't smell *sedo*." She cocked her head.

"You told me I did in the cabin. You specifically said I smelled ' *mostly* sedo.'" I got hung up on the word "mostly" until Faruhar leaned in close, inhaling along my neck, her straight hair shining in front of me as my senses sharpened to her proximity.

A slight smile played on her lips as her eyes rolled back. "Wood, smoke, and sweat. Strong. Isn't that what I said before?"

A heat rose in my cheeks, and I could have sworn I saw a mirror of that in Faruhar's eyes. "Not like that, you didn't."

"I'll get a sample tube," Mira said with a glance to Ash.

Faruhar sat back down, frowning. "Would that worry you? If you found out you were ... like me?"

"I just—I want to understand why it's happening." Rolling off a glove, I opened the cap of the lancet tube Mira gave me. "I don't like that I'm not in control, that I don't know what's going to happen next."

When I looked at her again, her eyes were distant, staring right through me.

"I understand," she whispered. She broke her gaze, darting her head to the sky. Two ravens, as large as the one I once saw perched on Mahakal's shoulder.

"Ash, don't look. We're killing something with a mind," I said as Faruhar drew her crossbow to shoot them down.

CHAPTER 46

Tea Shop

The last slivers of sun rolled away behind the horizon, leaving behind a spill of orange, pink, and violet light. We'd reached the roadside tea shop to intersect with Soren, and I felt like I'd stepped into a much older world than the one I knew. Low tables clustered under and between trees, lanterns flickering atop them. Children scurried and clung to the low branches in the outer courtyard. Among the many cushions on the grounds were living sofas, intricately woven from branches and soft moss. Underneath our feet, Oria shimmered and thrummed low, keeping the garden seats alive and vibrant.

Beside me, Faruhar kept the hood of her cloak up, unsettled to be near so many people. I gave her arm a reassuring pat as I pulled her beside me on one of the living sofas.

"They'll be out in a minute." Asher returned from inside, carrying an open bottle of wine and glasses. "Relax, we're *all* safe here," he said to Faruhar, pouring her the first glass.

Faruhar smiled, but did not lower her hood. Instead, she inched closer to me. I thought about putting my arm around her, kissing the top of her head, but I stopped myself. Mira passed me some wine. I took a hesitant sip, a frown creasing my forehead. "Wasted on me." I turned to Faruhar. "Does wine do anything for you?"

Her hand covered mine as she borrowed my glass for a sip. "If I want it to."

I looked up to see Soren and Telesilla, their pace slowing when they saw Faruhar, now sitting straight-backed under their sharp gaze. Telesilla saluted, then sat down at the end of the table, swinging her lone white braid in front of her.

She dropped a small, folded piece of paper on the table. I picked it up.

"That notice was delivered to nearby temples today, and Mahakal had his birds deliver them to major Asri businesses in the rural areas," Telesilla said. "And from what I understand, he also dropped one in front of the Underground entrance you last used, just after bombing it. Perhaps that last one was more for flair."

I swallowed. "I'm sorry."

Telesilla glared at Faruhar before she shrugged. "No one was hurt."

I picked up the note and read it aloud for the group. "Jesse Eirini and the Red Demon. You have three days to surrender in exchange for the lives of your friends. Asher Eirini and Mira, daughter of Solonstrong and Temar, can both be forgiven. You cannot."

Faruhar sipped her wine, looking between Telesilla and Soren. "Have you betrayed us already?"

Telesilla blinked at Faruhar's raspy voice, the first time she'd heard it. "No. We have kept our word to Asher. That being said, my mentor Reic urged me to be ... cautious with our arrangements."

Asher cocked his head. "Does that mean he tried to talk you out of the whole thing?"

Telesilla grimaced. "I expect his fire will cool when we tell him about the magic blocker you retrieved today."

Soren nodded at Mira, who sat straight, holding Asher's hand. "It's good to meet you," he said in Chaeten. "I'm encouraged to meet another person who escaped a Z'har pledge."

Mira offered him a tight smile. "If you asked me three days ago who was dropping SBO, I would have said you Underground rebels. But I trust Asher's dahn, and he trusts you." She turned to Asher, swallowing. "Watch them closely while I ask them these next questions, please."

Asher focused his attention on Telesilla and Soren.

"Do you have any part in distributing SBO, to anyone? At any time?" Mira demanded.

Telesilla leaned forward, her gaze sharp. "Of course not."

"No, friend," Soren said, furrowing his eyebrows. "No."

Mira drew a long breath. "If I could give you the code for an anti-SBO mod, could you help me broadcast it to other rebel networks in the nine islands, using Oria?"

"I might be able to help get you into an empire field station too," Faruhar added. She turned to Telesilla. "If I get you an ID tag to get you in the door, do you have anyone who could boost Mira's message to a higher security level?"

Telesilla blinked. Soren shifted back in his seat, staring at her as if she'd dropped from the sky.

"Possibly. We have a few people with the right combination of Chout and technological experience," Telesilla said.

"Good," Mira said. "Because if I give you that code, you would have the information to make SBO instead if you chose; to hurt people instead of helping them."

"*Niire Mai,*" Soren said, touching mind and heart. "I have only killed demons."

"Demons like her?" I nodded my head to Faruhar.

Soren swallowed. He moved closer, then reached out a glowing hand to her.

Faruhar stared at it, her body trembling beside mine.

"What's this?" I asked.

"I won't harm you." he offered his hand again.

Faruhar sat rigid, her hands shoved under her legs. "He wants to see inside my mind." Her gaze darted to me, fear in her eyes. I remembered Bria's frantic warnings, the fear that choked her voice when she spoke of Reic finding out about her. No one with a sword would scare Faruhar. Soren's glowing hand did, so much that she wouldn't tell him to fuck off herself.

"Why do you need to see inside her mind?" I said, my voice low and dangerous.

Soren flinched, his glowing hand retracting. "Just to understand. I want to trust her too."

Faruhar's lips tightened into a thin line. Then, with a start, she reached out and grasped Soren's glowing hand in hers. He jolted as if shocked, his brow furrowing. Faruhar's hand pulsed with a faint blue light. The glow from Soren's hand sputtered and died, leaving his eyes wide with disbelief.

"You can block me out," he said, his voice barely above a whisper. "Who taught you that discipline?"

Faruhar shuddered. "An Attiq-ka tried to train me once. Didn't work out."

Telesilla sat forward, whipping her braid over her shoulder. "Who trained you? To my knowledge, no one but the queen's mentor Marles has ever made progress with a Chaeten-sa."

Faruhar stared back, her jaw clenched. "Isn't Marles on the list of people the Underground wants to kill? Why give you another name?" Her gaze flickered to me again, a silent plea for help.

"None of this is your voided business," I snapped. "We're here to take Mahakal down. Can you trust her to help with that, or not?" When they delayed, I eyed the gate, the sunset road. I grabbed Faruhar's hand and stood.

"All or none," Asher said, with a nod to Faruhar and me. "You can keep the magic blocker when I'm done modifying it. We'll also make you as many anti-SBO mods as Mira's machine can produce. Or, with respect, we leave now."

Mira smiled, her eyes glowing at Asher as she took a sip of wine.

Telesilla's jaw clenched. Soren, however, continued to stare at Faruhar, his brow wrinkled in thought.

Faruhar squeezed my hand. I squeezed back.

"We will trust you all," Telesilla said, with a curt nod to Soren.

We let out a collective sigh. Telesilla ordered us dinner as we hashed out ideas.

"We need to plan the wording on the anti-SBO message carefully; ensure people trust it," Telesilla said a while later.

"Perhaps we pick someone credible and announce that they endorsed it?" Mira said.

Hums of disagreements from Soren and Ash.

"Who else do you want to kill?" Soren's voice was low and measured.

Crickets chirped, and children laughed in the nearby trees. I exchanged a confused glance with Asher. Mira, however, seemed to understand where he was going with this.

"If you give someone credit for this—generosity," Soren explained, "General Alexander may not believe them when they say they weren't involved in our hack. He's not known for his patience. He'll hunt them down. So, who do you want to kill?"

"No one. I'm trying to prevent more suffering," Mira said, her voice firm.

"Perhaps we are overthinking it," Asher said. "It only takes a few people to try it and confirm the mod works. Even with no name attached, word will spread."

Soren shook his head in disagreement. "Not everywhere."

Telesilla nodded. "Tomorrow. We'll sleep on this and discuss more then." She scanned the group. "But we must strike in two days, before Mahakal's ultimatum, before the General's ships arrive."

We nodded.

"Our network is willing to host you here. There are rooms above the tea shop." Telesilla eyed Mira and Ash, no space between their thighs on their moss settee, and then flicked her gaze at Faruhar and me. "Two rooms are sufficient, I assume?"

"Thank you," Mira said, when the rest of us delayed.

CHAPTER 47

Yield

It had been almost two weeks since Faruhar and I had been alone together.

In the inn above the tea shop, I opened an oak door to see a bed more luxurious than any I'd ever slept in—huge, with a thick down comforter and way too many pillows. Across the room was a large stone bathtub big enough for two, with no curtain to shield it from the rest of the area. I froze just inside that door, wondering how that night would end, studying her for any clues as to how *she* wanted tonight to end. Faruhar *could* have asked for another room. She didn't. Heat crept up my neck.

She stood by the sink, her back to me, running water. "Not the hospitality I expected from the Underground." She went back to washing her face with a sigh.

Wondering if she wanted privacy to wash anything else, and too pigeonshit to ask, I told her I was going to go downstairs to ask about towels.

There were enough towels.

Just outside, I pinched my eyes tight, considering banging my head on the wall to clear my thoughts. I concluded Faruhar would hear that if I did.

A woman cleared her throat.

I opened my eyes to find Mira watching me with a blushing smile. Relief washed over me, a lifeline thrown into the churning sea of whatever the fuck my brain was swimming in.

"Jesse," she said, a small bag in her hand. "I ... I'm glad I caught you. Ash told me not to meddle, but prepare yourself for meddling."

She pulled a small vial from that bag, her eyes darting between me and the closed door to my room.

I took the vial, its smooth glass cool in my palm. A label with typed script read "Silphium Y." My eyebrows shot up. "Is this what I think it is?"

"Probably." She bit her lip. "Shuts down fertility until you're ready to make Galen proud. I suspect he already picked out names for all your future children in his head."

A huff of laughter escaped me, then an incoherent sound. I shook my head, gesturing back at the room. "She doesn't... She hasn't..."

Mira's lips twitched, and she covered her smile with her hand. "It takes twenty minutes to be functional."

My cheeks burned. With a sigh, I uncorked the vial and downed the potion in one gulp, my thoughts as murky as it tasted.

The thing was, I was in deep shit, my thoughts more derailed from reality by the day. I'd been overthinking things, like how it was Oria that sealed Asri marriages, and I doubted the bionetwork was in the habit of blessing marriages for people it tried to kill. I took a shuddering breath, reminding myself I was the friend Faruhar trusted, someone she found "not ugly." That's all I had. I didn't know if she wanted to see me at all once this mission was over.

I wanted to crush that vial in my hands.

"Thanks, Mira. Tell Ash I'll wake him a little before dawn for training."

"Absolutely not," she said, turning away.

Laughing, I said goodnight, then retreated into my room.

Our room.

I kept my back to Faruhar, hesitating with my hand on the door-knob. "Safe to turn around?"

"Yes."

Whirling around, I froze.

There she was, perched on the edge of the bed, wearing Riverhawk's black Chaeten leather underneath her studded leather vest, her hair pulled back in a tight ponytail. She glanced up, expression intense as always. "I just got most of the blood off the pants. Up for night training?"

"Sure," I replied, letting out a breath.

We started into the starlit woods from either end, the game familiar. Far won the first two rounds as always, tracking and ambushing me in hand-to-hand combat before I found her. I felt confident as I started round three, rolling my feet over the ground to make no sound. For one, my night vision was more advanced than hers. For two, I'd gotten much better at predicting her next move.

She didn't like to be exposed on the ground. She'd strike from above in the tall trees unless there was a crevice to pierce from, and I searched for one that fit her style. From the branches, there were only so many ways she could descend safely. When I saw the branches on the way down, I could predict how she'd drop. So if I could spot her first, she was mine.

Then there she was, her outline bright enough to break through the grayscale, although I kept on pretending I didn't see a thing. I searched to the sides, checking empty bushes and brush, and walked under the tree to give her the moment she wanted. When she fell from the trees to take me, I shifted to meet her, using her momentum against her to pull her hard into the ground. She fought for her freedom, and lost.

"I have you," I said with a grunt, holding her against my body. She tried to break away, rolling us down the hill, but I held on, tangling with her until a tree stopped her fall. When her body hit the trunk, I hissed in a breath, and moved to cradle her head. "Fuck, are you okay?"

She kneed me in the jaw, then laughed at me.

But I reacted fast, wrestling until I pinned her lean body under mine, with her hands over her head. She looked up with wide eyes and mouth parted as I ground her to her place, not giving her a moment's reprieve. I grinned. This was the first time she was fully and truly at my mercy. I thought she'd glare and curse at me, but she just stared back, drinking me in, unused to defeat.

Or maybe she was speechless because I was a man, and I straddled her body with my hips lined up to hers. Could just be that.

Fuck, I needed to keep my focus. "Yield," I demanded.

I watched her chest heave under me, her panting breaths. My blood heated as I studied her face, so close to mine, lit by winter stars, and yet this was the edge of danger, where I knew I could fall and fall and never hit an end.

"I yield," she whispered with a hint of a smile, her tone only drawing me closer, making me want more.

When I released her arms, I expected her to scurry away, probably get a hit in for good measure. But she sat up, crawling backward a step to rest her back against a tree, trailing her feet inside my thighs as she did. She watched me, curious. I waited for her to push me away, to regain that cold focus, perhaps say something dry and sardonic to put me in my place. I was her friend, the one she trusted, nothing else. But the way she looked at me now, the subtle parting of her mouth, had me entranced.

"Jesse," she said. My eyes closed with the pleasure of my name on her lips.

That edge I mentioned. I was fucking over it.

I leaned into her, trailing my hand over her lips, questioning. She exhaled into my hand.

I brought my lips to hers, and she opened for me slowly, trembling in surprise. I tasted her desire as her hands came up to cradle my neck. She hummed as my tongue penetrated her mouth, and I fought to claim her, relishing her surrender even as I capitulated my desires to her. Faruhar laid her scarred palm across the muscles of my chest, her thumb trailing. She kept demanding, pulling me closer, her hand bold on my back.

I stood, taking her with me, not wanting to break the spell and risk a moment without her body against mine. When she arched into me, I rolled my hips forward to meet her. She groaned, leaning in. I drew one hand down over her shoulders and the kiss deepened, feeling the curves of her body under the armor. Way too much armor.

My hands moved down to her waist, my fingers probing just at the bottom clasp of her bodice. I searched for any rebuff, only for her arms to lace around my neck tighter. It only fueled my hunger when she shivered against me, her head to my neck.

"Jesse." She kissed my collarbone. "What are you doing?"

I could only laugh at that, holding her head to mine before I had to lift it and kiss her again. Words were hard; so was my cock. I smiled into her next slow kiss. "No idea."

She pulled my head away to look into my eyes, and I relished every detail of her beautiful scarred face under the moon and stars. "That's not reassuring."

"Far, do you want me?" I asked, knowing she did, believing it was as simple as that. I wanted her—this. It was impossible for me to pretend otherwise a moment longer. I moved my mouth from her lips, down to her neck, kissing, tasting.

She removed the last clasp from her studded bodice and pulled it over her head, unleashing her hair with it. I took that as my answer, mesmerized by how that hair cascaded around her shoulders and how her nipples peaked their tips under her linen undershirt. I flitted over those nipples with my hands, and her head rolled back as I cupped them through the shirt, my breath fogging the winter air.

Together we lifted that shirt up over her head to free beautiful, perky breasts that took my breath away. For a moment, all I could do was stare.

"You're beautiful, Far ... the most beautiful thing I've ever seen," I said, voice shaking as I dipped down. I gripped her back and swirled my tongue over a perfect mound of flesh. I gripped the other and massaged it between my fingers as she writhed, pressing into me with a soft moan. "Faruhar, do you want me?"

"Yes," she whispered, and I kissed harder at that. She rolled her hips to meet me. "I want you so much you should hate me for that alone."

"Tried hating you already. I'm terrible at it." I massaged those perfect little breasts one more time before I let go. My cock pulsed against my Chaeten leather pants, aching to be free. I stripped off my shirt, oblivious to the cold.

I know she'd bandaged me up before, but she studied my chest like she'd never seen it before—running first her hand then her mouth over the scar Ash gave me—licking and kissing over my heart and down, down. When her hands grazed over my leashed cock, I growled low. She stroked a shivering finger over the fabric of my pants, up the length of me. I closed my eyes so tight I saw stars.

She pulled away—without warning.

I felt like the ground fell away beneath me without her touch. Then I saw the tears reflecting those beautiful eyes.

"How can this be real?" she said. "You're—good, perfect."

I stepped closer, too slow to spook her. I cupped her face, tracing the maze of thin little scars with my thumb. "Far, I—" My voice gave out before I let out too much. All the secret desires that had yet to fade, promises I'd already made whether she'd heard them or not. I couldn't risk sharing the intensity of that to frighten her away.

"This isn't real," she said, voice husky. "If it is, you'll regret this."

"Will you?"

"No. But you should."

I smiled, leaning in for another kiss. "No."

She shivered, leaning into every touch in the winter chill with closed eyes. After only having her in my dreams and fantasies thus far, this felt just as unreal to me. And with each kiss, each touch...

"We'll make it real."

"I've hurt you too much to touch you like this. I killed—"

"Far," I growled, and tried to kiss her guilt away on the line of each scar. "I know. I can take it. You don't have to think about that now."

She sighed into my mouth, giving me access.

"Please."

"Just tell me this isn't insane," she whispered into my neck. "I trust you."

"Far," I said into her hair, my hands drifting in low circles down her back. "This is real. If you want me, I'm yours." *Always*, the part I knew not to say.

I watched her fear melt away.

"Far, you're safe." I raised her chin. Maybe she'd meet my eyes to see through all my secrets, all the things I couldn't say, and not push me away. "Yield?"

She let me kiss all her tears away. "Yield."

I could have cried with joy, and maybe I did. It surprised me how someone who fought with so much cold cunning could be gentle and malleable to my touch. It wasn't what I expected from her, but my cock responded to that contradiction with a throb. The hunger in her eyes was undeniable when I went to unleash her belt buckle with a clink. Her pants dropped to the forest floor. I wanted, needed, to be the one to taste her first. I dropped to my knees in front of her, a hand caressing her navel before I freed her from the last soft layer of fabric. She helped me, shrugging everything off to stand before me—a golden, stunning perfection. The lips of her labia parted like a budding flower under the moon.

I'd always thought that the first time I touched a woman would be as fumbling as the first time I touched a man, infinitely more so. On some level, I knew everyone would be different in how they wanted to be touched and tasted, whether they would lead or follow, but at least with a man I'd know where to start.

I hesitated, looking up at her from my knees.

"I don't think I've ever done this before," she confessed, running her hands along my jaw. "Any of this. Is that okay?"

I chuckled into her navel, tracing my fingers between her thighs with a feather light touch. She hissed in pleasure, so I did that again. "You're my first … woman."

She just smiled in relief, and I didn't let her say any more. With that first taste of nectar between her thighs, my fears melted away; her taste was a drug I got lost in. I lost all my inhibitions, listening for the change in every breath with every slow stroke of my tongue, every nibble.

She opened her legs wider, giving me room to explore. She bloomed for me as I arced my mouth, fluttering a kiss at her clit, my cock throbbing as she gasped above me. I buried my face between her thighs, unable to get enough. Her growl vibrated my face as my hand trailed up her body. I kissed and sucked until she closed her eyes, loving every sound she made.

"J-Jesse." Her hand in my hair was as gentle as I refused to be, reading her every gasp and twitch. She had enough of gentleness, responding when I attacked her bud with my tongue, bringing my hands around her to knead the muscles of her ass. She gripped the tree for balance, her thighs quaking around me. I looked up at her face lost in pleasure, and I was almost overcome right there. I had to close my eyes, focusing on the rise and fall of her breasts.

"Tell me what you want." I ran my chin against the soft, smooth skin between her thighs. "I'll give you anything you want."

"Y-You," she said.

I fluttered my tongue against her again, drifting one finger up and down her leg, tracing the trail where she'd dripped for me. I meandered up her leg, following that sweet drop all the way home, hesitating at her opening before deciding to swirl my tongue around it. I pressed one finger in, slow. She gasped.

"Me what?" Her walls were slick and warm around my fingers. I imagined my cock gripped there instead. But she was so tight around just that one finger. That wouldn't do. I worked the finger in and out.

"You, just you. Voids," she said, only after I pulled away.

"And what if I want too much," I growled against her, forcing in a second finger as she gripped me from within. She was still so tight. I needed her ready for me. She leaned into the tree, her chest heaving in quick gasps.

"I want too much, Far." I released her to grip her hips and devour her with my mouth once more. When her knees buckled and I worried she would lose her grip on sanity, I guided her down to the moss beneath a tree and positioned my face back between her legs, my fingers back into her. Her walls pulsed around me as I picked up a pace, thrusting harder. I could see her holding back with everything she had, gripping the tree, staring down at me in wonder. "Don't fight me, please yield." My teeth scraped along her inner thigh before I came back home, those taut muscles clenching with every thrust, and I heard her incoherent whimpers with every gasped breath.

"Yes," she whimpered.

"Yield," I demanded.

Her breath came in sharp little gasps as she arced from the ground. Her fingers clenched in my hair as she came for me.

I kissed her bloom with a smile, unrelenting as she cried out under me. She tried to pull back, shivering under my touch. I pushed the edge of her wave, building it higher, higher. She fell apart beneath me, her scream echoing in the woods. I made comforting sounds, letting her come down just enough, refusing to let go completely, refusing to ever let go.

"I want more Far," I growled, dipping my face down again.

Her back arched, as I had her come undone again on the floor of that forest, writhing under me until she sobbed with joy.

I pulled back, my fingers glistening with the proof of her pleasure, as she leaned back against the tree, gasping for air, her pert little breasts heaving.

"Jesse," she begged, looking down at me, but I lost myself in the simple joy in her face.

I swallowed. I wanted to see that look on her face forever.

"Please."

"Please, what?" I kissed my way back up her body.

She growled, then sat up, using every bit of her strength and speed to remove my pants, freeing the fabric covering my erection. Only when I was nude and wanting before her did she freeze, eyes wide as she looked between my cock and my face, hungry. She ventured one hand, then another to touch me, feather-light. I shivered.

"Good?" she asked, studying my face for the answer.

She could read me so well. I groaned in response as she gripped tighter.

She knelt before me, looking up with those beautiful eyes before her open-mouthed gaze flitted to my straining, pulsing erection. She stretched a finger up my length, cradling my balls with her other hand, bringing her face closer before her hot breath surrounded me.

"Voids, Far," I choked out, as she swirled her tongue around the head of my cock. "Slower—I'm so close already, Far."

She swallowed me slowly, halfway, cleaning every bit of pre-cum on the way back.

"Good?" she asked around a mouthful of me. I choked out a guttural sound as she swallowed me whole with relish.

"Fuck," I said, lost in the feel of her warm mouth surrounding me. "No, tonight you're mine." When she released, I wrestled her down below me again and spread her thighs with my knees, watching her face glow under my touch.

She gave my cock one slow stroke by her entrance as I hesitated, overcome with anticipation. But the moment her eyes grew wide under me will be frozen in my memory forever. We claimed each other, her slick walls gripping so tight around my tip I made myself stop, wait, pull back.

"More," she said, begging. I hungered for her, gripping her hips as I pressed forward, deeper. Again—halfway and already too much—I retreated, feeling her tense in surprise, wondering if I hurt her.

"Jesse." She said my name through clenched teeth, gripping my ass and pulling me down to the hilt, surrounding me with her heat. Her hand flew up to my face as we both cried out. She'd wanted all of me, taken all of me, and it meant so much that she did. I lost myself in those beautiful, miraculous eyes, her little smile.

I kissed her as I pulled out, and she held onto me so tight. Another slow thrust, and I needed her face to mine just as I needed all of her around me, joining me. We found a slow rhythm, and I watched the pleasure build with every perfect fit. She wrapped her legs around me, her fingers gripping my ass as she welcomed each stroke.

The way she moved with grace and power had always made everything inside me stand taller. But this hunger, her uncertainty—she'd let me close enough to see this. I would drive that fear away—all her self-hate. I would fill her with all the pleasure, be her hope—all the—voids. My mind blurred, and I don't know what came out of my mouth as I gave my body and soul to her, riding the edge of our wave before falling to the point of no return.

"Far, come with me," I said, between short, sharp breaths as I started a steady rhythm, my hips snapping with all my force.

She gripped me, pulling me deeper, deeper. "Wait for me," she rasped out. "Please."

I slowed, but hit harder, kissing as she thrust up at me. My tongue danced with hers, and she fought back hard, claiming my mouth, gripping me from within, driving me so close. I reached between our bodies, claiming a breast, drawing my hand along her heart, then lower. Her mouth opened in a silent scream as I found her clit, kissing her through a thrust. I felt her walls grip me so tight. I couldn't hold back.

"Jesse—"

"Yield."

She broke apart under me as we came together. The muscles in my back strained as I spilled every last thought into her with one last pounding thrust. She clenched around me, pulling me in to join her.

Far held me tight and did not let go as I collapsed, helpless into her arms.

"Jesse." She stroked my hair where I lay lost over her fluttering heart.

Her heart pounded a steady rhythm in my ear, while the locks on all my promises came loose. "I'm here. I'll always be here." The truth, and yet not all of it as her body gripped me in her aftershocks. She came again in my arms just from those words, her eyes crescents of pleasure as I stroked her face.

I couldn't move, couldn't break the spell where I was just a man, lost in happiness, and she...

She—Faruhar, the Red Demon, was the one I wanted, and I wanted her in a way I never thought I'd want anyone. I would never have enough, and she would always be enough. I would give my last breath for her happiness. That revelation, bright and unafraid of the winter dark, chased away every fear, leaving only the joy of her. She was happy; I'd made her happy.

With a laugh, I kissed her again, my head spinning. She smiled into me, tracing my back with her fingers, in the cool wind.

"You're everything to me, everything," she said, forehead into mine. I watched her eyes light up like twin suns, a proud smile on her lips. "No matter what happens, remember that."

"Put that in the journal just in case," I said.

"I—I won't need to."

My thoughts were stormy seas. I watched her smile ebb as I faltered—surrendering to the waves. Her eyes grew more full and uncertain as I fought my way up for air.

"Far, I love you," I said, using the Asri word—the one that means forever.

CHAPTER 48

Surrender

After leaving the cold forest behind, we knew we needed to rest in that warm and inviting room, to recharge and focus on defeating Mahakal. We also knew this time was finite. This might be the only chance I had to love her like this, before I joined the void with no regrets. We didn't sleep much that night. Sunlight, pale and tentative, fought its way through the curtains. I stirred, my muscles sore with welcome satisfaction. Faruhar nestled beside me. I brushed the hair from her face, expecting her eyes to flutter open with the usual fog—but she met me with startling clarity. A slow smile warmed the space between our faces.

"Faruhar, you're safe—"

She cut me off with a kiss, pulling back with eyes ignited. "I know."

She reached for my hand on her cheek. I let out a soft sigh as she kissed my hand, trailing the other over my fluttering heart.

"Everything is clear."

I asked her questions to make sure, the things she normally lost. She remembered Riverhawk and Eight, despite them being too unimportant to record in her journal. I asked her which wine she ordered last night, a trick question, since Mira and Ash showed up with it. She remembered.

"How?" I asked.

She shook her head. "I'd ask Bria, but she's not around."

My head cocked.

"I don't think she wants a front-row seat to my thoughts right now."

Her gaze locked on mine, heavy with unspoken desire. I leaned over her, my lips hovering a hair's breadth from hers.

It was well into late morning before we made it downstairs.

Mira and Asher had set up their workroom in the office, just outside the kitchen. Asher, hunched over a desk, organized meticulous piles of screws and pieces into rows, scribbling in a notebook. Mira, hair a wild halo around her face, tapped away at a tablet beside the code sequencer, with a tray of empty tubes beside it. Soren entered with a crate, bottles of biochemical substrates, and cleaning supplies.

Faruhar crossed her arms. "Is there anything we can do to help?"

Soren set the crate down. "I don't know. Practice killing demons. Telesilla will be back in a couple of hours."

"We did some training last night, but I suppose we could head back to the woods for more," Faruhar said, her voice rougher than usual.

I smiled at her, heat rising in my neck. *Voids, this Chaeten-sa was insatiable.* Then I caught Asher levying me Taam's pre-lecture glare.

"What?" I said, as nonchalant as I could manage.

"I just thought once you two ... became a couple, you'd stop..." he said, offering vague gestures between the two of us.

"'Eye-fucking' is the term you're looking for, Ash," Mira said.

Faruhar glared. Soren found somewhere else to be.

Asher sighed his agreement to Mira. "Yeah, you two are worse than before."

Mira snorted. "If the offer is still open to help, grab some coffee and help label these mod vials."

A day later, we huddled together like dying embers in a fire, just outside the town where I would turn myself into Mahakal. That was the best plan we had.

Ash wore Istaran on his back, his eyes steady on the snow-laden sky. Faruhar stood statue-still and tense, her eyes imploring me to back down. I'd left my Chaeten leather behind, unarmed.

We'd debated this plan a hundred times since yesterday, each iteration leaving a sour taste in my mouth. Mira and some tech-savvy rebels were already infiltrating a field station to do their part. Telesilla stood with us, tall and steady, as we prepared for ours.

"I still think we should wait," Faruhar said.

"Again, neither the Underground nor you have a location on Mahakal," Telesilla said.

"Then I'll go," she said. "Jesse can track me with Istaran."

I shifted in the cold. "They'll kill you outright, Far. They're more likely to question me first. Ash agrees."

Ash grimaced, eyes to the ground.

"Just be fast, Faruhar," I said. "Listen to those ghosts and come save my ass."

She clenched a fist at my choice of words, eyes going distant. I regretted letting some of my fear peek through.

"It's time. Say your goodbyes and take positions," Telesilla said, her hand going to her forehead, glowing a soft blue.

I offered her an Asri salute, heart and mind. "Thank you for your help, Telesilla."

I squeezed Faruhar's hand, pulling her head to mine. Pain flickered in her eyes as I brushed a reassuring kiss to her lips.

The warmth of Asher's hug was grounding. I gave Istaran a pat as well.

"Stay safe—I want you among the living at my wedding." Asher's eyes twinkled.

"Please tell me you'll give Mira at least a month before you propose again."

He laughed, a hollow sound despite joy in his eyes. "Brother, I already said yes. Telesilla said she'd do the ceremony as soon as this is all over."

"Voids." I had to choke my laughter into my hands to stay quiet this close to town, but I turned him around by the shoulders. "I'll be there."

"Faruhar, I want you there too, of course," Asher said, turning to her.

"Sure. Oria can only kill me below ground." Faruhar's bittersweet smile bloomed as she looked between me and my brother.

Telesilla nodded.

I took a deep breath and turned toward the little settlement, where lights twinkled on the stone gates in the misty morning.

I gave it a few minutes so the others could take their positions, my heartbeat pounding in my ears.

I entered the frosted clearing, giving a friendly nod to the guards. Removing my cloak, I shook out the blond curls I knew were on my wanted posters in the temple. With every casual step, with any words they let me speak, I planned to contradict Mahakal's lies.

Nearing the gate, I looked up to see the guard's crossbow trained on me. "Hi! Good morning! My name is Jesse Eirini. I'm here to—"

A crossbow bolt ripped through the air, stealing the air through my lungs where it landed with a thud in my chest.

My breath hitched as I crumpled to the ground, the bolt pressing deeper into my chest with a kaleidoscope of pain.

CHAPTER 49

Prisoner

My world blurred at the edges of the dark, my head pulsing. Pain lanced through my chest with each ragged breath. I forced my head to clear and hauled myself up from the floor, only to feel cold steel chains binding my wrists and ankles. A dank chill wove through the fabric of my undershirt and pants.

I'd been unconscious long enough to lose my sense of time. I pushed through the haze, realizing my wound would be a clue. No arrow pierced my ragged shirt, but my chest burned with each breath. I couldn't feel a bandage against my skin; it felt like my shirt clung to me with dried blood. A day? Hours, I decided—not days—but the darkness here was so thick I could practically choke on it. Even my eyes couldn't see with no light at all.

Long, fearful hours passed before footsteps echoed through the stone. The light from the door blinded me as an outline solidified. My eyes adjusted to the electric brightness overhead. Major Mahakal, wearing his glimmering raven-wing armor, smiled down at me, patronizing and hungry.

I knew then—with a hollow drop in my gut—that Plan A had failed. Although we'd planned for my capture, the Disciples of Reic were supposed to attack Mahakal en route to collect me, or attack on the road after he took me prisoner.

"It brings me pleasure to see you humbled, friend," he drawled, cold as the room.

I brought my head up, nodding at his pants before his face. "I'm sure it does." My voice sounded dry and weak to my ears, but I forced a smile. "How have you been, friend?"

His black eyes, devoid of any warmth, met mine, and I could not hide my shiver.

He crossed his arms, the silence heavy with malice. "The deal I offered you was yourself and the Red Demon in exchange for amnesty for your friends. Why didn't she turn herself in?"

"Ask her yourself."

He gave a feral grin at that, black eyes glittering. "Did she think she could track you here? How would she do that? We checked you for both tech and Asri magic, and found nothing." He stared a minute more. "Her ghost, I imagine."

I clenched my jaw. I steeled myself to remain silent as he unclipped his sword.

"Or maybe it's that nose of hers, sniffing you out like the mutt she is," he said, lowering himself down to get a good look at me. He gripped my chin, assessing, then ran his fingers through my hair. "But you're no mutt, are you, friend?" His low voice tickled my ear. "You just lack proper training."

He ripped my shirt away from the wound, reopening the scab that healed against the fabric. I closed my eyes tight through the pain, hating that hand under my chin most of all—his shushing tone, the gentle way he drew a finger down over my throat.

When I opened my eyes, I saw a predator savoring a meal. "Kane, get in here, please."

The door creaked open. Fuck, it was *that* Kane. When we'd sparred behind the forge, I'd thought his seastorm and gold Asri eyes captivating, his smirk something I couldn't wait to kiss away. I wanted to vomit as he studied me with that same smile.

"Kane, you have some history with our friend here," Mahakal said. "Does he strike you as someone who breaks under pain? He's too proud for what we have in store for him. He'll need breaking in."

Kane licked his lips, staring down at me. "I'll break him in however you want."

I tried to laugh in his face, but my lungs burned, wheezing out a stutter.

"That wasn't what I asked, Kane," Mahakal said. He slammed his knee into my ribs, and I let out a guttural sound, falling with a shudder over the area of impact.

"Fuck you," I spat.

"Yeah, that just sounds time-consuming to me. You want a turn?" Mahakal asked Kane.

I didn't expect him to go through with it. But Kane landed a stinging blow across my back with the flat of his blade. I kept my knees under me, my head trained on him.

"Fuck you too, Kane," I said.

"I see what you mean." Kane leaned against the wall. "But he deserves the pain."

"True. This is justice. He and the mutt killed good men, powerful, loyal soldiers," Mahakal said, his black eyes twinkling down at me. "Please gather the equipment for him, Kane."

My heart stuttered. When he left, Mahakal just stared down at me, with an expression I once mistook for caring.

"Does Kane know what you are really doing?" I wheezed out.

Mahakal moved closer. "Everyone in my squad is intelligent enough to understand how complex and fragile our world is, that difficult things must be done for the sake of our future. Kane appreciates my efficiency in releasing SBO to cull the herd, and make room for the best of us."

Asher thought no one would follow Mahakal if they knew.

"Why?" I asked. "Why hurt your own people?"

Mahakal scrutinized my labored breathing through lidded eyes. "My people are the ones that survive: the ones who deserve to survive, men like Kane. I gave you and yours chances to get out before the judgment came." He stared at me like a disappointed father.

Mahakal dropped to his knees beside me. "It pains me how wrong I was about you," he said, before trailing a wet kiss down where Kane's blade had struck. I rose against the bindings with everything I had, unable to do anything besides shrink away a hand's breadth—swearing.

Mahakal only laughed. "I suppose we know where to start breaking you in, but I'm afraid not all of this is pleasurable. I want you to understand your punishment, to know that what I offer you is justice after everything you've done."

The world tilted as Mahakal loomed over me, his voice a low whisper. "Friend, do you know why I offered you a place in my battalion?"

"I would have never been who you wanted," I said through my teeth.

"In some ways, you've yet to disappoint. You've survived, Jesse. You cheated death in Crofton, then Nunbiren. Do you even understand your uniqueness?" He leaned closer, his obsidian eyes glinting with a predatory hunger. "You have impeccable breeding, like all the men I choose." His words were a sickening caress.

I shrank inward.

"I first looked into your code when you told me you survived Crofton," he said, his voice dropping to a conspiratorial whisper. "That was my mission, and I made sure the death was quick, painless, ethical. To find a resistant survivor, well ... a fortunate surprise."

"I ... I don't understand."

His hands trailed my body. "There were some unregistered mods being used by the people in that town, choices that would build the wrong future. It had to be done. I didn't expect survivors."

I made myself stop feeling his hand trailing my back, focusing on his smiling face. "What do you mean?"

"I built the next round of SBO based on Crofton anomalies, you know. We had scientists rework some things for the next variant. Now the infected survive longer, to infect others. We can herd these ghosts from more populated areas into lands like Noé, guide away the useful citizens before attacks, and when it is over, replace the lost population with the loyal and strong, just like we did in the Bend." He kissed my fingers.

My mind raced, blanked. But I would not give him the satisfaction of cringing at his hand circling low on my chest.

"I'm fascinated by what I found in your code. You have no idea what lengths I went to protect you."

I tried to focus on his words, not his roving hands, to pull my consciousness away.

Kane returned, taking in the sight. "I'd expect you'd have the ungrateful traitor screaming by now, Major."

"Patience, Kane," Mahakal said. "Shall we show him who he truly is? Give me your knife."

Kane stepped forward, producing a sleek dagger from his belt, handing it to Mahakal.

Mahakal gestured toward me, the knife glinting in the electric light before he seared a shallow cut down my arm. "Have you ever heard of microchimerism?" He leaned closer. "It's nothing new, in its simplest form. A woman can absorb stem cells from her fetus. That foreign code can alter her body in both subtle and miraculous ways. She may find herself with curlier hair, or her cancer cured. Rarely harmful, but rarely meaningful."

He trailed his finger across my chest, his voice a chilling whisper. "Directed Microchimerism, that's the technical term of what the Crofton lab continued to produce after the queen outlawed the mod. You, Jesse, can quickly transmute foreign code into stem cells from almost any cell in your body. And it models the replication, trying out a change before it commits to a wide-scale change."

He brought the knife closer to Kane, the tip a hair's breadth from his skin. "I'll show you. A simple nick, that's all it takes."

Kane winced, but held still. A single crimson bead welled up on his arm before Mahakal collected it on the dagger, then kissed Kane's arm. When Kane groaned at that, I knew I'd never be horny again.

I watched in horror as Mahakal spread that blade across the wound on my arm, mixing Kane's blood with mine.

"There," Mahakal's voice was a low purr. "I'm curious to see if blood contact yields different results to more *intimate* forms of DNA exchange. After all, Kane tells me you absorbed code from him in a much more pleasurable manner."

My head throbbed, swimming with nausea.

"How'd you get the Red Demon's code, Jesse, when you were in our camp?" Kane asked. "You saw those scars and still fucked her?"

My eyes widened. Her blood met mine the first time we fought. The healing, the stamina, all of it, from her. I added that to the tally of how many times she'd saved my life. A fragile smile survived the wreckage of my shuddering breath.

Mahakal grasped my smile in the talons of his gaze. "It was nice of the mutt to leave some blood behind to test. Our first sample from her. The Red Demon's code is also—fascinating."

I growled, the sound echoing off the stone walls.

"He definitely fucked the mutt," Mahakal laughed to Kane, giving my cheek a patronizing pat. "But we won't be wasting your code anymore. Even an untrained dog can be bred."

CHAPTER 50

Choice

Mahakal's words echoed in my skull. *Even an untrained dog can be bred.*

"No." My voice constricted on the word.

Mahakal nodded to Kane, who left the room, the thick door creaking on its hinges. Acid filled my mouth.

Kane came back with a small, rickety table that he placed just out of my reach. Mahakal pulled me up by my hair, forcing a kneel. My vision turned over in dark seas, settling on the tablet Kane placed on the table.

"You should be excited," Mahakal purred as the screen flickered to life, revealing a grainy image that flickered into focus when the lights came on. Video from a prison cell, similar to mine.

A tattered figure hunched in the corner, a woman—dark skin, matted with blood and grime. No. *Mira?* But as the hunched figure shifted, a shock of auburn braid tumbled free.

"Ruan...?" My rasp echoed off the stone. I'd assumed she was dead, burned with the rest of the bodies in Nunbiren, my snarky and fiery friend.

My eyes clamped down. When I found the strength to look, Mahakal smiled down at me. He whispered a name I didn't recognize into the comm at his ear, his voice clipped and cold.

On the video feed, a soldier entered the cell, slamming his boot into Ruan's curled body, the dull sound echoing through the feed. Ruan reacted with a feral snarl, her body twisting in the corner against her manacles. I leaned in. It was a primal response—angry and devoid of fear. I studied her on the feed as she continued to rail, striking up at the soldier, mouthing unintelligible curses.

"She's still got a ruren-sa in her. Can you cure her?" I didn't know which answer would hurt more. Faruhar believed there was no cure but death. If she was wrong, then I'd killed people who could have been saved.

"No, this is all that is left of her mind." Mahakal's voice was smooth, savoring my pain. "But SBO is a virus, not a mod. Her flaw will not carry to future generations."

I stared in mute horror at Mahakal, my breath catching in my throat. "Have you touched her?"

I could have drowned in despair at Mahakal's smile. "Would *you* want to touch that, Kane?"

Kane huffed.

Turning back to me, arms crossed, Mahakal said, "I give my squad first choice of the spoils: traitors whose code is more virtuous than their deeds. No takers on your friend, I'm afraid, although I don't mind offering my feral dog the scraps."

I felt the weight of his gaze as I watched the screen. The guard kicked Ruan again and again. Her snarls grew guttural, a wounded animal cornered. I clenched my fist, and forced myself to watch, to not leave her alone by closing my eyes.

"I'll give you a chance to save her and her line," Mahakal said, his voice dropping to a low murmur. "If you'd like, we'll move your chains to her cell. Breed the bitch, or if you prefer, we'll kill her."

I dry heaved, tears stinging my eyes. "No." My world narrowed to the screen, Ruan's snarls and screams distorted through the speakers.

"As you wish," Mahakal said, a laugh in his voice. Mahakal picked up the tablet, typing, taking a moment to give me a broad grin before turning it around.

Another video feed; another cell. I recognized the vivid red hair, golden skin; the maze of intricate scars etching a map across her sleeping face.

No.

There was no hiding my reaction. Kane and Mahakal loomed, savoring my pain. From the looks of it, they'd already beaten her to the brink of death. All the air in my injured lungs left in a strangled gasp as I looked at the woman I loved, broken.

"How—"

Plan B failed too. Faruhar would track me to Mahakal's lair, and the Underground would attack. There was no Plan C.

"See, friend," Mahakal's voice was soft, taunting in its tenderness. "As smart as you thought you were trying to sow division in my battalion, I am smarter." He gestured toward the screen. "My ravens saw her coming. Their cortex is synched to command. I told you I wanted her too. I always take what I want."

On the screen, Faruhar lay crumpled and vulnerable on the stone floor, her lip split with crusted blood.

"What did you do to her?" I demanded.

"Oh, look at that fire." Mahakal's voice was honeyed poison. "The mutt is not worth breeding. But she'll be helpful to train you."

This was it. I'd failed her. Faruhar's breathing, shallow and uneven, was the only evidence of life. Shame burned in the depths of me, a black hole encroaching on my last vestiges of hope.

"Tell me," Mahakal said with an intake of breath. "Do you believe she lives up to her name? Is she a demon to you?"

"No." The truth slipped out, emptying me further.

"I worried as much. The things she's done, the good lives she's taken: I could multiply the crimes you've witnessed a hundredfold, show you all the evidence, and I doubt you'd believe a word." Mahakal flicked his eyes to Kane. "But I think we know how to make you understand."

I closed my eyes as Kane hummed his agreement, leaning on the wall.

Mahakal twitched his mouth into a sneer. "I didn't know before you told me that there was a paper leash on her demon, just a journal she used to contain her worst impulses. Time to slip that leash off."

I held my breath, biting down.

"You see." Mahakal leaned closer. "We've made sure she slept well. Sedated and woke her again and again. The last round should wear off shortly, and you get to meet who remains. It will be a hard lesson for you, but you will learn." He studied me, swallowing.

I looked between Mahakal and the video feed with frantic eyes.

Shaking his head, he touched the comm in his ear. "Open the door."

A metallic clang echoed through the tablet speakers. Mahakal tapped the display to split the view: one camera on Ruan, another on the sleeping Faruhar, a door opening between cells.

The weight of my helplessness pressed down on me, and I pulled at my manacles in impotent fury just as Ruan did, both of us unable to reach the sleeping Faruhar with her bruised face and split lip. Ruan cursed and railed.

Faruhar stirred, eyes still closed. Her lips moved, forming a sound I couldn't make out over Ruan's angry screams. Every shallow breath she took in the video was a shard of glass in my lungs.

Faruhar opened her yellow-green eyes, alert.

Then it happened. In a single, horrifying breath, Faruhar burst up. Two strides, then she launched herself atop Ruan's back with animalistic grace. A crunch filled the audio feed before Ruan's body fell.

I watched, my body numb, my heart shattered in my chest. Faruhar, my Faruhar, hunched over Ruan in a primal rage I refused to recognize.

"Ruan was dead already," I said. Faruhar's screams echoed in the confined space, a chord of pain and fury.

The screen flickered. So did the lights in the room. It barely registered in my numb state, I was just glad not to have to watch as the screen flicked off. Mahakal cursed under his breath, touching his comms.

"Command, repeat that please." Mahakal's face contorted in frowns as Kane's did the same. They exchanged worried glances.

Then, without another word, he and Kane strode out the door, leaving the tablet abandoned on the table.

It flicked back on.

I surged forward. My hands wouldn't reach, the chains groaning in protest. I was able to reach the table edge with a toe, inch it closer. There—I had the tablet in my hands. Maybe I could interface with something, a control.

I found a grim array of video feeds, grainy dim-lit cells. Most of the prisoners were women, many visibly pregnant. Horror gnawed at me, putting together the details of what Mahakal and his personal squad really did here.

A mechanical whirring filled the air, followed by a series of clicks. The prison cell groaned open a crack, but my mechanical manacles held. The video feed flickered off and on again.

It took forever for that tablet to reboot, and I was grateful there was no login prompt.

I flicked through the menu, desperate for any clues. It might be an attack—Telesilla and the Disciples of Reic. My heart lurched.

I found the video feeds of the cells again, all doors cracked open. Lights flicked on in every room, bodies lying on the ground, presumably sleeping. I kept scrolling until I saw the blood. A pregnant woman, abdomen ripped open. I looked away.

They weren't all sleeping.

I found Faruhar's cell—the same cell number in the top left corner: twenty-two. I scanned it, empty. Gone.

I found her in a frame, red hair flying as she crashed into a chained girl too young to call a woman, hands on her neck and twisting, then exiting the cell in a flash. I shuttered my eyes closed with wracking breaths, grateful for the pain in my lungs. When that girl's heart stopped beating, Faruhar crushed mine too.

CHAPTER 51

Strike Cold

My world shrank to the flickering tablet screen when I could bring myself to look again, to keep swiping and looking for something that wouldn't wreck me. Images blurred by: an empty cell, death, a grimy kitchen, more dead. A hallway patrolled by armed guards in Mahakal's black and red, sprinting down the corridor.

The prison's exterior, snow distorting the feed. Asri cloaks, blue-lit hands. At first I was too afraid to hope. But there they were. Telesilla had found us.

The rebels moved in a unified line, their engraved staffs glowing, the snow pulsing with the light of Oria under their feet. Magic, unblocked and unrepentant. The screen lit up with the flash of an aerial assault, the ground of my cell shaking. Mahakal must have launched artillery at them.

I braced myself before I looked at the video again. The rebels stood tall, standing in a ring of undisturbed ground when the dust on the screen settled.

Mahakal's soldiers came at a run, no doubt with fresh magic blockers among their gear. Yet I watched as the empire soldiers stumbled, clutching their heads as their faces contorted in pain. An unseen force, no more than a ripple of light, as the first wave of soldiers fell. The rebels pressed their attack.

Hope unfurled in my chest. Asher had done it. He'd reversed that magic blocker to break the other machines, allowing our allies to squeeze Mahakal with their full power. My eyes scanned the battle-field, flicking the exterior cameras, searching for Asher, the familiar glow of Istaran. He had to be here. He must have used Istaran to track Far.

There! Istaran flashed and cleaved through a line of twitching soldiers, the blade humming with power. A ragged sound escaped me—Asher, blade flying as he took to the front, his face determined and fearless.

And then, Faruhar.

She assessed from the edge of the fray. Soren gestured to her. She picked up a weapon from a fallen soldier, Chaeten tech—blade dull like the kind Mahakal had gifted Ash. Her eyes burned with fury, alert and devoid of recognition as she struck down a robed Asri rebel with brute force to the head. My throat opened, tasting the rank air of the cell. She picked up his staff next as its glow faded.

I didn't understand. I couldn't.

She lunged down the line as the rebels raised their blue hands in her direction, as the ground underneath swelled with light. Another black-robed rebel fell to the ground, silent on the video feed, but I felt the thud all the same. She found Soren with a swiped dagger, using her body to sweep him to the ground as she sliced his belly open.

He did not rise.

Faruhar turned, steel eyed, seeking her next victim. I could see mute screaming on the feed as the rebels charged in unison, meeting her with everything they had. Each encounter ended the same: a flurry of motion, stained snow. Another rebel down, and another, holding their line, their hands outstretched in denial of the fact that while

Mahakal's forces fell like harvested straw at their magic, she marched on, unaffected.

Horror stole my breath. Telesilla, her white braid flying, met Faruhar with furious grace, but not enough. Telesilla died with her mouth so wide on the silent video my mind filled in the sound. After piercing her chest with the dagger, Faruhar picked up Telesilla's Oria-threaded blade, dark in her hand, and hacked off Telesilla's head.

Then Asher.

Asher stood his ground, his sword low as she turned to meet him at a run, sword ready. I clamped my eyes so tight I saw red bursts of blood but I could not unsee Faruhar, my Far, painted with the blood of her allies as she ran for him. *Ash. Not Ash.*

I opened my eyes too late. Faruhar stood alone on the screen.

Mom taught me there will always be someone else to hold on to when a pillar of our life falls down, and she taught me to be that pillar in turn. The last pillar of my life was dead, and Far...

The world exploded into chaos as the door to my cell clattered open. Mahakal rushed in, snatching the tablet from the table.

With a snarl, he slammed the tablet onto the cold stone floor, crunching it under his boot. The screen flickered with mute colors before shuttering out on the next frenzied stomp. Then Mahakal's fist slammed into my jaw, pain throbbing through my skull.

"Traitor! Wild dog!" he spat, raining blows down on me. "I protected you! Shielded you! Do you think the queen would have let you live?"

He punched my back, and I retreated into myself as the blows rained down on me. "I saved this world for survivors like you. Millions died for your betrayal—" I lost the words, the sense if there was any, focusing on the manic glint in his eyes between blows. I didn't mind them, after a while. His fists hurt less than Ash and Far, and soon nothing would hurt me anymore.

The beatings stopped. Mahakal stood before me, catching his breath, a vial glinting in his hand. "This," he said, ripping off the top with his teeth. "Is the death you deserve." He took a sip, laughing.

"You don't deserve a quick death, you deserve one that is certain, with more pain than my fists can give you."

He yanked my head back, the metallic scent of blood filling my nostrils. He tipped the poisoned vial into my mouth, sweet and green and lethal.

This was it. I wondered how long it would take until the end, already starting to detach from the pain of my body. He reached out his hand to force my mouth shut, shattering the empty vial on the cold stone.

I saw my opening. I lunged my neck forward, my teeth snapping shut on his outstretched finger. A bone-splitting crunch, followed by Mahakal's roar of pain. He pried the mangled bit of flesh loose, spurting blood, but not before his blood dripped in my mouth along with any remnants of the poison I couldn't spit out. Disgusted, I sucked in what blood I could and spit the bloody finger out, my throat on fire.

Mahakal screamed at me with venomous hatred from the other side of the room, his face contorted in pain and fury.

I gasped for breath, falling to the ground. I saw the triumph in him as my body began shaking. The poison, working too fast. Pain I didn't know was possible, wracking me to a silent scream.

He spat at me, the wet saliva landing in my hair as he touched his comm with a scowl. Taking his weapon with him, he opened the door and left me in the dark. I hovered in and out of a pain so intense it consumed me—sliding into black waters to a place where there was nothing, where my fears melted and my senses loosened their grip to the Nara, falling up, up into the bright acceptance of death.

I'd done my best. I'd failed. *There was nothing left.*

I don't know how much time passed until the door burst open again, the sounds muffled, and I focused my dull eyes. It wasn't Mahakal. Kane, his face pale and bloody, stumbled into the cell, his hand clutching a nasty gash across his chest. I looked up, too dizzy and weak to rise from my crouch on the ground.

Beside him, Faruhar. She gutted Kane with her borrowed blade, and his bowels fell across the cell as he crumpled. She sliced his head next, smashing through his skull to spill his bleeding brains across the cold floor.

Each breath ached—my chest too hollow for fear, but I couldn't close my eyes. She turned to me, covered in blood, her eyes wide and alert.

"Far," I choked out.

She cocked her head, a bird of prey.

My mind raced, searching for the familiar script, the words I used to anchor her, to remind her of who she was. "Faruhar, you're s—" I started, but I wouldn't lie. No one was safe: not her, not Telesilla, not Asher. She'd shatter me too. She already had.

I met her blinding gaze. Tears streamed down my face, a silent plea to see any trace left of the woman I said I'd love forever. *But I didn't.*

"Kill me," I whispered, lost.

She blinked, taking a knee beside me, her sword below my chin. "Why am I your death wish?" Her whisper echoed in the small room.

Tears streamed down as I struggled for breath, tasting my blood, or Mahakal's. I wasn't sure.

She knelt beside me, her eyes scanning with sharp movements. "Who are you to me?" she rasped.

A new sob escaped my lips. "It's me, J-" I slumped under the weight of my wounds, the poison, my despair, but I formed the words clearly, certain. "Kill me."

She shivered, dropping the weapon. A single tear bled down her stained cheek. "I remember the people I trust." Her voice strengthened, gaining defiance through the cracks in her voice. "The people I love."

That was the first time she said it, but I couldn't smile. I didn't even look up.

She reached out, a tentative touch against my cheek. The warmth of her fingertips chilled me.

"Tell me your name, please." Her voice trembled.

I shook my head. My throat tightened, but I answered. "Jesse."

Her lips quivered into a smile. I thought I saw fragile recognition, at risk of shattering.

Words failed me as I looked into her yellow-green eyes. Intense, familiar. Beautiful. "You killed them—innocent women. Our allies. And Asher—"

I watched all the joy in her flicker out.

"My brother Asher," I said, forcing the words out. "You killed him."

A tremor ran through her body, her hand on my face shaking. "I thought—" She turned away from me, breathing fast. When she looked at me again, tears blurring her vision, she drew her borrowed sword, pointing it at me.

She threw all her weight into the struts, striking the bolt that chained my feet to the floor. Another strike, another. The metal screamed in protest before finally giving way, the blade denting under the stress. She turned to my chained hands, her jaw clenched and hair flying. The raw tang of blood and bowels filled the air from Kane's body in the corner as she hacked between ragged sobs. One manacle finally broke one. She pried open a seam of the chain on another that refused to dent, and it fell away with an uneven clang as the blade shattered, only leaving the cuff.

I winced as I sat up, my vision blurry with the poison coursing through my veins, a dull throb in every limb instead of the original fire. I stood, my head clearing as I held the wall for balance.

Faruhar backed herself into a corner, her mad eyes roving. She clutched her head as a strangled cry escaped her bruised lips, her hands torn and bleeding from the force of her swings. "Who did I kill? Tell me their names!"

I shivered through my thin clothes, at the ice forming over my heart. I couldn't answer. Her eyes darted around the cell, to Kane's body, then locked back on me. "Who was he? Please, tell me. Where's my journal? I'll write everyone down."

"Did you kill Mahakal?"

"No," she said, her voice tight, urgent.

The lights in the room flicked off.

"Far?" I tried to reach for her in the dark. "Ask Bria what's—"

The door opened. Mahakal's silhouette, a battle ax in his hand, a heat vision helmet on his head. The door slammed. Darkness again.

Panic raked my mind. I couldn't see, just feel the vibrations through the floor as he struck, hitting stone. Faruhar screamed and Mahakal grunted, then a clang of metal on metal. All Faruhar had was that broken sword. The ax sparked on the walls, giving me a flash of Mahakal's sneer. I picked up the chain, hearing Faruhar's choked gasp as the ax met something wet.

A body fell against me, heavy and male. Mahakal's ax shaved my leg. I pulled the chain in my hands tight before wrapping it around Mahakal's neck, rolling away from his swing, choking him. The ax sparked against the wall as we wrestled, my movements shaking with the pain of my injuries and poison, but I could push through. Faruhar roared, and I heard the ax clatter away.

Pain flared through my side where Mahakal elbowed the arrow wound in my chest. He rolled me. His weight pinned me to the floor, his breath refilling his lungs as the chain loosened in my hold, his arm leading on my neck. He pried a hand between his throat and the metal, as his heavy breath washed over me.

Faruhar lunged for him and he twisted, slamming her into the wall with his body as I wrestled for control.

The door opened, dim lantern light filtering in.

Ash. It was Ash.

Relief washed over me, an intense wave that threatened to drown me as Mahakal tried to prise the chain from my hands. Faruhar scrambled to grab the ax, bleeding from a gash on her side.

"Asher!" I said, my voice hoarse.

Asher set the lantern on the floor where our shadows tangled. And I had the chain tight against Mahakal's neck once more, holding tight as he tried to break me against the stone with his fists and knees.

Faruhar drew Mahakal's battle ax. Ash took his place beside her with Istaran.

Mahakal landed a blow on my jaw. But his eyes were unsteady, face blue.

Pulling the chain tight, I fixed my legs around him and rolled him over, driving his head into the stone wall with the chain, kneeing him hard in the groin. Far readied her swing.

"Far, no," I said.

She froze mid-motion as Major Mahakal purpled, his grip against the chain weakening.

"Let me, please."

With a nod, she tackled Mahakal from behind, her weight adding to the pressure on his already compromised air supply. She took the chain from me, loosening it only enough to hear him gurgle.

Fury pulsed in my head, rage fed by the relentless nightmares of everything Mahakal had done. Everything she...

I hefted the ax in my hand.

"You told me once you killed with justice, slow or fast, depending on what they deserved." Clarity stilled my ragged breaths. "I have some justice for you." I lifted the ax and drove it hard into his groin. His eyes widened. "That's for Faruhar's mom."

Faruhar blinked at me. She jerked the chain again.

"Then there's my mom." My voice held steady in the storm. I hacked off a finger in one shot, the metal grip on the ax cold in my hands.

"Bella was twelve!" I roared, arcing the ax down in a sickening squelch to Mahakal's foot.

Faruhar loosened the chain for his scream and tightened again, ensuring the death would be slow.

"Sora, Samantha, Cara!" I screamed, bringing the ax down again and again, this time connecting with more fingers, moving up his arm, severing a fresh sliver with each blow. A spray of crimson painted the stone wall behind Faruhar as he twitched.

"Iden, Mal, Oren." His feet, his remaining hand. Mahakal's struggles grew feeble, his grunts turning into gurgles as the stone welled with blood.

Asher's mouth was moving, forming words I couldn't quite grasp—nothing I wanted to grasp.

"Galen, Meragc, Atalia—" With each name, each face I loved, I hacked at his arms and legs, scything him bit by bit, a litany of the lost, a chorus of the wronged.

"Jesse," Asher said.

I ignored him.

"Plato, Ruan—" Each blow clanged to the stone floor, a rhythm as easy as the hammering of Galen's forging press. He was a mess now, his blood dribbling from stumps of limbs, but still breathing. Chaeten-sa did not die easy. I kept hacking, bit by bit.

"Jesse!" Asher gripped my arm, his face horrified and pleading in the flickering glow.

I shivered away. "Dr. Garla ... Juna ... Hector..." I said, sobbing between swings.

It was Faruhar's touch behind me that made me pause. She should be behind Mahakal, making sure he died. Making sure this ended. He'd get away.

"Don't get up!" I said.

But she blocked my arm when I brought up the ax once more, heavy, dripping crimson. My gasped breaths were ragged, my body quaking.

"You're not him," Faruhar said, her cracking voice an arrow between my ribs. "You're not me, either."

Faruhar stood rooted to the spot, her knuckles white on my arm until I lowered the ax. Her gaze flickered to Mahakal's ruined body. He breathed rapidly and shallow, pale with his one good eye unfocused. She stared down the storm within me until I broke.

"Strike cold, without malice," Asher said, voice breaking. "*Niire Mai.*"

I closed my eyes with a nod. "*Niire Mai.*"

Faruhar stepped away as I raised the ax for the last time, severing Mahakal's head.

CHAPTER 52

Mar

Asher placed his arm on my shoulder, his touch firm as I caught my breath. "Jesse."

Faruhar hunched on the far side of the cell, her gaze locked on mine.

A cold weight settled in my chest that I was too weak to carry. There'd be no moving from this room for me, not really, even when my feet crossed the threshold. Years later, I still find myself there, with Asher's disappointment, and something in Faruhar I still can't understand.

"Come on, Brother," Asher said, his voice tight. "It's over. Let's go."

I looked between the mangled flesh that had once been Mahakal, then Kane's corpse by the door.

Faruhar stared at me still, a tear tracing a path down her cheek in the lantern light.

"Jesse." Asher shivered when I met his gaze. "There's a healer still alive outside."

"Are you sure Far left her alive? I saw what she did." I gestured vaguely to the broken tablet on the floor. My eyes flicked up to Faruhar, who looked away.

I turned back to Asher. "I thought she killed you." For a moment, words failed me. "I saw Faruhar turn to you and—" I closed my eyes tight as Asher gripped my head to his shoulder, holding me tight as I forced my breaths to slow.

"Hey," he said, his voice weak. "She remembers those she trusts." But there was no conviction in that, and neither was there absolution.

"Far..." I said, when I felt strong enough. My words echoed in the small room. I wasn't sure what else to say. She seemed to shrink further into herself.

"Bria just told me the woman with the white braid was going to perform your marriage ceremony," she told Ash, then looked back to the ground. "I'm sorry, Asher."

I bit my fist to choke off a sob. "The rest of the rebels are going to kill her, aren't they?"

Asher looked at Faruhar, his jaw clenched tight. "Nothing they tried worked so far..." His voice trailed off.

With a flash of motion, Faruhar dove to pick up the blood-soaked ax, still dripping with flecks of bone and guts.

Asher reacted quickly, drawing Istaran.

Faruhar didn't even look at us, just the floor, at Mahakal. "Asher, where's my journal? Do you have it?"

Fear drained out of Asher's face before he let out a sigh, sheathing his blade. "My bag is at the treeline. Should I fetch it?"

Faruhar shook, her knuckles white on the ax grip. "I'll find my swords first. Mahakal has them somewhere. Just ... tell them all to leave me alone. I will defend myself if they attack." A ragged, hollow sound tore from her shuddering body.

Asher nodded to Istaran. "They heard you through the blade."

Tears mingled with the grime and bruises on her face. One quick salute to mind and heart, then she burst past us for the door.

Asher gripped my arm as I tried to follow. It took all my strength to break away from him, lurching after her as she disappeared down the dark prison corridor.

"Far!" Her name tore from my lips—all I had left. I didn't even know what I wanted to say. I released her name once more into the shadowed hall, letting my voice burn through the pain in my chest.

Outside the cell, heavy snowflakes drifted down over the carnage, blanketing the dead in an icy hush. Dozens lay in the field below the prison, many allies in their Asri cloaks, more in Mahakal's uniforms, all sprawled lifeless in the snow. My head throbbed, fogging, and if I didn't focus on pushing the pain away, it threatened to overwhelm me. Every breath felt like a knife scraping against raw flesh, and I suspected Mahakal had broken a few ribs in that last round of beatings.

I could push all that pain away though, if I concentrated. That was new.

Three figures, staff and Asri swords drawn, huddled near the prison gate next to a cluster of survivors, their faces obscured by their hoods. As we approached, most stepped back in fear. Three rebels took a crunching step forward, lowering their weapons. An older woman and man I didn't recognize, and Soren—with his green Chaeten eyes. I dipped my head under the weight of Soren's anger. I couldn't blame him for hating me.

"We saw you kill Mahakal, through your brother's sword." Soren's voice was deliberate, each word crisp.

"I'm sorry for your friends; for Telesilla." The words scraped against my dry throat. I saluted deep and heartfelt to the bodies behind him, shuddering. "I'm so sorry, Soren."

He offered a curt nod, his jaw muscles clenched in his weathered face. A silence stretched between us until the rage in his face dulled with a swallow of his throat.

Although Ash had swiped a coat for me from the complex, I stood covered in blood, still wet and cooling against my skin. Crimson stained my clothing and hair. I remembered what Galen taught me: look the demon in the eyes. Use the minimum force necessary to end suffering. Strike cold, without malice, to execute a clean death. I wore the evidence that I could not, that although I triumphed, I'd failed.

"Master Seyla, can you heal my brother?" Asher's voice tightened, turning to the older woman with brown and blue ringed eyes.

Seyla looked to the other two for their opinion, holding a cautious neutrality on her wizened features. Soren gave a curt nod, then turned away from me.

Seyla approached, placing her hand on my chest. A tingling blue light emanated from her touch, cool and bitter, a brush of soft velvet before a hundred needle pricks. I bit back a groan at the sensation.

"*Mar*." Seyla's brow furrowed as she pulled her hand away.

"What?" Asher's head whipped up. He'd been walking toward Soren.

Seyla met my gaze. "Hate, darkness," she explained in Chaeten. "Too much to burn away as I heal you."

"I know what '*Mar*' is," I said in the fluent Asri she should have heard me speak by now. "My Taam was an elder."

Seyla pressed her lips tight. "You don't need me. Heal yourself, Chaeten-sa."

"What?"

She scowled and stepped away.

Soren turned on his heel, his eyes cold. "Asher, your brother must leave by the morning. And if we ever see him at his lover's side, we will kill him too." The threat hung in the air. He took a long deep breath with eyes closed to control his rage, the snow melting into his black cloak.

I hung my head.

"The Red Demon won't stand a chance against my master, Reic, Keeper of Dreams. I'm confident all other networks in the Underground will unite around this. We will kill her." Soren shifted his stance, eyes on me. "How do you feel about that, friend?"

"I don't know, Soren." The words tore at my heart on the way out: the truth.

"Asher, if we need to speak more, we will do so in private," Soren said, before walking toward the huddle of prisoners, the few that Faruhar had not killed.

CHAPTER 53

Path

The Underground safehouse emerged from swirling snow, candlelight in the window flickering in the gathering dark. I knew what those candles meant to the Asri, lit to remember those they'd lost.

As we neared the entrance, the door swung open, revealing Mira bathed in warm golden light. I felt a wave of relief so powerful it left me breathless. She frowned, her chest heaving at the sight of the small party—until her gaze landed on me, then Asher.

With a choked cry, she fell into Ash's chest. He held her tight and lifted her bare feet out of the snow. I watched them for a moment, needing to borrow a little of their joy.

Her body went rigid when she turned to me. Ash set her down as she stared at my blood-soaked clothes, torn rags under the cloak, the crimson smears staining my face and arms.

"Yeah, you don't want to hug me right now," I said with a brittle laugh.

The concern in her eyes was a storm, and I turned away before it broke.

Inside, I took a long time in the bath, testing my new skill: feeling the pain of my cracked ribs already healing, turning the wave of pain away. But I let all that focus go, needing the judgment of that silence, lit only by candles inside my room. I knew Ash would tell Mira everything, and that I could not. My mind lay wounded and immobile, even if the rest of me would heal.

No member of the Underground would so much as look me in the eye when I walked down the creaking stairs to join Ash and Mira for a meal. Two cloaked figures promptly left the kitchen. But Mira finally gave me that hug, and I got a face full of her black hair as she nestled into my shoulder.

I winced, pain lancing my side. "Maybe go light on the broken ribs."

Her eyes scanned me again, lingering on my chest. I shifted my weight. Disbelief flickered across her features. "They wouldn't heal you?"

I shook my head, breathing deep. "It didn't work. They told me to 'heal like a Chaeten-sa,' whatever that means."

"Oh." She brushed a stray strand of hair from my forehead to look at a bruise, her touch feather-light. I wasn't sure if I wanted to smile or cry at that gentleness, but I knew I needed every bit of the love radiating from her. "Chaeten-sa can focus on a wound to heal it, with practice. They only keep the scars they choose."

I couldn't hide the panic at that, how deep I retreated, breathing fast, thinking of a Chaeten-sa who kept every scar.

With love in her eyes, Mira turned my head to face her, sensing my pain.

"I'm all right, Mira," I assured her, squeezing her hand. "Starving, though."

After some food in my stomach and a steaming mug of something herbal, I settled into the cushions. "How'd your release of the SBO code go, Mira?"

Mira straightened her posture in the booth across from me, a mischievous glint in her eyes. "Flawless. You will love this, I think." She dug around on the shelf beside her for her tablet.

I took another sip of bitter tea.

A wry smile twisted her lips. "Getting past the front door was easy enough with the ID card, but the real challenge was the security protocols. The Disciples of Reic are certainly stronger for allowing Chaeten into their network. Apparently, they are the only Underground network that does. They got it done."

She leaned back in her chair, her eyes gleaming with a spark of mischief before she passed the tablet to me.

The headline on the screen cut through the dim light: *QUEEN AZARA RELEASES SBO-PREVENTION MOD. INFECTIONS LINKED TO GHOSTS.*

I blinked, looking up at Mira.

"It's everywhere. Sent to every temple in the Nara, marked mandatory to post. Keep reading."

I did.

> *South Bend Outbreak (SBO), the disease that has ransacked the southern islands of Noé and Ment, will no longer be a threat to the citizens of the empire. The disease, which the queen reveals works by attracting the ruren-sa left from Nara Mnaet's civil war, had previously been a death sentence to those infected. The simple mod works by...*

"Why give the queen credit? She may be in on this, for all we know," I said, scratching my head.

Mira smiled, crossing her arms. "Let's say she is—that for some reason, she wants her people dead. The code is out there, and with her name on it, I guarantee it's already been sequenced, applied. She can't contradict something that works. And if she's been lying about the virus or its cause before now, she'll have some serious explaining to do to the empire nobles."

Asher kissed Mira's head. "Brilliant, isn't she?"

"Ash, stop eyefucking a sec," I said, just to be a dick. Once Mira gave my bandaged arm a playful slap for that, I followed up with, "Okay, what if Queen Azara is innocent?"

Mira's eyes sparkled. "Well then, she'll rake Mahakal's reputation over the coals, and we've just strengthened her position. She should thank us."

A genuine, full-bodied laugh escaped my lips, echoing in the small kitchen. "Yeah, I like it."

She scrolled down, her brow furrowing. "We should pay close attention to the next bulletins in the temple. General Alexander and the queen haven't responded yet. Even if Queen Azara tries wiping our bulletin and code schematics off the network, the Underground will supply me with reagents to keep producing the anti-SBO mod for them."

Asher's and Mira's faces glowed in the warm light of the hearth fire.

Sometimes, when things seem dark or hopeless, I set my brightest and most hopeless memories in my head, imagining them side by side to let the warmth of a good day triumph over the dark. A scared boy alone in the forest knew this day was coming, and I filled his heart with what overfilled me then; what I saw reflected in the faces I loved. When dark days come again, that moment has enough life to spare—Ash relaxed by the fire, his eyes full and content, Mira leaning into his shoulder, turning to smile at me too. This is all I needed.

Soren entered the kitchen a moment later, breaking the spell. "Asher, can we talk?" he said, ignoring me. With a sigh, I got up toward the stairs, mumbling about needing to get some sleep.

I could smell Faruhar in my room, a wave of salt and green and fire so strong I had to search the closet to see if she was hiding, but I only found her bag. This was a fresh gift from Mahakal's code—I realized—the intensity and color of an aroma I smelled for the first time but recognized at once.

Her bag, a worn and patched up canvas, was not her, but I hugged it tight to my chest all the same. Just two days ago, I'd told Faruhar I'd always love her. I'd held her to my body in a cozy room so much like this one, wanting a lifetime of nights like it. I gripped that bag, fighting sleep, fighting thought, knowing that there was no way to win.

A knock on the door, gentle.

"Come in," I said.

Asher, his face grim, Istaran's green and gold sheath strapped on his back.

"Jesse?" I could hear so much concern in his voice.

"I'm fine," I lied.

He stepped in and closed the door, leaning on the dresser across from me, gripping the wood tight.

"What should I do?" I whispered.

Asher shook his head. "You know your own path, Brother."

"Taam would tell me what to do." It was hard to speak. Blinking, I leaned my head against the headboard. "What would he say?"

Asher weighed that. He sighed, a deep sound, steady as the tide. "The soul has a path it must follow, and it will languish if it loses its way."

I rubbed my hand through my hair, the weight of the decision pressing heavy.

"Do you mind if I borrow Istaran again?"

"Borrow?" He swallowed, removing the blade from his back.

"Galen was your father first. Your blood, not mine." I choked on the words, unable to hide from them. "Everyone else seems to know the difference."

Asher paused a minute, giving me a moment to get a hold of myself. He pulled me into a tight hug. "Brother," he said, his voice thick with emotion. "Always." He pulled back, his hand gripping mine above Istaran. "Take it."

I stared at the sword, the weight of its history, letting it settle in my hand. It had never glowed for Faruhar, or Mahakal, whose code now ran through my veins. I was afraid to unsheath it with the hands that had tortured Mahakal at his death, the actions it would judge me for. So I told Ash about directed microsomething, the words tumbling out in a torrent.

When I finished, Asher pulled my forehead to his, his grip unyielding. "Nothing will ever change what you mean to me," he said, voice fierce.

I took in a long breath, borrowing his strength before he clapped my shoulder and pulled back.

I couldn't delay this forever. My hands trembled on Istaran's familiar hilt, pulling it a few centimeters from its sheath. A faint blue light emanated from the engraving etched along the blade.

"It's ... not as bright," I said, my voice barely above a whisper.

Asher's face softened. "You'll do better. It trusts you; so do I. But you need to get Istaran out of here. You can guess what Soren already asked me to do with it. They're going after Faruhar tomorrow."

I pushed the pain away, all of it, as the path cleared. I grabbed my bag from under the bed, shoving Faruhar's pack inside mine.

"Don't wait for me for the wedding. I'm sorry. I don't know how long this will take." I took a deep breath. "Where are you headed next?"

"Nunbiren. We want to say goodbye," he said, his lip twitching up. "And I'll dig up my century robe from the training clearing. Mira is happy you saved that."

I nodded, unable to smile back.

He frowned at that, drummed his hands on the dresser. "Mira wiped out all the records on the network about us she could find. No one will recognize our code if we're scanned somewhere," he said, a playful glint in his eyes. "Istaran will let you know when I've secured your couch."

I let out a huff of air.

For a moment, I thought about telling Ash just how stupid I was, to tell him about a life I dreamed up a few days ago. Faruhar, Asher and I would train in our clearing each morning, and we'd huddle together for dinner in the kitchen above the forge. We'd need to expand a bit, maybe build out that house next door that Galen had already chosen. Far would forage while we rebuilt the town, and Mira would make money selling unlicensed mods, and be smart enough to figure something else out if she got caught. I'd rebuild brick by brick in the soil where the ancestors knew my name, and Faruhar would stand with me for each step, healing a little each day until she never forgot anything again. Ash would play his mandolin over dinner for all of us, until sooner than was sensible, Mira would tell me I had a niece or nephew on the way.

I was a stupid, stupid man.

Looking into Asher's eyes, brimming with concern, I knew I didn't need to say anything. He knew me. He knew it all. I settled the bag on my back.

"Ash, I need you to promise me something," I said, low and serious. "If I ever…" I pulled out Istaran again, its glow reassuring. "You saved me a long time ago. Keep saving me. I—don't let me become a demon."

"Always." The weight of his gaze settled on me, unwavering. "My heart and mind are with you."

Chapter 54

Unshaken

Ice whipped at my sweat-soaked tunic as I jogged through the night, the edges of the sky paling. Istaran glowed in my hands and Oria pulsed under the snow, guiding my crunching steps to Galen's killer.

I knew she heard me coming, but she didn't rise from her curled heap, cradled by the eroded roots of an alder beside a frozen river. Her anemic campfire smoked more than glowed when she finally sat up, the bruises on her face unhealed despite my ribs no longer aching with each breath. Maybe she was too cold and weak to heal, maybe this was like her scars, a choice to ensure she remembered her crimes when the sun rose. Faruhar's eyes focused on me, weak.

"Have you even slept yet?" I brought Istaran's light closer to see her face. She shrank back.

"You've come to kill me?" She didn't go for her weapon. She could have, in the time it took her to say that.

Sheathing my blade, I sank beside her, keeping my movements slow so as not to spook her. "I brought your bag." She flinched when I set it down in front of her, the worn canvas dark against the snow. I waited for her eyes to calm. They didn't.

Watching her shivering form, those swollen yellow-green eyes, I reminded myself of every innocent person she'd killed. Telesilla, about twenty rebels, and about as many terrified women huddling in that prison, winking out whatever hope they'd clung to, the life they deserved to rebuild. I knew my path, to let the timbers of my life burn down, collapsing to white-knuckled ash. My foundation held as always, and I would rebuild on what remained.

Silence—heavy as the winter clouds and the blanketed forest. The silver river beside us sparkled and whispered while the smoky tendrils of fire grasped for more fuel.

"You're cold." When she didn't respond, I went to gather kindling, my voice rough with the effort of wrangling so many thoughts I didn't have words for. Faruhar sat numb where I left her, staring into the night.

Once I fed the fire to a crackle, I rolled out my camp blanket on the other side, far from a tangle of uncomfortable roots she'd been curled among. I gestured for her to join me, opening the cloak that could cover us both.

Fear flickered in her eyes, confusion at my outstretched hand. "Why are you here?"

"Let's get a little sleep, Far." I swallowed. "We'll talk things through in the morning." Sleep would unravel my grief. I needed to build strength to face this.

Hesitant, she stood, and her hands were frigid when I pulled her in, her back to my chest. Without thinking, I kissed her hair, tasting blood and dirt. I bit back the confusing mix of comfort and disgust, wondering whose blood it was as I drifted off to sleep, feeling the vibrations of her ragged sobs against my bruised chest.

The winter sky dawned pink and pale, too cold for birdsong. I settled into her, holding her closer, until Faruhar tore herself away. First

she went to the bag to flick through the journal, the snow crunching under her boots like glass as she angled down the riverbank.

With bleary eyes, I watched her break off the ice and strip off her shirt, scrubbing off blood and grime in the cold water with bared teeth. She shivered into clean, dry pants when I made my way down the bank to sit beside her.

"Morning," I said, my voice thick with sleep.

She stopped scrubbing to glare at me in silence. Just the gurgling river and the rustle of wind through dead leaves.

"Did Bria already fill you in?" I asked. "We shouldn't stay here long. The Underground is hunting us."

She paused, her back to me, dipping her dirty pants into icy water, staining it red with every scrub.

"Bria is more broken than before," Faruhar said, voice flat. "She defended me against the Underground, that *chout*..." Her eyes fell under the shadow of dark clouds. "She just keeps repeating the same non-sensible things over and over again. Something about three paths merging. There's so little of her left."

"I'm sorry," I said, clenching my eyes tight. I knew Bria would have done everything she could to reach Faruhar before she killed innocent people. Even she had been powerless to call her back.

Faruhar carried her guilt; I'd never hated her as much as she hated herself. I understood this now.

"You still have me," I said, unwavering. "You'll always have me."

She froze at that, eyes wide like the pain of a mortal wound. "No."

I settled with my back against a tree. "I'm stubborn, remember?" My smile died in the air between us.

Three quick breaths, eyes roving back to her bag by the remains of the fire.

"Far. Calm down. You're safe—"

She laughed in my face. "Safe? Do you think you are safe anywhere near me?"

"Far," I said, desperation seeping into my voice. "When I'm around, things are fine. If Bria injured herself, you need me more than ever. We'll stay on the run together, maybe get you on a ship to a bigger island, somewhere with more places to hide. I'll keep you from hurting anyone. This will never happen again."

Her gaze met mine, a storm swirling in her heaving breaths. "After we defeated Mahakal, you said you wanted a normal, boring life with the family you have left. With Asher, with Mira." A sob escaped her lips, raw. "Do you still want to know what I want? You promised to help me get it, remember?"

I nodded.

"I want that for you too, Jesse. You need to leave me alone."

My chest hollowed out.

"We'll have better days," I said, believing that for her sake.

A flicker of her fire sparked to life in her eyes. "Claim the life you deserve and leave me out of it." She stood up from the river bank, fists clenched. "Rip whatever feelings you think you have for me away and burn them before I do! I've killed the other people I loved. Never again. Not you." Tears welled up in her eyes, glittering in anger.

I took a step closer, reaching out a hand, but she flinched away, shivering in the cold. "No. You need me," I said.

"You don't."

A choked sound came out of my mouth. "We're going to find a way to heal your mind. I'll be right here beside you the moment you do."

Desperation tinged her laughter. "Heal me? How? Should we waltz into a Z'har hospital and ask about mods I've never heard about? Even if I made it through the gates, they'd kill me as soon as they scanned my face or my code. Or should I ask one of the Underground networks, see if one of the Attiq-ka on the council will forgive my blood debt?" She crossed her arms to her chest, shivering. "None of that is going to happen. Ever."

I fell silent under the weight of my dread. There was no plan to throw at her, just that blind and senseless faith that I always had enough of to spare.

Faruhar stared at my crossed arms, her eyes pleading. "Please, Jesse. Go. Let me go." Her voice dropped to a whisper. "I know what I am. I am the only thing keeping Bria alive, and when you told me I deserved to die—" She took a fortifying breath. "You were never wrong. The day I fail to protect my sister is the day I die, and I will not shy away from that. I have no life to give you before or after. This is all I am and all I ever will be."

My love for her, that weight in my chest, stood unmoved. "I will never believe that." I stepped toward her.

She grabbed her wet clothes from the rocks and bolted for our little camp. I followed her back as she shoved her damp things in her bag, clipping on her swords by the smoldering fire.

She turned back to face me in the dense forest, desolate against the towering ancient trees.

"I'll kill you if you try to find me again. I don't want to, but—that's never been enough to stop me." Faruhar's voice drifted into the wind.

I stood rooted to the spot as the last echo of her footsteps faded to silence. The world blurred around me, the stark beauty of the snow-covered landscape. Yet I recognized her lie for what it was, and I stood, unshaken.

CHAPTER 55

Epilogue: Candles

Faruhar

I'm a child, old enough to speak and not much more, starving in the forest when the man finds me. The damp moss squishes beneath my little fingers where I lay starving, only scarred by flame thus far and not weapons. But I know people like him will kill a child, because everyone will kill a child who looks like me. I'm afraid of the old man with the blurry face, a man whose name I can no longer remember. I am too weak to run away when he offers that name and asks mine, reaching to pick me up with the long blue sleeves of his Asri robe.

He winds our way through the endless green, hunger aching in my belly as I sit on his hip. His forest shrine stands stark and beautiful when we arrive, carved with wood atop the old stone foundations. There, he feeds me and wraps me warm in oversized clothes, giving me cushions in his sanctuary to sleep on. And when the night rolls over solemn sky, he doesn't make me go back outside to the cold and rain. Instead, I watch him light candles in the window, one by one.

I'm confused about the candles; emboldened by a full belly. He explains that he lights one for everyone he loved and lost, people too far away for him to hold close. He nurtures each flame, singing life into each name, his voice rustling like the wind in the dry leaves. When he asks my name and I can't remember, he gives me one: Faruhar—a name he says would keep me safe, explaining we all grow into our names.

When he asks if I have anyone to light a candle for, I say no. He gives me two. He explains I must have a mother and a father—everyone does. I don't believe him, but I clutch the candles anyway, asking him if, when I go, I might light one for him. And there is so much love in the gaze he gives me that even I know it for what it is.

Later, beneath a sky studded with all the lights scattered in the cold void, I can see a multitude of candles burning under the trees, candles I light for all the people I choose to love. Even if I don't know them, I feel there should be many, that I can make room for them all. The memory fades, crackling at the edges with the warm scent of burning green. The flames lick wild and hungry at the sky, claiming the lives of the trees. I see the carved wooden roof of the shrine groaning in protest before it falls into itself, and I find the man's bones in the morning, still inside. Bria tells me that to kill a star, you must make it turn inward on itself, like that burning shrine.

This is the first day I learn what I am, and I will hold onto that memory even if I lose everything else. There are no candles for me to light, only that man's bones, the ash of the first man who ever loved me.

I'll remember the last man too.

These memories are delicate, nothing to hold too tight. I stand too far away to burn him down, but I haven't always. I remember his curly blond hair is soft to my touch. The rest of him feels strong in all ways, unwavering.

I dream about him sometimes: nightmares I know are not real. A festival explodes before my eyes, a riot of laughter and music. I see him, a solitary figure sitting at the fringes amid the swirling colors, his eyes distant to the sky. I wonder if he knows how to destroy a star.

In those dreams, I'm shameless. I reach for his face and wrap my arms around his body. I flood him with my every secret and desire, drowning him with words and hopes that are not mine to give. He'll look right past me in those dreams—unseeing, unhearing, as if I am a ghost—an unsettling breath of wind. He never could see ghosts. A face flickers at the edge of the crowd, a sneer of twisted lips that reminds me I shouldn't be here, that I will never belong here. I slip away before they try to kill me, before I kill them.

But there's another dream I believe is real. He's strong, unchanged, and I find this strange somehow, because the years have come and gone. He's playing with several children, their laughter echoing through the trees. The children's sandy brown skin shines in the sun as they duck between trees, shrieking, collecting sticks they pretend are swords. A carefree smile stretches across his face as he darts and twists between them, until he surrenders, and the children attack him and beat him senseless. I can hear the thwack of those sticks against his body, tensing. But he's laughing; he was always strange like that. He looks happy, and I smile too, hidden in the shadows of his joy.

"Let's go," Bria says in her little voice.

"You could play with them," I offer. She looks like a child their age, her dark, shoulder-length hair whipping in the wind. But she's in rags, a frail child shaking beside me.

"No," she says.

I smile at her. "Bria."

"Faruhar, I need your help," she says, trembling as she looks up at me. I watch as the details of the forest shift, blurring. The sunlight through the trees breathes with me, and the ground wavers underneath.

"It will be over soon," I tell her, offering my hand. "Let's go."

We step into another dream. And another.

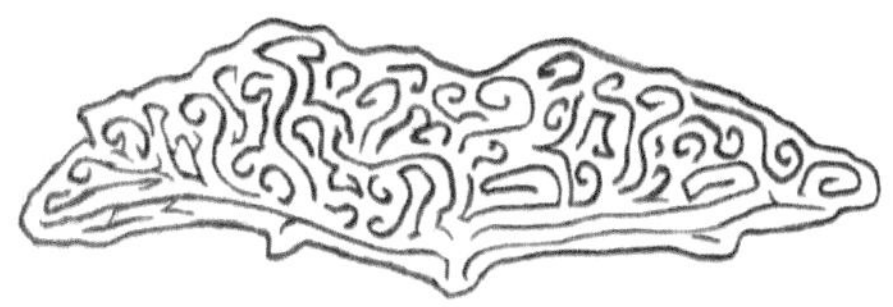

A Note From the Author

Hey. Sill here.

No, this is not the end. I hope. With your support, I'll continue writing stories—including ones where you'll see these main characters again.

Authors know that there are much more profitable things we can do with our time. Even the literary success stories are more often than not paved with a lot of *"nos"*, or *"not quite"*, or *"almosts"*, and many find they can be happier doing something else. Even New York Times bestsellers—which this debut is unlikely to be—are generally written by people who work full-time in order to afford to create art for its own sake. The people who keep going are people who found they can't live any other way.

This story—and a handful more—have both haunted and comforted me for years. I have come to a place where I can do nothing else but release it to the best of my ability, even if that means taking time and money away from things that seem far more grounded. This is too real to me.

I hope Jesse and Faruhar's story is real and meaningful to you too, and that will mean enough to you to tell others. Reviews and word of mouth are everything at this stage, so I hope you'll leave a review on Goodreads, Amazon, or wherever else you can. Truly, I am grateful for the support of every one of you who read this book, and I cannot continue without it. I've done my best to this point and poured my soul into every word, edit, and illustration—and now this book is yours.

If you want to stay in touch, you can join my newsletter at sillautho r.com. I will always make big progress announcements there (monthly to quarterly) before I make them on social media. I'll also periodically release free short stories and first looks to newsletter folks only. PS – I have a certain solstice novella idea with Red Demon readers in mind.